HUMAN TRAUMA II

By
PirateOPotato

Human Trauma II

Printed in the United States of America

Paperback ISBN: 979-8-9896069-4-8
eBook ISBN: 979-8-9896069-5-5

This story is dedicated to all my readers on Reddit, Royal Road, and the RFM community. I hope this lives up to and surpasses the standards you have grown to expect of me.

TABLE OF CONTENTS

ACKNOWLEDGMENTS

Thank you to Frannercakes, Dee, Two Heavens, and Kelly for assisting me as pre-readers and editors. Your contribution to all of my works cannot be understated.

Additional thanks to Guardbro, Sarah, and Gary. The three of you inspire me every day to be better, write more, and never stop grinding. I would not be the same without you three in my life.

LITTLE HUNTRESS

Lysa Veringal was slumped in a chair behind the counter of the Specialty shop she had worked at for the last few years, waiting for the final few minutes of her shift to end. The shop was filled with rows upon rows of merchandise; it had been that way for as long as she could remember. Hell, most products filling those shelves were the same; each was made by and for a specific species, so they could enjoy some pleasure of vice their unique anatomy allowed.

However, some of the chemicals contained within them could be consumed by many different species. But those cases were few and far between.

Her own species, Aviex, was one of the species in the Galactic Union capable of that and was considered quite hardy by many. However, regrettably, that was not her species' claim to fame—or, more accurately, infamy.

The Aviex species evolved on an incredibly barren planet called Aveion, many hundreds of lightyears from here. It had sparse flora, fauna, and sunlight, which led to her species having a few traits that others found unsettling.

Her skin was pale as a ghost, and she had four blood-red eyes that gave her incredibly keen sight, along with her species having what was by Galactic Union standards an extremely dense muscle mass and high endurance. Few amidst the galaxy could match an Aveix in pound-for-pound strength. So far, the only ones she was aware of were Humans.

1

Yet the feature that unsettled other aliens the most was her teeth. Her mouth was filled with incredibly sharp needle-shaped teeth. Though not incredibly large, they were strong and just as white as her skin. They were a physical representation of the cultural tendencies her species performed that led to them being mockingly called Vein Slicers.

The Aviex species had developed to drink blood as one of their primary forms of sustenance; there was so little to go around. What else would they have done? Wasted it. This need led to them treating blood as something somewhat sacred, even developing an analogy to Human kissing, mordain. A pair of either Ruh'ah, or Gra'hu would bite from the other and drink a small amount of blood as a symbolic gesture of trust and care, symbolizing giving a bit of themselves to the other.

Most species found the idea of them drinking each other's blood or the blood of different species as abhorrent and detestable. This brought about rumors that the Aveix would slice them open and drink from their veins, hence the unfortunate moniker. They were little more than hypocrites in the eyes of most Aviex. They were perfectly willing to call them monsters, vampires, or whatever analogy their species had to blood-consuming ghouls, all while stuffing their mouths with the meat of some lesser non-sentient.

Lysa yawned and shifted in the chair, pushing the stiffness out of her athletic figure. She stretched high to the sky, her black shirt pulling up ever so slightly, letting the cool breeze of a fan roll over her lean abs. Thankfully, no one was around to hear her groaning as she did.

It had been well over an hour since the last customer had graced her with something to do. Too bad, ringing up a shaking, somewhat fearful customer only took moments, immediately followed by them rushing out the door. She usually would message her Ruh'ah, Henry Martinez, during extended downtime at work. But she had recently changed to working a day shift like him, so her dear Human was busy working at the trauma center and could not be her source of entertainment while she waited.

Instead, Lysa was stuck here, pecking away at a little story she had decided to jot down on her datapad. She was in no way an incredibly talented writer like her mother and had just started this one. It was at least something to do, and it wasn't like anyone would ever read it.

Who would want to read what might as well be the ramblings of someone trying to recreate the magic of old Human fantasies? Lysa barely knew the Human Fantasy genre herself, but Martinez enjoyed them. So, through exposure, the fantastical dragons, epic quests, and dirty diminutive goblins grew on her. At least it was something to occupy her mind.

At least no one else arrived before the night shift clocked in and relieved her from working the register. She had managed to make at least several paragraphs that read somewhat cleanly. If only Galactic Standard was not such a complex language. With the amount of context and descriptors needed to have sentences make even a bit of sense, she had taken a few creative liberties when describing fantastical elements.

Sythen was a young reptilian alien working the night shift. Lysa had never bothered to learn his species. He was clearly afraid of her anyway, always keeping at least a few meters between them if he could. So, learning about him would be a waste of time and effort.

After handing off the shop and signing out for the day, Lysa grabbed the jacket she borrowed from Martinez a few weeks ago and tossed it on. She did have her own coat but preferred his because it smelled like he did—luscious fresh pine. That and the dark, near-black leather complemented her ensemble of blacks, dark blues, and whites.

She stepped out into the streets of Draun and shielded her eyes from the bright twin suns still high in the blue Renoural sky. Getting off work when it was this bright felt odd after having lived nearly constantly in the evening and night for the last few local years. At least with this, she could spend more time with Martinez or train more in martial arts at Teachers dojo. Though she only planned on doing one of those tonight. Seeing her Ruh'ah.

Lysa started on her way through the bustling city streets, which were seldom, if ever, too crowded for her. The moment any alien spotted her and realized what species she was, they would avert their course and make way for her.

Years ago, that treatment bothered her, but not anymore. At the time, she was young, angry and spiteful. Not at anyone in particular, but at the entire universe for the hand it had dealt her. Through Teacher's training and Martinez's comfort, all of that was behind her. Who cares if they don't want to be around her? They aren't worth her time or effort if that's how they feel. She had plenty of friends at the dojo, a man who wanted her. What else could she want?

She diverted from her usual direct route of weaving in and out of shops and highrises; instead, she wished to meander through the several-kilometer-wide park in the city's center. The many colors, building designs, and cultures that coexist in Draun were wondrous. It was something she adored and was a part of, even if it was a diminutive role. The city was considered an example of what the Galactic Union aims for its society to be like, though few ever reached this level of harmony. She wished to visit the city's park for some fresh air.

Traversing the rolling meadows of green grass and the lush autumn colors of the trees was far more enjoyable than the stuffy business district she worked within. Though not the same as where she had grown up, seeing this much flora was a comforting reminder about where she grew up on the far side of the planet. A little reminder of the town called Cellna, while she could keep a comfortable difference from there.

Lysa glanced across the small lake in the park's center, the waves rolling and glistening in the sunlight. Other aliens were lounging about, watching the trees sway in the breeze. She breathed the crisp autumn air, letting the sharp scent infect her lungs, filling her with subtle warmth. Without a doubt, autumn was the best time to live in this city. The summers were too hot and humid. The winters were nonstop heavy snow, while the spring was an unrelenting assault from insects and rain.

She slowed her pace to linger in the park a little longer and pulled out her datapad, sending a quick message to Martinez.

Lysa: Ruh'ah, will you arrive at your abode soon? I will be there in a little over ten minutes.

Martinez took a few minutes to reply, but that happened when he was at work. He usually was caught up with reports or was wrist-deep helping his coworkers with another patient. So, the delay did not bother her.

Martinez: I will be a little late, sorry. Give me, IDK, thirty minutes?

Lysa: Very well, I shall await you outside.

Martinez: Alright. :)

Little else happened until she arrived at Martinez's apartment complex. She had been told that the reddish brick building looked similar to what you could find on his home planet, Earth. Not that she had been there yet—but she would not mind seeing where her dear Ruh'ah had grown up.

His apartment was on the far side of the city from her home and had a very different vibe than the suburbs she lived in. It was not bad, but it was packed with aliens on each floor. Their potpourri of sharp scents was jarring the first time she arrived, but now, she was used to it.

She happily waved at a few of his neighbors while ascending the stairs, a gesture they returned. They had gotten used to seeing her over the last few months, and neither seemed bothered by her, much to her preference. If only all aliens could be like them or Martinez, open-minded and accepting, treating her just like everybody else.

She settled onto the windowsill just outside his door at the end of the hallway on the third floor. She shifted her muscular legs as she settled in, trying to find a position where she was not in some amount of pain. Her butt and thighs had been sore over the last week, the result of Teacher's training and her nightly romps with Martinez. Not that either was wrong; she just had to live with it.

While Lysa waited, she remembered she needed to call her Mother and inform her that she and Martinez were willing to come over and visit them soon, having agreed on a date. She had meant to tell her mother several weeks ago when she and Martinez had made up after their spat about Martinez not reaching out and being open with her. But life had gotten busy, and doing so slipped her mind.

She quickly dialed her mother, Nelya. She truly adored having the opportunity to speak to her; if only she was not so busy, otherwise they would talk more often. Unlike Lysa and her father, they had gotten along swimmingly throughout her life, a model mother and daughter.

Lysa and her father had difficulty getting along for as long as she could remember. His treatment and views ultimately drove Lysa away from Cellna almost six local years ago.

After a few quick rings sounded out from her datapad, her mother's smooth, ethereal voice came through. Lysa had to admit her mother's voice was something she found soothing throughout her life. After she comforted Lysa countless times, telling her that her father did not mean it or was only trying to protect her, hearing her smooth, somewhat resonant tones was like a warm hug.

"Hello, my little huntress. How are you doing today?" Nelya replied in Galactic Standard, which surprised Lysa because her mother usually spoke Aviex to her.

Little huntress, a pet name her mother almost always called her, although it was strange hearing her Mother say it in Galactic Standard. The translation was not clean in any way, but that was not her mother's fault. It was because the term was from the Aviex language, where it was used to refer to one's daughter, while hunter would be used for boys.

The Aveix language was strange like that. It placed a lot of emphasis on titles that quickly described one's relationship to others. From Ruh'ah for an intimate partner, Gra'hu for someone you had children with, and countless others to explain family members and those who were not. Even with those technicalities, the Aviex language was far easier to speak than Galactic Standard. If it was not, Lysa might not talk in such a formal manner and with her atrocious accent.

Lysa could already picture her mother's soft, heartwarming features. Her mother had four pink eyes, a full figure ready for a hug, and hair similar to Lysa's—raven black hair that she tended to tie back.

It had been a long time since she had seen them; she truly did miss her mother.

"I am well, mother," Lysa replied, casting her gaze out the window and watching the street below for Martinez's arrival.

They shared some small talk, going over the most recent events in their life. Nelya spoke of her current book and bemoaned her readers for incessantly writing to her about their desires to be loved by her main character. Lysa simply updated her on the new shift at work and the training endeavors. They continued this way for a while, laughing and sharing each other's recent strifes and triumphs—until Mother brought up the reason Lysa called her in the first place.

"So tell me, how was your conversation with your Ruh'ah? I was expecting to hear from you a few weeks ago," Nelya asked slyly.

"It did go quite well, though it was rather uncomfortable to force Martinez through my berating," Lysa sighed, thinking about the horrible, pained scowl on his face when she laid his sins bare and scolded him for what felt like hours.

"Hmm, well, as I said, ensuring he knows your boundaries and limitations is important and will benefit you two in the long run. If I had not done the same in the past, Kyroll and I would have separated long ago," Nelya said.

Kyroll, Lysa's father. She had heard the story of when he abandoned her and her mother for several weeks just after she was born, then came back, and her mother gave him a cold shoulder for months.

A part of Lysa wished he would have stayed gone; he had caused her enough pain growing up. Chasing off her few friends, yelling at her for dreaming of traveling the galaxy, and threatening the only man she had ever been attracted to, at least until she moved. Kyroll was abhorrent. A true example of how to be the worst father someone could be.

At this point, Lysa would tell others she hated him, but that wasn't right. She felt utter indifference. If he was burning alive and she had the only water in dozens of kilometers, she would sooner drink it than save that horrible man.

"Very well then," Lysa said, trying to dismiss the mention of her father. "I wish to inform you that Henry and I arranged some time off to visit you. He has a break from college in a month, so that is when we plan on arriving."

"That's wonderful. I will have your old room ready for you two." Nelya said chipperly. "I cannot wait to meet your Ruh'ah."

"I cannot wait for you to meet him as well; I'm certain you will adore him," Lysa beamed.

She was proud that Martinez was her Ruh'ah. The Human was strong, intelligent, and protective enough of her to melt her heart. Mainly because their first date involved them getting attacked by a pair of particularly Zeletous aliens, and he gladly came to her aid. Thinking about it even now made her heart flutter.

"Oh, make sure you do tell him about your father. I will make sure your father stays well-behaved, but just make sure he is aware of your—relationship," Nelya insisted.

"I had no intention of not informing him of that horrible man. If I am lucky, that monster will choose to stay at work for the duration of our stay," Lysa grumbled.

"Now, my little huntress. Your father loves you. He is just—difficult. Not unlike what you have told me about Martinez," Nelya said.

Martinez was nothing like Kyrol, as far as Lysa saw it. The only linking factors were they both were in the military and had combat experience. Other than that, they could be nothing alike; Martinez was giving and considerate and wanted to see her happy—unlike that bastard.

Just before Lysa expressed this to her mother, she spotted Martinez amidst the crowd. He glanced up, spotted her waiting on the windowsill, and waved with a brimming smile. Lysa waved and decided to put that subject to rest for now. He undoubtedly had a strenuous work day; her being in a foul mood from complaining about her father would not help.

"If that is what you wish to believe, mother. I shall not argue about it. However, Ruh'ah has returned, and we are going to make dinner. I shall speak to you later," Lysa said.

Nelya sighed loudly. For years, she had attempted to convince Lysa of what her father thought about her, but to no effect. As far as Lysa considered it, if Kyroll loved her and wanted forgiveness, he could reach out and attempt to explain, not use her mother as a broker.

"I hope you have a nice night, my little huntress. I love you," Nelya replied.

"I love you too, Mother," Lysa replied before she ended the call.

VAMPIRIC VISITANT

M artinez had a long day at work. The entire day was filled with a nonstop influx of patients who did not need to be at a trauma center. Most of them had sat on a minor complaint for days until they randomly decided it needed to be treated right that moment. Too bad the patients were wasting their time. Each required an extensive work-up; it could take weeks to diagnose their unprovable pain, and that was before treatment was ever considered.

Martinez, Shiksie, Ivorn, Harnsis, and Therin did believe the patient felt the pain they were at the shop for, but they were workers at a trauma center; if the patient's life was not in immediate danger or suffered some other grievous injury, they should not be bogging down the system—general medical practices were for that.

Martinez never would have guessed that malingerers, crazed hypochondriacs, and unnecessary patients would be problems on the far end of the galaxy. According to Shiksie and Dr. Harnsis, they were an issue no matter where you went in the Galactic Union.

Never in his life did Martinez think he would want to be treating Human Marines again. Those animals never wanted to see the doctor. Mainly because others would see them as a pussy and never stop berating them, but at least they generally did not malinger.

The patients who did not understand the trauma center's role in the GU's extensive medical systems were annoying for the shop. But they were not today's primary issue; That horrible glory was given to a Suulintal tweaking off their mind on some new drug sweeping across the planets and moons of the Rentix system.

This was Martinez's first time dealing with someone losing their mind on a drug called Visage. Not that their violent and paranoid outbursts were the patient's fault, at least for this specific drug.

Visage was a powerful broad-spectrum hallucinogen that, according to the police that escorted the poor patient in, was favored heavily by traffickers and other criminals. It was given the street name of Visage because of the nasty effects it initially showed and the side effects the victim would suffer for weeks.

Once it enters your system through inhalation, blood, or glandular contact, you will forget all faces that your mind has not committed to long-term memory and won't be able to recall any you do see for several days. It's a genuinely horrible drug, used for even worse practices.

However, the worst part was how it functions similarly to nerve agents and other chemical-based weapons. Mear skin contact is often enough to have someone be affected by them. Similar to ancient VX compounds used in the trenches hundreds of years ago in World War One.

Today's victim was tough on everyone mentally, especially Shiksie.

Apparently, from what the police were able to piece together, the woman recently had a clutch of eggs hatch, and her mate left the system for a week on work. She was the prime candidate for whatever ghouls decided to target her.

She was found in a panic, wandering the streets, clutching an empty swaddle in her wings, screaming that she could not find her young. She could not relax until the Draun Police sedated her.

By the time she was in the Trauma Center, the doctors had already decided she would be moved to the ICU(Intensive Care Unit) and kept under sedation until regular brain activity resumed—however many weeks that might be. The shop could not even reach her poor husband. The poor thing must have been horrified when she awoke from Visage's initial effects to an empty nest.

Martinez could not imagine the pain and suffering that family would go through once she was stable. Fuck—their kids were stolen from under their noses.

It was a shame that her story was not original; according to the GU, the police, and the hospital services recently, a massive spike in child trafficking occurred in the system and showed no signs of slowing down.

But none of that was his concern right now; Martinez was already on the way home. Spotting Lysa's bright, fanged smile next to his apartment and her happily waving at him was enough to push any of those looming dark thoughts away.

"Hey, Ruh'ah, how was your day?" Martinez smiled as he rounded the corner to the third floor, and she walked toward him.

Lysa, the woman he loved. Though it took him a few months to understand how genuinely he cared for her down to every last detail. Her cute accent when she spoke standard, her curvaceous but equally sporty figure, and her gothic way of dressing. Nothing was wrong as far as he was concerned.

She thought similarly to him despite them being different species.

Lysa did not fault him for his PTSD dreams caused by his time as a Corpsman in the Human Navy. She was always forward with him about her desires, something he needed because he was as dense as tungsten. She even found the extensive scarring covering his body attractive—something he doubted anyone would ever do.

Lysa draped her arms over Martinez's shoulders and gently brought her lips to his while he pulled her waist close, their warmth spreading to the other. After holding the kiss for several longing moments, they rested their foreheads together and briefly got lost in the eyes of the other. She had four beautiful red jewels, whereas he sported eyes as dark as tree bark, fitting for his deep pine cologne.

"My day was quite long. I am not yet used to being out and about during daylight hours," Lysa giggled while crawling her hand beneath his jacket to move it to the side.

It was time for the second half of their daily cross-species ritual. Something Martinez and Lysa adored beyond anything in the universe. Mordain.

Martinez had initially thought the idea of letting her bite and drink his blood was insane, but after it happened once, he understood why Aveix did this. It was intimate and something unique to their species. Well, now it was also a tiny part of Humanity.

They both gently kissed the other's shoulder before biting down. While for Martinez, electric arcs of pleasure coursed through his chest while Lysa's sharp teeth sunk in, he could only leave a hickey and a few teeth marks on her shoulder, not that she minded. It was all he could do to reciprocate the gesture for his lady love.

After several months of doing this daily, both had scars left on their right shoulders. According to Lysa, that is essentially one of the reasons it was done daily. The scar was a quirky status symbol they both could show off. Lysa tended to wear clothes that left her pale shoulders open to view, while Martinez generally wore more conservative garb. Thankfully Lyusa understood he was not rejecting the idea, he just preferred long sleeves.

After wiping blood and saliva off their Ruh'ah's tender shoulder, they quickly entered Martinez's humble apartment.

The inside of the apartment was something that Martinez had grown to love. Doctor Harnsis, his direct boss, was a Humanphile and decorated it before Martinez arrived at his current assignment to Draun. His obsession with Human culture but a general lack of understanding of it led him to decorate the apartment in a way that could be called eccentric in the politest terms. Still, Martinez described it as a knick-knack shop that had exploded inside and painted the walls with items from all over Earth, spanning thousands of years of Human history.

Martinez appreciated the insectoid doctor's effort. He did manage to get some things that Martinez adored: a massive collection of movies that were likely bootleg, a couple of plush bean bag chairs that Martinez and the few Aliens who swung by liked to lounge in, and a silk bedspread from Japan. He and Lysa definitely appreciated how soft, warm, and inviting the green silken sheets were.

Lysa tended to describe the small single-bedroom apartment as garish but quaint. That was not surprising for her, she was the daughter of an author and had a far more expansive lexicon of words in Galactic Standard. She also tended to speak formally compared to most aliens and definitely when compared to Martinez.

"Would you care to tell me about your day while I prepare dinner?" Lysa questioned while she tossed her jacket onto the back of one of the dining room chairs.

"Sure," Martinez replied after tossing his bag down and going to pull out the basics to set the table.

The two of them nearly always had this routine: One cooked while the other set the table, be it here or at Lysa's house across town. They really had no preference for whose home they stayed at; it usually came down to whether one of them had to go to work in the morning, with them splitting the difference if they both did.

The only days they did not sleep together was when Martinez had to study late and crashed at his mentor Shiksie's house, but that had not happened in nearly a month. Ever since Marinez got used to the routine of going to college while also having a full-time job.

Martinez was glad that was the case. Shiksie confessed her affection to him several weeks ago, and he utterly failed to let her down easily. Ever since then, the air between them was slightly awkward; she still seemed to be waiting for him to leave Lysa and run to her, confessing his undying love.

But that was not going to happen.

So Martinez still had to broach his denial of her feelings with the tall, athletic feline. Much to Lysa's chagrin, at least his Ruh'ah understood why he was trying to be tactful and that Shiksie seemed to be maintaining a comfortable and professional relationship—for now.

Lysa made Martinez well aware she would kill Shiksie if she tried to overstep with him. When he explained what happened between them, Martinez nearly had to hold her back from rushing to the trauma center and killing Shiksie. Thankfully, she was letting him handle the issue for the time being. Shiksie would not survive that encounter if Lysa had her way.

"So, where to begin," Martinez grumbled as he began to explain the day and its events.

They were both very used to recounting everything that happened to each other. They did so at least every day or two, especially when something eventful happened to either. By the time Martinez had walked Lysa through what went on at work, they were already settling down next to one another to eat dinner.

"Well, that sounds atrocious. I do hope the police manage to find that Suulintal woman's children. I honestly cannot understand what kind of monster would whisk away someone's young," Lysa growled while she lowered into her chair.

Martinez wished he did not understand why Aliens might do that. While Slavery was illegal in the entire GU, plenty of smaller conglomerates and independent systems out in the universe refused to abolish the concept. Along with the general areas within the GU, the government could not entirely keep them under their thumb.

Wherever there is a demand for some product, there will be a market. And with thousands of species in the Universe, each with unique traits and conditions they were adapted to, undoubtedly, some unsavory individuals would be perfectly willing to commit horrible crimes to snatch them up into trafficking.

Lord knew Martinez had seen enough examples of that type of thought while working with the Human Marines. It seemed wherever war went, child soldiers, slaves, drug runners, and merchants of war followed or led; he was never sure which came first after his dozens of combat deployments and thousands of battles and preferred not knowing what led people to such horrible acts.

"Yeah, hopefully they do find those kids," Martinez replied. "What is this meal anyway? Another Aviex dish?"

The meal was something Lysa had never made for him before. Usually, her meals were chock full of Iron and meat. This one was similar and looked like a large slab of red meat, slathered in one of the blood sauces she usually had with it. But unlike usual, there was what reminded Matinez of beans, but they were the size of Brussels sprouts spattering their plates, soaking up the sauce.

"It is. My mother made it regularly around this time of year. The tubers are called Irt'lin. They last an extremely long time when dried. We may use them in stews or anything else that could use starch," Lysa smiled, poking his side playfully. "Did you not witness me placing them in our shopping cart the other day?"

"I guess I didn't," Martinez shrugged. "Any particular reason why you wanted this?"

"I assumed eating more traditional Aveix food might be beneficial before we travel to my parent's abode. I would not wish for you to detest what my mother would likely prepare," Lysa replied.

"Makes sense," Martinez replied. "But if her cooking is anything like yours, I will like it."

"If my cooking is what you wish to compare my mother's against, I'm certain you will adore her meals. Although I fear you won't enjoy mine once you spend a few weeks with mother plumping you up with extravagant dining," Lysa jokingly said.

"Oh come on it can't be that good," Martinez replied as he started to dig into the meal.

"Believe me, my abilities cannot compare to her prowess as a chef," Lysa assured.

Martinez shrugged his mouth already full of the succulent fatty food. If that was true or not it did not matter. He loved Lysa's cooking as is.

"There we go," Martinez said after cleaning the kitchen after dinner.

"Do you wish to join me, Ruh'ah?" Lysa purred, gesturing to the black bean bag chair she had settled into, before sipping some Lorian wine they had picked up the other day.

"In a second, I have something I want to open with you," Martinez replied, wiping his wet hand with a dishrag and tossing it onto the table.

"Should I be excited?" Lysa questioned.

"Definitely," Martinez whispered into her ear, eliciting the cutest shudder as his warm breath caressed her neck. "Let me go get the care package the Marines sent us."

"Oh, it arrived?" Lysa excitedly replied.

"It did," Martinez said, heading toward the bedroom.

Lysa felt her heart pounding as excitement filled her. She could recall when they were cuddled up in bed and watched the video Martinez's old unit had sent explaining they mailed a care package filled with gifts for Martinez and his "Hot goth."

Ruh'ah and her decided to send one in response that same day.

That was an enjoyable project for them. Martinez selected specific items for individuals and regaled her with tales explaining why the item was either a joke or something they would genuinely enjoy. She had been charged with selecting treats and other items she might want or could eat. Humans' and Aveix's tastes were generally very similar, which was perfect for her, mainly because she was not intimately familiar with his old friends.

The standout tales Martinez told involved Dee, Johnson, and Raleigh. His genuine smile when telling her of their misadventures together was heartwarming and the most childlike she had ever seen her Ruh'ah.

A part of her wondered if he still could be that way after all he had been through. But seeing Martinez settle into the seat next to her with a large box in hand and a brimming smile assured her that Martinez definitely still had a bit of his inner child in his heart.

"Hopefully, they sent two specific items and not too many dick pictures," Martinez said, clicking open his pocket knife, slicing the package open, and digging through the items.

"Oh, come now, would they genuinely send pictures of their cocks?" Lysa genuinely questioned.

"They would, so be careful opening any letters," Martinez laughed deeply.

Martinez rummaged through the package further while Lysa scooted closer to peek inside. The Marines indeed went no holds bar when filling Martinez's gift. The box was overflowing with candies, treats, and various knickknacks. Spattered amidst them were several closed envelopes.

Lysa was surprised that Humans still sent letters at all. Most Aliens relied on video messaging or Email because they did not have to wait weeks or months for a response. But who was she to judge? Lysa still preferred to write using pen and paper instead of a datapad; too bad she could not lug around the supplies effectively.

"May I?" Lysa questioned, leaning against his shoulder.

"Of course, they did say it was for both of us," Martinez assured, shifting the box onto both of their laps.

Martinez was not worried about Lysa eating anything the Marines could have sent him. After Ezol had an adverse reaction to the hot sauce Martinez had negligently gifted him, Martinez screened her species thoroughly and ensured every bit of food he bought could not hurt her. These treats could only hurt his beloved if Lysa had some unknown allergy that neither knew about.

That doesn't mean he didn't have a twinge of fear. If Lysa was hurt by something he gave or did to her, he would never be able to forgive himself. The mere thought of hurting Lysa caused him heartache.

Lysa joined him and pulled out a smaller candy and one of the letters. Lysa opened the candy and popped it into her mouth without asking questions. It looked like crystalized green-dyed sugar covered in more sugar crystals.

When the round ball hit her tongue, Lysa knew it was nothing like the sweet treats she usually had at work and instantly regretted her decision.

"Baahh!" Lysa groaned, nearly coughing out the incredibly sour candy, but her mouth clenched, locking the ball in her maw.

Martinez dropped his search instantly and turned his full attention to her, fearing the worst. He grabbed her hand tightly, worry clear as day in his bark-colored eyes.

"Are you alright?" He questioned frantically.

"By the stars, it is incredibly sour," Lysa squeaked through her grimace.

Martinez paused momentarily before laughing so hard he was nearly crying. Seeing Lysa's scrunched-up face was adorable. He wrapped his arm around her and playfully jostled her. At least he thought it was funny, but that was not what she expected. Her entire body tensed up moments later as the taste overwhelmed her. It was foul.

"I'm sorry. I should have warned you," Martinez said, grabbing the wrapper from her lap. Oh, you had a Neutron drop. Don't worry, Ruh'ah. It's only sour for a few moments, then tastes like fruit."

She tried to reply, but her face refused to move from a tight clench. So only a light squeak escaped her while she nodded, trusting his judgment.

Why would Humans make this?

Candy should be enjoyable for whoever is eating it, not for someone watching. Then she remembered who sent them the package and their relationship with Martinez—Marines.

Fucking Human Marines.

Of course, the Humans he considered his brothers would have no issue sending off items that would momentarily be cruel to the other. They thought of each other as family, after all. Small, offensive jokes should have been expected.

"Here, watch," Martines said softly before he popped a similar candy between his lips.

It took a few moments, but Lysa started to chuckle, watching his face squeeze into contorted pain. Too bad she could not laugh as hard as her body was trying. The effects of the Neutron drop were still making it difficult to breathe, much less emote.

Lysa knew if she looked half as messed up as he did. She could somewhat understand why they would pass out these joke candy. Martinez's eyes were watering, and cheeks looked like he was trying to swallow them. He looked like a goof. Her goof, but a goof nonetheless.

"You look ridiculous," Lysa painfully squeaked through pursed lips.

Martinez chuckled and rubbed his head against hers, fully understanding the feeling. She looked ridiculous, too.

After a few minutes of sour candy hell, they both relaxed as the now unbelievably sweet flavors of the fruity candy overtook them, pressing away the tart taste. Although neither candy was as marvelous as fruit, it tasted like it was meant to resemble fruit—vaguely.

"Feeling better?" Martinez asked, placing a small kiss on her cheek.

"Indeed, however, I would much rather not be surprised like that again this evening," Lysa replied, sticking her now green-stained tongue at him.

"I will warn you next time," Martinez assured.

Following that surprise, the next bit of their exploration of the gifts did not have any more shocking revelations, other than Martinez quickly tucked away some pictures before Lysa had seen them. Most she saw, and they were expected. But Martinez assured her it was just the Marines sending him pictures of their cocks, or bare asses.

He had told her they would likely do that, but that they actually did was still unbelievable. But the slight blush on his face when she tried to steal them was cute. Not that she was too curious about them. She was well acquainted with Human anatomy, to put it lightly. Lysa just wanted to mess with her Ruh'ah after he failed to warn her.

"So, what did you wish for me to try?" Lysa asked, leaning against his shoulder and snaking her arm around his back playfully.

"This," Martinez said, pulling some of the final items out.

One was a small bar wrapped in foil, not much larger than Martinez's rough hands; the other was a bag filled with tiny green tubes about the size of her pinky finger.

"Coffee and chocolate," Martinez smiled while tossing the bag of tubes to the side. "We can have the coffee in the morning."

He opened the chocolate and smelled it deeply. His anticipation was palpable.

"Close your eyes and open wide," Martinez requested.

"Is this another trick?" Lysa asked, raising a brow.

"No trick, I just want to see what you think," Martinez smiled. "I can take a bite first if you really want."

The reassuring, soft look in his gorgeous dark brown eyes always got to her and rested her woes. Lysa swears Martinez, without a doubt, knew how weak she was to puppy dog eyes.

"Very well," Lysa said, doing as Martinez requested.

Lysa waited with bated breath, holding her tongue out. While Martinez was usually very close and more than willing to share, he never fed her. Hell, no one had fed her since she was a toddler. She knew this was going to be interesting.

Martinez placed a small chunk of chocolate on her waiting tongue. She involuntarily moaned when her taste buds registered the delightful, full-bodied, and rich morsel. It was surprisingly loud, so loud she would think it was only possible in their bedroom.

The delicious taste melted in her mouth and filled it with velvety sugar. Every muscle in her body melted with the chocolate while Martinez pulled her relaxing body close.

Human candy was terrific. The flavor was as complex as Martinez, nutty, bitter, sweet; all these flavors washed over Lysa's palette, gently bidding for dominance of the overall profile. She had never had anything this good, save for Martinez's Ichor-like blood.

"Oh, by the stars," Lysa moaned, her eyes fluttering open and peaking up at him. "Please inform me there is more?"

"Don't worry, we have more, but I wanted to savor it. There are only three bars, and that taste was a solid bit of one," Martinez replied, holding up two more sealed bars with the one he opened.

"May I have a bit more now?" Lysa pleaded, fluttering her eyes.

He gently smiled and took a small piece between his lips. He leaned in close and kissed Lysa, letting the piece slide from his lips. Lysa reached up and pulled his head tight, savoring him and the chocolate at once.

Now, this is how you kiss.

Lysa adored Marrtinez's usual salty, savory lips, but this set Lysa's body alight. Her panties soaked nearly instantly. There was no way Chocolate was just a candy. Lysa pressed her tongue into his maw, twisting it against his own. Both moaned as the succulent chocolate finished melting between their writhing appendages.

Once the kiss broke, the flavors of each other gripping their minds, Lysa sucked in a needed breath.

"Thank you," Lysa whispered, scratching the back of his head with her long nails.

"I'm glad you enjoyed the chocolate," he replied

"The chocolate was marvelous, however," Lysa smirked with a bestial hunger in her eyes. She dragged her hand down his abs and gripped his belt, claiming it and what lies beneath as hers. "I think I wish for another bit of desert tonight."

Martinez smiled, her favorite look overtaking his vision. It was a primal desire, the same one a hunter would use seeing their prized game caught in a trap.

"I think we can do that," Martinez whispered, tempting Lysa to rip his shirt off.

Before Lysa realized it, she yelped in surprise while his hand slipped beneath her muscular rump, pulled her out of the chair, and tightly cradled her in his arms. Her arms instinctively wrapped around his shoulders while she nuzzled into his neck. Taking in his deep pine scent, mixed with the lingering scent of his blood from his shoulder. Lysa's mouth watered, ready to bite into her dear Human.

"Let's go do that then," Martinez replied, carrying her toward the bedroom, leaving the remnants of the care package in the living room.

Lysa was ready for another beautiful night with Martinez. They did carnally enjoy each other every day they could. Each time was a blissful dance; their hearts intertwined as their bodies and minds were lost in bliss. She knew tonight would be no different— and Lysa could not wait for him to press her into the lush silken sheets.

"I love you, Ruh'ah," Lysa breathily moaned.

"I love you too—my Ruh'ah," Martinez replied as he pressed the bedroom door open, eager to spend more intimate time with the only woman he had ever loved.

VISAGE'S VICTIM

"I shall see you at my abode this evening, Ruh'ah," Lysa purred as she pressed her soft chest against Martinez, holding him against the wall.

Martinez smiled and gently caressed her cheek, leaning in and kissing her goodbye for the day. He liked that Lysa was forward like this; it was amazing to be wanted, and none of his previous lovers had ever been open and honest with him. While he would never tell the Marines or anyone at work how this made him feel, the way Lysa gently scooted in and guided him against the wall scratched an itch he never knew he had before.

"I can't wait. I will get us something to eat on the way home, alright?" Martinez said.

"Very well, just make sure it's not as spicy as you usually have your food. I still cannot bear that heat," Lysa said.

"I got you," Martinez nodded. "Lysa, please be careful out in town... with all the people going missing and this new drug..." Martinez started, but Lysa hushed him.

"Ruh'ah, worry not; I shall be aware of my surroundings," Lysa insisted.

Lysa stepped back, letting them both go their separate ways for the day. Maybe he was paranoid. Lysa could defend herself well, and it wasn't like he or Teacher would not notice her absence. Still, he was worried; this new drug and the disdain others felt for her species likely made her a prime target for whoever was orchestrating these abductions.

Martinez stopped at the door just before the streets began and watched Lysa as the early morning crowd parted for her. He knew they were afraid of her because she was an Aviex, but he did like that their parting gave him an excellent view of her swaying hips and long legs, barely visible in the morning fog.

Martinez held her in his sight as long as he could, but eventually, the crowd of listless drifting aliens returned and concealed her from sight. He smiled and turned toward the distance, ready to go to the trauma center. The last thing he should do is keep Shiksie waiting. The tall feline woman was stressed out enough and did not need to think he tried to hurt himself again.

Martinez ran his hand through his hair and stretched, spreading out any tender feelings from the multitude of fresh cuts and bites Lysa had given him last night.

"Henry, hurry up and finish that report. Another patient is arriving, and I need you to do the initial assessment on your own," Shiksie said.

Martinez looked at her from the data terminal he was working on like she was crazy. Shiksie never let him do an initial assessment alone. She always coached him because he was still not certified as a cross-species nurse. He had his Human EMT(emergency medical technician) certifications and a menagerie of different Human Naval schools. But he had only been working here at Draun for a few months and was forced to enroll in school by the director only three earlier.

Shiksie was hunched over at her own data terminal, tapping away at her report of their last patient. She was wearing the same scrubs Martinez did but built for her gymnast-like body. Her long legs were crossed, and her meter-long tail was tightly coiled in her lap, gently swaying as she focused on the information.

She reached up, scratched behind her radar-like ears, and scrunched her nose, squinting at the report she was going over. Her emerald cat-like eyes were barely visible in the dome-shaped trauma center's bright overhead lights.

"What do you mean do it myself?" Martinez questioned.

"I mean, you are on your own for this one. We have five more patients outside, and the rest of the rooms are all full. I need to handle these others. So, I am handing you this jail clearance. It should be simple enough that you don't need me, but call me if you do," Shiksie said in her flat, professional monotone.

Shiksie almost always had that cold professionalism since she confessed her feelings that had lessened around him from time to time, but that was not assured. In a way, she let her hair down when they were alone. But her emotions froze back over when it was busy at work, and the facade went back up.

Today was hectic; the shop was constantly bustling with life. The sound of heart rate monitors and various intravenous pumps chimed all day, but the grating sound had become background noise hours ago.

Because of how busy they were, Martinez had yet to take his lunch break, which was supposed to be hours ago. There was no chance to file all their reports for the first patients of the day.

But Shiksie was correct; a jail clearance was generally straightforward. All he needed to do was assess the patient, take vitals, and sign a paper saying the soon-to-be prisoner would not die if left alone in a cell. The process mainly existed for liability reasons but also ensured that any injuries the Draun police might have inflicted during the arrest were spotted and tended to.

"Alright, I will do my best," Martinez said, slightly nervous about being left alone to treat anyone.

"You will do well. I trained you, after all," Shiksie said with a slight smirk. "I'm forwarding you the file for their species; brush up on them, then head over to room fifteen, alright?"

Martinez nodded and twisted in his chair to look at the file.

Well, this was a shock. Martinez's first solo patient was another Suulintal woman. Hopefully, this one was not like yesterday. Martinez did not know if he could stand seeing another broken mother begging him to tell her where her children were.

Martinez quickly reviewed the Suulintal information on his terminal. Because he had treated one yesterday and reviewed all their species information, this was more of a refresh than Shiksie had likely assumed it would be.

Suulintal were an avian, semi-humanoid species classified as yellow. They were common but not seen every day. Most of their vitals were similar to Humans', though they had a slightly higher metabolism and an average temperature of 40 degrees Celsius.

Beyond that, their appearance was nearly Human, besides their reflective eyes, feathers, large talon-covered feet, and a pair of wings that spanned several meters on average. Nothing too surprising, Martinez was well used to aliens of all shapes and sizes at this point; few truly shocked him by appearance alone anymore.

After a few minutes of confirming any specific cultural needs the Suulintal had, he was ready to go. Luckily, there were none, unlike many patients who showed up where he had to dance around religious or other needs.

The Suulintal were well integrated into the GU, and most of their old cultural tendencies were well forgotten or waylaid to ease interaction. The only exceptions were those on their homeworld of Insyun, where they held deep issues with being seen by non-arboreal species and, god forbid, touched by those not of their kind.

Martinez got up and went toward the patient room. As he went along, Ivorn and Therin rushed into other rooms, checking on the patients who had been waiting a while. Meanwhile, Harnsis fluttered by going to discharge one of the patients whose treatment had been completed.

They all worked exceptionally hard today, and there was no sign of slowing down. Hopefully, a workload like this will remain an anomaly. Having this many people arrive for medical aid was concerning and pushed them all to their limits. If this keeps up, they might need to hire another nurse.

Martinez paused and stifled a gag when he entered the room with his first-ever solo patient.

The woman was at most only fifty kilos, her skin clung tightly to her body, and her skeletal structure easily visible even though her entire body was covered and caked in matted blood, shit, and other excrement. Martinez thinks her feathers are meant to be orange, similar to her vapid expressionless stare, but he could not tell.

Both were concerning; the data Martinez had indicated the Suulintal should be close to a Human in weight; seventy to eighty kilos would be more reasonable for someone living in the safety of Draun.

The more horrifying thing was that one of her wings was halfway gone; loose, filthy bandaging covered the nub sticking from her back as it oozed pus and plasma. She had the tattered remnants of the other wing clutched between her arms while swaying uncomfortably back and forth on the bed.

What the fuck happened to her?

"Took you long enough," the police officer snarled after glaring at Martinez for the last few moments.

Martinez looked over at the man he was regrettably acquainted with. Officer Surail.

Officer Surail and Martinez have a bit of history, namely that the man was adamant about arresting both Lysa and him after they were attacked several months ago. After that failed arrest, they periodically ran into one another when Surail needed a jail clearance.

Martinez was confident Surail was still salty about the night he and Lysa were released, especially because he was not shy about acting with the same courtesy as a live grenade around the Human.

Surail stood from the chair and to his full height. The man's imposing frame easily reached two and a half meters high. Something about the man always unsettled Maritnez, be it the reddish eyes, the jet-black fur, or the fact that he was always wearing the usual green and black uniforms of the Draun Police. He could not tell what combination of them set him off. But he did know that he did not enjoy that Surail was, in general, an ass.

"What, no one else available other than a vein slicer today?" Surail growled.

"Now is not the time for your petty shit; what happened to her? And what's her name?" Martinez rebuffed, stepping past him and tossing on gloves.

Surail always seemed to have the issue of speaking down to everyone. It especially bothered Martinez that he always referred to Lysa and him as vein slicers. Neither of them ever did anything to the man, but he still insisted they were no better than murderers waiting to happen.

"Found her rolling around in some gutter while on patrol. She never said anything or did anything. Other than being stupid and trying to get away, I had to toss her to the ground a few times," Surail replied with a sadistic grin.

"Oh, I can't imagine why anyone would want to avoid you," Martinez said, rolling his eyes.

Surail did not comment on that beyond a low growl.

Martinez carefully approached the shaking woman, paying close attention to where her long talons were. For all Martinez knew, she was whacking out on drugs and would lash out at him; she might as well have four kitchen knives on her feet.

"Hey, my name is Martinez. I am here to help you out. Is it alright if I see your injuries?" Martinez gently said while sitting and leaning close to her.

"You are wasting your time, vein slicer. Stupid thing won't talk," Surail grumbled, leaning against the doorframe.

Clearly, she didn't want to talk to Surail, a feeling he understood. But that was limited to the officer. A few moments after asking the question, the woman's dull, tired-looking orange eyes landed on Martinez, and she gently nodded.

So she was communicating; the dense police officer behind Martinez could not notice something subtle. Why the fuck is a shithead like him a cop? Does he have no empathy?

"Ok, just hold still and let me get a look at you," Martinez said, slowly moving to her missing wing. That was, without a doubt, what he had to look at first.

Martinez spent the next few minutes unwrapping the disgusting matted bandaging from where Jane Doe's wing used to be. With each wrap he removed, the scent of rotting flesh grew more robust; it got bad enough that he heard Surail gag and nearly vomit. Even Martinez had to admit this was a horrendous odor, and he already knew what was happening. She had to have an infection, a bad one at that. She wasn't even making noises as he touched the injury. Jane Doe was likely septic already.

Pulling off the last blood-soaked covering confirmed what he had feared. The woman's wing stump was halfway rotted. All the muscle and skin were red, damp, and covered in throbbing pustules. Not even the worst case of trench foot he had ever seen could prepare him for the swirling discolorations.

However, the worst part was the jagged piece of greenish-white bone that poked out from the center. Jane Doe clearly had befallen some amount of osteomyelitis. Just how much of the infection had entered the bone, he could not tell; she was so filthy that seeing her skin to look for discoloration was impossible. He could not even make out the fur beneath the thick muck.

Something was not right about this. Getting an infection this bad would take weeks of neglect, and plenty of people were afflicted by drugs around the city and would come in between their fixes. No one ever had anything this bad.

That, along with what broke her bone? It looked half smashed; little bits of shattered fragments clung to the surrounding flesh.

Someone did this to her.

It was not like she had been run over or slammed against a hard surface by a larger species. Her wing would still be there, likely mangled and in need of surgery, but still there.

Martinez put a thermometer into her mouth and almost dropped the reader. She was burning up with a temperature of forty-five degrees Celsius. There is no way this could be a jail clearance. Martinez would never sign off that she would be alright; she would die without being rushed to surgery to remove her infected skin and be put into a treatment room for several weeks.

"Go out there and get Shiksie. I need her to be washed, and cannot do that alone," Martinez told Surail.

"What do I look like, your servant?" the officer complained, lifting his nose at the Human.

"Do you want her to die? I need to check her infections and treat them. If she is filthy, nothing will change them," Martinez barked.

Martinez could order around the toughest Marines in the GU to do anything he wanted. That was the only real benefit of bearing the coveted moniker of Doc. When Doc told you to do something in his serious medical tone, you did it, no questions asked.

This cop would not give him any guff if the situation called for it. This scenario certainly did.

"Fine," Surail grumbled before lazily moving out of the door.

Martinez went over and closed the door. He did not want to deal with Surail any further. The officer's lack of care was not helping and was obviously making the woman uncomfortable. Her eyes kept shifting to the officer every few seconds while removing her bandages. After that, Martinez settled into one of the chairs and scooted next to Jane Doe.

"Hey there, can you talk? I have a few questions," Martinez asked calmly.

There was no response for several seconds, but eventually, she muttered a few words. It was so quiet that Martinez could not understand them. He had been blown up too many times; it was always like this. People had to speak up around him.

"I'm sorry I can't hear you. Are you able to speak a little louder?" Martinez asked.

"I can," the woman said just above a whisper while nodding.

"Perfect. Can you tell me what happened?" Martinez asked.

The woman shifted uncomfortably for several seconds. She grumbled and groaned, clearly frustrated. Then, she clung tighter to her only remaining wing, holding it like a kid would a blanket.

"It's alright. I'm just trying to help you be safe; I can't do that without some idea of what happened," Martinez assured.

She snaked her clawed foot out from under her body and grabbed Martinez's hand with her talons. Not much of a shock there; Martinez knew her species used their feet as a second pair of hands. She gripped it tightly, a pressure he returned, wanting to show her he was with her.

"I can't remember—I was at home with my family—then everything is a blur like I was in a fog. The first thing I saw clearly after coming to was that cop yelling at me in some warehouse, then dragging me to his car. Where are we?" The woman mumbled between long pauses to take breaths.

Well, that sounds like a story similar to yesterday's woman, so she likely was drugged with visage. But how long ago was that? Visage lasts a day or two; With her infection, she must have been afflicted weeks ago.

"We are at Draun City, on Renoural, in the Rentix system. Specifically the Trauma Center," Martinez said.

"No, that can't be right. I was on Minorun," the woman whined, pulling his hand closer. "How did I get here?"

Minorun—that planet was halfway across the galaxy from here. It was a relay stop for long-distance travel. The only reason Martinez knew about it was because while on the way from Verillon to here, the Jericho stopped there for a day or two.

"I'm sorry, but I don't know. We will figure it out, though," Martinez reassured, even though he had no idea where to start doing that. Likely, that would have to be done after the massive undertaking of tending her wounds.

Martinez did not want to freak her out any more than she already was, so he decided to end that conversation there, moving on to possibly getting more information about her and seeing what else she could remember would be better.

The woman could only remember her name and a few details about her family, so that was something. Her name was Ruhinley, and her family was a mate, Stuhlin. Together, they had four little ones: Manei, Ruhlet, Sarumit, and Caritlen.

When that was done, Shiksie arrived and asked him what was wrong, clearly worried he had messed up somehow.

"What happened?" Shiksie gasped, seeing the shivering woman clinging to his hand.

After a quick explanation, they got Ruhinley to agree to be cleaned up and washed so they could treat her.

It took Martinez a few harsh words to get Surail to stay out of the room. Surail was so persistent that it took Martinez threatening to tell Sergeant Feinel about Surail going against medical professionals to back off. The look on the man's face was flawless, a solid mixture of fear and frustration.

Serves the fucker right. Surail treats everyone like dirt. But Feinel was quickly able to put the officer right and get him to back off, even if it took some threatening. Although, the fact that Surail was alone was odd. He and Feinel usually worked together.

Cleaning Ruhinley took Shiksie and Martinez almost a half hour; it was horrible. Every bit of dirt and grime they cleared revealed more open wounds, bruises, and fractured bones. As they went along, Martinez felt sick and sinking.

This was not the result of some random violence; these injuries were calculated and planned. Every injury was terrible, but it would not kill Ruhinley outright. It was like she had been tortured. She reminded him too much of the Marines they found kidnapped by Farq's on Verrilon.

Every detail of what he saw was horribly familiar to what he had seen on Varilon of captured Marines. She was dehydrated, infected, and covered in more injuries than he could calculate. They even found a tourniquet buried under the dried bloody feathers around the stump that was her wing.

Someone tried to keep her alive. But why? The Marines on Varilon Martinez could understand. That was torture to extract information or stress the Human military's medical systems. This just seemed pointlessly violent.

Each time they revealed a new oozing wound, Shiksie shuddered and looked horrified. Her ears were tucked, and she kept looking between Martinez and Ruhinley, seeking some kind of stability here.

Ruhinley was no help. She was still delirious and barely able to talk. Martinez was focused and spoke to his patient constantly. Even if the topics were random, keeping her going was vital to her shaky situation.

Shiksie was always sensitive regarding kids and women in the shop. This was such a horrible situation that even Martinez was uncomfortable. He had to be their rock for the moment.

By the time Ruhinley was dressing in some extra scrubs and had the highest-strength antibiotics they could give her flowing inside her, she had nearly passed out from sheer exhaustion.

Ruhinley looked better, but not much. She lay down on her side, where she had the fewest injuries. The freshly bandaged stump jutted off her back, and the rest of her was somewhat relaxed now that it was an option.

"Thank you for getting me away from him," Ruhinley sniffled.

"What do you mean 'him,' Surail? Or someone else?" Shiksie questioned while taking the woman's vitals.

"The officer, I don't like him. He unsettles me, and I don't know why," Ruhinley said, looking pleadingly at Shiksie.

"Well, he brought you in for a jail clearance, but that's not happening," Martinez commented. We have you scheduled for surgery to treat your wing and follow up. Do you know what he brought you in for anyway?"

She shook her head and grumbled.

"Ok, hold on," Martinez said, stepping outside to speak to Surail. "Shiksie, keep her talking and watch her vitals."

This whole situation reeked; there was no way this sweet woman did something to get arrested. Even then, Surail said he had just found her. Martinez may not be a cop, but if what his buddy Feinel's word was anything to go by, the DPD(Draun Police Department) was short-staffed and had no real-time just to wander around.

How did he find time? And where the hell was Feinel?

Martinez found Surail just outside the room, lazing about and messaging someone on his datapad. Upon seeing Martinez, he tucked the datapad into his armor and looked over at him. "So, is that thing ready to go to jail?"

"Is that really your only concern? Did you not see the state she was in? Martinez said, crossing his arms.

"Yeah, it is. So can we go?" Surail questioned as casually as one would order a drink.

"Fuck no, I need to know what happened, and we have to get her to surgery," Martinez replied.

"Well shit, I guess that's it then. Call me whenever she can leave," Surail said, turning to leave.

"Where are you going? I still need answers," Martinez said, grabbing Surail's shoulder.

Surail whipped around and tossed Martinez's hand off him. "Don't touch me, you filthy vein slicer."

"What the fuck is your deal bud? I'm trying to help the person you arrested. I want to know why?" Martinez growled.

"That's police business, not yours." Surail rebuffed.

"It is mine; she is my patient," Martinez replied, pointing a thumb at his chest.

"Go figure it out then; she's just some stupid junkie," Surail growled, stepping closer to Martinez.

"Martinez, get back in here! She is going into shock," Shiksie yelled.

"See, go save your precious patient," Surail snorted. "Now move along, you filthy animal."

Martinez wanted to throttle him; he clutched his fists tightly, knuckles going white. Surail was always a lazy fuck, but this was something different. He was always more than happy to arrest anyone he could get his paws on.

This was not right.

"Fuck you, Surail. You are lucky I have to help her. If not, I would deal with you," Martinez said as he turned around.

"I would watch it, vein slicer. I could arrest you for insinuating threats," Surail boasted.

Martinez paused as he grabbed hold of the door. He took a deep breath to let his fury settle a bit. Surail was not worth getting arrested over. He could always message Feinel or file a complaint with the DPD later.

Surail's actions were flat-out criminal, but he was the cop and could get away with it—for now.

"Oh, is that so? I'm sorry for making you think I was threatening you," Martinez hissed through gritted teeth, each word venomous in his mouth.

"Good, make sure you remember it," Surail smugly said before walking off.

Martinez sighed and opened the door. He had to help the patient he had now, and dealing with issues of DPD would have to wait.

FELINE FRUSTRATIONS

Shiksie was on her way to Martinez's apartment so they could study tonight. The evening temperature was just above freezing. Her breath steamed out of her lips with each step through the frosted streets of Draun. This was the first frost of the upcoming winter, which was a shame. If the first was this early in the autumn, it would likely be a particularly frigid winter.

Hopefully, it was more pleasant than last year, when there was a meter of snow on the ground only a few weeks after the equinox.

Shiksie shifted the heavy backpack on her shoulders, not used to bearing this much weight. The slick ground made her usual jovial traversal of the bustling streets slow and arduous.

Shiksie had spent an exceptionally long time the previous night collecting all her notes for Martinez, ensuring she had the ones he would need on hand. He was doing well in the Interspecies Nursing Program, but he was staring down the barrel of his midterms in a few weeks, and those were a whole other animal than any test he had so far.

However, in this case, calling them midterms was a bit of a misnomer because Martinez's midterm was covering half a year's worth of lessons that Shiksie had taken. So, essentially double what she had while within the Nursing Program.

The Director, in his infinite wisdom, had decided to truly put Martinez through a trial by fire with the modified version of the course the Human was strong-armed into enrolling in. It varied greatly in every way from what she had; it was self-study, with no classes and just weekly tests. Oh, and if all of that was not enough, instead of the average two or three-standard year-long course of study, Martinez's course was only a year long.

That he was keeping up with the study tempo was mind-boggling. Shiksie doubted she could have done it without going insane. Mainly because, on top of the Nursing Program, Martinez has a full-time job.

He had been doing well, having made it almost a quarter of the way through the program the Director had cruelly devised just for him. Shiksie still did not trust the Director, saying that he was giving Martinez this opportunity to make the Human into an asset. Shiksie had known the Director long enough and had worked in the GU Medical Services for too long to be that naive.

The Director had to be playing from some angle or have some long con planned. He likely wanted to use Martinez as some political tool to propel his career forward. Shiksie just could not understand how he planned on using Martinez because she lacked the Director's perspective on the matter.

The fact that Shiksie could not find a reason had weighed heavily on her mind. She was worried about Martinez because of that. If she did not understand the Director's goals, how was she to keep him safe from any fallout? Or if the Director tried to screw him over? She was his mentor; Her job was to keep her mentees safe and guide them to prosperity.

However, that was not the only reason Shiksie was worried about Martinez. Shiksie also felt concerned about Martinez because she finally admitted that she liked him as more than just a casual friend or a coworker.

Too bad he shot her down—somewhat.

When Shiksie finally admitted to Martinez, she had taken the only approach she understood, that relationships were mutually beneficial in some way. She had not had any form of a relationship that was unconditional since her parents died when she was a kit. It was always that way, be it in Draun public orphanage and college—someone always wanted something.

Despite her trying to be honest and explain how she would not leave him in his time of need as Lysa did, he rebuked her, saying she did not understand that relationships were complicated. She did not see what was so complex about it. If you like someone, and they like you, you spend time together, giving effort to one another.

What could she possibly be missing?

She considered herself attractive, with an athletic figure and a healthy gray coat of fur. She knew Martinez at least thought she was somewhat appealing, having caught him glancing at her bust or rump while on their morning jogs or during their post-workout stretches.

Martinez had even complimented her clothing several times whenever she purchased something for the encroaching winter. She needed an opinion, and who better to ask than the male she only recently realized she wanted to court.

Ever since he told her to wait and see what happened with Lysa, Shiksie had been patiently waiting for Martinez to give her an answer to her feelings. She waited, hoped, and stewed in anxiety every day.

Then that damn Aveix started lingering around him again.

When it first resumed, Shiksie hoped she was mistaken about the smell on him, but after a few days of her bloody-lemony scent on him at all times, she knew they were back together. The thought of it put her hackles on end.

Why could Henry not see that she cared about him? She supported him by exercising together, helping him at work, and coaching him through schoolwork—not Lysa.

Shiksie grumbled, shifted her bag on her shoulders, and sidestepped some of the aliens lingering outside Martinez's apartment. Not wanting them to spot the scrunch on her brow or hear her grumbling about that foul woman under her breath.

Being back here brought back some memories. Shiksie and Dr. Harnsis had spent several days moving all of Martinez's furniture and other decorations into his apartment before he arrived. She had not seen it in several months.

The idea of seeing what changes Martinez had made to his apartment itched at the part of her brain that wanted answers. Perhaps getting to see how he lived might help her piece together some amount of an answer to what he meant by that relationships were complicated. After all, people's homes were them expressing their most honest selves, at least so long as they were not putting up a front.

Martinez was not like that at all. As long as Shiksie has known him, he has been generally honest. At least the Human had always been open in ways her keen Farun'se senses could easily perceive. Twitches in his gorgeous brown eyes, the slight pheromones within his intoxicating pine scent, or the subtle shifts in his body language. He was easy enough for her to generally read—save for a few odd quirks she had yet to decipher.

Shiksie nervously approached Martinez's door, her heart stammering faster with each elegant feline footfall. Ever since she admitted her feelings to him, she kept hoping the next time they saw each other would be when he told her the same. The anticipation was killing her. Maybe he just needed to spend more time with Lysa to see how she herself was more capable, reliable, and better—she hoped that much, at least. What else could it be?

She slammed her fist against his door and waited and waited. Seconds turned to agonizing minutes while she periodically hammered the door yet again. She shuffled nervously and checked her datapads time, wondering for a moment if she had arrived too early. It was the correct time for her to be here.

Where in the stars was he?

As Shiksie was about to message him asking where he was, as if guided by the universe itself, her datapad chimed a happy tune she had set for him. She smiled; he had beat her to the punch.

Martinez :): Hey Shiksie, sorry I ran a little late with other plans. I will beat my place in a few minutes. I am sorry about being late.

Shiksie sighed. That was unlike Martinez, he was usually diligent. But with how work had been dragging everyone down lately, she could understand letting time get a little bit away from you.

Shiskie: It's alright. I had just arrived. How long will you be?

Martinez :): No more than five minutes.

Shiksie: See you shortly.

Shiksie did not have to wait long for Martinez to arrive at his door. Seeing him drew a smile to her lips and had her tail immediately happily swaying. Being around Martinez outside of work sent butterflies loose in her stomach and gave her a warm, fuzzy feeling in her chest.

Shiksie wished she entirely understood what these feelings were, but no one had ever given her this experience before. He was the only being she had ever let her guard down around. Well, that's a bit of a misnomer; he simply had a strange calming effect emanating from him. She had never known why, but even with violent patients, they just did as he asked. It was odd.

When at work, Shiksie tried to ignore and suppress her feelings about him, along with most of her emotions, just to keep herself safe. Martinez was the only exception among her coworkers with whom she expressed genuine opinions while inside Draun's walls. For everyone else, it was strictly business.

Especially when it came to Therin, that stupid fucking bird. After what he did to Martinez she had to work especially hard to keep her composure around him; just thinking about that bird cowering below her still made her nearly smile cruelly and get a twisted predatory enjoyment. Something about seeing Therin cowering felt right. She still owed him for making Martinez cry. But Martinez asked her to let it go, so she complied; it was what he wanted after all.

Even if, as she saw it, that feathered monster deserved more than just being so afraid he shit his pants. She almost regrets that Harnsis stopped her that day. Shiksie had no doubt she would have gutted him then and there. How dare he do that to Martinez!

"Hey Shiksie, sorry about being late," Martinez said, awkwardly rubbing behind his head with a slight blush.

"It's alright, I don't mind," Shiksie shrugged. She would have waited hours if needed.

"Right, let's get started," he said, walking up and opening the door.

The heavy scent of Martinez's pine cologne poured out of the apartment like a tidal wave and made Shiksie's body ache and bathe in blissful comfort. How could anyone smell so heavenly? By the stars, the urge to grab him and hold him close was so tempting.

Stepping into the lush forest that might as well grow out of Martinez's apartment, Shiksie carefully analyzed every detail within, wanting to carefully compare what was there now to when she and Dr. Harnsis had set it up before.

To her pleasant surprise, the vast majority of what they had used to decorate the apartment was still there. The odd stacking dolls she picked out and the little wooden cutout birds were still perched atop the cupboards.

There were some minor additions he had made. The once-empty shelves over his sink and stove were now filled with dried foods, cans, and bottles of what she could only assume to be alcohol. But she was not sure about that.

Shiksie could not consume almost any ethanol, so she was not a connoisseur by anyone's imagination—she would stick to studying medical journals. She regrettably could not even partake in the drinks Martinez, Sursee, Ivorn—or Lysa enjoyed. Even Jurtoi would hospitalize her. Because of her lack of knowledge, the bottles were just a mix of colorful poisons, even if the blue twisting bottles were stunning.

Scanning the rest of the entry room and living area, Shiksie also spotted a collection of books on a shelf. Both she and Harnsis had not collected them for him.

Shiksie walked over to peruse the old-looking books. She had never known that Martinez was much of a reader, having always assumed that he enjoyed movies more than any other entertainment.

When she was a few meters away from the books, Shiksie shuddered as a horrible bloody scent accosted her senses, making her ears defensively fold. It was not just the bookshelf; now that she was further into the apartment, she realized every surface of the room had the subtle scent of blood. She instantly knew they had been marked by what was lurking inside the lush pine grove.

A life-sucking shade that reeked of blood and lemons.

Shiskie was well aware of the appalling scents Lysa gave off. Regrettably, she was also well aware of the scent of Martinez and Lysa's more erotic concoctions, with Martinez often having their infuriating mixture clinging tightly to him. To her dismay, the scent of that was also chokingly thick in the air.

Her claws begged to be released, to fight off who she knew was not currently here. But the mere reality that the woman's scent was within a territory Shiksie's confused brain, for some reason, claimed as hers set fire to her instincts to defend Martinez.

"Hey Shiksie, are you ready to get started?" Martinez questioned while he sat down at the table.

His sudden speaking ripped her attention from the collection of tomes written in Aviex and drew her mind from the beast lurking somewhere in the woods of scents.

"Yeah," Shiksie said, stifling a defensive hiss. "Just let me get some scent blocker on."

"Oh, sorry about the scent. When I'm not at work, I don't use that blocking soap. It feels horrible on my skin," Martinez apologized, his soft eyes genuinely concerned.

If only it was his scent, then there would be no problem. But that vile woman who was trying to steal away her apprentice was the issue.

What gave Lysa the right to weasel into her territory?

The fact Lysa had been here upset her, but the worst part was that Martinez was complying. He had to be. It's not like Lysa could just enter his home uninvited. That bugged her; she was always right there, eager and waiting. Why would Martinez go for another woman? Why? Why did he let her over? Martinez even allowed Lysa to move her books and undoubtedly countless other things into his house.

Did they become more intimate since she had confessed? Had Lysa moved in with him or something?

A grim thought crossed her mind as she watched Martinez pull out his books. Had he completely forgotten she had even requested an answer?

Shiksie settled next to Martinez for the worst few hours she had experienced in years. Nothing could have prepared her for what tonight would reveal.

No matter how much they studied or how warmly he smiled while succeeding in practice tests, she could not settle. It was odd, she loved to study and research, but this felt like torture. She was shifting, and fidgeting constantly under the table, trying to ensure he did not catch onto how upset she was.

Every second, she lingers in the heavy odors, even though her heavy-duty scent blockers do their best to suppress them. The odor of blood and lemon is always at the forefront of her mind. Each breath causes her to shiver from the haunting feeling of being hunted by that Aviex.

Like she was deep and lost inside that monster's territory.

Shiksie could swear that Lysa's four dagger-like eyes were looming over her shoulder and that she was one moment away from having her neck ripped open. After about an hour of her heart slamming against her chest, feeling like she was moments from dying, Shiksie needed a break; she craved a short respite.

"I will be right back. I need some air," Shiksie stammered, pushing back from the table and going toward the door.

"Alright, I will be working on this test. See you in a minute," Martinez casually replied, not even looking up at her.

Shiksie was in such a tizzy that she had not even been bothered by his short response. Before Shiksie even made it to the door, it parted, and her heart sank, claws extended, and eyes narrowed.

Standing in the doorway, a bag draping off her bare gothic shoulder, was Lysa. She was wearing her usual revealing dress, and his fucking jacket tied around her waist. Her four red eyes narrowed in a silent fury upon seeing Shiksie. The look perfectly matched what Shiksie had been feeling already. She hated that Shiksie was here; her four blood-red eyes looked her up slowly, pausing on Shiksie's claws for a moment. She locked eyes for a second and silently conveyed, 'Why are you here?'

A crawling fear shot up Shiksie's spine, knowing it was not a glare of questioning but of vengeful accusation. After a moment of agonizing silence, Lysa smirked.

"Good evening, Shiksie. I was not expecting you here tonight," Lysa smiled somewhat cruelly, her rows of dagger-like fangs on full display.

"Hi Lysa, yeah, Martinez and I are studying for his upcoming test," Shiksie replied, slightly nervous.

"Marvelous, it is so joyous that he has such dedicated friends," Lysa growled, clearly emphasizing friends.

"Yeah, excuse me for a moment. I'm just stepping out for some air." Shiksie retorted, trying to not sound as if she was afraid of the Aviex woman.

Shiksie had dealt with Aviex before at the hospital and held no ill will to the species as many did. But something was so freaky about that smile Lysa kept and the fact that Lysa had paused to look at her claws. Shiksie prayed Lysa did not think this was a fight. Shiksie knew damn well that if Lysa really wanted to thrash her, she would stand no chance.

Much like Humans, the Aviex were physically dense and, by weight, far more powerful and faster than most species. While in a test of raw agility, Shiksie might be able to best her, but in a brawl, there would be no contest. Shiksie might as well be fighting a Machine designed to kill.

"Well, before you step out, shall you be joining Ruh'ah and myself for dinner?" Lysa challenged, crossing her arms under her bust.

"Oh, uh, I am not too sure about—" Shiksie started, but Martinez had to join in. For once, Shiksie would have rather not heard him speak.

"Yeah Ruh'ah, you might as well make three plates. Shiksie and I have a lot to study today," Martinez interjected, clearly having been attentive to the tension between the two.

"I guess I am," Shiksie said, both glad and mortified that she had just been pulled into spending time around Lysa.

"Very well, I hope you enjoy kyulon. Ruh'ah and I have been trying to eat more Aveix cuisine to prepare for visiting my family soon," Lysa calmly boasted to Shiksie.

"Ah, I see. I have never had it, but I'm certain I will," Shiksie replied, going past Lysa and into the hallway, leaving the awkward tension behind—at least for a minute.

The entire time Shiksie was downstairs in the frosty air of Draun's streets, she was pacing. Passersby obviously picked up on her frustration; they shot her glances and muttered under their breaths, thinking she could not hear them. But she easily could.

They thought she was either on some kind of drug and was freaking out or that she was just some freak. She did not do drugs, other than that one time when they were celebrating Martinez's first test. While it was nice and filled her with a bliss she had not experienced before, that did not make her a junky. Right?

Additionally, Shiksie was no freak. Yeah, she had some issues and knew it. But this was the only way she could rip tension from herself. It's not like she could talk to Martinez right now, Lysa was right there and would undoubtedly challenge any claim, or statement she made.

As she paced back and forth near the apartment's entrance, questions circled her mind. Trying to figure out what was going on. Why did she feel like she was being hunted by Lysa? Why was Martinez not being forthright with her? Why did Lysa have a key to his apartment? And what in all the stars was the horrible hollow feeling in her chest?

Shiksie felt hollow the moment Lysa entered the apartment; before that, she felt troubled and odd. But now, this was different. It took her some time to recall when she felt this before. It was an old feeling and plucked at a heartstring she had cut long ago.

Loss.

This was the same thing as when her parents died, and she was in the orphanage. Yet Martinez was not gone. He was just a few floors up right now, likely diligently studying. But that Aviex was there.

Shiksie did not understand it; Martinez was her apprentice, her friend. Why could Lysa be so close to him, and she could not?

After nearly a half hour of mulling over the front and digging a deeper hole of whys and what ifs inside her own mind, Shiksie gave up. Her sulking was obviously not getting her anywhere, and Martinez needed her help to study. So she took a deep breath to steady herself and prepare to finish helping Martinez with his exams.

Too bad his preparations were not the issue at this point; it was hers. And no matter what preparations Shiksie had made in her mind, the sight she found upon returning to Martinez's apartment was unexpected. It was shocking enough that Shiksie froze like a statue and drew in a sharp breath.

Lysa was standing behind Martinez, and she bit into his bare shoulder. Simultaneously, Martinez closed his eyes, smiled, and ran his hand through her raven hair, gently caressing her cheek.

What the fuck? She drinks his blood. Shiksie might as well have screamed in her mind.

Lysa clearly heard Shiksie gasp in surprise. She peeked up from Martinez's shoulder and bit down harder, causing him to groan in enjoyment, rubbing Shiksie's face in the intimate display.

"Fuck, Lysa, a bit enthusiastic today," Martinez muttered softly to her.

Shiksie watched in stunned silence. Lysa moaned and wrapped her arms around Martinez's, holding him tightly to her. Her eyes never left Shiksie, staking her claim as clear as day. Time dragged to a crawl. Shiksie had no idea how much time had passed watching the display. Her mind screamed and begged for this to stop, for her to intervene, but her body would not listen to her command.

Before she knew it, Lysa slowly and salaciously licked the blood off his shoulder and moaned one more time before pulling Martinez's shirt back over his shoulder. Without missing a beat, she turned to Shiksie and feigned surprise.

"Shiksie, I am terribly sorry you had to see that! I know most species find that Aviex drink blood revolting," she exclaimed before whipping his blood off her black coal lips.

Shiksie fully understood the vile smirk Lysa gave. That was more than a claim or a warning. Lysa was marking her territory out in the open for Shiksie to see.

That was too much. Shiksie could not stay here and look at either of them. She felt like she was on the verge of tears. That hollow feeling twisted and grew into an all-consuming black hole inside her. It was not sadness, anger, confusion, spite. She felt empty, But why did seeing that make her want to cry?

Martinez shot up and looked over at Shiksie. "Shiksie, I did not know you were back. Uhh—sorry, you saw that."

"No, no, it's alright," Shiksie lied through gritted teeth, trying to ignore the broken feeling in her chest.

"Oh, Ruh'ah it's alright. I doubt your friend minded seeing us do that; it's only natural, right?" Lysa purred, walking her fingers along Martinez's shoulder before sauntering toward the stove where some pot boiled. Her gait was as graceful as a dancer but as assured as any true predator.

Shiskie paused and tried to steady herself momentarily, biting her inner lip and clawing at her pants, but that did not work. Seeing that broke her and any hope that tonight would be the night Martinez confessed was crushed to bits. She could not do this. Lysa made it clear enough that Martinez was hers and that Shiksie was the awkward outsider in their apartment.

"I'm sorry, Henry. I have to go," Shiksie squeaked.

"Oh, is something wrong?" Martinez asked, his worry evident as he stood and walked closer.

"I am feeling ill from the heavy odor," Shiksie lied. She just could not bear to see this anymore.

"Oh, that is a shame. Are you sure you don't wish to stay? Dinner is almost ready," Lysa said calmly, never turning to face them.

"I'm sorry to hear that. Do you want to study at your place later this week? We haven't even started for my main test this weekend," Martinez asked, now right up to her.

Being this close to him felt wrong, almost dangerous. Shiksie peeked up and spotted Lysa watching them intently from the corner of her eyes. Waiting for Shiksie to slip up. To step on her claim.

Martinez was correct that they had only focused on his recap of the previous lessons today and had yet to get anywhere with the newest topics. If he had any chance of getting high marks, they would have to move the practice anywhere but here. Not with Lysa rubbing reality in her face.

"Could we please," Shiksie nearly begged.

"Yeah, that's no issue," Martinez said. I will see you at work tomorrow," he finished with a bright, heart-warming smile that almost made her forget Lysa's glare.

Shiksie nodded before quickly exiting the apartment, scoping her bag up and practically sprinting for icy air.

By the time Shiksie made it home, she was beside herself. No longer having to suffer that looming odor or feeling like she was being hunted was good, but that hollow feeling was still there. If anything, it had only gotten worse.

Shiksie understood she would have to think of a new plan to get Martinez on her side and out of Lysa's arms.

Was it wrong for her to try and press the issue further? She did not know, but it felt just as painful to let things be.

Shiksie plopped face-first into bed and called upon what little she knew about relationships, romance, and seduction. Desperate to think of some answer to her now far more developed issues, she realized she knew virtually nothing about them.

Shiksie racked her brain, searching for answers to many obnoxious questions. What was different? Why her? What did Lysa bring to the table that Shiksie did not?

Shiksie was not so dense that she did comprehend that Lysa and Martinez were physical, something she was not with the Human. She also understood they performed caring and romantic gestures, having seen several delectable lunches Lysa had prepared for Martinez, along with them kissing, hugging, and now Lysa feeding on Martinez.

"Stars, dammit! What does she have that I don't?" Shiksie groaned to her pillow, starting to sniffle. It was all so overwhelming.

Shiksie gave into the hollow infection spreading from her chest, bawled, screamed, and thrashed. Each sob gave her some subtle catharsis. What else was she to do other than cry like a pathetic kit? The only person she ever opened up to was being guarded by the reason she felt alone. Why was the universe so cruel?

As Shiksie began to relax for the night, she continued to think about how to solve this issue. She had never liked anyone and had no real idea how to initiate anything beyond a hug, not that Martinez would even want that when Lysa was around.

Shiksie decided she would have to do some research on the matter. That was one thing she did know how to do. She prayed taking a more analyzed approach to the matter might help her bring some order to the chaos swirling in her chest. Shiksie also considered asking Miss Luan for some advice. However, it had been a while since they had spoken. Would Miss Luan even remember her at this point?

Shiksie relaxed fully, her wet, tear-filled eyes finally closed; one last thought ran by her again before darkness took her.

Why does her thinking about Martinez with Lysa hurt?

WEREWOLVES AND VAMPIRES

"Martinez, move faster than that!" Teacher shouted from off to the sidelines of her dojo.

Martinez slumped down and leaned against the wall of the padded fighting room, gasping for air. He wondered beyond everything else in his mind why in all the universe he agreed to come here and train with the roided out goblin esc woman. This was torture, not training at this point.

"Come on, Ruh'ah. We still have another ten minutes of jogging," Lysa purred, dragging her nails on his neck as she ran by with the other students.

Martinez looked up and barely spotted Lysa winking over her shoulder at him. Her tantalizing hips were well outlined by the short black shorts everyone was wearing, and her chiseled abs were easily seen as she turned back to run at full speed. Her raven hair was tied in a trailing ponytail, babbling up and down, letting him see her pale skin and those cute dimples just over her rump—similar to the ones on her cheeks.

Oh yeah, that's why.

Martinez usually did not attend the classes Lysa's Teacher offered, not because he did not enjoy Martial arts or because he did not want to exercise. Usually, he simply did not have the time between school, work, and spending time with Lysa. But today was different — somewhat.

Before Martinez and Lysa had some time away from one another after he fucked up royally, Martinez had agreed to try and help Lysa get ready to enter a competition representing Teachers Dojo. Today was his first day aiding her in that preparation because there was a small local competition at the end of the month, a few days before Lysa and Martinez were leaving for a few weeks— and that stubborn Teacher was insistent they prepared for that one.

Why the roid rage goblin was resolute in the fact Lysa should be ready for that one, not one of the undoubtedly dozens that would go on over the rest of the Local year, was beyond both Martinez and Lysa. Yet here they were, sweating, jogging, and training with one of the main classes hours before he would run their private lesson.

Martinez sucked in a sharp breath, jolting halfway out of his skin. Lira had just run past and slapped her heavy fur-covered hand on his back, "Come on, Henry, or do I have to thrash you again?"

Like Surail, Lira, and Feinel were Jurintik in all forms of outer appearance; they could be a stereotypical werewolf, but no, that was just a happenstance of their evolution. So Martinez did not have to worry about transforming come the full moon if they bit him. This was a boon for a few reasons; the planet of Aveion not only had twin suns over a dozen moons, but they also sported some wicked teeth, and he would prefer not to let them ever bite him.

Unlike Feinel and Surail, Lira's figure was far more feminine, from having fur as white as snow, a more rounded, gentle face, a longer, softer-looking tail, and a pair of eyes as blue as cobalt, unlike the two males who looked straight out of an old wolfman movie.

Lira was definitely attractive in ways Martinez could not deny. He could think of more than a handful of Marines who would jump at the chance to have her howl their name. But she was not Martinez's cup of tea—even if he would not deny that she filled out a pair of shorts very well.

"Yeah, yeah. That was a fluke last time, and you know it," Martinez gibed, resuming his run, doing his utmost to catch up with her, Lysa, and the rest of the panting, sweating gaggle of aliens attending today's class.

Oddly enough, Feinel was not in attendance today. As far as Martinez knew, the grizzled police Sergeant never missed a training opportunity if he could help it. He must be caught up at work. Lord knows, with all the Visage going around, they both had been busy.

Although, maybe he was lucky to not be here today. This was incredibly arduous.

No matter how much Martinez had been going on runs with Shiksie, it made no difference once he was inside these walls. Teachers' classes were just another breed of animal and made the most horrendous PT(Physical training) he had ever done with the Marines look like a walk in the park. They were long, grueling affairs that consisted of nearly constant exercises and sparing—Thank god that, at least today, Teacher seemed to be more in the mood to just PT the class to death instead of having them thrash each other in long bouts or a never-ending shark tank.

"Whatever you have to tell yourself, Lad," Teacher chimed in, not one to let anyone have their chance at making fun of her students without her.

"I will tell myself that," Martinez chuckled back, dismissing the doc-eared gremlin's remark.

"Good, at least it means you're breathin,'" Teacher ribbed. "Ain't that right, yah lazy bums!"

"Yes Mam!" The class sounded out in unison. A hallmark of these torture sessions.

The rest of the class took about an hour. It only consisted of more running, with five-minute breaks for the students to practice different techniques against either bags or mitts. The "breaks" were hardly that; the running around was the breaks.

But Martinez was taking what he could get for the time being and would not bring any complaints or gripes to Teacher. He liked his spine where it was, after all.

After class, Martinez, Lira, and Lysa were slumped against one of the walls, slowly drinking out of some water bottles while chatting and watching as Teacher sent off the rest of the students, hurrying them out the airlock doors and into Draun's streets. Not that Teacher was doing so in any malicious manner; she just wanted Lysa and Martinez to get to practicing as soon as possible, and the other students lingering about in the mat room would not help.

"Lira, shall you be joining us in preparation for the upcoming competition?" Lysa asked chipperly.

"If you are alright with it, Teacher kind of strong-armed me into attending this next one," Lira replied before sipping her water bottle.

"What, did she threaten to stop banking with you or something?" Martinez joked, knowing Lira worked as a teller at one of the local banks.

"Nah, it's nothing like that. Just know it's embarrassing," Lira replied, shaking her head and scratching behind her fluffy ear.

Martinez and Lysa both shrugged and left it at that.

He was not close enough to Lira to be comfortable prying or teasing her too much. Her life and business were hers. That and he wasn't exactly an open book to most people. He might as well extend the same courtesy.

On the other hand, Lysa was a close friend of the white-furred Jurintik. They spent quite a lot of time out of class together, regularly going shopping, dining, or heading out to some of the hundreds of thousands of recreational activities around the city. As such, Lysa already had heard the story from Lira and was not about to air her friend's dirty laundry.

Last week, Lira sought Teacher's council about how to ask Feinel out on a date and fumbled her attempt hard. She had stumbled over her words and ultimately failed to ask him properly. Somehow, during her abysmal attempt at asking him out, Feinel displayed a level of density Lysa had thought was only reserved for Martinez. The man somehow took her invitation to spend some alone time together as a desire to train. In her infinite wisdom, Lira ended up agreeing to train with Feinel at the shooting range.

Lysa did not see how that was a failure, but Lira did not see them spending time together, doing something as a date.

While shooting weapons was not what Lysa considered a flawless first date, it counted as far as she was concerned. Besides, Lira and Feinel got along well enough; how in all the universe she botched speaking to a man she spent several hours a day with was beyond Lysa.

That would be as embarrassing as if Lysa attempted to ask Martinez to Mordaine and ended up asking, "May I kick you in the balls"?

At least it was a start for Lira. She would fix it. The woman was sharp, after all.

They casually spoke for a few more minutes while Teacher finished up with the other students. Their conversation did not involve anything too eventful. Lira told them about a new clothing store opening, which she wanted to drag Lysa to—something, of course, she agreed to do.

Martinez bemoaned his recent stents at work and his encroaching midterms. At least, that was something Lira could understand, having graduated from Draun's college only a few years ago. So, the pains of midterms and finals were relatively fresh in her mind.

"Oi, lad," Teacher barked as she walked over to them, her bare feet plodding on the plush matting.

"Yes, mam," Martinez replied, giving her a joking salute.

"Go ahead and teach 'em some of your jiu-jitsu for the next hour or so," Teacher said, gesturing at Lira and Lysa. "I got some paperwork to do. Once I'm all done, y'all can cut fer the day. Alright?"

"Yeah, no problem, mam," Martinez groaned while he stood, both knees sounding like popcorn. "Anything specific I can't teach them?"

"Nah, just don't break 'em," Teacher replied before patting his shoulder and heading to her office.

"You two ready?" he questioned.

Lira and Lysa nodded, scooting closer to the center of the mats. Both of them quickly relaxed and started to listen to the explanation of the basic rules of their practice. Most of what they discussed was to be expected: no biting, intentional hair pulling, grabbing of digits, punching, or kicking—all things Teacher typically enforced with heavy punishment for rule breakers. Not that Martinez was going to do that part. Punishing his Ruh'ah would be weird as hell, and Lira would get the same fair treatment Lysa got.

Martinez would focus on grappling with them and defer to Teacher regarding anything involving striking. Yeah, he had experience in Krav Maga and the Human Marines Basic Martial Arts Program, but he doubted anything like the good old eye gouge or groin strikes would be legal during their competition—or enjoyed by the recipient. While only Lira had claws, Lysa certainly kept her nails sharp.

Martinez had decided to cover the absolute basics for them for practice. Because there was hardly a month left and they would only be practicing twice a week, focusing on escaping and maintaining the mount and guard would be a lot of their focus for the next few weeks, and anything he found they needed or could use.

Today, they would focus on some of the simplest forms of breaking out of the mount and guard. Everyone needed to know how to do those if they wanted to be any good at grappling.

"Alright, Lira, go ahead and mount Lysa, and I will explain what I want her to do," Martinez requested.

Lysa and Lira quickly got into position, with Lira straddling Lysa's bare stomach. He briefly explained the goal of each step as they went along. The steps of today's maneuver were simple and practical, but the Lord knows that the techniques would work as long as your opponent had two legs and no more than four limbs.

Lysa had to take several steps to get out of the mount and into a more dominant position. While ending up in Lira's guard was still not ideal, it was better than being in the mount where Lira could easily control the fight and press the attack.

Firstly, Lysa buckled up against Lira hard enough to knock her off balance and take one of her arms across Lysa's chest. From there, Lysa had to roll Lira to the side of the arm she now controlled. At that point, Lysa would end up between Lira's legs and in the guard and have control of a single wrist.

It went incredibly smoothly after having to re-explain to Lira to not resist too much and let Lysa get a rep or two in the first round of training. Martinez should have expected that she tended to get slightly too enthusiastic from the few times he had practiced with Lira.

Martinez did have to admit hearing Lira yelp in surprise when Lysa nearly bucked her off was funny, with Lira tumbling onto the mats. Neither Martinez nor Lira expected Lysa to generate so much power that Lira was essentially thrown out of the mount and face-planted. But here they were—for a few rounds at least. Lysa also slowed down to let her practice the technique and not just muscle Lira off her.

Once Lira and Lysa swapped, they, funnily enough, had a nearly opposite issue. Lira was not used to grappling, and because Aviex and Humans had incredibly high muscular density compared to most, the white-werewolf esc woman could hardly move Lysa. At first, each buck only moved Martinez's Ruh'ah's bulk only a few centimeters.

Watching Lira struggle was somewhat sad. She was clearly trying, but biology was just not on her side for this matchup. Martinez and Lysa likely were two of the few people she would have difficulty grappling or fighting. After a few meager attempts at dislodging Ruh'ah from her waist, Lira was already panting and clearly starting to get frustrated.

Lira's frustrations were not helped by Lysa's hints of snark and cruelty she had with her friends and him.

"I would have assumed you, of all people, would do better than this," Lysa teased Lira, a smug, toothy grin on her coal-black lips. She wiggled her butt back and firmly replanted it on Lira's hips from the gentle attempt at a buck.

Lira growled at Lysa, not in any way with legitimate venom. Either that or Lysa and Lira just practiced together long enough to understand one another subconsciously.

Martinez found it strange how Lira growled. He had heard Feinel and Surail growl before, their growls felt territorial, like a hard line in the sand was being drawn moments before they snapped. Lira's sounded softer, more refined in a strange sense. It reminded him of the sound a mother dog might make to their pup when they are out of line.

Lira brought her long legs up tightly to Lysa's butt, halfway kneeing her. All the way from her toes, she bucked as hard as possible, grabbing Lysa's hip as she did. Lira managed to send Lysa lurching forward with a surprised mewl, her butt sliding down forward on her stomach; where Lira snatched both her hands tightly when they landed on the ground to keep their faces from smashing together.

As quickly as Martinez expected Lira's initial attempt to go, she snaked between Lysa's legs and flipped her hard onto the mats. Lysa tightly wrapped her legs and Lira's hips and held her tight, setting up a powerful guard—as he instructed both to do.

"How about that one?" Lira jeered, sitting tall and proud, her trail brushing happily against the mats.

"Far more like you," Lysa chuckled.

"Yeah, a few more like that, and we can move on to the next step: escaping the guard," Martinez interjected.

Lira looked at Martinez with the strangest combination of surprise and a scowl. Meanwhile, Lysa slipped out and readied herself to reset for another attempt.

"Really, I have to do that again?" Lira bemoaned.

"Yeah, of course. Only completing one maneuver is nowhere near enough," Martinez shrugged.

Shortly after Lysa and Lira had repeated one of the methods for reversing the mount a few more times, they moved on to the next step of breaking an opponent's guard.

Martinez had several different options for breaking the guard he could teach them, but with Lira's slight variation in anatomy, he was unsure which ones would work. So, he had to spend a few minutes figuring out what worked best by trying a few of them. After ruling out a dozen options because they were not wearing Gi's and could not punch each other, Martinez decided to teach them two.

The classic choice was to press your opponent's hips to the deck, then shimmy back until their guard opened.

The other option Lira was in no way happy about having tested on her. A sentiment Martinez understood, having someone drive their knee into your gooch and increasing the pressure until the pain was unbearable. But most people let go quickly once a knee planted itself into their groin area—Lira apparently was not like most people and wanted to be stubborn, pigheaded, and had something to prove. Whether she was proving it to herself, Lysa, or Martinez, only she knew, but the end result was the same.

All three of them apparently had that stubbornness in common because Lysa was giggling like a sociopath, watching her Ruh'ah and friend struggle to see who gave up first.

"Fuck, for how long are you going to do that for," Lira groaned.

"Until you let go, you realize in practice once it hurts, you can let go, right?" Martinez retorted.

"I won our last round; I'm not losing now," Lira sneered.

"Lira, it's practice," Martinez replied, twisting his hips and driving his knee further.

Lira gritted her teeth, growled, and tried desperately to keep her legs locked around Martinez's hips, but this maneuver was perfect because no matter how strong you were, it both hurt like hell and forced your femur between their ankles and lock, preventing them from closing in more. It was only a matter of time until her locked ankles were forced open. Thankfully, that was only a few moments away.

"Fuck," Lira gasped as her legs finally released.

"Ha, I win," Martinez bragged.

Lira sat up and awkwardly shifted, clearly still in some amount of pain. "Yeah, yeah, you won that one. Now lay down. It's my turn."

"Go ahead and practice with Lysa a bit more. You both need to be on both ends of this," Martinez gestured to them.

"Nah, I want to try with you," Lira sneered, clearly having not given up on winning.

"You just wish to push your bravado," Lysa replied.

Lira simply shrugged, not denying the idea in any way.

Martinez looked to Lysa for some support but received none. She clearly wanted to watch this.

"Fine, the two of you can use me as practice for this part," Martinez shrugged, "Maybe seeing it and breaking the guard might be helpful."

The rest of their practice was reasonably straightforward but not uneventful. Apparently, both Lysa and Lira were enthusiastic about showing how quickly they could learn how to break his guard. It was too bad for him and his family jewels; both were a bit too quick, and each ended up kneeing Martinez in the balls multiple times.

Once, he could see it as an accident, even if Lira's sharp, bony knee made him see stars for a moment. Martinez could still believe it was an earnest mistake the second time around. But come the third and fourth, he was sure this was at least somewhat intentional. Their sniggers and sneers between the two alien women made it evident they thought hearing him trying to stifle groans of pain was hilarious.

"I'm glad you two are having fun," Martinez groaned.

Both paused, looked at one another, then back at him.

"Oh, Ruh'ah you are tough. I am sorry if you were hurt," Lysa said, patting his thigh.

"Sorry, we might have gotten a bit carried away," Lira affirmed, averting her cobalt eyes and adjusting her slipping tank top.

"It's OK. I think we have had enough practice," Martinez whined after Lira forced his legs open and shimmied back, escaping a guard he had given up half a minute ago. "I don't think the judges will let you intentionally knee your opponent's balls."

"What if it was actually an accident?" Lysa questioned.

"I have no idea," Martinez said, flopping flat onto the mats. "For all I know, your opponents won't even have junk there."

"Some will, some won't," Lira shrugged.

"Well, keep it in mind," Martinez said, the pain in his groin subsiding.

"Oi, you three, class is over," Teacher bellowed, her voice overpowering the entire room.

Teacher walked over to them, her heavy muscles glistening in the bright lights of the dojo. Her breathing mask was slung around her heavily scarred neck. She already had her jacket in hand and was oddly wearing long, loose-fitting cargo pants—something noticeably unlike her. Martinez could not recall a single time he had seen Teacher wearing anything but workout shorts.

"Oh, must we depart?" Lysa complained, pointing at her recovering lover, "I think Ruh'ah wanted to spar a little bit."

"'Fraid so, I got stuff to do tonight. You two can keep picking on the lad in a few days," Teacher said, sneering at Martinez.

"Very well," Lysa replied, tugging Lira to her feet. "Come on, Lira, we shall go shower and change."

"Righto, yall do that," Teacher replied.

The pair quickly exited and headed toward the lockers down the back hallway, leaving Teacher and Martinez on the mats.

"So, how was practice?" Teacher chuckled. "Did they at least learn something and not just knee your nuts for the whole hour?"

"Yeah, they did learn something," Martinez replied.

"That's good. I never took yah for the cock and ball torture type," Teacher laughed, hoisting Martinez up from his seat on the mats like he weighed nothing.

That was unsurprising. Teacher was built like a bodybuilder and likely weighed almost as much as he did despite only being a meter tall.

"I'm not," Martinez chuckled, gently tapping her on the shoulder with his knuckles.

"Could have fooled me," Teacher shrugged.

"Fuck you," Martinez joshed.

"I told yah lad, I like my men with more meat on 'em," Teach replied without missing a breath, deflating any ground Martinez might have tried to retake for his dignity.

VEHEMENT VALMIN

"**W**ell, all of that could have gone worse," Martinez whined about the rounds of bludgeoning he had just survived, still feeling a throbbing ache in his family jewels.

"I'm certain Lira had an enjoyable time with practice," Lysa assured, squeezing Martinez's hand slightly.

Martinez did not deny they both had an enjoyable time. He was not having a horrible time until they nearly made a game of seeing if they could make him give up by knee-striking his member. What red-blooded man would not enjoy spending time with the woman he cared about—even if she laughed at his expense?

"Probably, but can you two not use my groin as a target?" Martinez teased, " How would you like it if I used your tits like that?"

"I would be cross with you for at least the evening," Lysa assured, sticking her tongue out.

"Exactly," Martinez replied, lightly flicking her shoulder, eliciting the slightest giggle and flutter of her four ruby-red eyes to smooth over any hard feelings. Fuck she knew precisely what he was a sucker for—and how to use it. And it wasn't like he would hold it too much against her. Beyond that, instead of their usual tender love and care, he would likely spend the night icing his more sensitive area.

The area of Draun they were walking through was one of the main thoroughfares. If the city had what could be called an actual main street, neither knew where it would be. A massive grid was set up around the Medical station Martinez worked out of, with the rest of the city either organically winding around other buildings or just adding to that grid.

That made sense since the medical station was also named Draun, and Draun City grew naturally because the people working there and at the attached spaceport needed places to live, eat, and lay their heads.

Humans have done that for thousands of Earth years. That other sentients did similar things was not a shock to either of them; it was all they had known, so why question it—primarily when it resulted in this wonderous evening jaunt?

The autumn breeze played with Lysa's hair, brushing up and flicking his neck. Hundreds of alien species traveled from stall to stall and doorway to doorway while shopping or going to the restaurants and clubs the nightlife offered. Not that either of them went out much; they both were more of homebodies than not.

The fact the aliens gave Martinez and Lysa a wide berth was something he enjoyed. It made potential threats easy to distinguish, something his PTSD and paranoia took as a boon because even with the moon high in the sky and the wan LED(light emitting diodes) street lamps, there were heavy, all-consuming shadows every few dozen meters.

Martinez had enough experience in his storied career as a Corpsman to know to give any dark blotches of the street that put his hairs on end a deserved respect. Shadows like those were all too optimal to stage an ambush out of, grab hold of a target, or lie in wait for an unsuspecting victim.

It was a shame that the GU was not keen on letting anyone who wanted to walk around with a concealed pistol or some other ranged choice. Lord knows he would feel more at ease with an 11.5mm caseless in a holster.

As for less-than-lethal, it was complicated. There were too many factors for chemical options; they just banned them nearly outright. What was lethal for one species was a harmless annoyance for others; for some, it might as well be a summer breeze.

The GU did allow pocket knives, having accepted that with thousands of species with their own built-by-nature weapons or through readily available augments, giving those without them some cold steel was perfectly fine. The lawyers and lawmakers had long ago declared a knife as a tool, not a weapon.

At least he wasn't unarmed like his first date with Lysa. While the folder tucked in his belt was not ideal, it was better than grappling everyone. Even if he only carried it mainly for the intimidation factor, no one wanted to get cut, not even him.

Was shooting someone terrible, violent, and deadly—yes. However, those actions were over in an instant. Cuts and stabs took time and were never clean like they showed in movies for anyone involved.

Martinez also never forgot Sgt. Johnson's golden rule of knife fighting.

"You will get cut," even if you are the initiator.

As they kept going, Lysa kept catching hints that Martinez was overly paranoid and was trying to hold him closer to relax him. Attacks against even her as an Aviex were rare, so much so in the city they were pretty much as safe as his home. She was glad it worked until every muscle in his body flexed tightly, and any calm she passed to him shriveled and died when his name was called out.

The gentle voice was one Martinez hoped he would not have heard her again after what happened.

"Martinez, how are you?" Verni said from just off the side of the street; Lysa's clinging to his arm prevented him from seeing the pangolin-like woman. So, hearing her set off every ambush reaction he had for a split second.

They shifted to see her. Verni wore one of her usual apron-like clothes, which her species tended to wear. Today, it was bright orange and adorned with intricate angular stitching resembling flowers.

Clutched in her claws was a small sampling of food on skewers—a sign that Martinez honestly dreaded seeing because it meant somewhere nearby was Ezol.

"Oh, uh, hi there, Verni," Martinez croaked.

"You never answered my messages or Ezol's. Are you alright?" Verni questioned, tilting her head slightly while looking up at Martinez and Lysa.

Lysa gently squeezed Martinez's hand in calm assurance, knowing very well that his nearly killing Ezol was what led him to basically drink himself to death. Between the guilt of that, Verrilon, and him not fully trusting Lysa or the others at the time to let him vent, he had fucked up and knew it—so she wanted him to feel safe here. This situation was likely volatile, to say the least.

"Oh, yeah— That was nothing. I just–" Martinez cringed out, not wanting to have this conversation.

How the fuck was he supposed to explain to Verni he did not want to answer her or Ezol because he felt like an uncaring asshole. His ignorance and failure to show the care that Ezol as a different species had led to a dozen of their family being hospitalized and a handful never making it out of the ER.

"Would you please come and speak with Ezol? His cart is just over there, and we are worried about you," Verni insisted, gently stepping closer and grabbing Martinez's hand. Her bright eyes looked at him with an earnest, gentle expression that reminded him of a caring mother.

The mere touch of her claws made Martinez grimace and want to retreat. This was not planned and already put him on the back foot.

"Oh–I don't know," Martinez said, looking off to the distance for something to use as an excuse to leave.

Verni gently nudged Lysa with her other clawed hand, something Henry never noticed, but the look and nod told Lysa what Verni was asking. Lysa was smart enough and knew how much that event weighed on her Ruh'ah. Granted, that never meant she would force him to deal with something like that—she would recommend or possibly nudge him toward moving past it, but not force him.

"Ruh'ah, perhaps it is best if we at least speak to your friend. I know they have been trying to reach out often," Lysa said softly, emphasizing *we* and signaling her support.

Martinez whined, showing his apprehension while looking at Lysa. It took Martinez a few moments, but he eventually surrendered.

"Ok, let's do this," Martinez said quietly.

"Marvelous, come on you two," Verni said, guiding Martinez by the hand.

The walk to meet up with Ezol was maybe less than a minute's walk just around the corner off the main road and into a smaller section of the city where hundreds of little mom-and-pop shops lined the road, along with just as many food and specialty item vendors hocking their wares from carts.

The city's scent shifted drastically from its usual somewhat fresh but welcoming scent to something similar to Martinez's apartment building odor. It was filled with the delicate scents of foods of every kind and the sharp odors of their preferred colognes and perfumes.

The location even matched the usual welcoming comfort, filled with laughs and idle conversation of those both in and out of view. Filling the air with a cacophony of hundreds of languages.

However, Martinez was anything but calm, and he did not feel welcome. Each step was heavy and dragged. His heart pounded a million beats a minute, and both Verni and Lysa felt his pulse through his palms as he breathed heavier and broke out into a cold sweat.

"It is alright, Martinez, you are with friends," Verni assured when Ezol's cart came into view.

"Yeah—" Martinez agreed out of courtesy.

The cart looked almost identical to the last time Martinez had seen it, save for the lack of a crowd of jeering, eager-to-eat Valmin. The sign still had lights outlining the spicy, succulent meat skewers Ezol was known for around town. Food that, frankly, most species cannot stand to eat. Most could not, but those who could eat his food were regulars for the meter-tall Valmin man behind the smoking grill filled with skewers.

"Martinez, Lysa!" Ezol said, spotting the approaching trio and happily waving at them. "Come on over."

As much as Martinez just hearing and finally seeing that Ezol was still alive gave him a bit of comfort in knowing he had not killed his friend, his voice was all wrong. Instead of the relaxed, laid-back, enthusiastic tone, his voice was harsh and growl-like, as if the Valmin man had smoked three packs a day for years.

That change, coupled with the garish scar on his neck from the emergency tracheotomy Martinez had given to shove a breathing tube down his gullet, did not make seeing his old friend easier.

"It's good to see you, brother. Have you been busy? Oh, and Lysa, sorry about not stopping in as well; I've been trying to make sure I make up for some lost revenue," Ezol said as calmly as ever while flipping the skewers over.

"That's alright, Ez. Not many people come to the shop to buy your special peppers. Besides, I no longer work the night shift, so unless you arrive during the day, I will not see you," Lysa assured.

"Yeah, I've been a bit busy," Martinez said, still feeling awkward about being here.

"I can imagine. I've heard a lot about what was going on in the city with drugs and crime. Knowing you and the medical services, you likely have your hands full," Ezol shrugged.

Martinez quickly shifted from awkward to confused based on their reactions. He might be able to justify Lysa just accepting this odd tension he felt because she was trying to be supportive, but Ezol and Verni? Do they not understand he nearly killed Ezol? No, he did kill several of their extended family. Why were they so unsettlingly nonchalant?

Verni let go of Martinez's hand and scooted in next to Ezol, gently nuzzling his neck for a moment before looking back at Martinez with that same assuring look she had a little bit ago, though it included a wee smile on her snout.

"So Martinez and Lysa, would either of you like some dinner? It will be my treat," Verni asked.

"Do you have anything not too spicy?" Lysa questioned.

"If you're anything like the big man here, nothing would be spicy to you," Ezol laughed, his voice horse and painful.

"Ok, can we pause for a moment!?" Martinez blurted out in a half-shot, his confusion being far too much at this point.

Their attention turned entirely to him, With Verni jumping half out of her skin, surprised by his outburst.

He could understand trying to reassure someone all was forgiven and forgotten, but this was ridiculous. They were all acting like nothing had ever even happened, like he had not hurt Ezol and his family, nor that he had maimed Ezol to keep him alive.

"Yeah, what's up, buddy?" Ezol said, still cooking without pause. "You two got dinner plans already or something?"

"What—no—no. How are you so casual about this? I was nervous beyond belief; I was ignoring you and Verni because I was horrified about facing you after killing your family," Martinez protested loudly enough some of the alien's nearby attention was drawn to the short outburst.

"A little too loud, Ruh'ah, no need for yelling," Lysa whispered, drawing his attention to the few anticipatory looks.

Martinez looked around and politely apologized to the other vendors and patrons in the area. They were just as forgiving as Ezol and Verni, hardly even acknowledging him after seeing it was not a fight.

"Sorry, but Verni—Ezol, how are you two not furious at me?" Martinez questioned, nearly pleading for an explanation.

They shared a brief glance before looking back at Martinez.

"Brother, I don't think you realize exactly how our family, well, specifically Valmin families, works," Ezol almost shrugged. "I thought I explained it before."

"Clearly, I am missing some information here," Martinez said.

If anyone killed even his cousins, his family would likely never forgive someone for that. Hell, half his extended cousins would try to kill that person for years.

"I told you before how all those people from out of town were extended family. I will be honest: I only ever met half of them once or twice. Each Valmin has dozens and hundreds of brothers and sisters alone. Mine and Verni's extended family are in the thousands. I could only name our two little ones and maybe a handful of the others," Ezol calmly explained.

"I could never imagine that," Lysa commented, squeezing Martinez's arm tighter. Aveix families never got much larger than a few dozen, even at the far reaches of extended families. Lysa could not even comprehend having a dozen siblings because she was an only child.

"Yeah, most species can't," Ezol replied, pointing his spatula at them.

"Wait, those numbers aren't lining up, Ezol," Martinez prodded, thinking they were essentially gaslighting him. "If you two only have two kids, those population numbers could not be possible."

"Ah yeah, that," Ezol said, awkwardly scratching his snout. "Well, that errr—"

"I think I might be able to clarify. Ez and I had some difficulties with having the typical number of children," Verni interjected. "It's a bit personal if you would rather not dig into a medical issue."

"Ok, ok, a bit of a perspective difference for the first part," Martinez agreed. "What about the fact, I nearly killed you!" gesturing an on-safety knife hand at Ezol's neck scars.

"There was Nothing you could have done about that," Ezol said flatly. "It was an allergy, nothing to do with the capsaicin like I heard you were on about."

"But all the blood, the reactions? How?" Martinez interjected.

"Ruh'ah, perhaps wisdom would recommend you hear him out before you continue interrupting him," Lysa said, bumping her hip into him.

"Ok, sorry, sorry for interrupting. Ezol, please lay it out for me," Martinez agreed after realizing he was interjecting too much again.

"I don't doubt there will be some trouble getting around that part. So this is what happened—" Ezol began before explaining a series of astonishing, annoying, and upsetting events. So much so that Martinez was upset that he had not realized this was possible.

Ezol explained to Martinez the events that led to him being hospitalized, with them all having dinner for a visit. Followed by, as the Valmin's doctor said, "The perfect storm of symptoms".

There was an ungodly combination of Ezol's stomach lining being inflamed by the capsaicin and his own allergy to what they believe to be several chemicals in the hot sauce, causing internal hemorrhaging and anaphylactic shock. Additionally, the chemicals burned his vocal cords to a degree, causing his current issues with his voice.

According to the doctor, the allergy must run in his family because only those closely related to him were affected highly. In comparison, Verni and her side merely had a minor version of the allergy that led to them having a regrettable day-long case of food poisoning, but otherwise, no ill effects.

"So yeah, I'm still waiting on results for what it was in the sauce. Stars above know I can eat capsaicin," Ezol chuckled, gesturing at the food he had just moved to the warming section of his grill and off direct heat.

Martinez was beside himself, not angry at any of them. He was furious at himself for not thinking about any specified allergies with Ezol. Martinez did that with Lysa because he cared about her but never considered it with Ezol.

How shit of a friend and corpsman can he be? That's damn near day-one stuff. He checked for drug allergies with every patient, for god's sake.

"Dude–I—Fuck!" Martinez exclaimed, his rattled brain unable to make anything else for a statement.

Ezol handed his spatula to Verni and walked up to his Human

friend, patting his side heartily. "Brother, It's all good. It's just a fresh Oasis, as I see—and you should too."

"I have no idea what that means," Martinez replied.

"It means it's not that big of a deal. Was it a tragedy? Yeah. But don't kill yourself over it," Ezol assured.

"See, Ruh'ah, I told you you should have talked to them weeks ago," Lysa purred.

Martinez looked over at her and chuckled, thinking about how many nights she told him to go and message Ezol to clear the air. Insisting this issue weighing on him was only making his sleeping problems worse— and if anyone could know that, it would be her.

"Yeah, you did," Martinez admitted, regretting telling her he would not.

"Now, do you want to take them up on the offer for dinner?" Lysa said.

"Yeah, come on, I miss having someone who can sample new recipes coming around; you have left me high and dry for weeks," Ezol smiled, rubbing his claws together in anticipation of an answer from the only sentient the Valmin man knew could outdo him in hot sauce.

Martinez glanced briefly at them and Verni, who was already serving them food, assuming she knew the answer.

"Yeah—I can eat," Martinez said.

"Perfect. It was a slow night; I got plenty ready to go," Ezol assured, turning back to Verni.

SCHEMING SHIKSIE

Shiksie growled in frustration and looked over the ocean of papers on Human courtship and mating as she tried to relax in the simple living room of her comfortable home in Draun's suburbs. She had been working on this personal project for weeks but felt no closer to a genuine answer on how to make Martinez see her as anything but just his mentor.

Her eyes shifted from the notes on the table to the papers and active datapads strewn across the room and plastered to the walls. The fact that even with all this effort, she had no honest answer was mind-boggling, frustrating, wrong. Usually, she could find a solution to medical questions with a short afternoon of document perusing; this was starting to seem ridiculous. Her living room looked like the cork boards crazy people in Human movies used: pictures, articles, newspapers, and scrawled notes strung together in a web diagram matching her mind's attempts to grasp some logic of her feelings. While the light of the datapads illuminated the room in spotted clarity, the distances between wan and indiscernible.

Shiksie had to assure herself she was not nuts like those people. She still had her faculties. Her need to have all the relevant information she needed at her clawtips just ended up looking eerily similar to those conspiracy-ridden characters. She was just being logical about her approach, no more, no less.

Her research was as extensive and detailed as anything else that took her dedication. The page's scrawlings covered everything from gender roles, mating theories, romance novels, hook-up culture aids, erotic guides, anecdotes of success and failure, and relationship help books. They were just the basics she needed while wading through the hefty muck her heart had been trudging through lately.

They were the basics, then Shiksie looked up more explicit media over the data net, needing to grasp more than the culture but the physical aspects of Human relationships. By every star in the sky, she was not prepared for the amount of pornography she leaped headfirst into. Not just because pornography was something she had never taken an interest in, thinking watching material like that was a waste of time. At least now she knew Martinez and her would physically be compatible; she knew most things about Human anatomy, after all.

As repulsive and embarrassing as watching the videos was, Shiksie had to admit Humans were undoubtedly creative in their sexual efforts. Ever since delving into those areas of what felt like forbidden knowledge, she did her best not to picture Lysa and Martinez partaking in those bold acts; why did so much of it involve rope and other tools?

Imagining them holding each other tight and rutting was better ignored; otherwise, her heart had cold ice driven through it. Seeing those salacious acts of other Humans made Shiksie wonder what it would feel like to be on the receiving end. She had never done anything like that with anyone. Martinez was the closest she had ever been to Human kissing someone, and that was only a tiny lick on his head and a hug. But the thought of Martinez doing those things to her made her body flush, dreaming of him holding her with a tender caress and gentle, beatific smile. Never in all her life had Shiksie somewhat yearned to wear a collar or have lashings around her wrists. It's too bad his guard, Lysa, was always around.

The air was thick with the odor of her anxieties, confusions, and frustrations. To anyone else with a nose as sharp as hers, walking in here would be like entering a bog of vile death and decay after festering in her emotions for this long. The only reason the miasma did not bother her was because she was the originator.

She set her pen down and leaned back to stretch some of the fatigue from her tight muscles, having not slept well since delving fully into finding a solution to this problem, not just because of lewd dreams of Martinez but the exponentially increasing pressure that had been building in the trauma center. No one in the shop had gotten off work on time in weeks, and lunch breaks were a distant memory. Everyone slipped in snacks where and when they could, or as Martinez said, "Chow is continuous". It was an apt term for what they had been going through for sure.

Every day, there has been at least one victim of the horrible mind-altering drug—Visage. They had become so common that Harnsis and the other Doctors had ordered keeping sedatives on hand because some of the patients were still under the first-stage effects and could not see a difference between whoever drugged them and the nursing staff.

Ivorn, Martinez, and security had already had to subdue several patients for not only their safety but the staff and other patients several times this week alone. Whatever is going on with this drug, hopefully, the police and the wider GU investigators can get a handle on it soon. Everyone in the shop was starting to look like the walking dead. Gone were smiles, jokes, and laughs between them and with most patients. No, now everyone was to the point and just wanted to get through another shift.

It pained her that that mentality carried over when Martinez went on runs with her or studied. Neither had much energy for much else. But for now, that was not her issue, at least not directly.

Shiksie stood up and languidly went to the fridge to get a drink. She needed something to soothe her drying throat and just a break from reading; her eyes started to hurt hours ago. The last five hours had gone by so quickly she did not even notice the sun had gone down, and it was hours past when she usually would go to bed. But she needed to find a solution and then draft a plan to execute. Martinez was leaving with Lysa to her parent's home in only a few weeks, and once that happened, her window of opportunity was gone.

From all the books, articles, and hours of non-graphic videos, Shiksie had absorbed knowledge from time running out. She knew quite a lot about the typical steps in Human courtship and romance. When a Human takes the step of verifying a relationship and having received acceptance by their partner's parents, unless there is a massive jostling between the potential mates, their future might as well be set: cohabitation, marriages, and eventually children.

Shiksie did not know if Martinez and Lysa could have kids, but even if your species were incompatible, there were options for gene sequencing and other possible routes for a facsimile. Gene sequencing works for everyone so long as you can stomach that the child is, in a way, not yours.

The gene specialist will take each species' genes, splice a viable embryo, egg, or whatever the species needs, and force the traits of each onto their future child. The embryo or egg would then be inseminated into the mother.

The only universal constant of the process was that the child that resulted from gene splicing would always be of the mother's species.

For those without the stomach or money for that process, there was always adoption. Shiksie knows that better than most, having grown up in an orphanage after her parent's untimely deaths.

Shiksie sucked down her drink and breathed a sigh of relief, the burning in her throat abating. After a moment, she donned her jacket and stepped out into the brisk evening air. Going on a walk or exercising has always been good for her when it came to relaxing and processing haunting thoughts, so long as she was alone. When Martinez had been around the last few weeks, their workouts only made her yearn for him more: seeing his muscle flexing, bark-colored eyes, sweat rolling, and pine scent—made her body ache for him to grab her, especially after delving into Human pornography. It was strange she had never felt this way for anyone, but Martinez's boldness, confidence, and scent just flipped a switch in her.

She glanced around the vacant street, leaves feathering across the area, carried off by a caressing breeze. The deep, intoxicating scent of the browning trees and encroaching rainstorm filled her lungs with lush comfort. Shiksie always enjoyed this time of year; pleasant memories of her parents were constantly dredged up in autumn.

Her mother had always insisted on them going on picnics or hikes during autumn just to see the changing colors of the woods. Shiksie's Father did not care for it but did so to keep her mother happy. Even with that knowledge, Shiksie adored those happy times. Sipping warm drinks while they all cuddled under a blanket, the chill breeze trying to crawl in to ruin their evening, but neither Father nor Mother would let the tiniest breeze touch their giggling daughter's fur. By the stars, she missed them.

Her walk in the calming breeze was enjoyable and just what she needed, though it did not give her a new perspective or anything like that. The time stepping back and looking at the whole picture let her categorize everything and put into perspective what she did and did not control and what else affected her planning how to seduce Martinez.

Lysa was the main issue, blocking Shiksie from getting too close to her Ruh'ah. With her around, making any attempt was out of the question. Shiksie could hardly make eye contact with the intense gothic woman. Every twitch and subtle squint of Lysa's four eyes were threats covered by subtle hints of fangs and sharp nails. So, if she wanted to prise an answer from Martinez, Lysa could not be around.

The only thing Shiksie did control was the times they exercised or studied together. So she would have to make her attempt during those times. She could easily control the venue at her home or elsewhere through that avenue. Anywhere would do, just not Martinez's apartment; there was too high of a chance of Lysa being there, and she could take no other steps to stack the deck in her favor.

By the time Shiksie returned to her home, she had not settled on every detail. But she had made several choices already. Firstly, she would try to do it right after his midterm to celebrate his hard work. Then she could make an easy excuse to pose a dinner as them doing something else and lure him into a bit of a trap. Was it ideal? No, but it was the only choice she had.

Now, all Shiksie had to do was adjust her chosen course of study to focus on how to initiate being more intimate and cook food similar to what Humans enjoy. With such a short amount of time left until her day of reckoning, in lieu of going right to sleep, Shiksie returned to her studies. To lay out the details of her rough plan.

PREGAME

Lira and Lysa worked their way into the gymnasium, where their first competition was being held. They needed to reach the locker rooms and claim a locker before they were all gone. They had just left Martinez, Feinel, and Ivorn to find seats in the competitor teams section, with Teacher showing them the way. That area was where anyone dedicated to supporting or aiding the fighters was given seats right next to the mats so they could rotate ringside whenever their competitor was up for a match.

Teacher made a wise choice by liberally using their friends' roles within the city and the dojo to get them those seats; otherwise, they would have to be seated far away in the back rows and have a horrible view of the day's events.

The team rated specialized medical staff because Martinez and Ivorn were medical professionals, and Lysa was a classified black species. On the other hand, Feinel was classified as a secondary coach who was there to aid Teacher ring side and give advice between rounds.

Lira and Lysa appreciated the coaching, but Martinez had been training them for the last month. So they would defer to his wisdom and advice as they fought. Yet Teacher was the professional, and they were both, as she eloquently said, "green". So, neither would argue with her wisdom to have Feinel on hand. But a part of Lira guessed this was Teacher messing with her.

Finding the correct back halls took the two of them almost twenty minutes. This was mainly because they kept being distracted by food that was on sale. Neither had eaten before because Teacher had told them not to eat breakfast and now they were hungry. But they diligently resisted the urge to nibble on something, for the most part. A few crackers might have slipped past their lips on the way to the back halls, but Teacher would never find out.

Lira looked around the crowded hallway, suppressing her unease at how the aliens parted, squeezing themselves against the walls to avoid Lysa. "You know, it's still kind of skeevy watching them do that. It creeps me out," Lira said, adjusting her gym bag and gesturing at the cowering aliens.

Despite her and Lysa regularly going out to do things together for several years, this still was unsettling; it is not like Lysa would attack them. The only person she had ever seen Lysa bite was Martinez, which was them being romantic because Martinez bit her back. Even if she did not fully understand why Aviex found biting intimate, she knew that's what it was and respected her friend's odd ritual.

Lysa glanced around and shrugged. "Others cower around me so often, I do not pay it any mind anymore. If anything, when it is not occurring, I take note."

"No doubt, still, I don't like them treating you like this," Lira commented, glaring at one of the aliens.

"Pay them no mind. Either they are approachable, or they are not. How they behave is of little issue to me," Lysa replied.

Although Lysa said that, she could not deny it in the back of her mind, it did bother her slightly. But she knew any of her direct actions would not help their impression of her or the Aveix species as a whole. The others had to be alright with her; otherwise, confronting them about the topic would only cause further issues.

Each of them was surprised by the number of aliens lingering in the hallways. Based on the Teacher's description of the venue and event, they had expected a few hundred observers. Still, there were easily thousands in attendance today—a bit of an intimidating idea for a first competition.

Entering into the women's locker room, the entire place was packed to the brim with other bipedal aliens, the category of competition Lysa and Lira had been entered into. Lira nearly gagged as the hundreds of different scents slammed into her sensitive nose like a wall; thankfully, Lysa put an arm around her and kept her steady, her head going dizzy for a few moments.

"Thanks," Lira choked.

"It is no issue," Lysa assured her friend.

They noted how all the competitors were in various stages of undress. Fur, feathers, scales, rippling muscle, and other odd forms of skin were unabashedly displayed while changing from street clothes into shorts and t-shirts that bore the logos of whatever dojo or academy they attended for their training.

"Wow, there is a surprising amount of size difference between some of them," Lira commented, looking at a two-and-a-half-meter-tall Varintol struggling to squeeze her plush, squashy hips into a pair of spandex shorts.

"Of course. But we still have to be separated into weight classifications. Our competitions should not be drastically lopsided," Lysa assured, finding an open locker they could share.

"I suppose," Lira said, "I would rather not fight the big girl there."

"Likewise. I cannot even best Ruh'ah in open competition. Someone more massive than him would be—Troubling." Lysa quipped, opening her gym bag.

They both quickly began to change out of their street clothes and don the uniforms that Teacher had provided them. Unlike everyone else's sports attire, their shirts were, as usual, entirely black and form-fitting. Although unlike the soft natural materials, their practice wear was made of, these ones were made out of a synthetic fiber that was shiny and slick. The material reminded Lysa somewhat of silk in how light it was, but it was more stretchy.

Lysa and Lira glanced at one another with the shirts on; both could admit the cut was complimenting the other for other reasons. For Lira, it showed off her broad shoulders and strong collarbones. Meanwhile, Lysa, the fabric, hugged her bust and kept her mound up and perky, even without a bra. Lysa wondered if she should wear something like this for casual time with Martinez; he certainly would appreciate one less bit of clothing to remove.

But those thoughts were neither here nor there. It was just a passing idea, not one Lysa lingered on. This was Lira's first time, and she had some alone time since the two Lira and Feinel went out. And Lysa was dying to know how their date went.

"How did your romantic rendezvous with Feinel fare?" Lysa asked, pushing down her panties and tossing them into the bag.

Lira groaned while she did the same, but she looked clearly away from Lysa, with her tail tucked down low and ears folded tightly against her head.

"It was horrible. How can a male be so dense?" Lira complained, slipping her shorts on and taking a moment to feed her tail through a custom-cut hole for it. "I wanted to do something romantic or go out and do something neither of us could do."

These shorts were interesting compared to what they usually used in training. They reminded Lysa of Martinez's Navy PT(Physical Training) shorts: Silkies. They were light and allowed both of them a solid range of motion, but they were also ungodly short, their lightweight fluttering material barely reaching a quarter of the way down their thighs. At least they have a built-in underwear set, so their genuine modesty was not a concern.

"I believe you are also quite dense; we both are aware of your attempt at querying him for a date," Lysa chuckled while fixing the elastic band of her shorts. "You still had the opportunity to have him alone and instruct you on the usage of firearms; surely you must have had an enjoyable time?"

Lira grumbled a response so quietly that Lysa could not understand her. Lysa rolled her eyes, wondering why Lira was acting like this. It was not like they were closed off to one another about most things. By the Stars, Lira was the first to know about Lysa and Martinez; not even her mother knew they were Ruh'ah before she did.

"Would you care to repeat yourself?" Lysa questioned, poking Lira's side, eliciting the slightest surprised jump.

"Ugh, fine. I outshot him. Afterward, he acted embarrassed the rest of the time we were at the range. He was quiet and did not even want to look at me," Lira admitted. "I grew up on a farm, and I think he assumed I had no idea what end the bullets came out of. He did not look at me the same after I handled the weapon better than he did."

"How is that an issue? If I recall correctly, your species generally likes their mate to be capable and handy in a fight, especially males. Don't they swoon after women who can handle attackers?" Lysa commented, zipping her bag closed.

"They do, but I don't want that—I want to be dainty and soft, treated like a princess. Not some muscular brick, like a certain Aviex I know," Lira teased, slouching onto the seat. "Her and the wall of muscle she calls Ruh'ah."

Lysa closed their locker and set a combination before plopping down beside her friend. "It's alright. I'm certain he would be more than willing to comply with your wishes, assuming there will be follow-on interactions," Lysa assured. "Additionally, Martinez is not a wall of muscle. He is quite soft and gentle when it matters." She finished with a hungered growl.

"It's easy enough for you to say. You both enjoy the other being a dense fighter," Lira commented. "I only want to fight in practice and maybe here. Feinel and Martinez both actually fought for a living. It's not the same."

Lysa shrugged but agreed. She did not deny that they both generally did enjoy that the other could fight. Not that either sought battles, they had just found them so far. Before Lysa had the opportunity to make any further suggestions to Lira on possibly making Feinel see her as more of a dainty flower and not some powerful warrior, Teacher's barking voice overpowered the idle conversations of the other students in the process of getting ready.

"Oi, you two ready to get weighed in?" Teacher said in a near commanding voice.

Half the locker room's attention was drawn to Teacher's magnanimous presence, but once most realized they were not the subject of the buff woman's attention, they returned to their own preparations.

"I am as prepared as possible," Lysa quickly replied.

Teacher nodded understanding before looking at Lira, her starry eyes intently gazing at the white werewolf-like woman.

"What About you lass? Why do you look so down?" Teacher pressed.

"You know why, mam," Lira sighed, having already explained her earlier attempt at a date with Feinel.

"Right—well, we can discuss that later on, fer now, y'all can come with me," Teacher said.

Lysa patted Lira on the back and flashed her friend a reassuring, warm smile. "Perhaps throttling someone might make you feel better?"

"Maybe for you, you combat addict," Lira chuckled, standing and gently knuckling Lysa in the shoulder. "Hopefully we are in the same bracket."

"That would be enjoyable," Lysa replied, knuckling her back and moving to follow Teacher.

CAT AND WOLF

"Surail might have picked up an extra shift," Feinel said, slouching in the folding chair just off to the side of the foam mats in the center of the small stadium. "I was off that day, and he is not some trainee. If he wants to work alone, he technically can, even if it's stupid and dangerous."

With how Surail had acted over the last few weeks, Martinez could not help but wonder if Feinel meant that it was dangerous for Surail or for the city of Draun—Martinez was definitely leaning toward it later.

Martinez looked around the area out of his usual habit of trying to keep eyes on the doors and maintaining a secure perimeter. While he had been getting better about understanding that he was no longer in combat, being switched on like that for years eventually made it difficult to shut off, or outright broke the switch completely.

This conversation had not given Martinez any of the answers he wanted. Feinel could not really do anything about Surail recently dumping drugged-up people in the ER—beyond writing him up and reiterating protocol. Still, Surail did not care about reprimands, and everyone knew it. He had been demoted and promoted multiple times already.

"Still, that ass has been out of line," Martinez complained, with Ivorn nodding his agreement, having dealt with the officer several times over the last few weeks.

"I will talk to him, man. But this ain't the military. I can't control him like we could there," Feinel replied.

Martinez could not deny that. He wasn't expecting Feinel to go that far anyway, even if the idea of putting Surail on bread and water and restricting him to half-pay would be a just action.

But Feinel was right. This was not the military, GU, or Human; no one had that power over the rough officer, not even the police chief.

Because Feinel had at least heard him out, Martinez acquiesced, not wanting to press his friend for more than he could give or could reasonably be asked. With that issue as settled as possible, Martinez continued to gaze around the arena, taking stock of the competition his Ruh'ah and Lira would be facing for hopefully the rest of the day.

Hundreds of aliens were spread out amidst the bleachers in small groups, likely having broken themselves up by either what dojo or gym they were affiliated with, not unlike Martinez, Feinel, and Ivorn had done.

Their idle conversation bounced off every surface in the expansive room, congealing into an indecipherable cacophony of white noise. Martinez could not think of any time when being slightly hard of hearing had ever been a boon, but if by the somewhat pained scrunched look on Feinel's muzzle, it must be deafening. For the first time in his life, Martinez sent a small wordless thanks to the Human Marine Corps for giving him tinnitus.

Competitors trickled out of the entrance to the back hallways and locker rooms in a constant, seemingly never-ending stream. The multitudes of colors and brands on their clothing created a constantly shifting rainbow of colors. Different types of builds and skins were just as varied as the logos: scales, fur, hair, and skin with just as various levels of musculature. The only thing that they all had in common was that they stood tall, proud, and eager for the upcoming biped competition.

As they entered, each eye traced the crowds and competitors as they sized the others up. The sheer cutthroat desire to win flowing off them filled the room with palpable tension.

Sorting the myriad of species that were here to make any friendly bouts a fair fight must be arduous. Still, breaking the competition into amounts of limbs and weight classes like the organizers had was honestly the best way Martinez could think of, and that is precisely how today's brackets were laid out with humanoid-type aliens.

Although that's not how it was described in the pamphlet tucked into Martinez's breast pocket. Today was for bipedal, two-limbed competition, with two days before and after for other general builds.

With Lysa and Martinez having the next day off, he might drag her back here to catch a glimpse of whatever type of Martial arts Traditional flying aliens used. That was something he had no impact or idea of what to expect. It might be interesting, and Lysa would likely go for it; She loved martial arts after all.

After some more relaxed conversation between the men of Teacher's little ragtag dojo, Teacher, Lysa, and Lira appeared amidst the flowing group of competitors. It was easy enough to see them, all of the aliens giving them a wide berth because Lysa was there. That and Lysa and Lira were both just shy of two meters tall, so the trio stood out like a nail ready to be hammered down.

Martinez and Feinel could not help but stare a little bit; both appreciated the trio for almost identical reasons, but each had their eye on different members of the rest of the dojo's members.

Martinez, as per usual, could not get enough of his Ruh'ah; from her gentle womanly confidence, taught and well-muscled build, wan skin, and piercing eyes that languidly watched the aliens nearby. That and even he could not deny it, he still was a sucker for a goth, and her tight shorts and t-shirt screamed that. Plus, her biting and drinking his blood tugged at his heart, knowing it was something that was theirs.

Lysa immediately found them in the ocean of aliens, a brimming smile growing on her coal lips while she waved happily to them. Her adorable dimples were even visible from several dozen meters. She grabbed Lira by the arm and damn near started to tug the werewolf-like alien toward them, drawing her attention from a chat with Teacher.

Feinel's tail started swishing and batting against Martinez's leg as they got closer. Martinez glanced between him and Lira and stifled a chuckle; their expressions could not be further apart. Fennel looked enraptured by Lira, unable to take his eyes off the fit and tall white-furred woman.

On the other hand, Lira would not even look at the group, trying desperately to look elsewhere; she looked mortified to see Feinel wagging his tail. Her ears were folded, and her tail was tucked.

"So buddy, you got something going on with Lira?" Martinez asked quietly while elbowing Feinel.

Feinel seemed to have been pulled from a trance and shot Martinez a short glare. "Am I that obvious?" Feinel grumbled.

"Dude, you were just beating us both up with your tail," Ivorn chuckled, patting Feinel on the shoulder. "Fuck even Martinez is more subtle, and he and Lysa won't stop staring at each other."

Feinel grumbled in defeat and glanced back at Lysa, Lira, and Teacher approaching. Lysa was clearly trying to raise Lira's spirits for the upcoming fights, mimicking short shadowboxing while jostling her friend; Martinez did not doubt Lysa was well aware of whatever was going on between the two Jurintik.

Feinel and Lira were usually somewhat stoic when in crowds, so the fact that both were so emotive was somewhat perturbing. But having known both of them for nearly half a standard year, he doubted it meant anything dangerous. He would ask Feinel about it later, even if he had to liquor the police officer up a bit to drag the details out—besides, it had been a while since he, Feinel, and Ivorn went out for a beer, so they were overdue anyway.

Teacher, as always, was enjoying watching her students cringe and squirm. Since Martinez and Lysa were not on the docket of potential victims anymore since becoming steeled to her teasing, poking, and prodding, it looked like Lira and Feinel might be her newest targets of ridicule.

But whatever their relationship woes were, they would have to wait. Teacher had everyone here for the competition, and she would be damned if they could not focus for the few hours they had to compete.

"Righto, everyone," Teacher started once everyone was gathered. "So the two of you will be in different brackets due to your weights. Because of that, we have two brackets before you, feather and light, followed by Lira in the middleweight class. Then we have to wait through the welters, followed by the heavyweights with Lysa."

Teacher shook her head and jabbed at Lysa's bare abs gently with her papers. "Fer a lass who can grind meat on these. I don't know where you are putting all that mass."

Lysa simply shrugged, knowing Teacher meant no ill will by the comment. There were only half a dozen heavyweights at the gym, and most were not obvious at first glance. Just by the nature of their bone and muscular density, they were extremely heavy.

The group nodded confirmation of understanding, and then Teacher turned her attention to the men on the support team. "As for you two lugs and Ivorn," she said, slightly angling her head in a half-bow.

Teacher, same as always; so willing to pick on her students, then turn around and be prim and proper to everyone else, so long as they didn't piss her off. Martinez still enjoyed that about the bodybuilder like Goblinoid; she took no shit and backed everything said with wisdom and spilled blood.

"Feinel, you will be coaching Lira during her rounds. When Lysa is up there, Martinez, that is your job. For all of it, Ivorn thank you again for acting as medical advisor; we needed it. Not that I don't trust the ones the league has, but they tend not to push the fighters. Are there any questions about your roles?"

None of them had any questions about their roles, Teacher explained everything they had to do while the girls were changing over. And thankfully it was pretty simple.

If anything, Ivorn had the most challenging task: ensuring he balanced keeping Lysa and Lira healthy and at peak efficiency while they fought on and off for several hours. But he had on hand the STTK, a small cooler of ice packs, electrolyte-filled water, and a few packs of gummy candy for quick energy.

Lord knew they would need it. If the blocks were filled as much as possible. Lira could be fighting for up to two hours today. Lysa would only have two or maybe three fights, so about half an hour of actual brawling. Go figure, finding bipedal aliens dense enough to fight an Aviex or a Human was difficult. Hell, Martinez could not think of many others that fit the bill off the top of his head, and he damn near memorized thousands of alien's medical data at this point.

Scanning the crowd while settling in to watch the ultra-lightweight division, Martinez could see a few aliens that might be going up against Lysa. There were some glimpses of who she might end up brawling against, but he could not tell. Most of the coaches and fighters were all in sportswear, so telling them apart at a distance was impossible. Although there was one that looked like a grizzly bear on two legs, which he was sure Ruh'ah would fight against.

Lysa pressed her warm shoulder against Martinez and snaked her hand into his, resting her head on his shoulder so they could enjoy watching the first sets of fights. Teacher and Ivorn made idle chit-chat, with him asking if Sursee might be able to attend classes. If only he knew what he was asking to subject his chipper girlfriend to.

The only two not watching the starting competitions were Lira and Feinel. The two acted like teenagers who had no idea what to say or do on a date alone. Martinez paid them no mind; they would figure it out. But he had a passing thought about how it was odd. Feinel literally fought criminals for a living, and he could not chat with the generally calm, easy-going Lira—it was so strange.

Reaching out in front of her, Lira reached for her wiggling toes with Feinel behind her, pressing her slightly forward, helping her deepen the stretch, causing her to involuntarily let out a content near moan.

Now, this was more like how she wanted Feinel to treat her. After she got knocked out for a moment in the first round, he was no longer acting like a bashful pup. No, the confident, robust police officer who really made her tail wag was back.

He had been attentive to her needs every minute since she started her bracket an hour ago, helping guide her with solid coaching from the sidelines by correcting her when she messed up a technique.

But the best part was when she was between bouts. After each match, Feinel supported her with a solid, muscular shoulder to lean on, letting her recuperate and drink water without any effort.

Lira leaned back and returned to resting against Feinel. She took one of the candies from Ivorn, already feeling gassed from her fights. He insisted that having something sugary would help. Ivron and Martinez were the nurses. Who was she to question it? The sweet juice filled her mouth with tart, fruity flavors.

Maybe attending this competition was not so horrible after all. Although she could live with Teacher not hollering at her while standing atop chairs next to Martinez and Lysa. But if that's the worst part of all of this, today was turning out alright.

"Alright, Lira, your temperature is fine, and you can still track objects, so you don't have a concussion. I have no reason to stop the matches on our end so long as you wish to continue," Ivorn calmly explained, pulling an ice pack off her neck.

"Well, that's good," Lira smirked, "I have no intention of stopping now."

"Alright, thatta girl," Feinel praised, giving a thumbs up to the waiting referee, letting him know their side was good to go.

The man turned and looked toward the other side of the ring, waiting for the same signal from the other side of the mats.

"Alright, you got another four fights after this one. Are you gassing yourself out? Or do you need some more water? Anything?" Feinel asked, turning his attention back to Lira.

Was she gassing herself out? Yeah, she was. For fucks sake, she just went twelve rounds with others. Lira wondered if he asked because she might be leaning against him too much; she certainly liked him dotting on her. But if this is what it took to have this lovable himbo close enough that Lira could feel the heat rolling off him, she was not about to stop.

Lira could only imagine Martinez and Lysa chuckling at her awkwardly, trying to keep it together. She held her tail still in the hand Feinel could not see so she would not play her card too strongly.

A pang of jealousy rang within her while thinking about Martinez and Lysa. Those two just worked. Lira had never seen a couple click like they did, same species or not. If Feinel and her would work out, it would be an uphill battle.

He was strong, fun to hang out with, and a good fighter. But he was so dense that unless she was bashing him over the head with a brick shaped like a heart, he would never pick up on subtleties—not like she had not been trying that for months. Maybe her trying a bit more would help, but she did not know.

Many women in her species were fiercely territorial and eager to brawl. But not her; she was timid and wanted to lounge about most days. She worked as a bank teller for those reasons. Others could deal with conflict. That was why she wanted this lug to sweep her up in his arms and carry her like a delicate flower—he could be the protector.

"No, I don't right now. Thank you, though," Lira replied, her voice squeaking nervously, earning the slightest breathy chuckle from Ivorn, clearly enjoying watching her not just ride the struggle bus but build and drive it too.

Sadly, reality had to come crashing down on Lira's little taste of what having Feinel being her ideal man could be like. The referee came over and informed them the match was about to begin.

With a reluctant sigh, Lira got up, stretched her shoulders, and tossed in a mouth guard. As she approached the center of the ring, the team cheered her on, causing her chest to fill with pride.

Her mother and sisters were fighters, having competed for most of her life, and she never understood why they enjoyed it so much. Having friends and Teacher encouraging her to do her best and not give up was intoxicating and caused her to hold her battered head high. While she did not think this one time at a meet would change her opinion on actual fighting, she could see the sport in it possibly growing on her.

Across the ring, her opponent looked shockingly in good condition, like they had just walked in off the streets and had not already gone through five fights like Lira had. The Farun'se woman had bright orange fur and sported little golden dots randomly amidst. The only exception was large areas of cream-colored fur on her stomach and face.

Lira did not want to have to fight this hulking monstrosity of a woman. With Lira generally being a nimble, light-on-her-feet fighter, this Farun'se was probably her worst match-up. They were fast and had a lot of muscle mass for their size. The fact that the woman was half a head shorter did not make any difference. The reality was that this would still be a horrendous battle.

Lira assumed the woman was likely a grappler like Martinez; she drew this conclusion from how fresh her opponent looked. There were no visible bruises or anything else indicating the Farunse had been struck at all. That and that the feline assumed a lower crouched position, keeping two open palms toward her, just like the Human.

The referee stepped between them and confirmed that they were both prepared. After a nod, he stepped back and started the fight. Lira and the Farun'se began to circle to the right, gradually getting closer, waiting for the other to make the first move.

Although none of the onlookers had to hold their breath long. Like a beast unleashed on the mats, the woman rushed forward and tossed a straight punch at Lira's head, but it was a feint. Just as her guard went up and Lira attempted to backstep, the woman dropped low and tried to grab her legs.

Lysa and Lira's extensive training with Martinez over the last few weeks paid dividends. As if the action was built into Lira's instincts, she planted her rear foot and drove a knee forward, meeting the woman's jaw.

With a deafening crack, the woman recoiled and stumbled backward, a kettle-like hiss escaping her lips.

"Fuck yeah," Feinel boasted, "Keep light, and keep going."

Pressing the attack, Lira burst forth and shot a straight kick into her opponent's soft stomach, the impact hardly slowing her down. The woman did not even flinch. Lira pivoted quickly and tried to bring a back-kick into her opponent's head, hoping to drop the woman like in her last fight.

That was wishful thinking. This Farun'se was far more nimble and well-experienced than those other competitors were. Like lightning, the woman leaped forward, closing the gap while the kick was mid-arch.

"Gotcha," the woman hissed, pressing her torso to Lira. Wrapping her thick, heavily muscled arms around Lira's waist, she instantly brought her rotation to a halt.

Before Lira realized what had happened, the world was upside down, and she was looking off at the wide-eyed, cringing crowd. The woman suplexed her, slamming the wolfish alien clean onto her head, rattling her grape.

Like a cat playing with its prey, the Farun'se let Lira stumble back to her feet. The world was no longer one picture, and Lira swayed back and forth like a leaf, clearly rattled by the deafening impact.

Ivorn looked up to Teacher, not wanting to end the fight before the master of their dojo tried to call it. Teacher looked back and gave him a subtle headshake. With reluctance, Ivorn swallowed his spit and looked back as the Farun'se loaded her legs and shot forward like a bullet.

As soon as Lira was grabbed, the woman attempted to toss her in a similar way to what Martinez had done many times. Like then, she tried to leap with the force and land on her feet. But her equilibrium was just too far gone.

Instead of a graceful flip, it looked like she had become a ragdoll. The throw was far more of a slam, whipping her against the matting with a thunderous boom. Even Feinel and Ivorn could feel the air whump past them, causing both to cringe.

Without missing a beat, the Farun'se leaped atop Lira and dragged her arm up and over a propped knee, using it as a fulcrum to armbar her. Lira tried to pull out of it, but with her seeing stars and having no air left in her lungs, any attempt was futile.

The tendons in her arm screamed in agony as the pressure slowly increased, and the Farun'se woman resisted her wild thrashing like a cowboy atop a bucking bronco. Any training she had done was out the window; Lira was panicking, going only on instincts, unable to generate a coherent thought in her fogged mind.

"Lira, you have to calm down and roll into it," Feinel coached, not that it mattered.

The referee stepped in, able to tell by Lira's near glass-like eyes the fight was over, stopping it before the Farun'se snapped her arm like a twig. This was a competition, not a genuine battle, and no one needed to get needlessly hurt.

The moment the referee stepped closer, the woman let Lira flop to the mats. Sitting next to her. As Ivron ran in to assess the fighter, Lira's mind somewhat cleared, but not much. It was just enough for her to realize how badly her lungs burned and her head throbbed.

"Holy fuck, that hurts," Lira groaned, running her claws through the fur near her ears.

"By the stars, are you alright?" The Farun'se woman questioned, frantic worry in her eyes.

"I think," Lira groaned, trying to sit up, but was stopped by Ivorn.

"Hold on there, let me check you out first," Ivron insisted, having already pulled out the gear he wanted from the STTK.

It took Ivorn no time at all to ensure Lira was alright. She would be physically sore for a few days because her elbow was slightly hyper-extended, but not enough for concern so long as it was iced and treated gingerly. But that did not hurt quite like her pride. Lira wanted to win; even though she was strong-armed here by Teacher she had been having fun winning until now.

"Hey, you did a good job," the Farun'se said, patting Lira on the shoulder after Ivorn helped her stand.

"What do you mean you thrashed me?" Lira replied.

"Nah, don't sweat it. You will get me next time," The Farun'se said with a brimming, fang-filled smile, extending a set of knuckles for Lira.

Not wanting to be rude and having learned how important etiquette was during matches, Lira bumped a fist into the woman. "Yeah, next time—uh?"

"Sundet," the woman assured.

"Sundet, alright. I'm Lira, thanks for the match," Lira smiled.

"It was fun. Get some rest Lira," Sunset said before turning and damn near skipping to her team waiting just outside the ring.

Stepping and stumbling for a moment, Lira did the same, walking alongside Ivorn toward Feinel. To Lira's shock, Feinel did not look disappointed. His tail wagged, and he had an infectious smile as bright as sunlight.

The moment he was close, Feinel offered her a shoulder and supported her as they walked toward the rest of the team.

"Good job, Lira. You did your best," Feinel whispered.

Not even attempting to hide it, Lira let her tail wag as quickly as her fluttering heart. Even if she got knocked out of the competition halfway through and wanted to keep going, she was going to take Feinel's praise as a consolation prize.

Besides, she could get him to take care of her for the rest of the afternoon while Lysa fought. And if anyone was going to win their bracket, it would be that combat junkie. All Lira had to do now was rest, relax, and watch her best friend dominate the competition.

HEAVY-WEIGHT LAUGHS

Watching Lira's fights was enthralling. The dedication to practice she had shown over the past month was evident in her form throughout. While she still tried to use her nimbleness and more flashy moves than either Lysa or Martinez would use, she had leaned on solid attacks that were tried and true, leaving little options for her opponents to attack her.

But Lysa could not celebrate her friend's attempt at victory at the moment, the two other fighters in the ultra-heavyweight division had to be her focus. Unlike her, the two she would have to fight looked like they genuinely belonged in the division.

One of them was the jet-black Varintol woman from the locker room. She was a genuine beast in her own right, standing nearly two and a half meters tall and almost as wide. She wore a bright orange top and shorts, both just large enough to cover the woman's modesty, and practically screaming as her squashy build almost ripped the seams open.

The other one, Lysa was unfamiliar with his species, but like several of the students in the dojo, he was an insectoid. His yellowish gold carapace shimmered in the bright overhead lights almost blindingly. He was incredibly swift despite being taller than the Varintol by a solid meter.

The division running the competition had decided that weight was the only way to make the competition fair. Yet, having someone like him, who could not only reach farther but was covered in spines that had to be capped by padding lest someone impale themselves, and was born with an essentially bulletproof carapace, hardly seemed proper—since she was unable to use the one thing Aveix had as a natural weapon: their teeth and jaws.

At least the Varintol also had to follow that rule, having her bone-crushing maw and knife-like claws off the table for options. The last thing Lysa wanted was for her to get cut by them. However, because of that limit, the Varintol was essentially trying to slap the insect into submission.

They were brawling wildly, fighting in unique ways that fell within strategies to aid them. The Varintol was surprisingly nimble despite weighing easily two hundred and fifty kilograms. Meanwhile, the far taller and long-ranged insectoid alien did his best to stay out of her grasp and keep scoring points with quick punches and kicks.

It was a fair strategy because if that woman grabbed him, she could smother him into a knockout and could do the same come Lysa's match.

While Lysa watched she attempted to craft a strategy to win against either of them. Keeping distance and kicking was definitely how she had to win against the Varintol, for the same reason as her current opponent.

"What would you propose I do about the man?" Lysa questioned, nervously fidgeting, unable to devise a viable plan independently.

"I'm not certain," Martinez replied, leaning forward and resting his elbows on his knees.

"You definitely could press in on them. That seems to be what that Varintol is failing to do," Ivorn commented.

"I could see that as an option for Lysa. She is definitely faster than the Varintol. But the trouble is that other Alien's reach," Martinez replied before pausing for a few moments and pulling out his datapad. "What species is he, Ivorn?"

"He is a Burtex, likely from their warrior cast. Hence the tall figure, and all the spines," Ivorn said after a few moments, thinking through the thousands of species names and descriptions he had put to memory over the last ten standard years. "Either that or nobility. They are also extremely tall compared to the workers, but he is not burly enough to be a hive guard. Why?"

"I figured we might be able to look up some data on them and use it to our advantage. We have all their medical information after all," Martinez said, opening the Burtex medical information.

"Isn't that a bit unfair?" Ivorn commented.

Ivorn did point out that Martinez's actions might be considered unfair by others. Still, there were no rules against researching your opponent's anatomy and capitalizing on any built-in weaknesses.

The years Martinez spent in combat taught him that any point in the enemy's anatomy or defenses that could be leveraged should be. While this time, there are no lives on the line, Martinez would find something to stack the deck in Lysa's favor—entering a fair fight is something only idiots do anyway.

"Meh, they are already doing it. We just are planning ahead," Martinez shrugged before returning to the datapad.

All of the effort Martinez put into finding any form of weakness they could exploit in anatomy was not wholly useless. Still, it did allay any nervousness boiling in Lysa's chest, buzzing in her breast like hundreds of angry hornets.

Her Ruh'ah had given her a simple plan for the Varintol. The woman, who, before their fight began, Lysa had learned was named Perla, had similar weaknesses to Lysa and Martinez just based on their all having mammalian anatomy: prone to being gassed out, having the same vitals, and having identical points that would drive her to the ground, even if she was far more sturdy.

They had to strategize about the woman being thrice Lysa's weight and being a tundra-adapted version of the species, not the variant built for the steppes, mountains, arboreal, or equatorial deserts.

Those variants of the species were far leaner and more analogous to Lysa and Martinez: lean, dense muscle, high oxygen efficiency, and the ability to endure for astronomical amounts of time in a fight. On the other hand, the tundra variation, when temperatures were not usually any higher than zero degrees, was prone to overheating and could be drawn out due to their generally more aggressive demeanor.

Lysa just had to wear the woman down, strike from a safe distance, and keep Perla from grabbing her. Physics was still in effect, and the arctic Varintol could easily crush Lysa when all two to three hundred kilograms of fur, fat, and muscle were laid out atop her. That was an end state they had to avoid; it would be a sure victory for Perla if it came to that.

"Just don't forget the plan, Ruh'ah," Martinez said calmly while double-checking Lysa's gloves.

"I shan't," Lysa nodded, gnawing on her mouthguard.

"Make sure you tap out if you are feeling hurt. This is still just a competition," Ivorn interjected.

Lysa nodded her understanding. She does wish to win and get a picture of her with a medal in Teacher's dojo, but that does not mean she wants to be seriously injured during this. Martinez had explained to her and Lira over the last month that this was not a title fight. No money is riding on this; She just had to do her best.

After short words of encouragement from Martinez and Ivorn and nods from the rest of the team, Lysa stepped onto the mats and took a deep breath to try to steady herself in front of her lumbering opponent.

Being close to Perla did not hold a candle to how intimidating the Varintol was from a distance. She was gargantuan. Muscle, fat, and fur all offered her safety in a fight. Lysa felt almost naked before her inspecting red-eyed gaze.

However, Perla was in no way what Lysa had expected.

Based on the previous fight, Perla was quiet and highly focused on the task at hand. Now, the black-furred Varintol had a bubbly smile and offered Lysa a glove to bump without any hesitation.

Calling what Perla wore mixed martial arts gloves did not quite encapsulate what they were. They looked somewhat like gauntlets you would wear with traditional armor, but they had increased padding on all sides and fully encapsulated her fingers to keep her sharp claws from being a danger.

"Hey, I hope we have fun today," Perla smiled, showing off her fangs in a wide beaming grin. "This is my first competition. I hope you go easy on me. That last guy was no fun."

Perla caught Lysa entirely off guard with the offer and her general demeanor and appearance; neither matched what she was expecting.

Lysa had never considered fighting other than as a means of defense. It was simply a vital matter of survival for most Aveix to treat martial practices that way. She had never considered anything else since she and Martinez had been practicing and plotting before this. Wasn't this meant to be a somewhat violent altercation?

At the same time, if this Varintol held no contempt for Lysa or other Aveix on sight, like so many who had since the moment Lysa drew breath. And since Lysa had no intention of being anything but cordial and returning the courtesies, treating the match as just some friendly sparring was also somewhat liberating for Lysa. Perhaps Lysa had been treating a friendly bout as a bit too vital to her survival?

"It is my first competition as well," Lysa replied, gently bumping gloves with Perla. "I pray you extend the same courtesy. Let's try to have fun, but I'm afraid I still wish to win."

"Same here," Perla replied, stepping back, raising her gloves, and assuming a tight stance.

Lysa backed up and did the same, waiting for the referee to signal the beginning. Peering over her fingerless gloves at Perla, the need for her strategy was all the more evident. It was like staring at a pair of trees guarding a boulder of fur.

"Begin!" The referee announced, giving the pair a wide berth, a reason evident from Perla's last fight against the man in their bracket.

Perla, true to her bearish nature, was immediately aggressive, putting Lysa on the back foot. She opened with a barrage of mocked claw strikes that, despite her weight, were blindingly fast.

Doing her best and showing her skill, Lysa dodged each one gracefully and quickly, moving her head, bobbing and weaving under and around each attack. Perla's gauntleted hands only missed Lysa's head and shoulders by a few centimeters, flicking at trailing raven hair.

Lysa broke off the initial engagement by leaping backward, bouncing on her toes, and keeping her arms and upper body in constant motion. She did all she could to keep Perla from predicting a potential retaliation.

"Great head movement," Perla extolled while cautiously closing the gap.

"I appreciate the praise," Lysa smiled.

Perla opened up with another series of the same style of strikes, and Lysa continued to do the same, keeping herself just outside of the attack's range. If the attacks were tighter and coming from the front, they would be difficult to avoid, but because they needed so much wind-up and came out like a hook with nothing to feint first, it was a simple duck and weave to avoid.

Teacher had forced Lysa and Feinel to practice dodging far tighter strikes than this in Roilan martial arts daily. But the strikes were like this because Perla used a traditional form of fighting for the Varintol, capitalizing on their claws. It was optimized for attacking animals or other Varintol, built to rip through armor and thick layers of fat. But Lysa would not know this until after the competition.

Lysa led Perla around the fighting area outlined on the mats, focusing on her main strikes, rhythm, and occasional punches. After a lap or two, Lysa started getting the feel and picked up on the part of Perla's martial art skills that was lacking; it lacked defense low and offered massive openings to her enormous frame when the Varintol's retraction lingered.

It was just as Martinez had told her. Arctic Varintol were fast relative to their girth, but a well-trained Human or Aveix could easily beat them out in speed.

"Come on, Lysa, you have to get some points," Martinez commented as they passed. "Get in there."

"I understand Ruh'ah," Lysa replied through a sharp inhale, trying to control her breathing while jerking her head back to avoid another strike.

After a few more dodges, Lysa had finally spotted her opening for a powerful retaliation. Stepping to the side and letting Perla's glove travel through her trailing raven hair, Lysa loaded her legs and exploded upward, launching her padded foot into the side of Perla's head.

To the Varintol woman's credit, she attempted to step back to dodge, but the tips of Lysa's foot collided with her jaw with a dull thud. It felt like Lysa had just kicked a brick wall, the shock of the impact rocking one as much as the other.

"Woah," Perla snorted, stepping back and shaking the fog from her head. "I was wondering if you were going to start attacking back."

"I just had to get a gauge on you, is all," Lysa responded.

"Smart, my teacher recommends a lot of the same, but that's no fun," Perla replied, gesturing at another Varintol behind her. His arms crossed and a smirk on his face. "I wanna as the GU lads back home say, 'Get stuck in.'"

That comment caught Martinez's attention. He had only ever heard that turn of phrase from Humans in the military. Some GU military guys had picked it up, but they were few and far between. Who did she know where that was part of her lexicon?

"Shall we continue? We should attempt to not disappoint either of our teachers," Lysa replied, gesturing toward Teacher in the crowd. The goblin-esc woman was already yelling at Lysa to stop chatting with her and keep hitting her.

Instead of a verbal response, Perla just stepped forward and attempted to throw a straight punch into Lysa's head; in response, Lysa raised her front leg and drove it into Perla's plushy stomach, stopping her forward momentum, and performing a flawless Teep.

Pressing the attack, Lysa dropped her foot and exchanged blows with Perla. Most of the time, she avoided any of the Vartintols' attacks, but a few sneaked through her guard, hitting her like a brick.

Such was the nature of fighting in the blender.

Martinez had warned Lysa against being that close to Perla or anyone for that matter. But Lysa seemed to have failed to follow one of the critical parts of their strategy: to avoid being pulled into a direct threat. It happens to the best fighters from time to time.

Because Lysa was relatively inexperienced compared to Martinez. He could only encourage her to get out of that range before it was too late. But Perla and Lysa were both caught up in enjoying the fight.

They were laughing, bantering, complementing, and playfully jibbing one another. Enough so that both lost track of time, and before they realized it, almost all of the five-minute bout had passed.

The referee announced thirty seconds remaining, causing the crowd to cheer for their favorite and boo whom they did not enjoy. It was not missed on Martinez that Perla was the favorite to win—but Lysa was an Aviex, so it happened.

Both clearly heard the cheers and sped up their attacks. Through ragged breaths, both weaved, dodged, and chained strikes in and out of one another's guards. Martinez glanced at the referee and saw both were gaining points almost as quickly as the other, the man clicking his counter for points just as quickly for each competitor.

Who would take the win was up in the air until the last few seconds. Then Perla decided to press and win with one massive throw. Lysa launched a quick kick into her side, a resounding thump echoing. But Perla had intentionally tanked that hit and given Lysa the point just so she could step in and grab Lysa by the waist.

Rolling Lysa over her hip, Perla slammed Lysa to the ground, giving the far lighter Lysa a scrap of grace; instead of jumping atop and crushing Lysa, she stood and distanced herself, burning the last few seconds.

Martinez watched as his Ruh'ah was slammed flat on her back, gasping as the air left her lungs just as the match was called, leaving her gasping for air like a fish out of water. To his dismay, the referee counted the points, and a takedown like that was worth quite a few more than the strikes they had been exchanging.

"Time!" The referee announced.

Without pause, Perla helped Lysa to her feet, ensuring her opponent was all right. "Hey, that was a lot of fun."

"It indeed was enjoyable. That was a nice throw at the end," Lysa smiled, leaning on Perla's support while catching her breath. Although both of them looked utterly gassed, neither could keep steady without the other.

It was a surprisingly violent and giggly end to the match.

Shortly after the referee let them both catch their breaths, he took a moment to get them to his sides. Raising Perla's hand, he announced she won, much to the crowd's enjoyment. It seemed everyone liked the fight despite a cacophony of agreements and denials of the outcome poured out.

The outroar of the crowd was enjoyable for both coaching groups, filling them with pride. Their students had done well enough that both would likely be talked about later in the night. It was rare for two classification black species to fight in public, and it was a spectacle. A show of sportsmanship not all would give.

The pair of fighters laughing and having fun as they went helped for sure. Their laughter was infectious throughout the bout. Even Martinez and Ivorn were laughing at their small, playful jabs.

"Congratulations, Perla," Lysa said, tilting her head in a slight bow.

"Thanks," Perla responded. "Can I have your contact information? We could go get a drink or something later."

"Of course," Lysa smiled.

After exchanging their information, Lysa wished Perla a lovely night and turned about preparing herself for the next bout. She walked over to Martinez and Ivorn to rest for a few minutes. With Perla having taken first place, she and the Burtex still had to battle over second place.

While she had enjoyed the fight and thought the next one would be just as fun, regrettably, it would not happen. For reasons she was all too familiar with.

UNAVAILED AVIEX

"What do you mean he refuses?" Teacher barked at the referee, who was quivering under the short, stocky woman's magnanimous presence.

"I–I–I mean just that," the man stuttered, trying not to make eye contact with Teacher's jet-black, star-filled glare. "Mr. Seyer said that competing against a lowborn–errr."

"Oh no, lad, yah said it once. Yah, might as well call my student an abomination again. Maybe that will make yah feel like some big man," Teacher growled, gesturing behind her at Lysa.

To her credit, Lysa was doing her best to stay composed, even though Martinez could see a few cracks in her facade, uncomfortable twitches, and glances at some of the muttering crowd members, who were clearly enjoying the show. Most seemed upset by what seemed like an early end to the day's fights, while a few clearly agreed that the noble Burtex had no reason to keep fighting—especially with an Aviex.

Most of the passive treatment of other aliens to Aviex did not bother Lysa anymore and had not in years, but active discrimination was another story. That still crawled under her skin like vile, ravenous worms.

Why could they not be like Martinez, his friends, or the handful of people she genuinely held dear to her heart and could confide in? They cared not that she was Aviex or the past of slavery and oppression the

Aviex had experienced. To them, she was just Lysa, not a monster, a vein slicer, or an abomination.

Unlike so many others, Lysa did not know why the GU looked the other way regarding the Aviex species' suffering. What made her species different? Drinking blood? Having rituals based around blood? Most of the aliens in the universe ate meat with no issue, including hers.

Yet despite that similarity, aliens had attacked her in the past, trapped her into dates that were just a chance to ridicule her, or even a few attempts at her being abducted. Granted, those events were few and far between, but the way Lysa described them to Martinez, it was clear they were some of the lowest points in her life.

Lysa had tried to get answers from her parents in her youth and from her mother since leaving home, but they never gave her an answer. Lysa was not stupid and knew her Father worked in government employment as a soldier specifically for that reason; they had to know something, yet they would not illuminate the reason to her.

Looking at the referee, he did not need to call her an abomination again; the entire team and Perla's team had heard Seyer go on a several-minute tirade that Lysa was a lowborn monster not worth the dirt in his chiton.

The insectoid also included several long-winded compliments to Perla and her far more regal upbringing amidst the Varintol home moon of Baratin, with her being the daughter to some lower baroness bordering the tundra of the former Ursana nation and the steppes and valleys of the Jurual empire.

The man was so insistent that they were better and had no reason to even allow Lysa to compete against them—they were of noble birth, unlike her. Even though Perla insisted it meant nothing once you were off that moon, she was just a regular person and held no lineage.

But Seyer wanted to hear none of it. At least the insectoid's attitude answered whether he was a noble or a warrior. Fuck, it took Martinez until this point to realize the man's coaches were more attendants and servants. Standing behind or abreast of the alien and doing nothing to interject as he made an ass of himself and whatever house he came from.

As far as Martinez could tell, the rest of his team and Perla's team could not give a singular fuck about royalty or politics. Other than Perla, they all grew up in the wider GU or Earth, and those boasted far more egalitarian cultures. It is not something based on castes and set classes.

Because of the way the GU governs and allows species, planets, and systems a fair amount of autonomy to regulate themselves, royals and the concepts of regality were in no way dead. They all knew it, but running into anyone who still committed to those values with such fervor was few and far between.

Hell Martinez had fought against the Faruqua, who had a tribal society with religious leaders that were essentially royalty, caste system, and all. But meeting someone with the belief they were chosen by God to lead was new to him.

"Well—he–consi–considers her a–a–a—an abomination," the referee sputtered out as Teacher approached him with balled fists.

Martinez almost felt bad for the alien. He was scrawny, looked somewhat avian, likely only weighed half of what Teacher did, and was not much of a fighter. If he was a brawler, his cowering from the woman who looked like she was about to go off like Castle Bravo was unexpected. A wise reaction considering who Teacher was, but unexpected nonetheless.

"That slimy sonuva bitch. Where is he? I will rip his fucking carapace off," Teacher barked, jamming a finger into the referee's chest. The man squinted in pain with each tap.

"He said he is withdrawing if Lysa will not," the referee quickly explained in a near-pleading tone, likely just wanting this ordeal to be over with. "Will you?"

"Fat fucking chance. If that bastard thinks he is better than her, I will fight him and make sure he—" Teacher started without missing a beat but was cut off when Lysa gently touched her shoulder.

"I shall withdraw," Lysa said flatly.

"What, why would you?" Perla asked before Teacher or the rest of Lysa's team could comment. "Fuck that asshole, make him withdraw. You should get the medal you deserve."

"I simply hope for this to end cordially. Should I withdraw, this uncomfortable affair will simply die," Lysa commented, squeezing Teacher's shoulder slightly tighter. "And I do not wish for Teacher to make an ass out of herself, nor reflect negatively on her Dojo."

Teacher whipped around and looked up at Lysa, "Lass, what in all the stars are you on about? You would thrash that noble prick; if you withdraw, all your work was for nothing."

Lysa sighed and glanced around the room, noting that most of the crowd's eyes were still on all of them. Eager to see how this issue would resolve. Teacher followed Lysa's gaze and saw them watching, but that was not a deterrent for the Roid-rage goblin.

"I am aware. For my sake, please just drop it," Lysa sighed.

The Goblin esc woman grumbled and was about to comment but bit her tongue. That was something Martinez had never seen from the hot-headed instructor. Lysa quietly pleaded for this to end, and her agreement showed just how much Teacher cared about Lysa.

Martinez was all for her withdrawal, even if he wanted Lysa to rip the arms off Seyer; He would back up Lysa's choice no matter what. They supported one another throughout their issues, and this would be no different. Even if Martinez had to subtly wave to Feinel, Lira, and Ivron to stop quietly commenting. This was Lysa's choice, not theirs.

"Are you certain?" Teacher pleaded, not wanting Lysa to just surrender, having never known giving up to get you anything good.

"I am," Lysa said, looking toward the referee and slightly inclining her head. "I hereby officially withdraw. I am sorry to have caused these issues with my presence."

The referee nodded and used the moment to retreat from Teacher, heading toward the back room where Seyer and his attendants were likely waiting.

As Lysa turned and started toward the team, Perla rushed over and placed a hand on her shoulder. "Hey, I am sorry that this happened—if I wasn't some noble, I doubt—"

"This is in no way your fault. Worry not about it," Lysa assured flatly, " If you still wish some other day, reach out, and we can go get a drink."

"Ok," Perla nodded, still uncomfortable with this outcome.

"Have a lovely evening, Perla. Enjoy your gold medal," Lysa said, turning about and heading toward Martinez.

Perla slumped her shoulders and languidly moved toward her team, her ear folded and looking around at the crowd as they began to leave, most clearly having lost interest since the conflict was over.

"Lysa, why did you do that?" Lira questioned once she was next to the rest of them.

Lysa sighed and looked at Martinez, Lira, Feniel, and even Ivorn's near-anguished faces. Their concern for her was evident. None of them moved to look at the dispersing crowd or even acknowledged any onlookers; all of their attention was on her.

"May we please discuss this at a later date?" Lysa questioned. "I wish to return home for the evening; I feel unwell."

The rest shared a quick glance, knowing they had all planned on going out for dinner on Teachers dime after the competition for the day. But none of them wanted to press the issue.

"Yeah, here. Let me take you home," Martinez said, offering Lysa a hand.

The moment she took it, Martinez's concern for her grew. Her palms were sweaty and cold. And once she was at his side, she trembled slightly. She was either incredibly pissed or was breaking to the point of nearly crying, neither of which was good for her.

"Please, I wish to," Lysa said. "I will see the rest of you at practice tomorrow. Save for yourself, Ivorn; I hope you also have a lovely evening."

After Lysa retrieved her gear from the locker rooms, they left the sports facility and flowed out into the evening streets of Draun; her general attitude only got worse. She refused to talk beyond requesting Martinez wait until they were back at her house, not wanting to air out her feelings in public.

Martinez would not press her on the matter, especially because she clung to him harder than usual. It was not like she was trying to cuddle up to him for warmth or comfort. No, it was like she was anchoring herself to reality by clinging to him.

Once inside her home, Lysa damn near broke down. They did not even have a chance to close the door fully or set down her gym bag. She turned into Martinez and wrapped his torso tightly in a hug, clutching his jacket and shirt in tight handfuls.

Before Martinez even could ask her what was wrong, she buried her head into his shoulder and started to sob.

"Hey, hey, it's ok, Ruh'ah; tell me what's on your mind," Martinez said, hugging her back.

"Wh—why do they ha–hate us?" Lysa bawled. "I–I–try yo be po—polite—but the–the—they de–despi—hate me."

Martinez gently rubbed Lysa's back and pulled her as close as possible, not wanting her to feel alone. He knew she had been on her own for so long, and if it was in his power, she would never be on her own again.

"I don't know—I'm sorry," Martinez replied solemnly, hating that he had no answer.

That was likely the last thing Lysa wanted to hear from Martinez; it only increased her wailing volume. But that was the only answer Martinez had. His lack of an answer felt like a knife in his chest.

The Aviex weren't by any stretch of the imagination a beloved species in the GU, and Martinez had not been able to uncover any reason through his work at the hospital or the extensive medical documentation he had read over.

Most people he associated with seemed to not care that Lysa was an Aviex; they just treated his Ruh'ah like the wonderful woman she was. Because of that, he had never done anything to dig into why the wider GU was that way.

Lysa always seemed so confident and, for the most part, unbothered by the fact that others tried to avoid her, and he had assumed that she just brushed the issues off as reality. But it was clearly weighing on her more than he had thought.

"Come on, let's sit down. Talk to me about what's going on," Martinez said, running his fingers through her hair. "If you want to."

Lysa meekly nodded before Martinez led her to the nearby sofa. Once settled, he gave Lysa all the time she needed to settle down enough to explain and lay out her thoughts, worries, woes, apprehensions, and views on the recent events. Well, not just recent events, things from across her whole life; some Martinez was aware of, others he was not.

One of her main worries was their upcoming trip to meet with her parents, specifically her father. Lysa was horrified by how her father would react when he learned Martinez was not an Aviex. She told Martinez he would hurt her, him, or just flat out be horrible to Martinez every step of the way.

Kryoll, Lysa's father, was the opposite of the racist coin that was surrounding her species. Unlike Lysa or her mother, who just tried to live their lives as best they could despite the treatment of Aviex, where they avoided or ignored people. Her father detested anyone not of their species.

Lysa told Martinez about how she ran away from home years ago because he tried to isolate her from everyone out of their direct family through violence and threats, forcing her into seclusion, and she has not seen him in years because of it.

Now that Martinez would be tossed into that line of fire, she admitted that her stress was through the roof. She had been imagining different ways Kyroll would be cruel: trying to separate them, hurting him or her, or taking any number of other detestable actions.

That was all news to Martinez. He knew that she had not seen her parents in years, but knowing why revealed a lot about her, from why she was bitter when she met Teacher to why she was surprised that Martinez defended her during their first date. He had made close assumptions over the last half a year, but this news brought everything he knew about Lysa into an entirely new perspective.

None of that mattered to him. He still loved Lysa. She was the only person he had ever known who could look beyond his violent past and coerce him into opening up about it without judgment.

The main issue for today was Seyer treating her like a monster; it felt like a kick in the gut. Especially after she had done so well surrounding herself with people who treated her like a perfectly average person. It was like she was right back in the horrible place she was immediately after running away.

"Have you ever asked your parents why Aviex are treated like this?" Martinez questioned.

Lysa meekly nodded, not even moving her head from his shoulder.

"Alright, did they ever tell you why?" Martinez asked, leaning against her head.

Shaking her head, Lysa clutched him tighter.

After hearing and seeing the usually confident woman he loved acting like this, Martinez would discover what was happening with the Aviex, their history, and why the GU treated them like this.

They are just regular people. Plenty of other Aliens drink blood around the GU; he knew that. But something had to make them different. And if he was going to keep being with Lysa, he had to know and understand what he should do to support her.

He would likely have to devise a plan to ask her mother about Aviex history whenever they arrive for their vacation. For now, though, comforting Lysa through tonight was all that mattered; she needed him more than he had ever seen. And he would, without question, offer her the comfort she had given him when he needed it.

SALACIOUS SHIKSIE

Shiksie nervously rolled her tail in her hands and glanced around the room, ensuring all of her research documents were tucked away. She could not imagine how Martinez would react if he caught even the slightest glimpse at all the research she had done over the last month.

At least some of it, namely her extensive research on seduction, mating, and courtship. She doubted her mentee would care much about her learning how to cook Human meals and spending countless hours trying to actually craft the meals. But none of the papers or connecting lines were left on the walls. They had all been tucked away in her closet under lock and key.

With that done, Shiksie moved over to the oven, the smell of the roast filling the room. She wanted to make something close to what Martinez would have eaten when growing up, but that was almost impossible to pin down because he was from America, California, no less.

She knew his family was from what Humans called Hispanic, based on his name alone—that was easy enough to discern—but that led her down a rabbit hole of complicated histories: stories of war, race, colonization, and the melting pot America apparently has been for over four hundred Earth years—it would have been an impossible task to make something from his youth without showing too much of her hand.

What was called a pot roast, but there was no way for her to acquire beef from Earth, so she simply cross-referenced the animals and meat available on Renoural.

At least Renoural was a heavy agricultural production world. While it was not a bread basket for the system and was used more as a relay for travel to other more settled and active worlds, its significant export was still food. Because of this, she did manage to find a suitable substitution.

Peeking inside the oven, the pot roast looked perfect; it was golden brown and falling apart when Shiksie poked at it with a fork. The tuber, carrot, and onion substitutes were also soft and cooked well— exquisite.

Seeing the fruits of her labor, Shiksie could not help but smile and let her tail sway happily. Before she came up with this recipe, she had had so many failures —over the last month, she had dozens, if not hundreds, of failures. But Martinez was worth all the effort—maybe now he would see that she was putting so much time and energy into understanding him and Humans.

Likely far more than that Aviex ever would.

After closing the oven, Shiksie set the table, lit candles, and played Human country music. From the extensive cultural research before Martinez's arrival, she had a penchant for country, cowboys, and westerns, so she deemed the music scores from that genre appropriate for today.

As she pressed play, her data pad chimed.

Martinez <3: Hey, I just finished my test and am heading to your place. Be there in thirty minutes.

Shiksie: Very well, how did you do?

Martinez <3: I got an 87%

Shiksie: That is a respectable score for your midterms. I will see you when you arrive.

Shiksie quickly tucked away her datapad, a smile on her face and a nervous fluttering in her heart. Going over to her bedroom, Shiksie pulled out the clothes she specifically got for tonight and made sure her bed was made and clean, should they need it later.

Martinez knocked on Shiksie's door, having just arrived from his mid-term. God, he hated the tests; each was overseen by the Draun medical center Director. The man was intimidating, not like you would expect from a Human, such as being a cult of personality or cold, calculating professionalism.

In the Director's case, he was three meters tall, covered in dark armored plating, and had four yellow eyes filled with venom and cunning; all that was before you thought of the 15-centimeter-long claws on the end of each hand.

Although Martinez knew the intimidation the man gave off was just a matter of how he looked, behind all of that bulk was a man of drive, intelligence, and significant political cunning. One that anyone who befell it would likely be cut down.

If anything, Martinez was praying for some of that cunning today. He had to squash any desires Shiksie had to be in a relationship with him; his previous attempt to let her down softly did not work. No, if anything, she was only bolstered to get closer to him.

Today, failure was not an option, and Martinez had the drive to succeed—until Shiksie opened the door.

Her grayish silver hair ran over one shoulder and traced down to a skimpy, tight-fitting dark blue dress; both sides were open lattice, allowing a clear view of her flanks. The dress perfectly showed off her lithesome curves, long legs, and gorgeous blue-gray fur, and it was low-cut just enough to give an ample view into pert cleavage.

Wafting past Shiksie were mouth-watering smells of roasting

meat, her subtle flowery perfume, the light of flickering candles, and the melodic sounds of an acoustic guitar.

"It's lovely to see you, Henry," Shiksie purred, slightly fluttering her eyelids. "You look handsome this evening."

Unlike all the other times he had seen the usually ascetic Farunse Shiksie, she had lipstick on and even dark black eyeshadow, making their bright emerald color pop to a disturbing degree; Martinez had not noticed it until now having been distracted by his mentor's athletic build, and cleavage.

"It's nice to see you too; you look good too," Martinez said without even remembering why he was here today.

Shiksie smiled and purred momentarily while looking Martinez over, soaking in his details. Meanwhile, Martinez pulled his jaw off the floor and tried remembering why he was there—thankfully, he did, lest he do something stupid.

"Are you going to come in?" Shiksie asked, standing abreast of the door and gesturing in.

Martinez stepped past Shiksie; as he did, he could feel her staring at the back of his head. Her discerning gaze assessed him, causing a deep primal part of him to be on edge, something he had not felt since first meeting her. It was also incredibly likely she was also taking stock of the waves of pheromones oozing from him; if she noticed anything outstanding, she did not openly comment on it.

"Would you care for a beverage?" Shiksie questioned while sauntering over to the fridge.

"Sure," Martinez replied, going over to the table.

While Shiksie was retrieving the drinks, he did his best to reassess his action plan, let her down firmly, and ensure nothing was misinterpreted. He had his plan, and even though he could not deny Shiksie's shapely build, her figure being hugged by the dress made him nearly forget it.

His mind was also questioning something else about Shiksie; something was off—it took him a few moments to realize what it was. How she was speaking—it was stiff, unnatural, and forced.

"Beyond your test, was anything else eventful throughout your day?" Shiksie asked, putting a beer in front of Martinez.

Now, he put his finger on precisely what Shiksie was doing; she was attempting to imitate Lysa's languid mannerisms, speech patterns, and even formal speech patterns. While her imitating his Ruh'ah was concerning, along with the fact that she was not being subtle in propping up her cleavage, his eyes wandered to the relative safety of his drink.

Where in the universe did she get a proper beer? Martinez knew getting beer imported in small amounts was ungodly expensive, so much so that a company could go bankrupt unless it did so in bulk.

But this was genuine beer from Earth. According to the bottle it was from a small brewery that only crafted and distributed in Wisconsin.

"Shiksie, how did you get this?" Martinez questioned.

"Worry not about that. I simply acquired it because I knew you would enjoy it," Shiksie purred, leaning forward and smiling brightly. "Do you not?"

Martinez paused, trying to think of how to proceed here. This was surreal by any stretch of the imagination. He had figured this likely would be odd, but this was beyond anything he could have imagined. He had assumed Shiksie would have cracked a few awkward jokes, maybe made some queer attempts at seduction—not whatever this was.

"Shiksie, what are you doing?" Martinez asked, ignoring her question about the beer and deciding to focus on her out-of-pocket actions.

"Whatever do you mean?" Shikie awkwardly chuckled, trying to ignore Martinez's discerning gaze and her heart rate spiking from being called out for her mimicry.

Martinez sighed, leaned back in the chair, and looked around the room, noticing the meal-time setup: dinner clearly ready in the oven, romantic candles, an over-the-top dress, and a nearly obnoxious attempt at brownie points.

Opening the beer and sipping out the liquid courage, Martinez enjoyed the sweet, soothing hops and decided to press the issue. He did not hate Shiksie by any means, but her trying to act like Lysa this much was disturbing and took away all the unique charm she usually had.

"Please drop the act, Shiksie. This is supposed to be us enjoying dinner as friends. Not—whatever this is," Martinez said, gesturing at the table and her skimpy attire.

Shiksie's attempt at behaving salaciously slipped immediately, returning to her more casual stature and demeanor. She almost fell into her glacial facade in defense of being called out, but Martinez was likely the only person that she did not use that stand-off on regularly, so she did not.

Sitting up straight, the tall feline brushed her hair over her shoulders, crossed her legs, and sighed nearly defeatedly.

"Am I being that unsettling?" Shiksie replied, returning to her usual prim and proper tone, but nowhere near as formal as Lysa.

"Yes, you are," Martinez sighed, sipping out of the beer before pointing firmly. "What are you trying anyway?"

Shiksie nervously shifted in her chair for a few moments while grumbling no words in particular, or at least if there were any words in there; they were so intently mixed with yowls and sounds of her distraughtness Martinez could not make them out clearly.

"I still want to be with you," Shiksie admitted while looking at him earnestly, having next to no trouble admitting it. She struggled to tell Martinez once, but now that she already has, this was likely her last opportunity to convince him she would be a better option for his partner than Lysa—she was desperate.

"Shiksie, we talked about this—I am with Lysa," Martinez groaned, not understanding what Shiksie seemed to not get about this issue.

He knew that Shiksie's species practiced monogamy, and she had two parents—until they died when she was young, but that did not change the reality that for Farun'se and Humans alike, being with one partner was normal.

"I—I—I—know," Shiksie nervously sputtered and leaned forward slightly as if trying to double down on her attempts at seduction.

"Can—we forget my attempt for now—and at least enjoy dinner? I worked hard on it," she pressed, hoping that perhaps refocusing from her awkward attempt at being something she was not could help her recover from the situation.

In all reality, trying to be more like Lysa was not her original idea but one of the dozens she had co-opted into tonight's efforts.

Through her research, she came across some advice that told her to be confident, bold, and outgoing. While Lysa certainly wasn't how Shiksie traditionally thought of being confident, when it came to Martinez she obviously had success. Why would she not emulate her a little?

After all, according to the Human dating guru she had watched dozens of hours of—Sarina Halsen, a woman has to be confident and bold, grab what she wants, and hold herself to the level of or higher than the man they want. Since that was not working, it was time to shift gears to a more gentle, caring effort.

Another method that she had read up on was one of the reasons she had acquired the beer and learned how to make Human food—so she could possibly be more traditional in both Farun'se and Human standards.

"I don't think that's a good idea," Martinez said flatly.

"Please?" Shiksie nearly begged, grabbing his hands and leaning across the table.

Martinez tried to gently withdraw his hands from her soft grip, but Shiksie's claws gently dug into him, holding him there. Looking into her emerald eyes, her pupils were wide, and she had a gentle, pleading smile.

"Do you understand there is nothing between us besides being friends?" Martinez asked.

Shiksie let go of his hands and stood up, not replying verbally. Instead, she went over to the oven and pulled out the food. Serving a plate for Martinez and herself, quickly returning with two steaming helpings.

"Here, enjoy this. I have plenty more of it and beer for us," Shiksie purred.

"Us?" Martinez raised an eyebrow.

The Farun'se were barely able to drink any ethanol compared to many other species in the galaxy. Martinez knew she could drink incredibly weak beverages in small amounts, but even something like this 5% ABV beer would be pretty stiff for her.

While he wasn't sure of the exact amounts from what he knew about the Farun'se, it likely would be bordering on him drinking a quarter bottle of whiskey or any other hard liquor.

"Yes us," Shiskie said, using one of her claws to open another bottle. "I have done all the research needed. So long as I am not overdoing it, one beer should be perfectly safe. Although—I still tend to not consume ethanol—but I want to celebrate how you, Lysa, Ivorn, and Sursee could last time."

That made Martinez wonder: was Shiksie jealous that the others could celebrate in a way she could not? Last time she and Sursee enjoyed some grasses that they huffed, but Sursee only started to do that after having a few boozed-up drinks, granted those were only at most 2% ABV.

Could Shiksie handle any amount of booze? Much less an amount that likely would have her slurring after a bottle.

"Fine, I will stay for dinner, but Shiksie, can we just relax? Work has been hell lately, and I don't want to leave here with this being something either of us will regret," Martinez reluctantly said.

Martinez was undoubtedly tense at the moment, not unlike when he was ambushed while working with the Marines. He knew Shiksie had not given up; she was too stubborn for that and likely was just shifting tactics.

Shiksie slowly sipped at the beer as they ate dinner and talked about simple things: Martinez's plans for school and what he and Lysa planned on doing for their vacation starting the following day.

While talking about their plans tasted as horrible as the beer, she had to slog through it. Until she managed to figure out how to broach what was her last hope to keep Martinez as hers. But she needed some more beer before being that bold.

Plenty of the advice she had read from the Human Relationship gurus included asking someone you are interested in if they might consider a more polyamorous relationship. Although some called it sleeping around, others open relationships, the end result did not seem different in her eyes.

"So, what did you think of the pot roast?" Shiksie asked after finishing her beer a bit faster than she had expected. Any bitter flavor of the acrid beverage had faded halfway through her first bottle.

"It is perfect," Martinez replied, surprised by how well Shiksie had recreated the Human dish, especially because she had never had the true thing before.

Then again, the fundamental cooking processes could not be too different even here on the far side of the galaxy. They involve rendering fats, saturating, and boiling tubers, as well as finding a suitable substitute for onions and garlic.

Knowing his mentor, she likely researched beef and the other ingredients down to their chemical makeup to ensure dinner was as close to the genuine article as possible. She did, without a doubt, get incredibly close.

"Would you like some more?" Shiksie asked, gesturing to his already empty plate.

"Sure," Martinez replied, having not missed the slight slur in Shiksie's voice.

Shiksie pushed back from the table and grabbed both of their plates. Martinez paid keen attention to her as she moved, looking for anything to pick up on her next play; beyond her peeking back at him while serving him a plate, she gave no accurate indication of what she was going to try until she sat back down, a fresh beer in her hand.

"Here you go," Shiksie said, having sat ever so slightly closer to Martinez, a detail he did not miss, but she was not so close it was raising massive alarm bells. She was just close enough to reach his shoulder if she desired, but nothing more.

As they slowly ate their next serving, Shiksie continued asking

Martinez more about his life back home on earth, his hobbies, and other things. He answered earnestly, not that there was much to tell.

He grew up in the ruins of Los Angeles as a result of World War three and the mass amount of strikes at cultural and civilian locations that had been caused. Luckily, Humanity had managed to recover and reach for the stars again before the GU found them, but the warrior and hardy culture that the survivors of the war and his grandparents had been to thank for that desire to recover.

If not for it, the GU likely would have passed Humanity by then.

Shiksie was cute when she was slightly sloshed; even Martinez had to admit it. She was almost disturbingly expressive. Her tail was waving, her ears fluttered, and even her painfully slurred voice expressed that she wanted to learn more about his hobby of video games and Martial arts.

Despite the cuteness, she never does any of that.

"Henrryy, I wanna know." Shiksie slurred, sipping from her drink now that they both finished a second plate of pot roast.

Martinez looked at her and considered pulling the drink from her hand. She likely was the most drunk she had ever been and likely was going to do something stupid if he did not stop her.

Once she found her train of thought once again, she leaned closer. She lightly plucked at the top of her dress with a claw, likely trying to be seductive, but with how sloshed she was—Martinez would not consider it, and that's before the issues of their professional relationship.

"Have yah ever heard of an open relationship? We could share you." Shiksie questioned. "Me und Lysa."

Now Martinez had heard of that before, never in a way that would work well for anyone not entering a relationship with that in mind, and both himself and Lysa were not keen on anything like that. That was all well before crossing the bridge of how inappropriate him and her having a relationship like that would be.

"Shiksie—I have already said I'm not interested," Martinez said flatly.

"But why noot?" Shiksie pouted, reaching for his hand that he quickly retracted, not letting her get a grip on it.

It was time, Martinez had put up with enough of her attempts for the day, and if she was going to try to ask him for something so stupid, he was just going to put the drunk cat to bed, call her an ass in the morning, and ensure she realized how out of line she was then.

He just had to be prepared for Shiksie crying, begging, and possibly attempting to drunkenly kiss him when he escorted her to the bedroom. Nothing in his wildest dreams could have prepared him for what a drunk Shiksie was willing to do.

"Come on," Martinez said, grabbing her arm and trying to lead her to her bedroom so she could crash; she was the equivalent of half a handle in and definitely was not used to drinking and needed someone to be responsible here.

As she stood, she did far more than Martinez ever expected her to do. Shiksie pulled him in close, propped a leg up on the table, and pushed her hips against him. She purred loudly and ground herself against him, pushing her warmth into him.

"Coom on Henree," Shiskie purred, in what she undoubtedly thought was a sultry tone, but only sounded like she was trying to twist a tale to an equally drunken lover—but Martinez had only had one beer and was not the demographic to be trying that with.

In fact, he was downright pissed, his fist already clenching, readying to clock her. A sloppy kiss from her would have been one thing, not her fucking dry-humping him against the table. Martinez pulled out the remnants of the NCO he had inside him and barked orders.

"Shiksie, stop, right god damn now!" Martinez snapped, trying to gently push her back, not wanting to genuinely hurt his mentor and friend.

Any amount of his prissing did nothing to dissuade her; if anything, it pressed her further and brought some of her kinks to the surface he would rather not know about.

"Oh yiis, I want it roof, tie me up baebee" Shiksie growled, hiking her dress up and leaving her, now apparent to him nude, womanhood to rub against him.

With no thought, Martinez just reacted violently. This was not just a step too far; it was leagues off the acceptable mark. Martinez never imagined Shiksie, of all people, could end up like this.

Due to the difference in density between the Farun'se and Humans, Martinez outweighed Shiskie by a solid 20 kilos. Most people think your reach matters most in what might be a fight, and that is true for striking; grappling was a whole other ball game. You want to be shorter and heavier.

He grabbed Shiksie's leg over his side and pressed forward, driving her fully backward while moving his leg behind hers. In one deft motion, Martinez folded Shiksie in half, her back slamming into the deck while her head knocked hard against the fridge.

Shiksie yelped in pain and immediately gave up on attempting to seduce him after having her brain rattled. Instead of pursuing him further, she clutched at her bruised and likely bleeding head, wailing loudly.

Martinez did not even glance back at the Farun'se woman as he rushed out of the room. He could hear her crying about how she was broken and always wrong, but that did not matter to him. He could broach that in an environment where others were there to back him up. He was alone, and at this point, Martinez knew he had to leave.

The only thing he did for Shiksie was text Ivorn to go check on her, telling him he would explain what happened to him later, but Martinez had to leave her in her home like that for now.

Thankfully, Ivorn was understanding and did not question him for the time being.

DRAUN AT YOUR BACK

"I will slaughter that fatuous feline!" Lysa shouted, attempting to push past Martinez and out the door, her rows of needle-like teeth fully bared in indignant fury.

Lysa was taking the news about what Shiksie had attempted to do far better than Martinez imagined she would. More accurately, it was precisely what he had expected his Ruh'ah to do, trying to slaughter his mentor. On the bright side, Lysa heard him out and did not choose the worst-case scenario he imagined: Blaming him like one of his previous flames would have.

Martinez did not genuinely believe she would do that to him; while somewhat territorial about him, Lysa was more level-headed than jumping into the deep end of wrong perceptions. And she especially took the news of him folding Shiksie in half very well, a bit too well in Martinez's mind, but she always had a bit of a cruel sense of humor.

"Ruh'ah move! I must skin Shiksie alive," Lysa hissed as Martinez pulled her in front of him.

"No, you're overreacting," Martinez said firmly.

"I'm not in any way. That filthy hussy was rubbing her cunt on you!" Lysa replied, stepping back and gesturing up and down at him, then crossing her arms defiantly. "I knew that whore would try something again, but this is insanity."

Lysa was right about how insane this was; Martinez did not think Shiksie would attempt anything so brash. His mentor was calm, level-headed, and in no way the sexual deviant he saw a few hours ago—at least, he thought that.

Ruh'ah had been suspicious of Shiksie for almost two months now, especially right after they all went over and helped Martinez when he disappeared in a drunken PTSD-induced binge. During that time, Shiksie was confrontational and was constantly trying to keep Lysa from Martinez, using her experience as a nurse, his mentor, and the fact she spends so much time with him as leverage to keep Lysa distant.

Now, Shiksie had finally played her hand and given Lysa all the vindication she could ever want. She was far too eager to kill that abhorrent hussy—even if she had to fight her way past Martinez, Shiksie's pelt would be a throw blanket on their bed.

"Ruh'ah, yes, you are overreacting," Martinez said firmly, grabbing her shoulders.

He did not manhandle Lysa by any means; he merely got ahold of her tightly enough that she could not easily slip free and out the door. That Martinez was putting his foot down here did not help him; Lysa shot him a vicious glare and damn near growled at him.

Fuck, that made his heart skip a beat. Martinez was used to violence and fighting, but that was when he dealt with aliens the Human Navy sent him to war with. He could just shoot them—he could not do that here; peaceful resolution was his only option.

"I am not; that vestigial whore thinks just because she is helping you study, she had the right to do that. I will show that filthy man-stealing slut just who she is fucking with!" Lysa snapped.

Martinez damn near rolled his eyes at that comment; Thankfully, he did not. Lysa would be furious if he did not take her emotions seriously. Just that phrasing was almost comedic to him and showed off Lysa's odd speech patterns flawlessly. Lysa always had a colorful vocabulary, but calling Shiksie rudimentary and having evolved past usefulness was something he, as a medical professional, could not help but find amusing and creative.

He wrapped Lysa in a taught, warm, welcoming hug, running his hand through her silken hair while she thrashed bitterly, still trying to get past him.

"She did not steal me, Lysa. I'm not going anywhere. Shiksie made a drunken mistake, and the issue has been dealt with. I don't need you getting in trouble for doing something you would regret afterward," Martinez assured.

Lysa grumbled and growled for a few more moments but eventually stopped struggling against Martinez and joined him in a calm embrace. "Do you mean it?"

"Yeah, I mean it. I'm not leaving, we are going to meet your parents tomorrow after all," Martinez replied, leaning his head against Lysa's while she clutched tightly to his shirt, clinging to him as if he was moments from fading away.

Lysa's behavior was not surprising, considering the horror stories she had told him about her previous attempts at romance being little more than opportunities for others to mock or belittle her. Martinez was the first real relationship Lysa had ever had.

"Still, I do not wish for her to steal you away. I refuse to trust her," Lysa pouted.

Lysa did have a point; Shiksie crossed a rigid no-go boundary with Martinez. He would have to do something to assure Lysa everything would be alright, and that Shiksie understood how wrong what she did was.

"I will figure something out. Maybe Harnsis can change my shift," Martinez replied after racking his brain for a few moments. "But we will have to see about that when we get back."

Lysa sighed and nodded in agreement. "If we must. Considering how late it is, I doubt anything could be done about it now."

"Exactly. Don't worry, I will handle it," Martinez assured, leaning back and giving a reassuring, warm smile. A gesture Lysa returned, although Martinez could still see the worry in her four ruby-red eyes and the gentle upturn of her plush lips.

His Ruh'ah had much to worry about. Between Shiksie's attempt, her new work shift, and them going to meet her parents after years of isolation certainly gave his Aviex lover many things to juggle in her mind.

"Come on, let's get some rest; we have a long day tomorrow," Martinez said, kissing Lysa's cheek and softly guiding her toward the bedroom.

The following morning, Martinez and Lysa were up early, far earlier than usual on their day off. Typically, the happy couple was more than happy to sleep in until well after noon when they had no pre-existing commitments.

Today, however, before the twin suns were high in the Renoural sky, Lysa poked at Martinez to get him up and at 'em. Martinez rolled over to see why she was awake so early but kept his mouth shut, seeing the look in her eye and the odd way she carried herself.

Almost all of her usual grace, tranquility, and soothing aura were gone, replaced by quick, jerky motions. Additionally, unlike her typical morning smile, she was blank-faced, with deep bags under her eyes.

If Martinez was a less tactful man, he would tell her she looked like hammered shit, but he was at least wise enough to know you should not tell your girlfriend that under any circumstance. Much less when she likely did not sleep at all.

"Did you not sleep well?" Martinez questioned, rubbing the tiredness from his eyes.

"I did not," Lysa yawned, "I was too nervous."

Martinez propped back against the headboard and wrapped Lysa in a one-armed hug, letting her rest on his shoulder. "Do you want to try to sleep more? We don't have our flight for a few hours."

Lysa snuggled closer, her bare chest pressing tightly against his arm. "No, I would not sleep anyway," she admitted. "I will try to get some rest on the flight. We will be in the air most of the afternoon anyway."

That was true; the shuttle flight from Draun to Cellna would be six standard hours long, so Lysa would have plenty of time to sleep there. Lord knew Martinez had spent many shuttle flights blissfully napping, either that or reading.

Martinez hoped that reaching Cellna would ease Lysa's tension. He believed this would be the case because Lysa always spoke fondly of the town and surrounding mountain ranges, even if the topic of her father would sour those memories.

"Alright, I suppose we should get ready then," Martinez said.

"In a moment," Lysa replied and nuzzled against his neck. "You're warm, and I do not wish to let you go yet."

Smiling widely, Martinez leaned closer against his gothic lover and ensured the blanket covered them entirely. The Human had no reason to argue about some time snuggling; with how hectic work had been lately, their usual nightly cuddling had been reduced to a few days a week—to both of their discomforts, so savoring this before packing and squeezing into a cramped and crowded shuttlecraft was perfect.

Eventually, after both had their fill of gentle beatific cuddling, Lysa's house became a flurry of activity as they got ready to rush out the door to get to the shuttle port on time and with all the essentials on hand.

Because Martinez had already packed and left his luggage at Lysa's the previous day, he prepared them some easy-on-the-go meals while Lysa packed her suitcase, diddy bag, and anything else she wished to bring along.

Lysa leaned in a bit to some of the customs and courtesies her mother had ingrained in her soul, specifically the tradition of bringing gifts to one's parents when visiting. The custom was a holdover from the desolate planet Verrilon, but it was still regularly practiced as a sign of care and love to those letting you stay within their abode.

Her form of tribute took her some time to consider, mainly because she knew so little about her father that it was impossible to give the horrible man something befitting his taste that she was willing to buy.

For her mother, Lysa imported a bottle of Human wine, specifically a bottle from Martinez's home state of California. She placed the bottle in her carry-on and carefully wrapped it in clothes to ensure it did not break. Mother did adore wine, and gifting her a sample from Martinez's origin home would be perfect for his future, Jaru'ha—hopefully future Jaru'ha.

Her father's gift received no such care or reverence. Lysa had purchased the cheapest Hemozin possible and tossed it into her checked bag, uncaring if it survived the journey. Unlike Mother's gift, his was still wrapped in the cheap brown paper bag from the convenience store.

As Martinez cooked, he regularly peeked over at Lysa in the bedroom, trying to gauge her state of mind and how she was affected by all that was happening. What he saw was both concerning and unsurprising.

Lysa was trying to look composed but was clearly off in the stars. Periodically, while folding a piece of clothing, she would stare at the garment as though it would tell her the mysteries of the universe.

When she returned to Draun and resumed packing, almost all of her fluidity was gone. She was ambling listlessly around the bedroom and would have to look around for each item. Both behaviors were significantly out of place for the usually composed and assured gothic woman.

Martinez was unsure how much of it was nervousness about reconciling with her father, Shiksie's debacle, or sleep deprivation. Either way, seeing her like this was depressing, but Martinez knew there was not much he could do about it in the short term; all he could do was help her through the day and the next two weeks.

Shortly after eating the simple steak sandwiches Martinez had prepared, Martinez double-checked that everything was packed, paying especially keen attention to Lysa's gear. Once he had a warm and fuzzy feeling that there was nothing vital being left behind, they hailed a taxi and were on their way to the shuttleport.

The ride there was uneventful but somewhat strange. It wasn't until they were almost at the port that Martinez realized why it felt odd, and a thought came across his mind: How long had it been since he had been in a vehicle?

Draun was built from the ground up with pedestrians in mind, with separate streets for vehicles and foot traffic crisscrossing and alternating within the skyscrapers. Doing his best to recall, he realized it must have been at least half a standard year since he was in any vehicle, and that was a military truck, not a plush taxi.

That thought made him have another idea. What about Cellna? Would it be the same? Would they rent a vehicle? Or would Lysa's mother drive them around?

"How are we going to get around once we are there?" Martinez questioned.

Lysa took a few moments, and Martinez repeated the question several times before she focused. "Oh—we can rent a vehicle at the shuttle port. I have a license and can drive anyway."

That was good news; Martinez knew Cellna was an out-there, more country kind of place. It was called a city because it met a certain population threshold, not because its description was anything like Draun, Los Angeles, or New York. According to the pictures Martinez had seen, Cellna was a small, humble place that was welcoming.

Once at Baribla Shuttleport, checking in and loading up was smooth and straightforward. The air transportation inspectors scanned their luggage and checked identification cards and tickets before ushering them aboard the civilian transport craft and to their seats.

Lysa settled into the window seat while Martinez took the adjacent one. Like all the other civil transport shuttles Martinez had seen, this one only had two rows of seats on each side, with an aisle in the center.

Not unlike the airplanes still used on Earth.

The chief difference between Human airplanes and this shuttle was the propulsion and aerodynamics. Instead of diesel-fueled turbine engines and a well-designed airfoil, the shuttle was powered by four rotating noise-suppressed repulsers and was shaped like a brick.

Martinez had been on plenty of aircraft like this during his stint in the Human Navy; most non-human-designed aircraft were similar in their shape and function because when your engines were so fuel efficient, they had to be refueled every few decades and not after each flight. The efficiency of the building and replacing parts took precedence over a sleek exterior. At least the interior was comfortable enough, if not a bit cramped.

Just before take-off, one of the flight attendants worked their way up and down the rows of chatting aliens, ensuring everyone was buckled and seated, and asked if they wanted a snack for the trip.

Upon reaching their row, she asked Martinez if he could wake Lysa and ask her to put on her belt. He had not even noticed she had fallen asleep already, having instead kept a close eye on the other passengers as they were loading.

Martinez acknowledged the request but did not wake Lysa up. Instead of interrupting her foray into dreamland, he buckled her in and turned his attention to his datapad, pulling up one of the novels written by Lysa's mother to pass the time on the flight. He had promised Lysa he would read her novels.

While the book was not in the genre Martinez would usually read, preferring to read thrillers, he would still push on. The stories of *Kirkai Lourin* were not written with him as the target audience; they were romance mysteries with a James Bond-esque character targeted toward women.

At least Lysa's mother was an outstanding novelist, and having something to read was better than him sitting here and stewing in what was making him nervous, meeting the parents. Martinez had never been in a relationship that was serious enough for him to meet the family. So all of this would be new unmapped ground for him. And nothing made him more worried than having no idea what he was about to walk into.

Lysa had already briefed him on her parents, their lives, and the situation that caused her to leave, so he knew the big landmines going forward. However, that left a lot of the area a gray space—possibly filled with dangers to him or Lysa.

Martinez sighed, flipped to the next page of the novel, and did his best to focus on the story, trying not to let his mind conjure up thousands of violent scenarios with Lysa's father. A man that all he knew of was former special forces and was more than willing to be cruel to his daughter.

NO PLACE LIKE HOME

The SUV that Martinez and Lysa rented for the trip rumbled down the dirt road, the gravel crunching beneath the heavy vehicle's tires. It was the perfect choice for their needs as it offered plenty of storage space and was more than capable of traversing the potholes of the backwoods.

Despite this, they had to admit the rental was extraordinarily plush and cost them next to nothing. It had heated seats, individual view screens, built-in GPS, automatic tinting windows, and an automatic drive function—that Lysa refused to use.

That was all before the incredibly soft faux leather seats and well-colored gray and white interior tied the luxury vehicle together.

It reminded Martinez of several old Human-designed cars his grandfather restored and owned in Los Angeles.

Being in an excellent vehicle made Martinez question why he had not bought a car since arriving on the planet. Then he looked up the cost of the Pysotric model M and remembered why. With that many zeroes at the end, Martinez expected the damn thing to suck him off and do his taxes while driving him to work.

Martinez surrendered to the fact that he could not afford a car anytime soon, so he turned his attention to the trees on the side of the small dirt road Lysa had just turned down. The scenery changed slightly since they left the shuttle port a few hours ago.

The shuttle port was centered in a wide clearing in one of the valleys and was surrounded by rolling foothills covered in thick green coniferous trees. They had already diverted before they reached Cellna proper, so the town itself was still a mystery to Martinez. But he knew they would visit it soon enough.

Unlike the route toward Cellna, the little road they were on now had no buildings, streetlamps, or signs of sentient life along its borders; it was quite the opposite. The occasional meadow, babbling brook, or small gulley broke up the endless oceans of trees; beyond that, nothing but bountiful nature.

The area was downright gorgeous and put several worlds the Human Navy had sent Martinez to fight on to shame regarding its pure, peaceful vibe.

This place made Verilon look like a piece of shit, but that was not saying much. That desert world offered little to anyone other than the local Faruqua. Those lizards were so well adapted to the heat and dry climates they likely would die being somewhere this lush.

The only place he could think of that came close was Harudeth. The section of that planet he had fought on was a gorgeous mountain range with stunning purplish dirt and blue foliage.

He would not mind returning there someday and taking Lysa on a grand hiking and camping trip. But that was a pipe dream as far as he thought of it. The last he heard, Harudeth was still being restored to its former glory and had many minor guerilla wars raging across its surface. He would never bring Lysa to a warzone. She did not need to see how cruel the universe and GU could be.

After taking in the scenery and feeling, for the first time in months, if not years, like he did not have to keep an eye over his shoulder for a potential threat or IED on the side of the road, Martinez looked over at Lysa. She looked far better after having slept the entire shuttle ride here.

Gone were the bags under her eyes and most of the languid, sluggish movements he had seen earlier in the day. She almost seemed to be back to her usual self—almost. If not for Martinez knowing his

Aviex girlfriend so well, he would miss the slightly blank stare and the white knuckle grip on the steering wheel, a detail that was difficult to see because of her pale white complexion.

But he could not deny that she looked leagues better than this morning. He hoped that was a good sign for the trip.

One thing Martinez could not understand was why Lysa insisted on actually driving. The car could have driven them to her parent's house without issue, and she could have laid back for more rest. He assumed it had something to do with them circumventing Cellna by turning onto this dirt road a kilometer before the town's borders, but she would not give him a straight answer when he asked.

"How much further is your parent's place, anyway?" Martinez asked. "I haven't seen any neighbors, and this seems out of the way."

"We arrived at their property almost an hour ago," Lysa replied, turning down the music slightly so they could chat.

"How much land do your parents own?" Martinez inquired.

Lysa pondered the question momentarily, trying to recall the exact answer, but it had been so long since she had lived here that she was unsure. In the past, she was little and only left their property to go to town and school. That and for all she knew, her parents had purchased more land, expanding their dominion greatly. Knowing her father's desire for privacy, that was highly likely.

"I cannot recall the number, but we can ask Mother about that when we arrive. Just know you can walk all day in any direction from the house, and you would still be on their property," Lysa said assuredly.

That revelation made Martinez wonder something he had not since meeting Lysa: how wealthy was her family? The idea just had never really crossed his mind. Both he and she were well off and could be considered lower middle class in the GU, living comfortably and with little issue on their incomes.

Martinez knew that her Mother was a successful novelist and that her father used to be in the Aviex military before being medically retired and becoming a lumberjack. He had assumed they were middle class, upper middle class at best. But apparently, they were far more affluent than he had ever imagined.

While Martinez would not say it outright, that they were so rich set a few alarm bells off in his head. He had dealt with plenty of shady politicians and twisted former operators in his day. He did not want to believe it, but with Kryoll's shady and likely well-connected background, he could see the old Aviex leveraging his experience for some kickbacks.

Evidence that Lysa's parents were firmly in the GU upper class was only made more apparent when the vehicle crested a small hill and entered an open glade, revealing the true grandeur of their property.

From this high vantage, nature's bounty spread from horizon to horizon. Three buildings were plain as day, with glimpses of the rest of the Veringal compound peeking out from the trees.

Two structures looked like houses and had the most area cleared out around them. Both were somewhat rustic in design and reminded Maritnez of log cabins, but neither was small enough to be called one. They were twice the size of Lysa's home back in Draun and could likely comfortably house six to ten people.

The other building in sight was a detached garage of some kind. That was evident because the road led right up to the large doors in front of it. If it weren't that, the only other thing Martinez could think it was would be a barn, but with no servant animals in sight, he doubted that was the reason.

After another hour of driving, they parked in front of the garage; the serenity and true isolation of Nelya and Kyroll's home were only more evident when he stepped out of the car. Martinez could not see it from the top of the hill, but from here, the small stream running along the side of the house was easy to see.

It was gorgeous in the evening sun. The oranges and reds glistened on the crystal clear water and oddly brightly colored rocks. Martinez was not sure what type of geology had caused the kaleidoscope of color, but it was certainly welcome.

Additionally, the blissful sounds of Renoural were all that could be heard. Birds chirped, the brook bubbled, and the wind whistled through the gently swaying bows. Martinez could not fully express the joy of being somewhere the sounds of modern society did not reach.

In his youth, he had dreamed of living somewhere like this, and his time in Los Angeles, and now Draun only galvanized that wish. While he would not deny city living had its appeal, the isolation and tranquility of the woods almost called to him, giving him a sense of warmth.

"Wow, this place is amazing," Martinez breathed, gesturing at the deep forest on the far riverbank. He let the clear air fill his lungs and invite him in.

"Indeed it is," Lysa replied somewhat solemnly.

"Oh, my little huntress. Welcome home!" the pair heard shouted from toward the house.

Martinez and Lysa tried to turn to face her excited mother, but Nelya was deceptively quick. Nelya rushed out of the house in a deft, elegant motion and went straight toward Lysa, pulling her into a warm embrace.

"Hello, Mother," Lysa gasped, barely managing to return a weak hug while Nelya attempted to squeeze the life out of her. "It is marvelous to see you."

"I missed you so much," Nelya praised, leaning back and looking Lysa up and down. "Have you been eating well? You look thin."

"I missed you as well, and yes, I have been. Martinez here has ensured that," Lysa replied, gesturing at her Ruh'ah.

Nelya let Lysa go and stepped closer toward Martinez. Her four pink eyes scanned him intently as she slowly sauntered closer.

Martinez was surprised at how Nelya looked. Lysa had told him what to expect, but his Ruh'ah failed to encapsulate it well, likely because it had been years since she had seen her mother.

Unlike Lysa, who dressed like a traditional goth, Nelya wore tight red leggings and an equally revealing tank top. Each fiber of both garments screamed and struggled to contain her nearly overflowing figure.

Martinez was not the most subtle man in the universe, nor was he a man with deep lexicons of words to describe everything around him. Nelya pushed his abilities to the limit as he tried to categorize her looks in his mind.

Every ounce of Nelya oozed confidence, and motherly grace, from the slight pout in her lips to her buxom figure to the way she defiantly popped her hips while walking, and the judgmental narrowing of her eyes.

All those traits, combined with the fact that she looked like Lysa but with a fuller figure and slightly more mature, made Martinez's dumb grunt brain scream and declare that Nelya was a milf—not that he would ever say that out loud. He was not that stupid.

Despite his horny grunt mind telling him that Nelya was clearly older. Their similar looks were uncanny, enough so that Martinez could believe they were sisters. They would be sisters with different eye colors and drastically different ideas of what fashion was, but sisters nonetheless.

With that similarity in mind, Martinez wondered what Lysa would look like in a few years. If she ended up anything close to Nelya—he had a lot of fun in the bedroom to look forward to, especially with how flexible his Ruh'ah is.

Once Nelya was within arms' reach, she paused and momentarily continued her intent scan of Martinez. Once satisfied with what she saw, a coy smirk crawled onto her blood-red lips.

"It is nice to meet you—" Martinez started, realizing he was standing there like a dunce. He offered a hand for Nelya to shake, knowing the gesture was relatively similar between Humans and Aviex.

Nelya had other plans for her future family member and her daughter's Gra'hu; The older Aveix grabbed Martinez's hand and tugged him into a tight, well-meaning hug.

"By the stars, dear, there is no need to be so formal," Nelya gushed, "If Lysa brought you along, there is no way you are getting off without giving me a hug."

After a brief moment of being surprised by Nelya's strength and speed, Martinez returned the gesture, going with the mentality of 'when in Rome do as the Romans do' and not wanting to set himself up for an incredibly awkward start to their stay with Lysa's parents.

"Thanks for having us over—mam," Martinez said, slightly unsure how formally he should refer to her.

Martinez knew that her name was Nelya; Lysa had told him that much, but he also knew that Aviex had a plethora of terms and titles to refer to others in and out of your direct family. Because of that, his mind defaulted to the training the Human Navy had ingrained in him. Namely being extremely formal.

Nelya leaned back slightly and looked between Martinez and Lysa, looking to Lysa for confirmation if Martinez was genuinely like this. Lysa responded by simply shrugging, knowing that Martinez was willing to touch others but was often uncomfortable if he did not engage them on his terms.

In retrospect, she should have informed Nelya of that particular quirk, but that ship had sailed.

"Oh, Henry, please don't be that way," Nelya giggled, looking back at him. "Calling me mam makes me feel like more of a biddy than I am."

Martinez stepped back and awkwardly scratched behind his head, looking to Lysa for some assistance with what he was finding to be an awkward introduction to her mother. Thank God Lysa's usual sharpness came to his rescue.

"I am terribly sorry, Mother, I neglected to inform you—Henry is uncomfortable touching people he does not know. He likely feels somewhat taken aback by your hug," Lysa explained.

That was not the most elegant way of phrasing one of the issues Martinez had developed after dozens of combat tours, but who was he to argue with putting it out there? At least that made the reason he felt bolshie known.

Nelya stepped back, and now it was her turn to blush. In an almost childish way, she averted her eyes and brushed her hair behind her shoulders. "Oh—I did not mean to make you feel—well, I am sorry either way."

"It's alright," Martinez assured, waving the event away with a hand.

"Thank you for the forgiveness. But for now, you two are likely exhausted from the trip. Let me show you two to the guest house," Nelya nodded before turning around but pausing before she stepped off. "Do you need any help with your luggage?"

"No need, I got it," Martinez said, opening the trunk to the SUV and pulling out their bags, quickly taking all four of them in hand.

"Thank you, Ruh'ah," Lysa nodded while following her mother around the side of the house, toward the backyard.

Following the mother and daughter, Martinez kept an eye open, scanning the area for Lysa's father. He spotted several deer-like animals grazing on the far side of the river and a few dozen birds watching them from a closed porch on the main house, but there was no sign of Kyroll.

"Where is Kyroll?" Martinez questioned as they entered the guest house. A deep part of his lizard brain was uncomfortable with not having tabs on someone he knows, is incredibly well-trained, and has shown negative feelings towards Lysa's past relationships.

"Gra'hu won't be back for a few days. He got caught up at work." Nelya replied. "Don't worry, he will be on his best behavior."

"The past makes me doubt that," Lysa quipped.

If it wasn't for Nelya having solid pink eyes, you would have been able to see her roll them. She and Lysa must have talked about how Kyroll acted many times over the years. The tension between the two was palpable. It was not hostile by any means. It was more of a reserved understanding, with both willing to end that conversation there.

Nelya believed her dear husband would do better than he had in the past, whereas Lysa was firmly in the camp of she would believe it when she saw it.

"Either way, we can still have an enjoyable time while he is out," Nelya assured. "Tomorrow, we can go out in town. Some people would love to see what a beautiful woman you have become. Miss Numla would adore seeing you after all these years."

Miss Numla was a name Lysa had not heard in years. Honestly, she had forgotten about her former tutor, assuming the older Hyltra woman would have done the same. But if Mother says Numla wants to see her, perhaps she was mistaken.

"That does sound lovely," Lysa said, looking around the simple guest house. "When did you build this?"

While not lavish, the guest house was pleasant. Guests were in a central foyer and could easily see an attached living room and the kitchen. The living room had a davenport and a lovely wooden coffee table. Additionally, paintings of animals grazing along the side of lakes and grand vistas adorned the walls.

Martinez was unsure if there was food in the kitchen but could see hanging pots and pans over an island in its center. But he would have plenty of time to figure that out later. He did not doubt they would cook at least a few times during their stay.

"Kyroll and I had this commissioned a few years ago; we needed it when a few of his old squad mates were moving into town and needed somewhere to sleep while they house-hunted. Having them around was so good for his well-being," Nelya smiled.

But her smile quickly faded as if she had just said something she should not have. "That is not me implying his friends at the lumberyard aren't good people; it was just different," she corrected with a more assured tone.

That sudden shift in tone caught Martinez's attention. Not because it seemed like Nelya was afraid or anything like that. No, it seemed like she was trying to respect her husband's feelings even though he was not here.

If he was correct, it told much about her mentality and beliefs about being in a relationship.

Before Martinez had much time to consider the meaning of her tone, Nelya continued her grand tour.

"Here, let me show you your rooms, and then we can relax. I

ensured the sauna was clean and ready for us all, and I got a bottle of my favorite wine. Assuming you all would like to," Nelya said, walking them down the hallway.

"Of course we would, Mother. Would we not, Ruh'ah?" Lysa asked, passing the buck to him.

"Sure, it's no hot tub, but it sounds nice," Martinez shrugged, having been in more than one sauna in his days.

As they went down the hall, Nelya showed them the bathroom laundry room and finished by showing them the room they would call home for their stay.

Their bedroom was very basic. It had a king-sized bed with posh covers and a walk-in closet against the far wall that was open and empty. But the most fantastic part of the room was the view. Just over a wooden desk was a double wide window, beyond which were rows upon rows of trees and the river.

It was a sight any of them could see on a postcard advertising a rentable bed and breakfast. Or, to be frank, Martinez's dream home.

Lysa walked in and took in the entire room. Martinez scanned it from the fatal funnel, having paused inside it, letting the women lead. Lysa ran her hand on the bedspread and grimaced slightly, feeling the coarse material. It had nothing on the elegant silken bedding Martinez had in his apartment but was still softer than most would ever own. But after having spent months sleeping in them—she was spoiled.

"Thank you ma— Nelya," Martinez said, dropping their bags next to the door, having noticed Lysa's slight scowl.

While he understood Lysa's reservations about returning to her parent's home, he suggested she make a little bit more of an effort to enjoy it. Her father was not here at the moment, souring the mood. Hopefully, this was just some initial nerves.

"We are glad to have you here," Nelya said, "I will see you two shortly; don't forget to grab towels from the bathroom."

"We shall not, Mother," Lysa smiled somewhat blankly.

After Nelya had left, Martinez and Lysa began to unpack. As they did, Martinez looked at Lysa and saw she was still somewhat scowling.

He set down his shirt and walked over, pulling her into a hug. "I know it's difficult, but your mother is trying t—"

"I am aware Ruh'ah—please forgive me if I'm a bit dour," Lysa replied, hugging him back.

"I will, but your mother clearly noticed your scowling," Martinez replied.

Lysa released a deep breath and looked down and away, thinking back to a few minutes ago. "I suppose I should attempt to loosen up before the truly uncomfortable part of these—events comes to pass."

Martinez smiled and let her go, believing in his Ruh'ah. She would do her best here, even if some of it sucked. To try and lighten her mood slightly, Martinez decided to tease her just a little bit, nothing harsh, but a firm pat on her rump, causing her to giggle and return the gesture.

"Now you just are not playing fair," Lysa stuck her tongue out at Martinez.

That was more like it. Lysa, being a coy, somewhat snarky woman, was far more enjoyable. A mood she kept throughout the rest of the time they were unpacking.

Once they were ready, Lysa grabbed towels and waited for Martinez at the door.

"Should I bring my swim trunks?" Martinez questioned.

Instead of outright telling Martinez no, Lysa gave him a snide grin, grabbed his hand, and led him out the guest house door toward a small shack attached to the main building. Steam and smoke billowed out from the chimney, and the slightest glimpse of Nelya undressing from the window in the door could be seen.

Initially, he thought nothing of it until Nelya hung her shirt on a hook. He looked at Lysa, who picked up on what he noticed.

"What is wrong Ruh'ah? It's not like you haven't seen me naked before," Lysa chuckled, reveling in the deep blush on Martinez's face.

As the distance narrowed, Martinez had one question roaring in his mind. What the fuck did he just agree to?

RELAXING REVELATIONS

Lysa quickly stripped and got ready to shower once she shoved Martinez into the first room of the sauna. It was a simple location with a single shower and a few cubbies for clothes and towels, Nelya's revealing clothes neatly stacked in one.

Once she had turned on the faucet and doused herself in the flowing water, she looked back toward Martinez, who was bashfully pondering the idea of taking off his clothes.

It was cute that Martinez, a trained and combat-experienced Corpsman, was embarrassed by the idea of being in a sauna with her and Nelya. He was a man who had faced the perils of the enemies of the GU with valor time and time again, but her mother naked was too much for her dear Ruh'ah.

Lysa knew they had open-bay showers when he was in training, so it's not like public bathing would be new to him. Aviex were incredibly social in their families, so group baths and nudity amidst each other were common.

"Don't worry about feeling awkward; we are all going to be naked," Lysa assured, gesturing toward the door leading into the sauna room.

"That's easy for you to say; I am about to go into a sauna with my girlfriend and her mother," Martinez replied, gesturing toward the door Nelya had just entered.

He was thankful that he only caught the slightest glimpse of Nelya. The idea of being in the same room as her while nude was overwhelming, especially when it came to having Lysa around as well.

Martinez never went to strip clubs, slept around, or did anything along those lines. To him, being that exposed with someone was reserved for intimate moments, save for the showers in training, you had no choice but to shower together—but those were his brothers in arms, not his girlfriend's bombshell of a mother.

Where was he allowed to look anyway? Could he look at Lysa and not piss off Nelya? She seemed reasonably nonchalant about Lysa and Martinez's relationship, but that was only from his understanding that Lysa told her every detail of their relationship.

That idea made looking at Lysa all the more fiddly. While Martinez roughly knew what Lysa had told Nelya, the precise details of their conversations were unknown. Did she know every intimate detail? Or just an overview of what they do in the bedroom?

Then there is Nelya. The idea of looking at her and chatting while nude was beyond awkward; no, it felt like a social faux pas, downright sinful. She was his girlfriend's mother, for god's sake. That she invited them to the sauna did not change the fact that he was raised not to look at any other girls naked—much less your Ruh'ah's fucking mother.

His grandmother and grandfather would have beat him with a switch and disowned him if they ever even thought he cheated or looked at another woman—not that they were alive or knew about Lysa, but he had seen it happen to his cousin Jose.

Seeing Martinez still in a bit of a tizzy, Lysa clicked her tongue and shook her head. If Martinez was ever going to become her Gra'hu he could not feel this shy about being naked. But she also had to be an excellent potential Gra'hu for him and support his shortfalls.

"Don't worry about feeling awkward," Lysa said while stepping closer, the water dripping down her muscular body. "You are the only Ruh'ah that I've had. I am certain my Mother is not quite sure of how to behave. Frankly, neither am I."

Martinez smirked slightly. He doubted what Lysa was saying there. She was generally proficient at holding her composure and knowing how to behave. Her mastery of those skills comes from being an Aviex in a large city. You had to know how to adjust your actions on the fly to not piss off an angry alien.

He was not sure about Nelya, but he would have to spend more time with her to take her mental pulse at a glance as he could with Lysa. Either way, he still appreciated the reassurance, even if it did little to ease his pattering heart.

"Head on in. I will rinse off and be there in a minute," Martinez said, having decided to treat the situation like pulling off a bandage—just get it over with.

"Very well, Ruh'ah," Lysa replied before leaning in and kissing his lips softly.

Martinez nearly instinctively wrapped his arms around her, pulling Lysa tight and deepening the kiss, completely forgetting that she was soaked. Not that either minded the water.

Once the kiss broke, Lysa smirked, one of her dimples forming. "Well, now you must change; you are sopping," she purred, plucking open his top button and stepping back. "We will be waiting for you."

Martinez took a deep breath once Lysa was inside the sauna. The rush of damp air filled his lungs and pulled out some of his rattled nerves, but it was enough to get him to continue.

He stripped, dropped his wet clothes in one of the cubbies, and stepped into the surprisingly cold water. The chilly liquid pulled goosebumps up on his skin.

While he rinsed off, he could barely hear Nelya and Lysa chatting. The running water and the closed door made all but their laughter indecipherable. It was a good thing they were laughing; Lysa needed this trip to go well, and he wanted it to.

To him, family was vital in a relationship, and it was not like his family was a few hours away. If Martinez ever wanted them to meet Lysa, they would have to take several weeks to travel to Earth; that would be both expensive and difficult, so they would have to wait until they had more money and were further on in their relationship.

Once Martinez showered and was in the suit God had given him, Martinez slowly opened the door. He damn near knocked but caught himself before rapping against the wood; he was already going to likely make an ass of himself during the next few minutes; doing something he knew the women could get a chuckle out of would not help him.

Inside the sauna was about what Martinez expected: simple wooden construction composing the walls and long benches teared up to the ceiling. The dead center of the round room was a metal stove filled with hot rocks.

Next to Nelya and Lysa were glasses and a bottle of wine. None of them had poured any inside the glasses so far. But Martinez did notice one detail that made him raise an eyebrow. Why were there only two glasses?

Before he could ponder that, Nelya reached over and cast a ladle of water onto the rocks, with steam erupting off them, causing the already near-scalding air to be overbearing. The heat was insane and pulled sweat from Martinez instantaneously.

But none of those details were what Martinez's monkey brain focused on. He looked hard left and concentrated on the empty bench. Whether it was him being genuinely curious about what they looked like right now or his stupid habit of needing to know what was happening in the room, he glanced over at them, blushing and seeing them intently watching him.

After years of combating the Farq on Heavalun, Martinez had developed keen senses and the ability to take a snapshot glance of what he looked at, allowing him to instantly assess dangers. Usually, that was beneficial to him. It helped him and his teams stay alive—now, not so much.

The Human hoped he did not see what he did but knew what was witnessed was true; it always was.

Nelya was leaning back against the wood, her arms propping her up. Her plump, voluptuous chest almost made him gawk, but thank God he could keep himself composed. While her chest certainly had no budget cuts, neither did the rest of her.

Her thighs looked soft and plush, along with her long, trailing black hair resting on the bench. Unlike her daughter, Nelya's pink eyes scanned Martinez with curiosity. It's likely a reaction to finally seeing how similar Humans and Aviex are firsthand.

Nelya had what looked like a tattoo on her upper thigh. It resembled a band of brambles, with a flower blooming just over her hip.

That was curious; Martinez had not expected the gentle-acting Nelya to be the type to get a tattoo. That and Lysa never showed any interest in tattoos, even the Human Marine tattoo he had on his right shoulder.

He might ask about it later but knew he likely would not—ink not out in the open was generally for the wearer, not the observer; at least, that is how he thought of it.

Lysa was sitting less than an arm's reach away and just as hypnotic, but her natural form was something Martinez was comfortable with; seeing her abs glistening with sweat and her athletic build was homey.

Though, unlike her mother's more laid-back posture, Lysa sat erect with her hands gracefully resting on her lap. She had a wide grin on her lips as she looked at Martinez with the same reverence he gave her.

"Henry, come and take a seat," Neyla said, patting the area between her and Lysa with a snarky smile. "You should sit beside your Ruh'ah, not over there alone."

Nelya and Lysa giggled when Martinez's spine went ramrod straight after being called out, not that it changed his plan.

He slowly worked his way over to them, not looking directly at them. However, instead of sitting between them, he sat to the side of Lysa, with her acting as a barrier between Nelya and him.

For several seconds Martinez was silent, sitting forward and staring straight forward, focusing on the water bubbling on the hot rocks.

"Come on now, Ruh'ah, you should try and relax," Lysa whispered into his ear; her usually hot breath was a chilly breeze in the steamy room.

Martinez glanced over and nodded, trying to assure Lysa that he was making some effort; this situation was a lot for him.

"So, Mother, do you recall me telling you about Henry's military service?" Lysa said, trying to pull Martinez into a conversation, hoping that getting him to involve himself would assist him in finding solace.

"I do," Nelya replied before leaning forward and looking over at Martinez. Her long hair draped down and nearly touched the floor. "Are you still in the service or not? Lysa tried to explain it to me before, but I could not make heads or tails of what she said."

"I made an earnest effort," Lysa insisted.

"Yes, yes you did," Nelya replied, acknowledging Lysa but still wishing to chat with Martinez despite her knowing his situation very well. "So, could you try to explain your situation to me?"

Even Martinez was unsure of that. He was on loan from the Human Navy to the GU medical service, so while he technically could be considered still in service, he was in no way acting like it. Hell, he might as well be a civilian, despite the threat that the Human Navy could recall him at any time they felt like it.

God knows that the Human Navy is fickle and that the Human government does not care about one soldier's happiness.

Martinez did his best to explain his situation to Nelya and answer any follow-up questions. She mostly asked a little about his time in service and what he liked and did not like about it.

Both were easy enough to answer, and he did not hesitate to reply despite his environment. A detail Lysa and Nelya noted, both understanding they just had to be casual and keep him talking and involved.

Martinez briefly reviewed how he went to basic training back on Earth and was then sent to Mars for follow-up training, where he learned to be a Corpsman; after that, he explained his nearly six years of constant warfighting or support operations around the galaxy.

He told them the rough gist of the fighting on Verilon and Harudeth before he was assigned to relief efforts in some of the outer Human colonies, specifically his near year of helping relocate and treat refugees of a repelled assault from the Bulamric empire.

The details of that campaign were all too vivid for Martinez. The remnants of those aliens rampaging across the planets were impossible to forget. There were so many bodies, destroyed houses and cities, along with gruesome treatment of the prisoners of war.

How could he forget the bat-like alien stay-behind troops and their odd social existence? Unlike most of the other members of the GU who were republics or other democracies, they were still a hereditary monarchy, just not in the traditional way humans had used it.

The Bulamrics had a strict caste system, the only exception to that system being when someone was born with white fur. Anyone born with white fur out of the traditional upper crust was filled into their church and allowed vertical movement.

Nelya shocked Martinez by mentioning that she knew about the empire's assault on Human colony planets; the nocturnal chiropterans had supposedly claimed hundreds of standard years before Humans had stepped foot on them.

It was not surprising that she knew of it. Humans were the talk of the GU at the time. No, it was the details she knew.

Nelya mentioned how they fileted members of outposts to display as warnings, shot down several of the planetary defense forces spacecraft, killing thousands, and even outlined how the Human Navy, Marines, and Army kicked them to the curb by bringing the full weight of their might upon the Bulamrics small attack fleet.

All of those details were things only the Humans directly involved would know. Nelya could even explain the warrior caste and their vampiric origins, drawing a clear line of how they even had something similar to Mordain, even though it was far more bloody and brutal.

"How do you know all of that?" Martinez questioned, knowing the Human government did its best to keep the events of the war quiet, likely to strong-arm the Bulamric empire into a trade deal instead of a GU sanction.

"Indeed, Mother, you seem quite well versed in politics on the far side of the galaxy," Lysa commented, genuinely curious about why she would know intimate details of Human wars.

Nelya smirked slightly and attempted to cover it with her hand, but both Martinez and Lysa saw it clear as day. "Well—I read up on them for novel research," she explained, trying to avoid eye contact with the duo.

Martinez noticed that and knew Nelya was not being forthright. There was no way it was just that. But he would not outright call her a liar; for all he knew, she was just researching to include Human characters.

"Seems like an odd thing to research since you write spy por—er romance thrillers," Martinez said, catching himself from calling Nelya's novels outright porn.

"Don't worry, I've heard plenty of critics call my novels porn, and if some of my reader's reviews are anything to go by—they enjoyed it in ways I did not intend," Nelya shrugged.

"Oh, come on, they aren't that pornographic," Martinez insisted, having finished her debut novel on the shuttle ride over. "I like your books."

Her first novel, *Kirkai Lourin, and the Rutiral Apprentice,* only had three sex scenes in its six hundred pages. He did not think it was terrible, even though the book was strewn with sexual innuendos and tension between Kirkai and his trainee Urenta.

Though he only thought it was not that abashedly sexual because the porn scenes were well-written, easy to visualize, and were not out of nowhere. They had a good build-up. Even someone like him who did not read books laden with sex could tell that much.

"Lysa, you were right; I was going to like him," Nelya smiled a toothy grin, gesturing up and down at Martinez, eliciting a heavy blush from him as he looked away, having not realized during the casual chat about his time in service he ended up looking right at Nelya.

"I know," Lysa complimented while patting Martinez's shoulder. "Ruh'ah is amazing."

That did not help Martinez relax; he had never been the type to enjoy praise, and getting it from Lysa and Nelya only made him feel more like he was taking what he should not receive.

"So, Henry, what else did you think of my first book?" Nelya questioned.

"Well, I enjoyed the setting. I think the city you placed it in was fun and felt alive," Martinez replied.

That response was not him just trying to be nice to Nelya. The city of Roqural, the setting of the novel, genuinely breathed atmosphere. Her vivid descriptions filled the world with motion—not so much that it was overbearing, but just enough that he thought he was seeing what she did.

"Oh, please continue," Nelya insisted after Martinez explained what he enjoyed about the story overall.

Martinez chuckled at the obvious attempt to fish for compliments, but he was not one to belay praises because he was in front of someone who deserved it.

The three of them began conversing about some of the books they enjoyed and their favorite genres to read.

Nelya explained how she started writing because she was bored sitting at home waiting for Kyroll to return from missions. Initially, she began by writing what she called horrible, barely legible short stories on the data net until she finally managed to cobble together her first Novel.

That sounded similar to what Martinez had heard from one of the Human Marines he knew, Aura. He had done something similar toward getting published.

"I'm certain Lysa will do something similar if you stay in military service and are sent off to another war," Nelya casually commented.

"I am uncertain if Ruh'ah intends to return to the Human Navy," Lysa said, patting his thigh. "I pray he stays and becomes my Gra'hu."

"Well, we can't have that until you two have your own hunters and huntresses running around causing havoc. On that subject, did you two go to a clinic to see if our species can reproduce naturally? I am eager to know how long it will be. I'm not getting any younger after all." Nelya mused, tossing another ladle of water on the coals, steam wafting up and filling the area.

Martinez looked over to Lysa, expecting her to explain what Nelya meant by they had to have kids, but Lysa was motionless and blushing while she damn near glowered at her mother.

This was not the first time Martinez had heard the word Gra'hu, but he understood it to mean something similar to husband or wife. Now, he was starting to question what the word precisely meant.

This was bringing to light some of the differences between Humans and Aviex. Some that Martinez was realizing he likely overlooked, having been swept up in his romance, work, and other issues at Draun.

It took Nelya a few glances between Henry and Lysa before she said anything to break the silence. "Oh— I see; well, I think I will leave the two of you alone—here, have the bottle," Nelya calmly said, leaving a bottle and two glasses on the bench and then quickly slipping out of the room.

It was now that Martinez started to piece together more about Nelya. She was cunning, and his little thoughts about her were confirmed. Like a politician steering a conversation and a meeting— she planned this interaction between Lysa and him.

"So— do you want to explain what she meant by that?" Martinez questioned.

To his surprise, Lysa did not initially respond; she was not even looking at him. She pulled the glasses over, poured some of the wine, and handed him a glass.

After taking a few sips of the wine, she sighed, hung her head, and spoke, "To put it bluntly—"

RUH'AH GRA'HU AND ALL BETWEEN

L ysa paused for a while after she initially started to speak, biting her cheek and swirling the wine in her glass, looking at it like the rose liquid would answer the question Martinez had just posed to her, for her to clarify what Nelya meant by that they had to have kids to be Gra'hu.

Being a Human with little experience with the Aviex and the GU at large, Martinez assumed it to be with a title for marriage, but apparently, it meant something closer to parents.

"I wish to begin by stating I fully intended to explain it to you—just—just," Lysa started before growling at herself.

This conversation was something Lysa was not ready to have at this moment. She planned on following a more traditional Human style of relationship development, assuming she had months, if not years, to explain the concept of Gra'hu entirely.

Thanks to Nelya's intervention her hopeful timeline was rushed to right now.

Lysa would have to chastise or argue with her mother about that later. She did not need to toss a wrench into the plans she and Lysa had already discussed. That and Lysa knew Nelya, and there was no way Nellya did not know what she was doing by implying she and Martinez needed to hurry and have kids.

"It's just what?" Martinez prised, pouring himself a glass of wine, preparing for what likely would be a long or uncomfortable conversation, unsure of where the ball would fall for the time being.

"The difference between our species—relationship development might be too much, and I don't want it to be taken as that I was trying to mislead you," Lysa said, fidgeting her legs, trying to keep tension from building in her further.

"Well, I'm already aware there is something vastly different. So can you just say it? I'm fairly positive of what it is anyway," Martinez sighed, leaning back and sipping his wine, letting the heat pull tension from his sore muscles.

Lysa let out an exasperated sigh, one that is uncharacteristic of her. "Very well, but as I said before, I was not trying to deceive you."

"I never said you were," Martinez interjected, not out of malice but trying to assure his Ruh'ah he was attempting to understand.

"As I was explaining—" Lysa grumbled, somewhat annoyed, not taking his words to mean what he intended. "We, Aviex, have a different social understanding of pairing, mating, and life. Especially when compared to Humans," She explained, gesturing up and down at herself and him in contrast. "Humans—had a far more hospitable world than Aveix. Because of Aveion being a dark, barren place—we consider what you call marriage to only exist once children are sired."

From his research on their biology, Martinez knew about the Aviex homeworld but nothing in-depth like social strata. Still, he was already aware their world lacked resources on all levels, and without the GU, they would have never risen to the stars.

"For us—due to the lack of supplies and safety, it was rare for Aviex to be conceived, much less carried to term. The defined vocabulary for what we mean to each other is a byproduct of that rarity," Lysa grumbled before sipping her drink and looking over at Martinez for a moment.

"Ruh'ah technically means we have tried and failed to have kids," Lysa sighed, hanging her head, sounding almost ashamed. "It doesn't mean we have just slept together."

"Well, that's certainly something," Martinez replied, unsure of how he should take that.

"I'm sorry—I–I meant to explain, but with how we are different species—and likely could not have kids naturally—I thought the original context did not matter, so I leaned on what I learned about Humans through my readings, and chats with you," Lysa slowly said at nearly a whisper, each word feeling like venom in her mouth.

Explaining this to Martinez was horrendous; it was like she was breaking everything she and Martinez had built up to this point. She legitimately never intended to deceive him, and with his knowledge of medicine, she assumed he knew they could not have kids anyway.

She had tried to justify it by telling herself she was giving him close-to truths. But that was wrong. She wasn't kidding Martinez, not even herself, now that the cat was out of the bag.

She lied for her own sake; she did not want Martinez to leave once he learned that Aviex only considered relationships legitimately sanctified once they had kids, and nothing up to that point mattered in tradition.

Lysa glanced up from her wine toward Martinez and could hardly look at him for more than a breath. His genuine look of concern for her might as well be glass carving her soul to shreds.

He did not look furious at her; seeing the gears in his head turning was evident in his bark-brown eyes and scrunched, almost pained expression. But she could not predict his conclusion or how he would act.

In her mind, Martinez was reflecting on everything they had ever done and judging it all under this new light, likely not one that would benefit her.

Deep in the vortex of scenarios she could cook up in her head, they all resulted in Martinez walking out that door, getting in the car, and leaving. She betrayed his trust in her and could not justify why he would remain loyal to her.

"I—I—I'm sorry," Lysa sniffled, averting her eyes, not wanting his bark brown stare to rip her apart anymore.

Looking over at her, Martinez sighed and leaned forward. He had not reached out to make physical contact yet but was just aiming to be nearer to his Ruh'ah. Yeah, was she technically not his Ruh'ah in the true meaning, but that did not matter.

They were not the same species; having kids naturally was less likely than being struck by lightning multiple times.

Martinez felt somewhat betrayed by her bringing him here under a false pretext. Not because she lied to him, but because he could not have met her expectations and desires in a partner.

Martinez grew up in a traditional Latino household and was perfectly comfortable with having kids with someone he loved. He would be lying if he said he had not thought about having kids with Lysa at least once.

Still, she should have told him, not let him lie to himself or her family. If he had been introduced with the idea that one day they would have kids after meeting a genetic specialist, he was game—but now Martinez almost felt dirty, Like he was introduced as a broken product. Someone they would never accept and never want as their family.

Stewing on that idea, they sat there for a while, silent and each dwelling in their minds.

Martinez almost wanted to go full Marine, or in his case, Devil Doc. Still a Marine in attitude but not in name. A part of him wanted to be mad, wanted to yell at Lysa, scream, break a wall, and ask what the fuck was she thinking.

Another part wanted to silently stand up and walk out that door. The Human Navy, his family, and himself held honesty in high regard, to the point the trait was cardinal to living an honorable life.

His entire body tenses, all of his muscles ripping themselves apart. After years of combat trials, a part of him could not help but feel the slightest twinge that Lysa was a threat, even if he did not want to.

He knew she deceived him, and the only people or aliens he knew who did that meant him harm in some form.

Looking over at her and seeing a tear rolling down her cheek and dripping into her wine glass pulled him back to the here and now, not thoughts of what might be or what he should do.

Doing anything brash would only cost him the only woman he had ever loved, so Martinez swallowed the first horrible instinct years on Verilon had taught him, and simply rested his hand on Lysa's shoulder and sighed, "Why?"

After almost recoiling from the sudden contact and ripped from her imagination, Lysa reached up and clutched his hand tightly, enough so Martinez winced. Lysa looked toward the coals and damn near sobbed. "I–didn't want you to go."

Lysa then reiterated why the Aviex were hated in the galaxy, that she had never had anyone other than her family and a few friends, and how she had been treated like a monster for years since running away from home.

Outside of the few empires of aliens that drank blood exclusively, the Aviex were unique because they ritually consumed it.

Martinez doubted that was the only reason the Aviex were hated in the GU; there had to be more going on after all. Many aliens ate meat, and he could not understand why blood drinking was the linchpin of generations of hatred.

The idea seemed almost hypocritical if that was all it was.

That thought was why he knew something else had to be going on in the GU; whether the Aviex were a useful boogeyman to the GU or just so happened to be the victims of decades of stigma, he did not know. However, he did know the GU at large was wrong about the Aviex and her.

Lysa was kind and understanding and never once drank his blood without his consent, a far cry from the uncontrollable, blood-hungry monsters the GU populace at large treated the Aviex like.

"I'm not mad," Martinez said, pulling her close, wanting to be a rock for her, feeling Lysa needed him right now.

Lysa clung to him and squashed her plush breasts against his chest. "But–I," Lysa shuttered but was cut off by Martinez interjecting.

"Stop. Yeah, I am slightly peeved that you did not tell me, but I understand why you did what you did," Martinez assured. "If you told me after the first night you were trying for kids—I probably would have thought you were nuts," he said with a slight chuckle, fully imagining how off the walls that would have been.

"Can you forgive me?" Lysa pleaded, wanting nothing more than him to. She would do anything to even hear there was a chance of him doing so.

"I already said I'm not mad; forgiveness is not an issue, but will you explain more clearly how this usually works for Aviex? At least then I won't get blindsided by your dad in a few days," Martinez requested.

Lysa clutched him harder, burying her head into the collar. That he was even giving her a chance was beyond what she had hoped for. If they were able to just reconcile, she would tell him anything.

"Come on, let's have a few more drinks while we clear the air," Martinez said lightly, pushing Lysa back so he could give her a beatific smile, one she thankfully returned, even though she had to wipe a few tears from her cheeks.

"Indeed, let's," Lysa replied, shifting so she was sitting beside Martinez again, though there was no gap between them now that Nelya had left them alone, and they were somewhat on the same page.

Martinez wrapped his arm around her waist, holding her tight. While they were both sweaty from the sauna, neither minded it; they were used to it.

After the next ten minutes and a glass of wine, Martinez was introduced to a new world of her culture. Lysa had left details about Aviex courtship in her previous, far more passive explanation, but her new clarification made it far more straightforward.

As far as a traditional Aviex was concerned, Lysa and Martinez might as well be single and not involved at all; Ruh'ah was precisely what she had just explained: Martinez and she had tried and failed to have children.

Both of them could quickly agree that they had not really tried because they had not been to a fertility clinic, nor could they likely have children naturally. So they wanted to continue to use the title to refer to one another; they had done so for months at this point, and it only felt natural to keep doing so.

With the understanding of what Ruh'ah meant out of the way, Lysa explained that Gra'hu meant that a pair had children; Lysa did not even have to explain that, but she did anyway just for clarification.

The only things she explained that Martinez wanted further explanations on were what you called kids and how conservative her father was.

Martinez's interest in what their eventual kids would be called made Lysa happy—hell, beyond happy. She was both turned on that he was interested and overjoyed he was willing to listen to the idea.

If not for her being in the middle of explaining and reconciling, she would have jumped his bones already. They were dressed for the occasion and alone.

But she would act on that in a few minutes after Martinez had all his questions answered.

Aviex children were called Yha-re or Yha-ru, translating to hunter and huntress, respectively.

Lysa was unsure why her Mother referred to her with the Standard equivalent of those words, explaining that she had always done that. Martinez assumed it might have something to do with Nelya not being incredibly conservative, unlike her Father, Kyroll.

He would be an issue in ways Martinez had expected and ones he did not.

From what Lysa was able to extract from Nelya and her past interactions with Kyroll, several things were guaranteed about the old veteran: he detested non-Aviex almost across the board, he hated Lysa ever dating in the past, and he was incredibly protective of his daughter.

He could agree that a Father should be concerned for his daughter, especially when she is an only child until she gave an example of how overprotective he was.

"Well shit," Martinez muttered, hearing Lysa tell a story about her father scaring off some of her friends by sitting on the porch with a rifle.

That he is so willing to even threaten violence against Lysa's friends and potential lovers was horrifying. Martinez knew about Humanty's past of racism and bigotry but had assumed that type of genuine hatred was mainly dead in the GU.

Some of the members of the GU species might have a bit of a stick up their ass, believing themselves truly better. But the GU rarely worked with those members, finding them prickly and stuck up.

"It will be fine," Lysa assured, sipping her drink. "Mother has made it clear she won't accept any treatment like that toward you."

That did not make him feel any better; everything Martinez had learned about Lysa's father only made him more concerned about the inevitable meeting. He had money on that violence was unavoidable, even if Nelya and Lysa were there.

Kyroll was dangerous, specist, and was more than willing to defend his little huntress from anyone, including him. Along with his background, Kyroll would be intelligent and capable.

"One can hope," Martinez said, leaning over and kissing Lysa's cheek.

Both had agreed to see a fertility clinic in the future; when? They were unsure but knew it would be at least after he completed his schooling. With that clear, they planned to continue going on as they have, supporting one another, cooking, and damn near living in each other's houses.

An idea Lysa took to heart a bit more than Martinez had anticipated, considering they had just cleared the air.

"Well then, Ruh'ah—since we have this alone time—care to pretend we can have our own Yha-re and Yha-ru?" Lysa purred, rubbing her palm up against his inner thigh.

Martinez looked over at Lysa, about to tell her no and that he was not in the mood after that heavy conversation, but Lysa surprised him.

No, surprised was not the right word, stunned him. Lysa smiled, clutched his hand, and brought it to her supple lips, treating two of his digits like a lollipop.

"I researched a bit of your species—pornography. While I know it is a bit taboo, I have been practicing not letting my teeth get in the way," she purred after leaving his fingers wet and slick.

How Lysa practiced was beyond him, but her sharp teeth barely touched his skin as she teased him with the idea of her trying to suck him off.

"Are you sure that's a good idea?' Martinez asked, remembering her telling him she should never try that and recalling how much she bites in sex.

Lysa paused for a moment after pulling his hand close to her breasts, "do you not trust me?" Lysa questioned, sounding almost hurt by the question.

Martinez was about to crack a joke because she just finished clarifying a lie she had told him. But she genuinely was looking at him, breathing heavily, and eagerly awaiting his answer.

Lysa then kicked any ideas of him not being in the mood out the door when she leaned close to his ear.

"So long as it's just me pleasing you, you are safe in my hands, mouth, or pussy—My Ruh'ah" Lysa purred in his ear, her purplish tongue licking him slowly between her words. "I won't bite."

"Just take it easy," Martinez gasped when she slinked her hand toward his groin. Her nails tickled his scarred skin, pulling a shiver down his spine, much to her enjoyment.

SODDEN SAUNA

Slowly, Lysa ran her tongue in circles around Martinez's ear while she rubbed her hand on his inner thigh, gradually nearing his already rigid member.

By the stars above, Martinez is remarkable, not only because he accepted how Aviex relationships work but also because he shuddered and buckled when she showed her more animalistic desires.

She snaked her hand around Martinez's cock and agonizingly slowly started to move up and down its length, eliciting at first a sharp, deep gasp from her Ruh'ah; followed by his breathing deepening.

"Relax, let me handle it," Lysa whispered before nibbling on his ear.

Lysa wanted to lead Martinez into the idea of her attempting to suck his cock. So, her showing the control she had been practicing on his ear first would likely help, and based on his shuddering, it was making a point.

"I will," Martinez moaned as she massaged his throbbing cock with deft intentional control, her thumb running laps around his tip faster by the second.

Without ever slowing her tender care of his manhood, Lysa meticulously kissed down his body, stopping to nibble, kiss, and lick as she went. As she rolled his nipple in her lips, he arched his back and grabbed her raven hair, not to hold her there, but to massage her scalp, matching the rhythm her hand was moving at.

It took Martinez and Lysa a moment to realize how loudly he had moaned when she teased his nipple. Once they did, Martinez blushed slightly, but Lysa helped him not feel embarrassed.

"I suppose I'm not the only one who finds pleasure in that," Lysa chuckled, looking up at Martinez.

"That—was something els—" Martinez started, but bit his tongue when Lysa, as gently as she could, bit his nipple, causing a lighting shock of pleasure to wrack him. "Fuck!" He said in a shuddered gasp.

Lysa giggled, enjoying that everything she had been trying was paying off. She then kissed down Martinez's abs until she was resting her head on his inner thigh, having slipped off the bench so she was kneeling between his legs.

For his part, Martinez enjoyed all of it. Lysa was always good at giving him attention in and out of the bedroom; now was no exception, especially when he looked down and could not help but smile as their eyes met.

After all the warnings she had given him initially about her not being able to go down on him, the sight of her rubbing his cock with it millimeters from her lips was one he never imagined he would see. In all reality, when they had first made love, Lysa would have never imagined she would be considering doing this—that was why she paused to rest on his thigh.

This moment of looking up at Martinez, his muscles rippling like waves as she stroked him, his heart beating rapidly, and vibrant brown eyes staring at her was a reminder of how much he trusted her.

"Are you prepared, Ruh'ah?" Lysa purred, licking her coal-black lips.

"Be careful," Martinez breathed, ready to see how this would go.

Yeah, he trusted Lysa, but she might as well have hypodermic needles for teeth. Their French kissing was already an intimate dance of care that they still occasionally messed up, resulting in little cuts on his lips or tongue.

He just prayed whatever practice Lysa had eluded to would pay off, and they would not have to explain to Nelya why they must rush

Martinez to the hospital. That was an awkward conversation neither of them wanted to have with her mother.

Lysa kissed up his shaft, eager to show him what she could do. Once at the tip, she wrapped it in her plush lips, the warm satin texture causing Martinez to grab her hair and almost help her along, wanting more than just her tongue running laps on his cock's tip.

Lysa, however, realizing what he was about to do, stopped and reminded him, "I shall be the one moving."

Lysa did not wait for Martinez to confirm his understanding before continuing to roll her tongue around on his cock.

After readying herself for the moment of truth, Lysa brought Martinez's girth further in, engulfing him in her wet, warm, velvety mouth.

Martinez reacted immediately, curling his toes and gasping with each head bob as she pulled more volume out of him; Her plush mouth and slick tongue attacked every millimeter of his cock with scrupulous intent, her sharp teeth hardly causing any issue.

Fuck, if anything, now that they were this far, it was, in a way, thrilling to have Lysa's razor-sharp daggers just barely making contact with his most sensitive organ.

Lysa pushed him onward, grabbed his thighs, and brought him as far into her mouth as possible, nearly causing her to gag. But her sensibilities won out in that battle, knowing if she coughed, it would be a disaster.

So she sucked like she was trying to pull his balls out through his cock. That was the step that pushed Martinez off a cliff into warm bliss. He tossed his head back against the pine boards as her throat and mouth rolled in waves, every muscle working in unison to bring him pleasure and bliss.

As Lysa continued, she could not help but feel switched on; all that effort practicing with different fruits, her fingers, and other tools was finally paying off, and it was intoxicating.

Her dripping, ready womanhood was eager to the point it ached, feeling her heartbeat in its swollen form. Lysa had not felt this ready since Martinez had first teased her after his first test several months ago.

But then she was begging, near demanding him to bed her. Now she was in control, and for his safety, she could not lose it, not slip her hand down and finger herself, not bring herself closer to climax.

That she could only give unto him in a way she had never felt before made each moment agonizing and equally spirituous.

Each time his cock pressed against the deepest part of her throat, she felt damn near drunk on the edge, wanting to bite her love. But she could not–despite her desires and nature demanding so.

She wanted Martinez to grab her, shove her against the wall, and make her legs weak while she clamped her jaws on his shoulder. Treating her with that unique caring dominance, he always treated her too, making her feel oh so loved and safe.

But knowing she could not have pleasure herself or stop now giving unto him made each breath all the more intoxicating. Her pride would not let her give up now-she had to finish this.

Martinez was close to painting her throat white, something she could tell by the salty taste of his pre-cum teasing her palate.

Pulling back on the throttle slightly, just to tease Martinez a bit and gauge her performance, she went up on his cock, releasing it from her velvet mouth, stroking its now spit-slick surface and admiring Martinez's reaction.

Her Human looked at her with damn near puppy dog eyes, as if he was pleading for her to continue and not just stroke his dick so slowly she could feel his heart racing.

"I thought you had never done this before," Martinez squeezed out through ragged breaths.

"I have never. I must be passing my oral exam with flying colors— At least based on your face," Lysa winked before kissing his cocks tip. "I am faring well?"

"Gods, yes. I'm already close," Martinez replied, rubbing his hand on her soft cheek, her dimple revealing as she smiled. "You don't have to keep going if you don't want to."

"I intend to see this through Ruh'ah; I wish to feel it all," Lysa purred before welcoming his cock back into the plush prison that was her mouth.

Lysa grabbed the base of his shaft, stroking the bottom and massaging his balls while she unleashed lewd fury upon his member.

When one part of her beatific mouth slowed, every other part increased its efforts to drive him into a blissful fog.

Lysa's ferocity increased as her body begged Martinez to fill her mouth with his hot seed. Just the sample of his precum rolling down her throat was making her mouth water, only causing her blow job to be all the more slick and impassioned.

That slight increase in speed was what it took for Martinez to give her what she wanted.

Martinez grabbed the bench hard enough that his knuckles went white, following Lysa's instructions to let her handle things.

At the same time, an arching pleasure shot from his groin throughout his body, making every muscle tense and scream in joy.

Lysa was not slowing down and pleased her Human as hot thick cum poured into her mouth with each cock twitch. She sucked, pulling more cum from him than she had expected, keeping Martinez's bliss high until he released the bench and sat there panting.

Once Martinez had settled and stopped painting Lysa's mouth as white as her skin, she released his member and sat between his legs.

He watched in awe as Lysa rolled his cum in her mouth for a few moments, sampling it like a fine wine. It was odd; from her reading, she had expected it to taste like salt, but it was not quite like that. It was almost nutty, reminding her of his blood's full fatty flavor.

Lysa noticed him staring as she pondered the taste. She smirked, knowing he was not expecting her to do that, so before swallowing his seed, Lysa opened her mouth and let him see her reward for the effort.

That was beyond sexy. Martinez had never had anyone give good head before, and now Lysa was reveling in what she had done.

She swallowed, lightly moaned and clambered into his lap, wanting to be closer to her love.

She paused once she straddled him. "Was my performance acceptable?" she whispered, pressing her supple chest against his.

"That was amazing," Martinez replied, bringing his lips to hers, holding her close, uncaring of how sweaty they were.

While they kissed, the fire burning in Lysa only grew; while it always burned for her Ruh'ah, now she needed Martinez to take her.

She was about to break the kiss and ask, but Martinez was already a step ahead of her, knowing her desires and tendencies without words being needed.

Using some of his Jujutsu skills, Martinez twisted them around in a flash of movement. Lysa ended up against the wall, the hot surface just warm enough to cause slight pain but not enough to truly harm her.

He pressed his slick body against her, taking her breath away as she gave into his forceful care.

"By the stars, yes!" Lysa gasped as Martinez's rough hand pinned her hands over her head while his other slowly kneaded her breast, the rough texture causing her back to arch in pleasure.

"Relax, I got this from here," Martinez whispered before kissing Lysa deeply, their tongues writhing against each other. Each blissfully enjoyed the other's candy-sweet spit and comforting presence.

Lysa squeaked in anticipation, nodded, and writhed as Martinez pulled one of Lysa's legs between his, spreading her wide open.

After the last ten minutes of sucking Martinez off and denying herself physical pleasure, she was wet, to the point she could feel her love dripping down her ass and onto the pinewood bench.

"Henry—Please—let—me," Lysa pleaded through her rapid breaths, wanting to have his blood rolling down her throat.

Martinez smirked and moved so he was upright, letting her crane her head and Mordain. Without hesitation, Lysa licked at his skin, finding the salty sweat to be a fun pallet cleanser before his rich, full-bodied blood.

Just as Lysa began to gently bite Martinez, letting his blood flow, he rolled his fingers across her throbbing clit. Wracking her body with pleasure, enough to have her teeth sink deep, far deeper than she intended.

Martinez winced surprised by her latching onto him like a vice and would have commented but she moaned and backed off slightly her teeth leaving bloody holes for her to drink from.

Moving his fingers along her wet womanhood, Lysa tried to shift her hips forward, bringing him inside. But Martinez pushed back with his total weight, doubling down on pinning her to the wall, making her gasp and stop drinking his blood.

"Plea—please," Lysa damn near begged, licking at his bleeding wounds, barely able to keep her thoughts straight.

Martinez did enjoy teasing Lysa, but now was not the time for that. She had shown her care, and it was his turn.

Not wanting her to wait any longer, Martinez pushed a finger into her sodden, tight pussy. Her body welcomed him in without question; the moment he started to push inside, she clenched and pulled his finger deeper, lightning pleasure spreading through her core.

Unlike Lysa, who favored slow, meticulous motions, Martinez used short, quick hand movements to keep Lysa on edge. Be it in and out, rotations, or a come-her-gesture, each brought louder and louder moans, matched in intensity by how Lysa squirmed in bliss.

Lysa's body was not just squirming; no, her wet tunnel was collapsing and squeezing tightly. Each time his fingertip found the furthest reaches of her womanhood, he pressed her against the wall, making her struggle to breathe in the overbearing heat of the sauna.

Each moment was pure bliss; Lysa's body burned like fire. Slick love poured out of her faster and faster, her volume shaking the pine boards Martinez pressed her body against.

It was all too much—far too much.

"Fuck!! Bite me!" Lysa screamed to high heaven, feeling the end coming any moment.

Obliging her tastes, Martinez bit her neck, just hard enough to make her pale skin pink. That did it. Lysa Thrashed like an animal and howled in ecstasy as wet love poured out of her, soaking Martinez's palm.

As Lysa's high slowly passed, she shuddered, breathing in the saturated air, struggling to regain her sensibilities in the heat. Eventually, her four red eyes meekly fluttered open, landing on Martinez, who smiled lovingly at her.

"Welcome back," Martinez teased, letting her hands go.

Without wasting a moment, Lysa draped her arms over his shoulders and hugged Martinez, with him pulling her off the wall so he could do the same.

They clung to one another as their bodies gradually calmed down from their little romp. After a while of snuggling, kissing, and Mordain ensuring each had their needed tender aftercare, Martinez stood up and stumbled slightly.

He knew they had been in the sauna for far longer than recommended. They have been in the sauna for almost an hour at this point, and that time limit was before you included that they were doing far more than just relaxing.

She also tried to stand, but her legs halfway buckled underneath her. She was still feeling like jelly after Martinez's love brought her such bliss.

He quickly supported her and chuckled, one she joined in with. Neither was upset about it; it was just funny how they were always there for one another, even in these little ways.

"Let's get ready for bed," Martinez said, rubbing his hand on her back, "I think we both could use it."

"Indeed," Lysa smirked, feeling fulfilled at this point.

FAULTING FATHER

The next few days were just what Martinez and Lysa pictured them to be: calm, relaxing, and filled with fun activities to bring Martinez and Nelya closer and allow Martinez and her to galvanize their relationship.

It was refreshing and just what they needed after the last few hectic months in Draun. There were no medical emergencies, racist assholes, or strangely horny nurses they had to deal with.

Each day has been filled with short morning walks and small activities Nelya had suggested they do while in town. So far, they have been fishing in the river near the house, where Nelya easily slaughtered both Lysa and Martinez handily.

Of course, the woman who lived right next to the river would win, knowing all the excellent fishing holes and secret locations nearby.

Martinez learned something about Nelya, Lysa, and the Aviex species he was not entirely aware of, namely that they were more willing to eat raw meat.

Nelya and Lysa needed to work together to convince him to even try a slice of raw fish.

Martinez knew of sushi and other raw meat eaten around Earth but had never tried it. It was not bad by any means, but he decided not to have more than one piece. Thankfully, Nelya and Lysa understood that raw meat was an acquired taste and texture and thus did not mock him for nearly throwing up when he first took a bite.

They also took some time to visit some of Lysa's old friends and teachers in town—not that many recognized her.

The last time they saw his Ruh'ah, she was more tomboyish and angry at the world, but this time, Lysa was smiling and laughing and was even embarrassed by stories of how she acted in the past.

That was a feeling Martinez and Nelya understood. After all, who was not embarrassed and cringed at their behavior from the past? Lord only knew that if Martinez had met himself in high school, he would have wanted to die.

Back then, he and the crowd he rolled with tried to emulate the gang culture of Los Angeles and southern California, specifically the look and mannerisms of Cholo.

At least none of his friends at the time genuinely got tied up in legitimate gangs; they were just stupid kids, and the actual gangsters knew it.

The last major thing they did was spend a day on the far end of Nelya and Kyrolls' property, having traveled to an area Nelya wanted to show them. The day was filled to the brim from dusk till dawn with strenuous hiking.

Martinez and Lysa were fit and capable of keeping up with Nelya, even though the older Aviex woman slowed down for her daughter and him. Neither were conditioned for the steep hills and loose rocks; they appreciated her giving that little grace.

All that effort was worth every ounce of sweat and heaving breath. By the time they stopped for lunch, they had reached the destination Nelya had in mind: a grand vista overlooking most of their property, including a beautiful view of a massive waterfall on the border.

Ether falls spread nearly a kilometer and fell just as far down into the main river running through their property. From that river, a vast delta of interlocking streams wound through the pines, offering the trio an astonishing view of a herd of Renoral stags lazily scrounging the water's edge.

It was a wonderful time, and they were glad they chose that day to make the hike; if they had not, the first winter snow would have made the already challenging hike impossible.

But they had made it home just before the snow began to fall. With a winter wonderland descending on them, the last night before Kyroll returned was spent indoors, with Martinez catching up on some studying—something he had ignored over the last week.

At the same time, Lysa and Neyla settled in on the sofa nearby, typing away at their own stories and happily chatting about some feedback they had gotten.

Lysa referred to her readers on the forums, whereas Nelya referred to several letters and Emails she had been sent over the years. Having Nelya to help coach her directly as an author was pleasant, settling Lysa's debates over what feedback to focus on.

Overall, the final night before the day of reckoning was flawless, allowing them all to feel themselves getting closer. Something they wanted before Kyroll tossed a wrench in the pleasant vacation.

Sweat rolled down Martinez's brow and cheek, clinging to his growing short beard. It was not that he was attempting to grow facial hair or anything like that; it was just that he was on vacation, and there was no need to shave.

It was not like Nelya or Lysa cared about him being clean-shaven. Nelya even commented that his slight stubble made him look a bit more rugged. Her approval and Lysa's agreement had him considering keeping the look. It wasn't like some senior chief would rag him for not looking professional, and if those two liked it, why would he not?

Martinez would consider that once he returned to the house and showered. For now, his focus was enjoying the snow crunching under his shoes, the flakes fluttering down through the shifting bows, and the chilly air infecting his lungs during his jog.

The exercise was refreshing, to say the least, although he had a slight pang of almost guilt in his chest. Every time Martinez went running for the last few months, it was with Shiksie; not having his mentor by his side left him feeling something was missing.

Even though he knew he likely never would be able to return to that little comfort—not after what she did and that he failed to prevent it.

Cresting the hill leading down to Nelya's house, Martinez paused because he spotted several new tire tracks leading down to their home, which were not there when he ran up the hill an hour earlier.

That caused his ingrained instincts to scream at him to look around and assess the changes. Needing to find out if there was some danger or issue.

Doing so, spotting the change was easy enough. Down next to the mansion were several trucks, including Nelya's truck and his and Lysa's rented SUV.

Kyroll must have arrived—and was not alone.

Nelya informed Martinez that her husband would return sometime today, but he expected him to do so in the evening, not around lunchtime.

Either way, he must have arrived, meaning Martinez needed to hurry up and get down there. He was not about to leave Lysa alone to face whatever her father had in mind, especially after the horror stories of his past behavior.

Jogging down the hill, it took Martinez only about half an hour to arrive; even then, that was far longer than he wanted it to take.

In sheer paranoia, Martinez peeked inside the unfamiliar trucks while passing by, wanting to know if there was anything dangerous that the unknowns had brought along.

Inside the truck beds and cabs were a mishmash of supplies. Most of it was benign and expected of anyone living in the woods: heavy work jackets, warming layers, chainsaws, lunch boxes, and miscellaneous supplies he could not identify but were obviously not weapons.

The only thing he found concerning was the healthy mixture of firearms hanging in racks on the back windows; they were all alien in design, so he was unsure of their capabilities, but based on shape alone, he could tell some were rifles and others shotguns.

Additionally, empty holsters were in the cabs. All were placed in locations to have them handy for the driver: tucked next to the consoles or between the seats.

Where were the pistols?

Martinez assumed the owners of the vehicles were carrying them, but that did nothing to put him at ease. If anything, the fact that a former special forces soldier and his friends who were of a similar background were armed only made him worry more.

He headed inside without knocking because Nelya called him family and insisted he didn't need to ask permission to go anywhere in the house except the basement where Kyroll has his mancave—not even Nelya went down there.

Finding Nelya and Lysa was quick and easy enough. The happy mother and daughter were in the kitchen chatting while cooking lunch. Both had cute blue floral aprons on and were quickly working to cook what looked like steak sandwiches.

For Lysa, wearing that bright apron looked odd, especially because she was wearing a tight black long-sleeve coupled with gray yoga pants, letting him get a solid view of her muscular legs and firm rump.

For Nelya, the apron was fitting because everything she wore was brightly colored, covered in flowers and other natural motifs. Even now, flowers covered the wool-like sweater, hugging her full figure.

Lysa heard the door shut behind Martinez, turned around, and offered him a faint smile before draping her arms around his neck and pecking her dear Human's cheek. "How was your run?" she questioned.

"It was good," Martinez replied, looking around the room for anything that indicated who else was here and where they were.

"Gra'hu is down in his lounge with friends from work," Nelya interjected, looking up from the cutting board at Martinez.

How she knew that was his first question was beyond him, but Nelya kept up with her uncanny abilities; as if reading his mind, she prepared for his follow-on question about how she could have known that was what he thought.

"Deary, with how long I've lived with Kyroll, military men's minds are not hard to figure out," Nelya smiled. "Most of the time that is," she finished, slightly twirling her chef's knife.

"I can agree with that," Lysa sniggered, lightly poking his side after releasing their hug.

"Oh, come on, I'm not that bad," Martinez replied.

Lysa and Nelya shared a short glance and chuckled with each other. Both likely having assumed he would say that as well.

Instead of being angry about them mocking him, Martinez just laughed with them. He regularly teased Lysa, so it was only fair that he was more lighthearted about when they returned some grief.

"Come on, Ruh'ah, help us finish preparing lunch. It is almost ready," Lysa said, stepping back toward the island in the kitchen and pulling a plate of mostly made sandwiches over.

"Yeah, we are making some for Gra'hu and his workmates, and then we three can have our meal," Nelya added. "They always spend the evening relaxing after being up in the woods for a few weeks. I assumed Kyroll would not have had them here because you two are in town." She finished, sounding slightly annoyed.

"It is no trouble they can stay down there," Lysa said, carving into another slab of meat.

Nelya sighed and shook her head. Instead of mentioning that Lysa was not trying to bridge the gap with her father and would not make their meeting any easier if she was standoffish, she turned to Martinez.

"Can you two finish these? I am going to grab them some drinks," Nelya said, pulling her apron off and tossing it to Martinez.

"Sure," Martinez said, while Lysa harrumphed slightly, seeing her mother's disappointed sigh.

Once Nelya had left them alone, Martinez gladly helped Lysa with cooking food. But it did not take him long before asking her one of the questions she and Nelya had not assumed he would ask.

"Were there any issues when your dad came home?" Martinez questioned, slicing a sandwich in half and tossing it onto the pile.

"Surprisingly, no. That vile man would not even look at me. He arrived, Mordained with Mother, then followed his friends downstairs," Lysa huffed. "Could he not have at least welcomed me?"

In a way, Martinez felt better knowing nothing had happened. Even though it would have been far more beneficial if Kyroll could have at least attempted to bridge the gap between them.

"He could have, but I honestly don't doubt Nelya has a plan," Martinez assured.

Lysa uncomfortably shifted her feet and paused slicing fresh meat. After a few seconds, she looked over at him, opened her mouth to speak, paused, closed it, and then tried to return to making their food.

"What is it?" Martinez questioned.

"Mother indeed has a plan," Lysa admitted. "While you were out, Mother told me she wished to introduce you to him while bringing them lunch. It's the reason we are preparing these."

Well, that was not ideal. Martinez would rather not enter a room filled with who he views as a group of armed thugs. But if Nelya insisted it was the best course of action, he had to show his trust in the wise woman.

Nelya knew Kyroll better than anyone else in the universe and had been assuring Martinez and Lysa all would be well since arriving.

"What do you think about it?" Martinez asked.

"Do you even need to question that? I believe it's horrible. He will not be cordial; if anything, he will just insult and threaten you," Lysa replied in a near hiss without hesitation.

That reaction was unsurprising, especially with Lysa's background with Kyroll.

"It will be fine," Martinez replied, trying to assure her by patting her shoulder. "Surely Nelya knows what she is doing."

That did little other than make Lysa want to grab Martinez and drag him back to Draun. The Human was her rock, and the idea of him going into danger pissed her off and made knots form in her chest.

"I do not doubt Mother does—Still," Lysa replied but bit her tongue when Nelya returned, lugging a small keg over her shoulder.

Does she keep kegs in the garage? If she did, Martinez had not noticed. Nelya had only been gone for a few minutes, so she did not go into town.

"How are the preparations?" Nelya questioned, dropping the heavy metal keg on the ground.

Martinez looked at the food, a platter overflowing with pre-cut sandwiches, slices of meat, pickled vegetables, and cheese slices. "Do you think this is enough?" he asked her.

Nelya looked over the work momentarily, smiled, and nodded, unaware Lysa had spoiled her plan. "It should be. Lysa, will you make our lunch while Henry and I take this downstairs?"

"I will," Lysa replied solemnly, having already been convinced to follow her mother's plan.

"Flawless. Henry, please grab that keg," Nelya purred, picking up the plate and heading toward the hall.

Before Martinez walked around the island and picked up the keg, Lysa grabbed him from behind, pulling his back tight to her. "Please—please—be careful," Lysa whispered, resting her chin on his shoulder.

"I will," Martinez assured, leaning his head on hers and standing with her momentarily, allowing their hearts and breath to match.

Once Lysa was willing to let Martinez go, he grabbed the keg and followed Nelya, waiting just around the corner.

"I was wondering if you were coming," Nelya teased, bumping her hip into him, similar to what Lysa does. "You're not getting cold feet, are you?"

Smiling back at her, Martinez assured her he was not. In all honesty, finally seeing Kyroll would likely be a good thing for him. After hearing about him for the last month and hearing all the horror stories Lysa told him, Kyroll was a monster in his mind.

To Martinez, Kyroll was a twisted man who, through the fires of war, had become a vile, pulsating abomination. Lysa's father was an atrocity given flesh, whose word would spread pain and hatred.

Meeting the man Nelya insisted he was uncannily like would hopefully kill the wild imagery his imagination had crafted. He did hope that Nelya was wrong about them being alike.

Yeah, Martinez was not a good man after his time in war—but Kyroll drove Lysa out and threatened people unnecessarily. He was more tactful and kind than that—Right?

Nelya led Martinez down the stairs, the simple concrete walls covered with no decorations; not even the ground had carpeting. It set a tone for who he was meeting. These stairs were Kyrolls to do with as he pleased, and they were ascetic, hinting at his mentality around comfort and care.

He thought the den would be like this entirely until they reached the bottom, and a roar of happiness came out from several voices. Everyone down below greeted Nelya in Aviex, so he did not know what was said.

She happily spoke back and turned toward him as he breached the bottom of the stairs, introducing him. He only knew that for two reasons: firstly, he could pick out his name in the sentence, and because everyone down there fell deathly silent.

The den was not what Martinez had expected based on the stairs. It was warm and inviting. The ground was a lush brown carpet, and soft velvet sofas surrounded a large television on the wall.

The walls were covered with military memorabilia: uniforms, medals, plaques, weapons, flags and photographs. It was a surplus lover's dream den—not that Martinez was one, but he could see the appeal.

If not for the five rough-looking Aviex men staring daggers at him, he might have gotten a better look at the awards, flags, and photographs, trying to learn about the near-mythical man who owned them.

But with them there, Martinez only noted two flags he knew by heart. One was the GU standard. It was gold with a black representation of the Milky Way front and center. The other was the Human Marines flag spread out on the wall.

Instead of focusing on the odd fact that Kyroll had that on display, Martinez traced the cold eyes of the men around the room. Each man's eyes stared at him with venom. Most still had all four bright red eyes, but one did not. The man he knew was Kyroll based on the pictures upstairs.

Kyroll sat in a chair, his burned face and missing eyes denoting him easily. Unlike the other men, he had no facial hair, likely because of the intense scarring. Uniting them all was that they were all Aviex, had pistols in holsters, and half-drank mugs of some type of booze in hand.

"Who the fuck is he?" Kyroll growled in Aviex, pointing a knife hand at Martinez.

Kyroll's voice sounded like he had been smoking four packs a day since birth, something Martinez had been informed of, but genuinely hearing it was still surprising.

"Now, Gra'hu Martinez here does not speak Aviex. Can you please refrain from that while he is here?" Nelya replied, setting the plate on the table. "Henry, will you set that keg over there while Kyroll introduces you," she continued, turning around and gesturing to a corner with another keg.

Martinez stood stock still, looking back at the men; it was long enough that a few whispered to one another in Aviex and gestured at him, earning them a glare from Nelya. She would not stand them making fun of him or making snide comments he could not understand.

"Henry, please," Nelya insisted. "Gra'hu, please introduce your friends to Lysa's Ruh'ah—now."

"Yeah, I will," Martinez said, swallowing his spit.

Crossing those few meters felt like walking through a pack of ravenous wolves. Each footfall felt like a lead weight was in his shoes. He heard Nelya and Kyroll arguing hushedly in Aveix as he set the keg down.

"Fine, you stubborn man," Nelya sighed, walking over to Martinez's side and half-hugging him.

"Everyone, this is Martinez, Lysa's Ruh'ah. He is a medic in the Human Navy," Nelya explained, gesturing up and down at him like Vanna White, assuring none of them ignored her.

Martinez was not a Medic but a Corpsman; however, that was semantics. To the average person in the GU the words meant the same thing, and knowing Nelya, she chose that word because the squad of men would understand that term.

That announcement earned him a few nods of approval from the Aviex, save for Kyroll, who glared at Martinez like he was about to thrash him.

At least that announcement got the others to introduce themselves and give the Human a smug smile. Gradually, they went around the room telling him their names and, oddly enough, rank.

Martinez did not know the ranks the Aviex military used, but based on their looks and what he knew about Kyrolls friends, he assumed they were enlisted men like him.

Once the short introductions were done, Nelya and the others looked toward Kyroll, waiting for him to do the same. But instead of that, he clicked his tongue and sighed.

"Dear?" Nelya prised him along, waving at him.

"Kyroll," Lysa's father growled, looking like saying those words hurt him deeply.

"Well, Nelya already said my name. It's nice to meet you all," Martinez said awkwardly, never taking his eyes off Kyroll's hand, which had drifted to his pistol over the course of the introductions—an act he made no effort to conceal.

"Thank you all for that," Nelya said, letting Martinez go and scanning the men who, funnily enough, almost blushed under her discerning vision. "I hate to do this to you all, but after lunch, can you leave? I wish to have a Family dinner tonight."

"Of course, we can Nel," the burliest of the group, named Grula said with a smile, gesturing at Kyroll to his side. "I'm certain Kyroll will want to get to know Martinez better."

That prodding joke clearly almost got a rise out of Kyroll, who, with his two good eyes, glared at Grula.

Martinez almost chuckled, seeing Grula hold his hands up in a joking defense. It was funny that these men from a military half a galaxy away from here acted like the Marines he knew.

Rough jokes that poke fun at each other's flaws.

If not for his presence, Martinez had no doubt they would start laughing and mocking Kyroll about his little huntress bringing a man home, who looks surprisingly close to Aveix to the point it was uncanny.

This thought was given credence when Nelya halfway dragged Martinez up the stairs, assuring him it was time for them to eat. He could hear them all laughing and speaking in Aviex again, with Kyroll's rough voice standing out. He was clearly arguing about their comments.

"We will get him to warm up to you," Nelya assured, giving Martinez a slight hug at the top of the stairs.

"Don't worry, he is only so stubborn," Nelya assured, letting him go and turning toward the kitchen. "For now, your Ruh'ah is waiting for us and likely wants to know how that went," she winked.

THE SLAP HEARD AROUND THE WOODS

Off to the side of Martinez, Nelya and Lysa sat sipping some kind of mushroom tea. The Human initially had no idea what the mushroom was, but after a short search on the data net for its name and chemical composition, he screened that information against what was safe for him to consume.

So he agreed to also partake in the sharp, gray tea.

Nelya noticed his initial hesitation and search, allowing Martinez to explain how his dear friend Ezol was hurt by some food he had given him. Since then, anytime he bought or ate new food, he looked it up.

Martinez did the same thing for Lysa when introducing her to anything Humanity created, but she never saw that part.

Nelya understood his hesitance and expressed some appreciation for his care of Lysa, even though she thought it was unnecessary because most species know the chemicals and types of food they cannot eat.

However, Humans were relatively new to the broader Universe, so needing to research was understandable for him.

After they ate lunch and had a few cups of tea, Martinez volunteered to take their plates to the kitchen and refill the tea kettle, not wanting to interrupt the giggling duo's relaxation.

It was an incredible sight for Martinez; Lysa seemed nervous and frantic before the trip and when Kyroll first appeared. But now that Nelya kept his Ruh'ah's mind occupied, she seemed far more expressive—acting more like the confident, proud, vampiric woman he loved.

A part of the Corpsman hoped that the trip would not sour. Maybe Nelya's plan would work out; it was so far.

As he washed the extra sauce off the plates and put the kettle on the stove, Lysa and Nelya giggling was joined by the sounds from the basement growing louder. Glancing over his shoulder, Martinez tracked the men exiting the stairs and proceeding toward the living room.

The rough men did not even spare the Human a glance, not that he minded. Their staying apart was likely for the best.

The men spoke in Aveix once in the other room and assumed it must have been them saying their goodbyes; the rough group of flannel-clad men seemed fond of Nelya and likely were keeping her informed of the goings on in her house.

After Martinez finished drying off the plates and putting them away, a hand landed on his shoulder, making him jump out of his skin. He whipped around and backed away from whoever just managed to sneak up on him.

How in all the universe did they manage to do that?

Martinez had been paying keen attention to all the noises from the living room; no, not just there, the whole house since Kyroll returned. He even heard the men speaking Aviex in the basement the entire time he ate with Nelya and Lysa.

No one should have been able to sneak up on him.

Standing behind Martinez, holding his hands up, was the burly Aveix man from downstairs. His red eyes glowed with concern, and his lips were barely visible through his thick charcoal-black beard.

Martinez remembered his name was Grula since Nelya had introduced them less than an hour ago.

"Whoa there, killer. Chill out," Grula horsily chuckled, lowering his hands now that Martinez had realized who he was. "I did not mean to scare you."

"You could have fooled me," Martinez replied, lowering his fists and allowing his heart rate to do the same.

Grula, for his part, waited patiently for the Human to calm down entirely, having trudged through his fair share of the fires of combat and likewise hated being snuck up on.

Still, unlike Martinez, his time as a machine gunner in the Aviex army was years ago, with the Human's experiences in far more recent memory.

The former Aviex special forces member knew that because he quietly asked Lysa while the rest of his former squad was in the living room.

"Bud, come on; follow me," Grula said calmly, speaking in a slow, strange tempo and stepping away from Martinez toward the door.

Martinez paused and looked over the man's back, scanning him for any weapons beyond the pistol he wore proudly.

Grula noted Martinez's hesitance, turned half about and smirked. "You can take my gun if it means you come."

Without missing a beat, Grula pulled his gun from his plastic holster and twirled it to offer Martinez the grip, an offer the Human had never expected.

That was a dangerous gamble from Grula's point of view. Not because he believed Martinez would intentionally fight him, but no one recently out of combat liked it when someone pulled any weapon.

"What?" Martinez said, quizzically, not understanding Grula's angle here.

"It's just for a chat," Grula replied, shaking the pistol grip. "Take it."

Martinez took the gun and checked the chamber for brass like he had been taught to do over the years.

It was loaded, but that was no shock; why would you have a weapon without having it condition one?

Martinez followed the man, taking the sign of peace as a reason to do so. If Grula or the rest of the squad had a plan to harm him, why would the Aviex give him a weapon?

Once outside, Martinez scanned the area around him, something Grula noted and chuckled, treating the Human's vigilance like a joke.

"Brother, chill out," Grula insisted, lighting a cigarette.

Though it was not tobacco, it was Hyrala, a similar narcotic Martinez knew what he lit—Hyrala was the universe's more common way of giving species nicotine. Tobacco was more potent and had not become popular outside military units attached to Humans.

After Grula lit his cigarette, he offered the just-lit one from his lips to Martinez; following a moment of pause and jamming the pistol in his belt, the Human grabbed the offered smoke.

Martinez was not the type of man to smoke, but if it was offered, why say no? Grula was clearly trying to break the ice between them. Martinez and many other Human NCOs have done similar things when they want to chat with someone.

"So what do you want?" Martinez said, cutting to the chase and taking a drag on the cigarette.

"In all honesty, I wanted to chat with you and try to convince you that Kyroll is not as bad as he seems," Grula replied. "My old squad leader—is a troubled man."

Martinez did not actively reply but rolled his eyes and leaned back against the truck bed, letting the Aveix veteran continue.

"I know you have heard about him from little Lysa and likely Nelya too," Grula continued. "How he is cold, distant, and uncaring?"

"I have, what about it?" Martinez replied flatly, flicking away some ash.

"Brother, I just want you to give that stubborn ass a chance—as big of an ask as that is. I know how this will likely go once the squad leaves," Grula sighed, cracking his neck and open-palming toward the house.

"Even if he is troubled, what he does will be his problem. Hell, it will be more of an issue for Lysa and Nelya than it will for me," Martinez shrugged. "I really do not care about how he feels. But I do give a relative rat's ass about those two."

That was something the Human truly believed in; his safety could get bent, and Kyroll's health could likewise go the way of the dodo. The only thing that mattered inside those walls was Nelya and Lysa.

Granted, they did for different reasons, but it was an issue of blood between the two lovely women.

Grula lifted his boot and stamped out the butt of his cigarette while sighing, "Yeah—I figured you would say something like that."

"What else would I do?" Martinez questioned as Grula clambered into the cab and held his hand out toward Martinez.

Without being asked, Martinez put the pistol's grip into Grula's hand. Grula was wasting his time trying to ask much of the Human. He was regrettably aware of the History between his god-daughter and her father.

They were silent as the Aviex's other meaty gripper moved the slide, checking the chamber for ammunition. "Try not to kill one another," he chuckled, slipping the weapon into the dash.

"That's easier said than done from what I've seen," Martinez replied, gesturing back at the house where Nelya and the other troopers were filling out.

"Yeah—I know, brother—I know," Grula sighed before pausing and waving goodbye to his squad and Nelya, who did likewise. "Just don't let that ass get to you," he continued after turning over the powerful engine in his truck.

"Fuck man, call me if you need a hand with the old snot weasel," Grula said, leaning over and handing Martinez a card.

It was not some special digital chip with his contact that would be thrown away after downloading the information; no, Grula had given him a genuine paper-printed contact card. Martinez had never seen one in person. Sure, they existed in the fiction media he and Lysa watched. But they were not used on earth even before the great uplifting half a century ago.

Holding the hard print in his hand drove home how truly backwater this section of the planet and universe was. You could not get this on earth without having a bunch of money, or it was for some specialized product—like the hard cardstock that came with his silken bedding.

"Sure," Martinez replied, still not entirely trusting Grula, something the professional man noted with a simple grunt before pulling away, his tires crackling on the stones.

Martinez did not respond as Grula drove away, watching his truck's rear lights vanish over the horizon. Turning around, he was shocked and unnerved that the others were watching him in their trucks, knuckles whiter than usual due to the Aviex's pale complexion.

Most of them gave Martinez a genuine smile and a quick nod before starting their vehicles and departing. Offering him a goodbye in standard as each pulled away, something he likewise did.

Until the only one of the squad who did not seem to be happy about his presence was left, Kyroll withstanding.

He was the older-looking Aviex from downstairs who sat immediately off to Kyrolls side earlier that day.

Unlike the others, this man had grayish hair, tired-looking, nearly black eyes, and wrinkles as deep as canyons across his scowled face.

This guy was still glaring at the Human when the others were mostly staring at him cautiously, or with a nearly overflowing curiosity.

"Burkla, you should head home—Frela won't want you out too late," Nelya said, interrupting the awkward stare-down.

He sneered toothily at Martinez for another moment before looking over at Nelya, "Yeah, I would hate to keep the Gra'hu waiting," Burkla nodded before putting his old rattling truck into gear and rolling forward.

Burkla ensured Nelya could not see the gesture he sent Martinez's way while rolling past; unlike the Aviex language, Martinez needed no translator to understand what running your thumb across your neck meant.

Some gestures were universal, and that threat sent a shiver down his spine.

What in God's name was wrong with that guy—and Kyroll? But Martinez had no doubt tonight would answer most of those issues.

Martinez walked over toward Nelya and was going to ask what he had missed between the conversation in Aviex earlier that day. He also wanted clarification on how Grula had implied they had chatted about her grand plan—but life had other plans for the duo.

Flowing out the open door and filling their heads with panic, Lysa and Kyroll yelled at one another in Aviex. Sharp curses, a smashed glass, and what Martinez prayed was not the sound of someone eating a hit followed right after.

Hearing that put Martinez's ass into gear.

"Ah fuck!" Martinez exclaimed, running past Nelya, who flowed in behind the Human.

Nelya was glad Martinez could not understand Aviex; hearing Lysa or Kryoll launch such venom at one another was unreal. As they rounded the corner, she had already heard them calling one another brain dead, bastard, whore, and she hoped she misheard Kryoll calling Lysa a Vuric's whore.

That would be beyond even his moronic ass. Nelya at least prayed it was.

She had expected that they could have been left alone for a few minutes without any issues, especially after her firm warning to Kyroll that Lysa and Henry were only giving him this one chance to not be an asshat.

But apparently, her Gra'hu must have thought his snide comments about Martinez would have been far more well-received than Lysa was or should tolerate.

"You waste of air; How fucking dare you!" Lysa hissed in Aviex, jamming her sharp nail into his chest.

"You brought that fucking thing into my house, around your moth—" Kyroll started to reply, but because of his train of thought was interrupted by a mixture of the other halves of the two relationships encroaching, even if they were approaching the issue in two drastically different ways—namely because Martinez could not have heard him calling the Human a freak, monster, animal, or Vuric, an Aviex word that is used similarly to the rest of the universes term Vein-slicer.

"Kyroll! Stop right now!" Nelya snapped, grabbing his shoulder and ripping his attention from Lysa—and Henry who forced himself between them and was making no effort to shield Kryoll from Lysa, giving Kyroll and Nelya his back.

That was something that Nelya had more time to focus on, and it would have melted her heart. Lysa had made it well known over the last few days that she would have no issues with her argument with Kyroll becoming physical—and with her training, age, and just that Male and Female Aviex are in no way less hardy than the other, that could not end well.

That and Nelya regrettably could see Martinez joining in and thrashing Kyroll because her husband likely would fight back. If they both fought Kyroll— at least one of them would need stitches, and it would assuredly be Kyroll.

"Whoa, whoa, Ruh'ah, it's okay," Martinez assured, gently holding Lysa's shoulders and getting between the pair standing over a shattered mug in the living room.

"Don't you dare use that word, you filthy animal," Kyroll replied in Aviex, having not bothered to change back to Standard.

"Pound sand, you old bastard," Lysa hissed in Aviex, ignoring that Martinez and Nelya were even there. Both had to actively keep the others apart, though Nelya was more gently trying to get a word in to get Kyrolls attention, while Martinez might as well be keeping Lysa from skinning her father. "Don't you have even the slightest amount of care for me and my joy?"

Nelya looked at Kyroll, who honestly looked slightly shocked by the comment. She and Kyroll had spoken about how much he regretted what had happened in the past and how his main goal with Lysa, which was her safety, had only caused issues—he just had the emotional flexibility of a rock.

"Don't you say a word," Nelya softly interjected, taking advantage of his pause. She spoke loud enough that Kyroll could hear, but hopefully not so loud that her emotionally charged daughter.

Not that her not hearing genuinely mattered. They were pulled tight like piano strings and were one wrong move from soiling any chance of them salvaging their relationship.

"Oh no, Mother, let the fucker say it!" Lysa hissed, having heard Nelya and venomously remembering the last time they spoke when Kryoll had essentially expressed that she could never date or be around anyone non-Aviex. "If that dalcop thinks he knows anything about me, Ruh'ah, or our lives, he can say it."

"Don't you dare," Nelya reinforced, before looking back at Martinez and was about to ask him to please get Lysa out of here for the moment so she could speak to Kyroll.

But her dear Gra'hu, just had to be himself again: an old, stubborn, stupid man, who had no idea how to deescalate anything, nor had any relevant understanding of Lysa's emotional issues.

"What do you know? I'm trying to keep my stupid daughter safe from these fucking monsters who will be more than happy to—" Kyroll started but was stopped by a deafening slap across his face from Lysa.

Martinez tried to wrangle her back after she slipped past him to strike her father. But it was not needed; she did not speak, or even look at him after leaving the non-mangled half of his face as red as his eyes.

Fuck, none of them moved, breathed, or did anything for the next few moments. The world had fallen silent, leaving only their orbit high heart rates as an indication they were still alive.

If a nail dropped in the room right then, it would have been more voluminous than a gunshot and just as deadly.

Lysa paused and looked at her hand, unable to accept that she hit him back, then toward Martinez for reassurance. But her Human's look of anguish did not help. No, it cracked her heart like ice on the pavement.

Lysa knew she crossed the hard line of no return; they all knew it.

Instead of pressing her attack or begging her father to try to understand—she sniffled and rushed out the back door, all those years of hate overflowing in that one millisecond-long strike.

Martinez rushed after her, not even waiting to hear Nelya asking him to watch after her daughter; the Human did not need to be told to do so. The older Aviex knew he would.

Neither Nelya nor Kyroll spoke or breathed until the guest house door closed loudly.

Nelya sighed, stepped back, and took a deep breath. This was an unmitigated disaster. How in all the universe did she mess this up so badly? What happened? What could she have changed to not have her family despise one another?

Kryoll stepped closer and was about to speak, but Nelya placed a firm hand in the center of his chest to stop him, "Sit down now!" Nelya said as calmly as possible.

She did not need to yell or hiss right now. Neither would help, after all.

But Nelya doubted this could be salvaged. For all she knew, Martinez and Lysa were packing already, both about to leave her and her Gra'hu's lives for good.

The wizened woman hoped that blunder would not be the final wedge between her daughter and Kyroll—But she needed answers before that fortune could even be guessed at.

A PAST BEST FORGOTTEN

Martinez paused Inside the guest house once the door closed behind him, wanting to think about what to do next.

Yes, he knows to follow Lysa into the bedroom, but after she slammed the door so hard that paintings fell off the wall—he wanted a rough plan of action.

Breathing deeply and stacking the fallen artwork against the wall gave Martinez enough time to prepare.

After all of what he had seen and what Nelya had told him, Martinez knew he had to be the problem. He was sharp enough that even with the language barrier, he could tell Kyroll was focusing on him: pointing, glaring, and snapping teeth.

If Martinez were a betting man, which he was, he would bet that Lysa was trying to stand up for him.

If her standing up for him led to her doing something she already regretted—it was his turn to confront her Father, well, after he settled her aching heart. Lysa deserved that much support and more.

Slowly opening the door, Martinez could barely make out the sounds of Lysa sniffling. For a moment, he wondered if she might not be crying, but he thought that until he was close enough for her meek noises to overcome his tinnitus.

His Ruh'ah was sprawled out on the bed, burying her head deep into the plush pillows. Her hair draped around the pillows, engulfing her shoulders, upper torso, and the surroundings. If not for seeing her heaving chest, he could think she was trying to snuggle up because she was cold.

Walking over and sitting beside her, Lysa's body sunk against his back. After sitting down, Martinez laid a hand on her shoulder and gently rubbed it, shockingly causing her to recoil as if he was about to hurt her more.

Thankfully, after a few moments of soothing contact, Lysa seemed to realize it was Martinez giving her beatific reassurance and not her mother, father, or some other specter she conjured in her mind; at that point, she somewhat settled once again, but her hammering heart was like a fist repeatedly striking his palm: it was steady, powerful, and unyielding in its presence.

"How are you feeling?" Martinez questioned, unsure of any more appropriate way to broach the topic.

Lysa looked over her shoulder at him. Her usually soft face was contorted with puffy eyes and was as sopping wet as the pillow. With an almost anguished look, Lysa attempted to smile, hoping doing so would help her look strong and capable, but that lasted only a heartbeat at most.

"Henry—am I detestable?" Lysa questioned with shocking earnesty.

It did not seem like the other times when she called herself a monster; at those times, Lysa was parroting the treatment from the aliens surrounding her. This was in no way like that. No, it was a question pulled up from the darkest dredges of her soul. The mere act of asking the question burned her throat.

It was the result of years upon years of doubt, self-hatred, and external hostility finally catching up to the vampiric woman. Her finally lashing out against the core of her hatred shattered any bulwark against the thoughts like glass.

"I don't think you are," Martinez replied, genuinely smiling at her, finding the question frivolous.

He would not have laid with her, cared for her, or traveled half a planet away to know her family if he believed her to be detestable.

That was not the answer Lysa wanted to hear. In her state, she was likely reaching out for his assurance—even if it was for a delusional reason.

Instead of looking uplifted and happy, Lysa twisted back to the pillow and screamed into it, unleashing her fury at the plush silencer.

"Babe, it's alright. It was a moment of passion," Martinez said after a moment of pause, wanting to phrase it to not sound like he was laying the blame at her feet.

Lysa whined and grumbled, pulling the pillow tighter, kicking the bedspread, trying to release all the pent-up emotions.

"After that?" Lysa questioned, barely peering out of the pillow.

"Yes, it's alright," Martinez assured. "We can get through this."

Martinez only assured her of that because they still had each other. In a way, both were alone, but they still were there for one another.

"Genuinely?" Lysa sniffled, shifting around in the bed and grabbing Martinez's waist while laying her head across his lap.

She wanted some amount of skinship from who, at this point, seemed like the only person there for her. Yes, Nelya would not abandon her, but Lysa would never want to bargain with the idea that it was her or her father.

"Of course," Martinez replied, running his hand through her hair.

Lysa fell nearly silent save for a few sniffles every few seconds, enjoying Martinez's tender touch, warmth, and support. At this point, he and her Mother were undoubtedly the brightest stars in her life.

Yeah, she had Teacher, Lira, Feinel, Ivorn, and a few other acquaintances she enjoyed having around. But with them, she found them and tried to go out once living in Draun.

"Can we go home?" Lysa whined, "I don't want to be here anymore."

Martinez sighed and looked out the window, enjoying the babbling brook past the portal. He personally did not want to go back yet. They were barely halfway through the time off both took, and Martinez genuinely wanted to know Lysa's family, even if her dad was an ass.

His own desires to stay aside, Martinez believed Lysa would

regret leaving now and not giving her Father another shot. All he had to do was get his foot in the door so he could help her. As it stands now, there was no way they could make up without both him and Nelya there.

"Can I try to meet your dad first?" Martinez questioned.

"Why? He hates you—and me," Lysa argued.

"I doubt he hates you. Me, I could see. But what father isn't protective of their little girl?" Martinez replied, looking down at his Ruh'ah, "Even if he hates me. I won't know unless I try."

"Please make no attempt; that man is not worth the effort. We can pack and be home by tomorrow morning. At least then, we will not have wasted our trip; we could do plenty of things closer to home. Perhaps camping?" Lysa argued.

Moving his hand from the top of her head to rub a thumb on her soft cheek, Martinez knew he could not accept just giving up. "Let me try. If I can't get him to at least give me a chance by tomorrow night, we will leave, alright?"

Lysa clutched his waist tighter and grimaced, trying to think of how she could convince Martinez not to. They could just vanish into the night like she had done years ago—Mother would get over her just vanishing again, and it was not like Father would care.

"Fine, I will trust you to try, but I am not returning to the main house," Lysa said.

"Alright, I will bring you some food then," Martinez replied, moving to find Kyroll. However, Lysa stopped him by not letting him go.

"After I have some more cuddling?" Lysa cooed, pouting slightly. "I wish for more."

"Alright," Martinez replied, laying down and snuggling until she had entirely calmed down.

They lay there for several hours, and Lysa initially vented and told him more about the treatment Kyroll had done to her; the stories were not treading new ground, but she wanted to say to them, so he listened and listened and listened, never interrupting his loves stories until surprisingly Lysa ended up muttering a few incoherent phrases and passed out.

Martinez slipped out of the guest house after wiggling out from Lysa's loving clutches and covering her with the blankets. The cool air and light snow on the ground were refreshing after having a living heater clinging to him.

It was not that he did not enjoy it, but after an hour, he was sweating, yet he would not say anything to interrupt Lysa's enjoyment of the moment.

Martinez had not even closed the door leading to Nelya's kitchen before she had already gotten his attention.

"How is she doing?" Nelya questioned, looking up from her datapad and the small snack platter.

Martinez was surprised to see her sitting in their luxurious dining room. It had a long oak table, chandeliers overhead, and well over a dozen pre-set dinner sets. He had expected Kyroll to be here, with Nelya forcing her husband to apologize or at least reign in his bullshit.

But no, it was just her, dressed as casually as normal and likely pecking away at her next novel while waiting for Martinez and Lysa.

"She is asleep for now," Martinez replied, sitting in the chair across from her.

Nelya relaxed her shoulders, her sharp four pink eyes setting into their typical ease. "That's good; I was afraid she was about to slip off into the night again."

"Well, she did mention wanting to do that," Martinez awkwardly admitted.

At this point, Nelya knowing what Lysa was thinking was in no way a shock; the two seemed to be able to read each other's minds. Her guessing her daughter's desires was to be expected, especially since it would not be the first time Lysa scurried away in the dark.

"I was afraid of that," Nelya sighed, "did you convince her otherwise? Or are you just telling me you two will be leaving when she wakes up?" She finished with a depressive drawl.

Today was stressful for the poor woman; just after her daughter finally returned, her husband had ruined it and undone any progress made at reconnection from the previous week.

"We aren't leaving yet. I convinced her to stay another day and let me attempt to break the ice with Kyroll. It was easy enough to tell after that screaming match he was focusing on me—So I figured that would be the best course of action." Martinez explained, looking around for Kyroll.

"He went out," Nelya replied, annoyance oozing off her lips. "But how did you understand the fight? I thought you didn't speak Aviex."

"I don't, but he was glaring at me, not Lysa." Martinez explained, "But that's not important right now; I need your help."

The older Aviex woman tilted her head curiously. "My help? Are you certain, my plan fell apart before even starting?"

"I'm aware. Honestly, whatever you had planned before told Lysa and me little. But now it's my turn to try and make a plan. I need you to tell me everything that was your plan, why Kyroll is so hateful towards non-Aviex, and anything else you think is useful," Martinez implored Nelya.

Nelya sighed, and a forlorn look came over her face as she looked almost sheepishly away from Martinez. "Will you tell Lysa what I tell you?"

"Yes, I'm not going to lie to her," Martinez replied without hesitation.

"I will tell you everything, but once I do, you might understand why I would rather you not tell Lysa," Nelya muttered, barely loud enough for Martinez to hear.

Martinez doubted anything Nelya could say would have been that horrible. Almost every Aviex he had met was kind, cordial, and fit well within the GU. Sure, they had their cultural quirks, but so did every other sentient across the galaxy.

That was until her plush lips parted, and she weaved him a tale that might as well have been an Arthurian tragedy.

Nelya explained that the Aviex is one of the oldest species in the Galactic Union. If Martinez's understanding is correct, they have been in the GU for several thousand years.

At one point, they were not the species in shambles that the GU knows today. Over five hundred Standard years ago, they were the mightiest individual military force in the galaxy.

That power naturally led the Aviex to a particular sin Martinez was all too familiar with—Pride.

Pride led to a feeling of superiority, allowing an Aviex man, whom Nelya refused even to say their name, to come to power. She declined to name them because the GU and the Aviex government have taken drastic steps to wipe that history section out of existence.

Why was evident when she explained what this mysterious Aviex did.

He and the armies of the Aviex attempted a rebellion against the GU, dragging along with them anyone who was just as prideful and power-mad. This led to a war that, to her best knowledge, lasted over a hundred standard years.

On the low end of estimates, that war led to quadrillions of sentients dying. Be it from direct combat, planet cracking, starvation, or, worst of all, why the Aviex remnants have their horrible modern moniker of Vein Slicer.

The Blood Camps.

They were locations where slaves were used as cattle, ready to be slaughtered, harvested, and consumed by the ever-growing mass of the Aviex militaries—and their allies.

The Aviex military did not use solid food for the war, opting to use their uniquely efficient blood-processing organs to fuel their armies. They did this for two reasons, at least Nelya hoped it was.

The look of shame and guilt on her face made it evident which one she could stomach, and it was not rooted in twisted logic.

Firstly, eating and drinking your enemies saved on logistical needs, and not having to ship food with your army resulted in no long logistical lines.

Letting slaves act as blood bags until they died was more accessible on long campaigns. The first reason was barbaric, twisted, and vile, but Martinez could, in a fucked up way, understand the logic, even if the idea made him sick to his stomach.

The Aviex of that time were not ravaging the local flora and fauna; no, those were people they were eating for god's sake—that's something entirely different.

Martinez thought the idea was bad enough, but it held nothing to the second reason for Aviex's consumption of the other sentients.

Although Nelya only knows the few details Kyroll was willing to tell her or what she could dig up through the dataset, it painted a picture.

Women, children, warriors, commanders—it did not matter; all were fair game and sought after for their own reasons. The higher-ups in the Aviex military essentially granted accolades for their favorite types of sentients to try to draw power from drinking from and eating them.

What kind of fucked up tribalistic warfare was this? Yeah, Martinez had heard of the messed up things Humans did to each other in the past, from African cannibal warlords, the mass slaughter of farmers, all the way to horrible death camps from all sides of the world wars.

Did the Aviex leaders of the time genuinely think they were taking power from eating other sentient creatures?

"What the fuck?" Martinez choked out, picturing scenes of Aviex soldiers stringing up helpless victims over vats to drain their blood.

"After the war ended and the Aviex were reduced to our current numbers, the remnants of the Aviex and the GU eventually came to an agreement." Nelya sighed, undeterred by the Human's shock. "At least as far as I am aware, this knowledge is not commonplace, so I only know what I do because Kyroll was at one point a bodyguard for the Aviex GU representative and overheard this."

Nelya leaned in close as if she was telling him the most dire of secrets despite them being alone. "All public knowledge of that war was to be suppressed so the few hundred thousand Aviex remaining would not be slaughtered to the man. The Aviex could never rise above a red status species, and of course, from our end, we could maintain only two military forces: a small planetary defense force and the section of special forces that works under a joint Aviex and GU command. That is where Kyroll and his team worked."

"So what did they do?" Martinez questioned, grasping at straws and drawing lines to similar Human history. He guessed that there might have been some suppression force or possibly a force meant to show the best of the Aviex to new species; that might explain the Human Marine flag in the basement.

"I am not certain; a lot of what Kyroll and his team did they keep quiet about—I'm sorry," Nelya said. "But I know he treats other species like he does because they regularly run into the remnant effects of that old war. Finding sentients who were out for revenge hundreds of years later."

"So he hates me because he thinks I will do whatever he saw to his daughter?" Martinez questioned.

"Yes," Nelya nodded, "I know you won't hurt our daughter. I wanted to introduce you to him, with you and Lysa being sweet to one another to put him at ease—when he showed up, that fell apart. I'm sorry, this is all my fault," She finished hanging her head.

Martinez stood up and walked over to her side, reassuringly patting her shoulder. "It's alright. I know you meant well. But I need to go and be more stubborn than your husband. Where is he?"

Nelya told Martinez where to find Kyroll, an old military bar on the far side of town. It would be easy enough to find, and the name "Battle Booze" was distinct enough.

"Thanks, Nelya. Don't worry; I won't mess this up," Martinez assured, turning toward the door.

As Martinez pulled the keys to the rental SUV off the hook by the door, Nelya stepped up and stopped him. "Henry, before you go?"

"What is it?" Martinez asked, turning toward her.

Nelya gently pulled Martinez into a hug, attempting reassurance. He would not be alright with most people making such sudden contact, but Nelya's was different. Like her daughter, her mere presence was calming and put him at ease.

"Do your best, little hunter," Nelya softly whispered as Martinez returned the gentle embrace.

Having Nelya call him what the equivalent of a son in Aviex indeed held weight for him. The gesture made him pull her plush body a bit tighter, wanting to show some return of the feeling. While he was not ready to call her mom or anything, this short time together meant a lot to him.

"I will do my best," Martinez said, separating from the buxom woman and opening the door. Before he left, Martinez turned around. "Can you make sure Lysa has some dinner? And tell her not to wait up?"

"Of course, I can," Nelya smiled.

SOLDIER TO SAILOR, MAN TO MAN

The history Nelya had told Martinez about the Aviex was beyond anything he had initially thought it would be. It was horrible, and he understood why their species' government wanted it forgotten.

At least the drive gave Martinez plenty of time to think. During the last half hour of driving over rocks, around blind corners, and through the snow-covered pines, one question regularly forced itself to the forefront of his mind.

Should he tell Lysa that reality?

His Ruh'ah was already troubled about being an Aviex and how most aliens treated her species. Would knowing the reasoning behind it make her feel any better? He doubted it because if what Nelya said was correct, those aliens likely did not understand the root of their hatred just as much as she did.

If he did tell her, yeah, she would have a grasp on the reasoning why she had been exiled on sight, but that might just make her more vindictive to others because they just hated her because of generational spite toward a species which, yeah fucked up in the past; but now were broken, beaten down and regulated to never being allowed to reach the glory of their past.

Martinez groaned and scratched the back of his head, wondering why in all the universe everything had become so arduous lately.

He was supposed to be on loan to the civilian sector; problems like racist allies, vindictive blood feuds, and the horrible results of wars past were not supposed to be his issue; that is the military and government's problem.

As he saw it, life was supposed to overflow with milk and honey. The worst thing that should land on his plate would be the occasional trauma red or GSW at the trauma center.

Life was not supposed to be whatever the fuck it was right now.

Bringing up whether he told Lysa was something he would speak to Nelya about after he dealt with Kyroll; opening that can of worms right now would just be rubbing salt in her freshly opened wounds.

To keep his mind occupied, Martinez decided he needed to listen to music—anything was better than stewing in his nervousness and anger at Kyroll.

He quickly activated his datapad and synced it to the radio. Once it was, the wonderful roaring guitar and heavy base of Supplicant roared through the speakers, drowning out the dull crunch of the snow and rocks under the SUV tires.

While he had hit shuffle, Supplicant, being the band that came on, was perfect. As the name suggested, the heavy metal band was a religious experience for him. He and the Platoon played this band daily over the loudspeakers of their FOB back on Verilon.

It was the soundtrack for the tenth war on Verilon, at least for the Marines. And who does not like having a good song to pump you up to kick in a door, shoot some Fark, or frag their nasty tunnel networks till nothing but dust remains?

Without this band and several others keeping spirits high, he and the Marines would not have survived that war. Having them on prepared him for this new war—not one of bullets, blood, knives, and boots, but one of tears, forgiveness, care, and understanding.

The rest of the long drive was done at a slow patrolling pace, at most 25 kilometers an hour. It was a downright crawl in reality. Martinez was not doing it for any specific reason; he just dreaded what was coming and wanted this little bit of peace until the moment of truth.

But all things must end, and his drive only lasted a few hours, which was more than enough.

He pulled the SUV into the parking lot of the battle booze, parking on the far end of the lot away from the entrance so he could get a good look at the place while he approached. Some habits will never leave you, and combat awareness certainly is one that will stick with you like a foul scar.

Slowly scanning up and down the empty road, Martinez felt a sense of solitude. Other than the occasional street light and dark, closed-down shop, the skittering of a tiny animal digging in a nearby trashcan was the only sign of life.

Celna was strange like that. There was no real main town; instead, it was a sprawling network of building clusters loosely connected by roads tucked deep in the bows of pines, with the Battle Booze being an isolated node.

Slowly moving toward the doors, the bright neon sign over the wooden structure bathed the snow in bright orange light, along with what Martinez could recognize as a long row of some type of repulser bike.

They were not as robust or spartan as the ones he had seen used by the GU military or in the boonies of some of the planets he and the Marines had visited. Quite the opposite; each bike was a custom-built work of art.

Similar to what you would see on biker gangs back on Earth, the bikes were covered in chrome, leather, and decorations. No two were the same; each was an expression of the owner's unique personality and mechanical capabilities.

While Maritnez was not a fan of motorcycles, he could still appreciate the work that must have gone into keeping them in such mint condition despite their obvious use.

The only other vehicle in the lot was front and center next to the doors inside. It was Kyroll's hulking monstrosity of a truck, nearly two meters tall and twice as long. Unlike the bikes, the old Aviex's truck was beaten down like an old dog.

Dents ran up and down its surface. The front windscreen was cracked, the spider webbing obvious in the glow of the lights. To give himself a warm and fuzzy feeling, Martinez peaked inside and was glad to see Kyrolls' pistol tucked into the center console.

At least the old bastard did not carry when drinking unless he was at home; Martinez had seen that first hand. That still was not a good thing, but it was better than confronting an armed and angry drunk.

Opening the door, the warm air rushing out greeted Martinez. The room was thick with smoke, the sharp odor of hard liquor, and the raucous laughter of who Martinez assumed to be the owners of the bikes.

Most of the room was dark and dreary, with little overhead lights dangling over tables, casting any occupants in a vanta black shadow, making their eyes impossible to track. The bartender was flicking away at a datapad and glancing back at rows of liquor while occasionally chatting to the group nearly overflowing from the bar.

The bikers were a group of Kuritla, all clad in leather jackets and nursing some kind of greenish drink. They are members of a hardy mammalian species whose short heads, bulky frames, and brownish fur reminded him somewhat of a gnoll from traditional fantasy. However, unlike gnolls, they were generally pleasant to be around and had a very social disposition.

The other main difference was that unlike, say, the Farunse, Jurintik, or the Varintol, who sported snouts or maws, this species had more of a flat, humanistic face, save for the four short ears, slitted pupils, and flared slits for nostrils.

Their species did not bother Martinez in any way. Over the last few months, he had treated dozens of the orange classification species. Overall, Martinez had a favorable opinion of the Kuritla; they were polite, cordial, and very wise of those with experience or in positions of authority.

Additionally, he had never seen any Kuritla cause an issue; if anything, his patients were more concerned about bothering Martinez and the others in the Trauma center than their life-altering injuries.

While loud, this group seemed just as welcoming.

When Martinez walked up to the bar, having not seen Kyroll at any of the tables, one of the drunk aliens patted his shoulder. "Hey there, bud! What in the Pack Mother's name are you? And more importantly, can you drink?"

"Oh, hey there," Martinez started, taking a slight step back so the man stopped groping his shoulder. At least the man seemed not to mind, likely because he was clearly sloshed. "I'm a Human. I can drink, but I'm looking for someone."

"Aren't we all?" the man cackled, gesturing at his friends with his glass, which spilled all over the counter.

He likely thought he was being prophetic, but as far as Martinez was concerned, the man was just another drunk person. After babysitting Marines and patients for years, the Human had a surprising tolerance for odd drunk antics.

"Curin, leave him alone," the golden-furred Bulmeric bartender said, her voice as smooth as butter while cleaning up the spill with the hands at the end of her membranous wings.

Her hands were nearly the size of Martinez's entire chest, which the Human found shocking considering that otherwise, her build was lithe, muscular, built for flying on those bat-like wings, but somewhat smooth in a lot of the right places, save for her top which was flat as a day old coke.

"I'm just being nice," Curin replied almost defensively.

"Yeah, yeah, I know. But you gotta play anyway," the Bulmeric said, turning toward the man, pulling some dice from her form-fitting apron, and tossing them on the table.

Martinez had only heard about the Bulmeric from some Marines. The chiropteran species were odd in both form and function in the GU.

From the Marines, he knew the Bulmeric warrior caste was insatiable about how much they wanted to couple with Human Marines. According to those devil dogs, the warrior women of the Bulmeric specifically prided themselves in finding and locking down warriors to have children with—and Human Marines were the new species in the GU and were quickly making a name for themselves as fighting like animals.

This fascination and desire to copulate led to an odd revelation in the Human military, one that must have caused more headaches and safety briefs than anyone should ever tolerate. Most species' ability to hybridize was unknown to the GU and the Human government; there were just too many species to make testing all of them a simple process.

The Bulmeric was an exception to this unknown and the only one, as far as Martinez was aware.

If tales in the smoke pit were to be believed, several dozen Human Marines from the 1st regiment proved that the universe was not as vast and lonely as Humanity once believed.

Though none of the Marines he had ever served with could say they saw the natural Hybrid of the Bulmeric and Humanity, stories of Marines knocking the Bulmeric warriors up while on campaign were prolific throughout the Human militaries; there had to be some truth to it.

Running into hundreds of Marines, all with the same story, gave the legends some credence.

But those old tales were neither here nor there. The bat-like humanoid in front of Martinez was not a warrior, looking to jump his bones, nor was his type; even if he could admit her golden fur, short blonde hair, and vibrant yellow yet nearly dead-looking eyes did not look unappealing.

Martinez could say that if he somehow managed to string together a series of words to quantify how it felt like she could see into his soul.

"Was he playing anything?" Martinez asked after the drunk took the dice and turned to roll them.

The Bulmeric turned back, letting him see her name tag—Bodah.

"Nah, he won't notice; it was just a bartender trick," Bodah winked casually, opening a wide-wing hand toward the man while leaning on the bar. "So I take it, you are looking for Kyroll?"

What she meant by a bartender trick was beyond Martinez. He just assumed it meant something along the lines of how he uses some clever verbiage to talk people down from violence at work. He would never know; there were more important issues to deal with now anyway.

"What makes you think that"?" Martinez raised a brow, genuinely curious as to how she knew.

Bodah scoffed and shook her head, her short blonde bob cut refracting the light around her. "I'm a bartender. I know my patrons—even his stubborn ass."

"That does not really answer my question," Martinez remarked.

Bodah rolled her eyes and rubbed her hands on her tall ears, brushing against their short fur. "Yeah, yeah, I was getting to it." She scoffed, "If you gave me a moment, I would explain."

Martinez blushed, realizing he had once again cut someone off for no reason. He shut his trap and let the woman speak.

Bodah pulled down a bottle from the bar and gathered two glasses; after scooping up some ice, she resumed speaking. "You are the spitting image of him. More accurately, you Humans look a lot like Aviex, but I know about you, Martinez, right?"

Bodah's on-the-nose call out, along with her already knowing his name, earned her a nod, even if this was unsettling.

"Good, well—That old callus talks, just like my other patrons," Bodah chatted while pouring ice and filling the glasses with booze and some mixer. "That stubborn man has been ranting and raving about you arriving for weeks, and based on how depressed he looked when he came in, I was expecting you."

"Do you have any idea how creepy that is?" Martinez interjected while Bodah was adding slices of fruit to the drinks.

"I suppose it might be, but fuck it," Bodah shrugs, pushing the drinks toward him. "Grab those and follow me; you will need them."

Still slightly perturbed by the woman's insight, Martinez picked up the cold drinks, followed her as she left the bar, and told one of the Kuritla to watch the bar for a second.

Bodah led Martinez to the bar's back door and turned about, giving Martinez a slight smirk. Her tiny, sharp teeth peeked through, showing her heritage as a descendant of the warrior caste of her race. "Your man is sitting out there," she said, jamming her winged thumb toward the closed door.

"So what are the drinks for?" Martinez questioned.

"You might be as hopeless as Kyroll was telling me if you don't realize why I gave you two," she chuckled, putting her hands on her hips and leaning forward slightly. "You both will need them."

"Oh," Martinez said, slightly blushing, realizing that Bodah was trying to help him.

"Glad you are getting it," Bodah said, pushing open the door, "Good luck."

"Yeah–" Martinez replied, swallowing his nervous spit. "Got any tricks for talking to the old man? I've only met him for maybe a minute."

Bodah sighed and scratched one of her fingers across her sharp jaw. It was oddly cute despite the massive bat-like ears flicking at every sound and her membranous wings stretching. "I would say maybe find common ground? He only talks to me once he is good and liquored up; otherwise, he keeps to himself."

That was honestly not the best advice; Martinez knew to do that much, but hey, if it's all she knows, it's all he's got to work with. "Thanks, I will be back for another drink in a bit," Martinez assured.

"Feel free; it's on your father-in-law's tab anyway," Bodah snickered, ignoring that Martinez scowled at the insinuation of his and Kyrolls relation.

Outside, underneath the Veranda, Kyroll sat sipping a tall, heavily alcoholic drink. The overhead heaters glowed bright orange, illuminated the area, and kept snow from collecting on the ground and benches.

The darkness around Celna was barely held at bay by the lights, making the little backwoods bar feel like a lone bastion of safety in overwhelming gloom. The only sound other than Kyrolls rasped, painful breathing was the occasional hoot or yelp from creatures lurking in the skyward grasping pines just beyond the radiance.

"Are you going to fill up my glass, Grulah?" Kyroll said when the door shut behind Martinez, not lifting his head from the nearly empty glass.

Seeing the old man like this was strange; Kyroll stared into the amber liquid like it held the answers to the universe. Considering how brash the man had been before, him sitting here nursing his issues with a drink was oddly humanizing. Lord knew Martinez had done that plenty of times in life.

For a moment, Martinez thought that maybe he was wrong about Kyroll; maybe Nelya had a point that he was just troubled; then the older Aviex man turned his head so his two remaining eyes could see Martinez.

His eyes widened when he realized that it was Martinez walking up to him, not his usual bartender. Kyroll's muscles tensed, and he gripped the glass hard enough that tremors started. That was probably not the best sign, but Martinez was a man on a mission and would not be deterred, even if it killed Kyroll.

"What? Not who you wanted to see with your next round?" Martinez said, setting the glass down in front of Kyroll and plopping into a seat nearby, not allowing the old man to complain about or deny his presence.

"No," Kyroll growled and looked away, grabbing the fresh drink in hand after shotgunning his first.

Kyroll, with his damaged vocal cords, always growled at least a bit, so Martinez had difficulty judging his mood based on his tone alone. Which currently was not standoffish; it was almost dismissive with his back toward Martinez.

The only break in his slumped, denying posture was occasionally turning his head, confirming Martinez was still there; he would then look back into the dark veil beyond the veranda and mutter to himself in Aviex.

The two sat there sipping away, watching the snow beyond the veranda. It was a shame both of them might have a lot in common, at least if Nelya and Bodah were to be believed. So far, the only thing that Martinez could see they were like-minded in was being stubborn and dense, neither wanting to start the uncomfortable conversation.

But someone had to be the bigger man here, and Martinez had already decided that backing down was not an option. Instead of trying to open softly and lure Kyroll into opening up, the Human decided not just to surprise Kyroll; he was going to ambush him, putting the Aviex secrets out as an opening gamut.

"So, about why the Aviex are called "vein-slicer" and why you hate me," Martine smirked, setting his glass back down.

Kyroll whipped around in his chair and glared soul-cutting daggers at Martinez. "You don't know anything," he hissed.

At least that got Kyroll to quickly engage in the conversation. Having this opening act of both refusing to talk was already tiresome.

"You wanna bet?" Martinez raised a brow, finding Kyrolls defensive action rather amusing. It was not like Martinez planned to fight him, even if he wanted to as revenge for making Lysa cry.

"What do you know, you filthy—" Kyroll started but bit his tongue and adjusted his composure. "You Human."

That Kyroll held his tongue from insulting Martinez was surprising. He was well aware of what the man had called him during the previous altercation—granted, he only knew the rough translation from Nelya and Lysa—but the sentiment did not change.

What the hell was with Kyroll? The man was an enigma. His wife hardly knew anything about what he did for work. He despises other species, and somehow, a woman like Nelya married someone so coarse.

Compared to his wife's bubbly, fill-the-room personality, he was a rag soaked in gasoline, ready to burn.

Martinez sighed and explained what Nelya had told him about the history of the Aviex, Kyroll, and his past with Lysa. At first, Kyroll sat there and silently listened, simply nodding. That was until Martinez mentioned that Kyroll was a member of some kind of special forces and that after seeing all the horrors of the after-effects of that war, he now hated other races.

For some reason, Martinez's claiming that he hated other races entirely based on a few bad apples caused Kyroll to grimace and look away, but he did not interject.

"Now, with what is going on with Lysa. I'm worried about her. She wants her dad to not hate her and to treat her better than the assholes you used to deal with, but apparently, that's too much for you," Martinez said, taking a break to sip his booze and let Kyroll have a chance to comment back or do anything at all.

"Kid, you don't get it. I'm protecting her and It's for her own good," Kyroll replied after sighing, stalwart in his stubborn ways. "If I don't she will go out there and end up in some hole having been dragged away by some slavers, or worse just a vindictive group who will kill her. And having you around is not going to help."

"That's fucking rich. You are doing a lot of things, but protecting her is not one of them; if anything, you are only hurting her," Martinez chuckled, causing Kyroll to grumble angrily, having heard something similar from Nelya earlier.

"Besides, what makes you think she needs it? Lysa can kick the ass of anyone I've ever known, fuck she regularly kicks the crap out of me when we spar," Martinez continued.

"That's because you are just some medic; you aren't a fighter," Kryoll replied, "I don't give a fuck if you were in war. You can't keep Lysa; all you are is a danger."

Martinez rolled his eyes and sipped from his drink, seeing that this conversation was not going anywhere at this point. He needed to press Kyroll harder, crack his walls, and make him face the reality of what was going to happen.

"Brother, I'm just going to tell you the honest truth, with no sugar coating. I can't make you do shit, but right now, I'm going to talk to you, man to man, sailor to soldier." Martinez started.

"What makes you think—" Kyroll started, but Martinez vocally barreled over him, not caring that he started to talk.

"Lysa hates your guts and probably wants to kill you. If we can't make up and get along in some way, we are leaving, and you will never see her again," Martinez finished his short statement of reality.

Kyroll looked at Martinez, almost flabbergasted. "There is no way she hates me. I'm her father; she will understand when she is older."

"What are you not understanding about this asshole? If I go back to your house with no solution to tell your Gra'hu and daughter, we are leaving in the morning; no ifs, ands, or buts. So work with me here. I know that Nelya explained this to you before we arrived." Martinez said, pointing a loaded knife hand at Kyroll's two good eyes.

Kyroll looked pissed after having himself called out. If a look could kill, Martinez would have died on the spot. Kyroll's two remaining blood-red eyes went nearly black with rage. He snarled momentarily before Martinez outright laughed at him.

"Dude, just stop. I want this to work, and right now, I'm the only thing keeping the possibility of you ever having a relationship with your daughter, my Ruh'ah possible," Martinez laughed, having gotten tired of Kyroll's posturing.

That shift in Martinez's demeanor seemed to have gotten to Kyroll. Martinez thought it might have been because any other friend or past boyfriend Lysa ever had was scared away by a few snarls, growls, and bared teeth.

But Martinez was different; He had faced the Faruqua, the Hrikala, and the Sputral; nothing Kyroll could do would intimidate him.

In the worst-case scenario and they did come to blows Martinez was experienced in a brawl and was half Kyrolls age; neither would walk away unscathed. Even Kyroll had to understand that their usual method of being violent to problems would not work.

"Fine, what do you have in mind?" Kyroll mumbled, tapping his finger on the glass rim.

"First, you are going to apologize to Lysa and listen to her, after that, I don't know. We just have to try and get along; maybe we could go out and do something together, get to know one another a bit," Martinez replied. "I just want Lysa to be happy. Help me out here."

Kyroll shotgunned the last of his drink and stared off into the snow, trying to think of what he should do. What did he have in common with some random Hwasan who was trying to take his dear little huntress from him?

After a short while, Kyroll smiled in a way that unsettled Martinez to the core. He had seen smiles filled with venom before; the last time was a few months ago when he was dealing with Chloe—that horrible spook of a woman. Martinez knew it was not an issue of his teeth; the Human was fine with Nelya and Lysa's bright, vibrant smiles.

It might be because his face looked like it had been sent through a wood chipper and he had a constant glare, but Martinez was not sure.

"I think I have an idea," Kyroll said, rolling his hand in the air to no one in particular.

"What is it? I will do anything to make this work," Martinez said, still suspicious of the man.

"I hope you do mean anything; Lysa deserves a man who will put in that effort." Kyroll sneered.

"Of course I mean it. I'm here with you, aren't I," Martinez scoffed.

"Good. Have you ever been hunting?" Kyroll questioned, not missing the subtle insult but choosing to ignore it. Leaning in and looking Martinez up and down for a few moments. "I have a few extra tags. We could head out in the woods and find a stag or two."

"No, I have not. I am willing to try it if you apologize," Martinez said.

"Perfect. We can leave tomorrow—after I talk to Lysa tomorrow," Kyroll explained. "Sound good?"

"Alright," Martinez replied, unknowing of the trouble his willingness to try to bridge the gap with Lysa's dad would bring.

FORGIVEN, NEVER FORGOTTEN

Martinez and Kyroll went their separate ways shortly after Grulah brought them another round. They did not talk much other than Kyroll explaining the deer-like animals they would be hunting and where they would be.

The Human left before Kyroll finished his next round of drinks. It wasn't like Kyroll really wanted Martinez there as is. He tolerated his presence at best and despised it at worst; at least he was not directly attacking or referring to him by some slur.

Once back at the house, Martinez found that it was as dark as the forests surrounding the compound. Instead of waking Nelya and bothering her with a late-night update on the issues with Kyroll, the Human went to bed.

Moving as silently as a ghost, he circumvented the main building and scurried into the guest house, wanting to hurry because the snowfall was increasing in intensity by the moment. Once inside, Martinez brushed off the fresh powder and entered the bedroom.

Lysa was already curled up under the blankets, the moonlight only letting him glimpse her pale skin. Her plush coal-black lips and hair shined brightly in contrast to the other shadows around her.

Once he stripped and was inside the covers, he chuckled slightly. Even when she was passed out, Lysa instinctively snuggled up, having shimmied closer, pressing her bare back to his chest and sighing contently. Wrapping her waist in his arm, Martinez joined her in beatific comfort and quickly fell asleep, savoring the company of his gothic angel.

Martinez wished that the talk with Kyroll was the worst part of the night, but no, his dreams were far worse.

He spent the night delving in and out of consciousness, being constantly awoken by his frantic mind, imagining Kyroll standing over him and cutting him down time and time again.

Strangely, unlike his typical nightmares, the method of his execution was not always the same. Each time the weapon or method changed: tossed off a cliff, shot with a rifle, throat slit, fed to wolves, beaten to death, garroted, hung by the neck, and countless other more twisted, slow, torturous methods.

By the time the witching hour rolled around, Martinez was half convinced it was God warning him to be cautious of Kyroll, but that might just be his own biases talking—even he could not ignore that possibility.

If it was anyone else subjected to this torment, it might have been concerning, but Martinez was used to restless nights dealing with nightmares of his past; that and each time he woke up from tossing and turning, Lysa would cling to him, pressing an overwhelming feeling of safety and comfort that slaughtered any baleful specters after a few minutes.

The next morning, the thing that pulled Martinez from slumber was not the winds of winter battering the window, or the wan light shining on his face, but a gentle nudging against his neck.

Forcing his eyes open, feeling like he was weighing anchor, Martinez was welcomely greeted by Lysa, who was straddling him beneath the covers. Her warm, nude body pressed tightly against him, her body practically melting against him. At the same time, her four ruby-red eyes stared at him, barely visible through her shiny coal hair.

"Good Morning to you, too," the Human smirked, still tired but conscious enough to clutch at her muscular hips, pulling her up slightly higher.

"Indeed, may I? I am feeling a bit peckish," Lysa purred, licking her lips.

It was odd. Lysa had been craving a lot of blood lately, an abnormal amount even for her. Hemopacks, his succor, or even fresh animal blood Nelya had at the house were never enough, no matter how many liters she consumed.

Part of Martinez wondered if she might be going through a growth spurt. His lover was only in her mid-twenties, and female Aviex and Humans could still be growing at her age. But he doubted it was that; having a growth spurt was so statistically irrelevant that most people did not consider it a possibility.

Her hunger was not causing any issues for now. Unless she started feeling sick, Martinez assumed it was likely just a stress response. He had seen plenty of Marines suck down food like no other just before deployment, so that made sense to him. And she had plenty to be stressed about.

"Yeah, it's not a problem Ruh'ah," Martinez whispered, kissing her head.

"Thank you. I don't know why I've just been ravenous as of late," Lysa whispered, scooting up and out of the blankets, letting them fall off her entirely and onto his thighs.

Lysa gently bit down on Martinez's shoulder and started to drink his blood. Just as usual, she moaned and clutched tightly to his shoulders while her lover held on tightly, letting a feeling of safe acceptance flow down her throat.

As she drank more blood from Martinez than was likely healthy for him to lose every morning or night, neither noticed the sound of the guest house's exterior door open nor the soft plodding and chipper humming traveling down the hall. They were too enraptured by the other to care.

They did not notice until Nelya opened the door to their room and exclaimed at seeing both of them naked with her daughter drinking Martinez's blood.

"Oh my, am I interrupting something?" Nelya giggled, feigning covering her eyes.

The second Nelya spoke, Lysa's head snapped to the door, and her face flushed as red as the blood on her lips. Martinez likewise blushed a deep red and pulled the covers up, covering Lysa's bare back up to her shoulders.

"Mother, you could at least have knocked," Lysa groaned.

"It's nothing I haven't seen before," Nelya teased, leaning against the door frame and adjusting her cardigan. "You have seen myself and your father Mordain plenty of times."

"That's not the point," Lysa replied hurriedly, wiping Maritnez's bloody shoulder off with the blankets, uncaring that she would have to launder them later.

"Well, if you are worried about Henry, worry not; he might as well be an Aviex in many ways. There are a few he is better in—at least from what I saw," she finished with a wink and a subtle eye shot toward where their hips were meeting.

"Mother, don't say that!" Lysa bemoaned, sinking beneath the covers, trying to hide from her embarrassment.

"Nelya—" Martinez interjected, feeling Lysa trying to crawl off him to use his body and the blanket to hide from Nelya.

"Yes, little hunter?" Nelya smirked, popping a hip out and giggling at her daughter's light suffering.

"Is there something you need?" Martinez said, trying not to slightly laugh to relieve the awkward tension of having who might be his mother-in-law see his johnson.

"I just wanted to tell you two that breakfast is ready. I also packed you and Kyroll some food for your expedition," Nelya smiled. "But I will leave you to it; take all the time you want. I still want those grandkids," she finished before closing the door and slipping out.

For Lysa's part, hearing her mother insinuate that they should resume earned a pained groan. Yeah, they both knew that Nelya wanted grandkids and was not shy about it. But that was a bit too forward, even for Lysa.

Once the door leading out of the guest house closed, Martinez lifted the covers and chuckled, seeing Lysa cupping her face and blushing so hard even her ears were showing it. "So, do you want to continue?" He teased.

"Henry, please don't," Lysa whined into her palms.

"Sorry, I just wanted to tease you a bit," Martinez assured, gently rubbing her shoulder.

Lysa sighed and shook her head. They teased one another often enough, and she supposed this was only fair after dragging Martinez into the sauna on his first day here.

At least her Mother would not go squawking to others about seeing her naked, moaning, and drinking Martinez's blood. Nor would she likely bring up what she saw of her Ruh'ah to her writer friends or anyone else for that matter.

"Come on, let's get dressed before she decides to return," Lysa said, hurrying out of the bed and standing. "What did Mother mean by your and my Father's expedition?"

Martinez got up and out of bed and began explaining the agreement between Kyroll and himself while they got ready for the day ahead. Martinez packed a small backpack with enough clothes for their planned three-day trip.

Martinez was not incredibly happy about leaving for three days, nor was Lysa. Her desire for him not to spend that much time alone with Kyroll was evident in a few sharp growls while he spoke.

Lysa included in her reasoning that Martinez would be alone with Kyroll for multiple days while he was armed and was days away from assistance.

Martinez fully understood the danger of what he was agreeing to do. But he would make it through the event. Kyroll could not shoot him in the back and get away with it.

The police would quickly figure out what happened, and Lysa would throttle and likely kill her Father. Then there was Nelya; she loved the man, but even she would not turn her eye away at blatant murder.

There was no way Kyroll would be so stupid as to think either of them would accept if he Mozambique drilled Martinez in the back.

After explaining those factors, Lysa was somewhat assured that he would survive the trip and that Kyroll genuinely wanted to attempt to reach out to him and her. But the underlying distrust was still there, festering like an old wound.

When Martinez said Kyroll would apologize and reach out to her before they left, Lysa scoffed at the idea until Martinez explained that he agreed to apologize to her before they left on the trip—under the threat that they would leave entirely if he did not.

"There is no possible scenario in which he genuinely will do that," Lysa argued, wrapping a dark purple scarf around her shoulders and brushing her hair out over the top of it.

"Nah, he said he would, and we know if he does not, we are leaving," Martinez replied, tossing on his jacket.

"We shall see about that," Lysa rolled her eyes, not believing that man had a single ounce of introspection in him.

Lysa sat in silence, leaning against Martinez while seated on the Davenport. Across the coffee table from her was Kyroll, holding his head down, damn near begging Lysa to forgive him and let him try to reconnect.

Nelya was catty-corner from them sipping some tea, overseeing the entire thing. For the most part, Kyroll needed no prompting and laid out his sins individually for Lysa to judge. Nelya only had to remind him of a few things he either forgot or chose to omit, but after the reminder, he added them to his list of transgressions.

The bright morning sun poured in through the window, giving the entire room a warm glow—a warmth that reflected the strange feeling in her chest. Kyroll—no, her Father did it. He actually just asked Lysa to try and forgive him, along with explaining that he and Martinez will try to make things work.

Lysa's mind was plagued with a stricken pain. After all these years of treatment, she wanted to despise her Father, to tell him to go kill himself and stop causing herself, Nelya, and now Martinez so much pain. In a way, she believed that was the least he could do.

On the other hand, Lysa was finally getting what she had wanted since she was a little girl: for her father to accept that she was not him and was more open and willing to work with other species.

Having these two conflicted voices screaming in her mind pressed her to silence. Unable to speak of the roaring beast in her soul, each demanding she responds to him by following their whims.

Kyroll raised his head and looked at his daughter; his two remaining eyes were vapid, blank, and devoid of life. As if saying all that sucked the fury, anger, and malice from his soul. "Can you try to forgive me?" Kyroll questioned. "I don't want to lose you."

Martinez looked over at Lysa, who was not quite glaring at her father but was close. She clenched her fists atop her lap and grinding her teeth. After resting his hand atop hers, he looked toward Nelya, who gave him a slight nod to press him onward.

At this point, the ball was entirely in Lysa's court, but that did not mean Martinez could not assist her to the best of his abilities.

"What do you think, Lysa?" Martinez asked, leaving the question open enough for her to interpret it as she saw fit.

Lysa looked over at Martinez and Nelya, taking in their supportive smiles and brimmed with pride having them here. Without their presence, Lysa would have assuredly listened to the voice demanding she hate Kyroll until the day she died.

She would have stood up and shoved his head through the wall, savoring that she was finally ending the man who caused her more anguish than anyone else. But with all she had learned from Teacher, that would not be right.

Executing your problems was only putting a bandaid on a stab wound. Would it somewhat help for a moment? Yes, but ultimately, that is not the treatment one needs.

"Father, do you genuinely wish to attempt to be forgiven by me?" Lysa questioned, looking back at him.

"Please, Yha-ru, I just want you to be safe and happy. I made mistakes in the past, but if being with," Kyroll paused, glancing at Martinez, his eyes souring for a moment before looking back at Lysa and continuing. "Henry here genuinely makes you happy. I will try to get along with him."

That Kyroll was still using the Aviex word for daughter was unsurprising; after years of avoiding using standard, it was to be expected. His venomous look at Martinez was also to be expected; at least, he seemed to be trying.

They sat in silence for a few moments while Lysa pondered what she should say to make the point he was still untrusted, but that she would at least show her trust by allowing him near her Ruh'ah.

It took her a minute, with Nelya and Martinez genuinely wondering how this would go. Both knew Lysa did not have to try, but they hoped she would agree for her sake.

"Fine," Lysa flatly replied, sounding almost angry.

"What do you mean fine?" Kyroll replied, "That could mean anything."

"I simply intend to convey that it is acceptable. I will never forget what you did, but for the sake of Mother and Martinez, I will attempt to forgive you. Despite my reservations against you, my desire to hate your very being, and the fact that I do not believe you are truly genuine, I will extend just enough rope for you to hang yourself with," Lysa explained before leaning forward and pointing venomously at him. "I do truly mean that I will let you dig your grave here, and I hope Ruh'ah and Mother will agree with me and happily let you jump into a hell of your design."

Martinez was unsure about the precise look Kyroll gave when Lysa said she did not trust him, but it looked almost guilty. But he could see that from any father's perspective, having your daughter say she distrusts you would sting.

"I understand," Kyroll grumbled, "I would not forgive me."

"Then we have an understanding," Lysa replied. "Mother, you mentioned breakfast is ready and that they are leaving for their bonding experience, correct?"

"I do have food ready," Nelya smiled, standing up and walking toward the kitchen.

Martinez and Lysa stood up to follow Nelya, both hungry and wanting to put this moment behind them. But Kyroll had one last thing he wanted to attempt.

The old Aviex stood up and walked over, attempting to hug Lysa. She was quick to react, which made her hatred of him apparent.

"No! Just No," Lysa hissed, pushing a close fist into Kyrolls sternum hard enough to make him gasp but nowhere near full strength.

Kyroll looked like he was about to lash back out, but Martinez stood between them and helped the man stand back up and catch his breath. "Try again after we get back."

Kyroll would not even look at Martinez then; he did not even make eye contact with Lysa. He simply accepted the helping hand and grumbled an agreement that maybe he would try later.

DOUBLE DEALING DAD

Kyroll's truck lumbered down the dirt road heading out the northern exit of Celna. The old red pickup's engine struggled to keep time, occasionally popping like a gunshot when a cylinder misfired. Along with the horrible tuning, the otherwise calm evening's sounds were interrupted by the squealing timing belt and the grinding clutch.

If it was Martinez's own vehicle, he might have some concern for the old beater, but it was not, so it was in no way his issue. If Kyroll did not want to give his vehicle proper care and maintenance, it was his problem. He would have to pay for it anyway.

Lord knew he and Nelya had enough money to fix the truck; they were loaded beyond anything Martinez could genuinely fathom. Yeah, he had a rough Idea, but he grew up in an LA ghetto, not on a massive plot of land that took an entire day to traverse.

Part of Martinez thought that the dereliction of care was just another example of Kyroll being stubborn to the point that it was detrimental—but that was likely just his negative bias against the man barking its objections to the man's existence.

Martinez looked back into the truck bed at their backpacks strapped down tightly, the light snow falling and sticking to them, the bed, and the road behind them.

Martinez could no longer see Celna, having left the outskirts of the town almost a half hour before. All that filled the truck's wake was cold, frozen over grass browned from winter.

Those dormant plants were juxtaposed with the coniferous trees crawling against the rugged road. The lush greens, blues, and whites breathed life into the otherwise glacially lonely forest.

"So where are we going anyway?" Martinez asked, turning back toward the front and looking at Kyroll. "It seems odd that we aren't going to hunt on your land."

"Do you have to ask questions?" Kyroll grumbled after shaking his head. "I get that you are trying to make this work, but it's not like we need to chat."

Martinez rolled his eyes at the comment. Why did Kyroll have to be this obtuse about these concepts? Not only were they attempting to find common ground, but also the question itself. Even a layman would wonder why they were not going to utilize the thousands of square kilometers he and Nelya owned.

In Martinez's mind, it made no sense at all. Why own all that lush, untamed wilderness if you would not traverse it? Nelya, Lysa, and he had already been on a hike to the far side of their property. It was beautiful, and plenty of stags were out there; they saw thousands in a single afternoon.

"Yeah, I kinda do if we are going to make this attempt work. I genuinely want to get to know you," Martinez replied.

Kyroll sighed in annoyance, a grimace crossing his face for a few moments before he waved his hand flippantly, "Fine, I will humor you."

That was not the ideal way Martinez wanted the old soldier to treat his attempts, but he doubted their propinquity would improve fast enough for him to get much better, so the Human would take what he could get.

"Alright, so why are we not using your property as a hunting ground?" Martinez repeated but a bit more poignant.

"I have a better place. Just past my job site, there is a reservation; no hunters have been there in years, and they won't be for longer," Kyroll explained, pointing at his datapad mounted to the dashboard, which showed off a large area labeled as Iritala reserve.

Martinez looked at the map, taking in the details of the sprawling forest they were deep inside. Funnily enough, unlike the map Lysa used when navigating from the airport, this one was set up using good old MGRS (Military Grid Reference System).

Martinez chuckled slightly at that; maps using this system are uncommon unless you plan to travel long distances overland, not roads. Hopefully, Kyroll will handle the map when they reach the reserve. Martinez could shoot an azimuth and use a compass, but it was not his specialty.

"So besides your company, no one can make it there?" Martinez questioned, following the roads on the map to the reservation, noting that all of them passed through sections labeled logging with several standard years going forward and back in time distinguishing zones.

"That's right," Kyroll nodded. "It will just be you and me for the next few days. Sounds great, right, big guy?" He finished tapping Martinez's chest with the back of his knuckles.

Martinez wondered how genuinely great that would be. He assumed the trip would likely be as pleasant as pulling teeth or possibly closer to getting kicked in the gooch.

His assumption of how pleasant things could be was only soured further when Martinez tried to break the next bit of awkward silence with further conversation. To his dismay, Kyroll seemed to have burned out his willingness to chat. No matter what he did to keep the old salt talking, all that was returned were curt answers that ended the conversation attempt quickly.

Do you like Music? No.

Do you enjoy your work? No.

What did you do while in service? I can't tell you.

Eventually, after growing tired of Kyroll's repugnant personality, he decided to ask something stupid to get a rise from the old salt.

"Do you have a barbed stick up your ass?" Martinez questioned coyly.

Kyroll shook his head and sighed before answering in his familiar cold monotone, "No."

Jesus fucking Christ, what is this guy? A fucking robot? He did not even smirk at the snarky comment.

Martinez had met drill instructors with more personality and gravitas. Even they could laugh at a joke or at least make fun of you back. But not Kyroll. No, it was all business all the time; that or he just truly did not care about the jab.

It did not matter at this point. Martinez had been trying to bridge their gap for thirty minutes, and if anything, they were drifting further apart, namely, because Martinez was starting to get pissed at the cold bastard.

If Martinez continued to slam against this brick wall of a man, he would flip his shit. That would do him no good at this point. So, instead of losing it on Kyroll and emphasizing yet again the importance of them being capable of basic cordialness, Martinez simply gave up for the time being.

Was it the best thing he could do? Likely not. Would the Marines back on the Jericho ever let him live it down if they learned he simply folded? Not a snowball's chance in hell.

Kyroll was not a grunt Martinez could order around with the weight of the title Doc. Pushing any harder would make the tumultuous situation even more volatile, so taking the tactical retreat was likely the wise option for the time.

Leaning back against the seat, Martinez flicked open his datapad, hoping he could doom scroll on military forums or possibly watch a video, but no dice. This far out in the boondocks, there was insufficient signal strength to send a text, much less do anything over the data net.

He should have seen that coming; Nelya's house was the same way, and wherever they were going was even more remote. His only other option was to read the medical journals Shiksie had made him download.

Perusing those was an option, but with recent memories of Shiksie being dredged up when he attempted to open them, he chose a wiser choice. The Human leaned on the oldest and most sacred traditions of any military man with time to kill.

Sleep.

The Marines especially deified the act, having mastered its practice beyond any reasonable amount. In the dirt, rocks, hammocks, spare tires, up-armored roofs, and even waist-deep in a muddy foxhole, Martinez and the Marines had slept like babies in them all.

Because none of those seraphic options were available, he laid the seat back and told Kyroll to wake him when they arrived. A sharp grunt was all he got in response—at least, it was something.

Watching the powder fall outside, and the bows pass like a movie, it did not take long for Martinez's eyes to weigh on him like anchors and sleep to find him.

Vehicles were a soft spot for the Devil Dolphin; sleep came easy whenever he was not driving. He was unsure if it was the rumble on the engine, the subtle rocking of the frame, or that he could go with the flow for those few moments. But what he did know was he found them as hypnotic as a lullaby.

The thunderous slam of the driver's side door ripped Martinez from a blissful dream of him and Lysa lounging on a beach. The metallic clang instantly crushed the scenery of the crystal clear water, bleach-white sands, and Lysa splashing in the water while wearing a micro bikini.

Why was it that whenever Martinez was getting blissful sleep, something had to ruin it: ambushes, injured grunts, drunk morons, incompetent leaders, and now his pseudo-father-in-law.

Did God have it out for him or something?

Martinez's ingrained reactions caused him to shoot up and reach toward the dashboard, where his STTK and rifle would be staged in an up-armored vehicle. But after jamming his knuckles into the nonexistent equipment, he yelped like a beat dog and realized where he was.

He was not in some dusty ambush on Verilon, readying to repel an ambush from the Farq. It was just Kyroll being an asshole yet again.

"Vuric, wait here. I'm going to tell the supervisor where we are heading," Kyroll sniggered, relishing Martinez's pain with a cruel grin. "And try not to beat up my truck anymore. It's not trying to hurt you."

"I know what that means, you ass," Martinez winced, rubbing his hand, feeling the sharp pain of soft tissue wounds. At least he did not break or dislocate his finger.

"I know, and I don't give a flying fuck, Lurip," Kyroll shrugged and walked toward some building on the far side of the clearing he had parked them in.

Lurip? That was a new one. Based on context and the vile hiss in Kyroll's voice, it was an insult or slur, but he had no idea what it meant.

After triple-checking his aching finger, Martinez looked outside the cab and spotted Kyroll amidst the bustling work area. It was strange, to put it mildly.

The camp almost looked like a military outpost, but enough details were different to make it evident that was not the purpose.

The dull khaki building Kyroll was heading toward was a prefab used often by the GU, the Military, and penny-pinching companies. Prefabs were enjoyed because they were cheap, could be folded into a half-meter by half-meter cube, and could be carried by two men.

Overall, the buildings worked fine in what they did. Just don't expect to live in the lap of luxury.

The rest of the camp was bustling with life. Trucks filled with logs went to and fro, weaving into the dozens of roads linking to the camp. Expertly traversing the massive industrial transports, men traveled between the other amenities scattered on the outskirts.

Circling half the clearing were a chow hall, barracks, Gee-dunk, head, motor pool, and what looked like some kind of recreation center. These were all built of massive timber, likely made by the workers.

Based on what Nelya had told Martinez about the lumberjack job Kyroll had, it made sense that the outpost had all these amenities. It would be difficult to sell such a dangerous job to people without them. You had to meet all the B's to keep people happy, which was universal regardless of the species.

Peeking behind him and over the bed, Martinez saw the rest of the camp, almost a mirror image of the other half. But unlike the other side, this one had a detail that instantly drew the Human's attention: an armed guard of all things.

Lazing about in a chair facing halfway in and out of the camp, the brown and green-furred alien let their HR-8 carbine lay across their lap. Now, that was a weapon Martinez had not seen in a long time— not since his unit's last stint with the GU Army.

That carbine is the primary weapon of most GU forces. While the Human military opted for the man-made C-7, he did not detest the laser blaster. It just did not compare to good old-fashioned gunpowder and lead.

What the Guard was protecting against was a complete unknown, but it could not be the threat of someone shooting back; he wore no armor, helmet, or camouflage—instead, he wore a simple bright orange jumpsuit with a belt bursting with charge packs.

He likely was charged with something similar to how Humans in the Arctic had guards for wolves or polar bears. What megafauna was out there to justify the presence was beyond Martinez; he did not know enough about the area's ecology to even guess.

Now that his mind was keyed in on the details of weapons, Martinez quickly realized that it was not just the guard who was armed; Everyone in the camp was. Every lumberjack had a pistol on hand, either in a drop holster or tucked dangerously into their waistband.

The excessive armament was not the only thing that raised a red flag in Martinez's eyes.

Why were there so many Aviex?

Besides the guard, every person he had seen at this camp was of that rare platinum species.

The sheer quantity, while odd, was not the unnerving part about it. No, they were all watching him and were not attempting to hide it. Thousands of blood-red eyes stared at him with suspicion as they flowed past the truck and to their destinations; each look was coupled with pointing and conversations centered on the stranger in their midst.

Being in the open with all these armed men made Maritnez feel like a fox stuck in a trap. What he would not give to have a loaded rifle right now, but the weapon Nelya lent him was in the truck bed, and he barely knew how to operate it.

Trying to escape the stares, Martinez sunk into the seat, hoping the men outside would just forget he existed. But he was never that lucky. That only made the men adjust their paths to get a peak at the interloper in their midst.

Martinez knew the glares, glowers, and curiosity had to be because of Kyroll. His squad knew about him before they had ever met, and because these lumberjacks lived together for weeks on end, they also had to know about him.

It only made sense. The military operated the same way. Word had its ways of getting around, be it the E-4 Mafia, the Lance Corporal underground, Barracks parties, or hours upon hours drinking together. At times word seemed to travel faster than the speed of light if you used those methods.

Hell, Martinez had used that effect to his benefit more than once, spreading around hints of surprise inspections just so the Marines could be ready. Was it morally right? Martinez could not say, and he did not care. The Marines were his boys, and these Lumberjacks were Kyrolls, so whatever lies he spread around were reality to them.

After almost half an hour of trying to ignore the Aviex stares, Kyroll exited the prefab control building. Martinez could barely see him initially step outside and turn around, but once he did, the Human sat up, hoping Kyroll would not see him cowering from the judgemental stares.

It was odd; Martinez was perfectly fine with getting shot at, stabbed, blown up, going wrist-deep in guts, or fondling a dude's balls and checking for stragglers after a nasty night with a barracks bunny. But hundreds of people staring at him like an interloper skeeved him out.

Martinez watched Kyroll hoping the old man would pull the lead out of his ass and get him the fuck out of this camp. If Kyroll had spotted Martinez's pleading look, he did not acknowledge it.

Instead, he turned about and waited as Burkla slinked out of the prefab and walked up to Kyroll. They chatted for a moment or two. The two men made almost no motions or gestures, so determining what they were talking about was impossible, but something unsettling transpired.

Burkla handed a massive black duffle bag to Kyroll while accepting a credit stick from Kyroll.

"What the fuck?" Martinez muttered, wondering what they were doing that looked like a drug deal.

Both looked right at him as if they heard him speak, causing a shiver to crawl down Martinez's spine. Without missing a beat, Burkla smiled that same Cheshire grin as when they first met—when the Aveix man had insinuated a desire to kill him.

After Kyroll snapped at him, Brukla crawled back into the prefab, leaving Kyroll alone in the snow. Kyroll took a moment and looked out over the camp, at his datapad, and then toward Martinez.

Even at this distance, his sigh was visible and full-bodied. Whatever thought just crossed Kyrolls mind was something he was not happy with, but after tucking his datapad away, any hesitance melted instantly, replaced by his usual stony demeanor.

Kyroll was up to something. Martinez hoped the man could look past his issues for the sake of Lysa and Nelya, but this smelled dirty. And as the good old saying goes, if it smells like shit, looks like shit, it probably is.

Whatever Kyroll had planned for him, Martinez would be ready even if he had to stay up for the next few days and keep his pocket knife under his pillow.

For now, Martinez knew one thing—he had to get into that duffle bag.

AFIELD CONFLICTION

B irds croak loudly overhead, gliding from bow to bow, as the wind made each snowy pine ache. Looking up from the snowy ground, Martinez tries to spot one of the avian interlopers.

Be it their natural camouflage, the density of the trees, or the encroaching end of nautical twilight, hardly a glimpse could be seen as they flickered overhead past the starlight above.

It was unnerving that he could not see the murder only a few meters away. But on occasion, he spotted a pair of vicious, sharp gold eyes flickering before vanishing. It was like millions of eyes were watching him and Kyroll march further into the woods toward death and destruction.

At least that was the thought niggling in the back of Martinez's mind. He was well aware the birds were not crows, ravens, or even some distant cousins. They just sounded so similar that he could not help but think of the little harbingers of death back on Earth.

That eerie similarity had been on his mind since they got back on the road and up into the mountains. The other thought that kept his hand firmly on the cold knife in his pocket was what the hell was in that duffle bag.

Not knowing the contents of the bag was taking its toll upon him, letting his idle mind wander to the worst possibilities: Poison, bait, guns, and drugs were only a few of the things that he believed may be within his companion's possession.

With his limited knowledge of the grander universe, Kyroll could bring millions upon millions of possibilities to bear on him. Not knowing all of those possibilities made Kyroll's protectiveness of the bag all the more unsettling.

Kyroll had certainly been keen on keeping it out of sight of Martinez—or at least out of his reach. The moment their feet hit the snowy dirt a few kilometers down the hill, he scooped it up and never let it leave his shoulder. He always kept it abreast of Martinez. That fact remained constant even now, traversing through pitch-black darkness.

At least if Kyroll did try something, Martinez was armed with his knife and Nelya's bolt action, which was chambered in the galactic standard sniper round on 12.7mm caseless. He ensured that the weapon was fully loaded several times before setting off and following the old man. You can't be too careful, and it pays to perform your pre-combat checks.

For the most part, their walk up toward camp was an uneventful affair, filled with a quiet understanding that neither trusted the other. The only odd thing that occurred surprised both Martinez and Kyroll, thrusting them into ingrained military actions.

When they were only a stone's throw from where they would go to ground a massive bear-like animal emerged in the path before them. Surprisingly, it was as silent as the wind and as graceful; the snow around it and even the bushes were barely disturbed as it emerged.

How something that massive could be that silent was beyond Martinez, but whatever this thing was had gotten close enough that he could smell its choking musk.

Kyroll reacted fast, dropped to a knee, and tossed his fist high, giving the GU and Human militaries a silent command to halt.

With a reaction that is built into his very soul, Martinez followed suit by tucking down off the side of the trail using a downed log as cover. The cold snowpack bid him welcome as it crunched beneath his body and heavy backpack, soaking through his gear nearly instantly.

Both trained their rifles on the mass of lumbering horror as it turned in their direction, its jaws snapping and breath billowing in the breeze.

Now, to call what Martinez would later learn is called a Milurt a bear was not accurate, but it was the only thing that Martinez could compare to.

Unlike a bear on Earth with fur, four limbs, and a rather ornery disposition, this thing was something totally different. Its pelage was far too heavy to be called fur; it was like a mat clinging to rippling muscles.

Each step caused a low vibration in the dirt, shaking them to the core.

Even in the low candela of the Moon overhead, the creature's grotesque lips were easily visible as they slopped open trailing spit. Each appendage was lined with jagged, backward-facing teeth. Tendril-like tongues caressed their surfaces and flicked at the air, tasting for their prey.

The pair waited with bated breath, hearts careening against their ribs as though they would break out at any moment. Slowly but steadily, they curled their fingers onto their triggers and began to take up the slack, ready to rely on their oldest and boldest reaction to a threat from a military man.

Good old violence of action. When in doubt, being faster and more violent than any threat will lead you to victory; how intact you will be at the end is always up in the air, but being battered is better than death any day.

Violence was always an option, especially amidst violent men; go figure, the two warriors were violent men through and through.

While Martinez might be an individual who does more saving lives than taking them, the stack of ribbons and medals on his dress uniform showed his ability to do both.

Kyroll, on the other hand, had lived his entire life in violence, though the Human only had the slightest inkling of it. What little Nelya had told the Human of the older man's life barely scratched the surface— hell, not even she had a good scope of everything he had done.

Dark deeds should be done in dark theaters and kept there, and Kyroll was not about to tell his bubbling starlight of a wife all of that. It would only upset her and cause him more issues.

"Don't you move," Kyroll hissed, slipping down next to Martinez, doing his best not to alert the creature of their presence.

"Wasn't planning on it," Martinez whispered back, shimmying down to allow his rifle to rest upon the log.

The Milurt curiously stepped closer, rooting through the bushes and snow while Martinez glanced over at Kyroll, trying to gauge his reaction and understand how royally screwed they were.

A cold sweat rolled down the mountain brow and lingered ever so slightly on his scarred face. He wetted his lips and rolled his shoulders like a boxer preparing to brawl.

Kyroll's nervousness told the Human that this was undoubtedly the region's apex predator if its bulk, claws, and rows of saw-like teeth weren't enough of a hint.

After a few more plodding steps, Martinez caressed the safety of his rifle, readying to launch a slug straight into its gullet. At the same time, Kyroll had decided the beast had gotten close enough; his announcement of that objection was opening up on the beast with blistering gunfire.

Round after round roared, their defiance as hypersonic pills were launched in salvo. Each fiery report gave them a brief snapshot of the creature's scarred and bulky body. It was twice the size of a polar bear and likely just as uncaring of fights.

The Milurt roared, grunted, and flinched as each bullet splattered on its thick armor-like fur and hide. The bullets initially only appeared to be a minor annoyance, barely causing the beast to change its course—but by the time Kyroll's rifle bolt locked back on an empty mag, the only sign of the animal was its bellowing and the thunderous snapping of trees falling in its wake while it retreated from the duo.

While Martinez could understand the sudden shock and surprise of being ambushed in the dark, something so massive having that much of a reaction was still surprising—he did not even need to fire a single shot.

But he could compare the idea to someone throwing a million stones at you. Even if it weren't killing you, you still wouldn't wish to be there. Death by a thousand cuts was still death at the end of it.

"Thanks for that," Martinez sighed, watching the treetops a distance away from them shudder as the animal crashed through their bases.

"Don't be. I'm not dying for your sorry ass," Kyroll grunted while sending a new magazine home; the hefty thunk of his bolt emphasized his distaste.

That's it? It was just a cold statement that he was in it for himself. Martinez was starting to think his brain might have been a broken record. Why else would he always ask what the hell was wrong with Kyroll?

He didn't even give an "Are you all right?" glance to check on him, nothing—just the cold fact that he did not care about the Human one way or another as he turned and continued up through the verdant pines.

Martinez stood stock still for a moment as silence fell over the forest, the last vestiges of the sound of the beast running away deafening in the snowpack. Kyroll did not even notice that the Human was not following him for several seconds; he just continued to be himself and moved further up the hillside, vigilantly scanning the trees.

Sighing dejectedly, Martinez stepped off to follow the man, not wanting to encounter anything that might be in the woods all alone. Only once he resumed following him did Kyroll occasionally look behind him at Martinez, keeping him well within his patrolling scan.

A detail Martinez noticed. Does Kyroll have some niggling of fear for him knowing something is up? Or is it something else entirely?

Once at the site Kyroll had chosen for their campsite, Martinez could not help but go slightly slack-jawed. Even if this short trip with Kyroll did not work out, the site alone would make it all worth it.

The moon barely crested the treetops across a smooth-as-glass lake, reflecting every detail with exquisite precision. Dancing around the shore, little insects flew, giving off a faint greenish-blue glow.

The tiny illuminators pranced from icy frond to frond in pairs, spiraling around one another. The insects, Stars, moon, trees, and all of the universe reflected in the water's surface almost made Martinez forget about his dower companion—until Kyroll just had to rain on anything joyous around him.

While Martinez gawked, Kyroll calmly doffed his backpack and retrieved a small metallic object. It was no larger than an apple and just as shiny as chrome. Pressing a button, it blared, sounding like the alarms aboard HNS Jericho, warning him it was time to abandon ship.

The repeated cry was shrill and deafening, an insult to Martinez's peace of mind and the tranquility of the locale.

"What the fuck," Martinez grimaced, gripping his head and watching the insects flee the area running from the waling object.

"Relax. It will be over soon, so quit your bitching," Kyroll said just loud enough for Martinez to hear while laying the contents of his backpack on the ground and beginning to set camp.

"What the hell is that thing?" Martinez yelled.

If Kyroll had heard him, he did not acknowledge the question and just kept working on preparing his gear.

The horrendous sound only lasted for maybe another minute; during that time, every creature within a kilometer of the gem-like lake fled far away, attempting to escape what sounded like a cross between a dying animal and an evacuation alarm.

Once the sound had ended, Martinez could finally breathe. The overbearing sound waves kept his diaphragm in constant motion during the activation. How Kyroll was so unaffected by the deafening cacophony was unknown and did not matter; before Martinez could dwell upon the thoughts in slight differences of Aviex and Human constitution, Kyroll spoke.

"Are you going to set your shit up? Or do I have to show you how to do that?" The older Alien sneered, shoving his duffle bag and backpack into his tent.

"Fucking bastard," Martinez muttered under his breath while finding a spot a distance away and beginning to set up his bivvy sack.

Unlike Kyroll, who used a proper tent and sleeping system, Martinez used an old-fashioned rolled-up bivy sack with a sleeping bag that fit neatly inside. He knew many of the Marines he had worked with did not enjoy being issued these, comparing them to sleeping in coffins, but he kind of liked it.

Bivy sack systems were lightweight, and they took a few seconds to set up, not minutes like most civilian tents. Curiously, Kyroll's did not seem to take minutes to set up but mere moments. Martinez was a bit distracted and didn't see him pitch it. Maybe it's some grand technology that he was unaware of. It wouldn't be the first time the GU had surprised him.

By the time Martinez set his bivy sack up, tossed his backpack inside, and turned around, Kyroll was already preparing for sleep, putting on a watch cap, staging his boots and socks, and reviewing his map.

Curious, Martinez began to step closer, wishing to ask him about where they would be hunting in the morning. But as soon as Kyroll noticed that he was approaching, the map was quickly shoved into a pocket, and the rest of his gear was tucked into a corner of his tent out of sight of his Human, would be his son-in-law.

"Are you ready to rack out?" Kyroll asked. "We will be getting started early in the morning, likely in only hours," he finished, glancing down at his watch.

"Pretty much, but where are we going to be going in the morning?" Martinez questioned, undeterred by the apparent standoffishness.

"There's a valley up over the hill," Kyroll said, gesturing off to the north. "Over there is damn near the dead center of the area my company has claimed to. It's the furthest from anyone in the region. I can guarantee we'll find something interesting there."

Interesting—even Martinez, as dense as he was, could not miss the slight hiss in the man's gravel-like voice. While he still wished to give the other man the benefit of the doubt, too many factors were just not adding up. Something was on the old man's mind, and the more he interacted with Kyroll, the more curious he became.

Back at the logging camp, he looked somber; he looked heartbroken when Lysa slapped him, and at the bar, after Nelya dressed him down, he looked like a beat dog.

Kyroll had something bubbling under the surface; despite having picked up on this, Martinez couldn't help but feel that the man in front of him was as much of a predator as the Farqs were on Verillon: cunning, unyielding, and perfectly ready to stab a Human in the back if it meant they got what they wanted—or were coerced by the rebels to do it.

Back on Verillon, the young Corpsman had changed plenty of bandages for Marines and GU soldiers alike who had been stabbed in the back by their so-called allies, friends, or family. But that was an active warzone, and they were the invaders.

Here, nestled deep in the GU, he should not be questioning if his future father-in-law was going to try and cut his throat like a Farq.

They were supposed to be learning to get along. Maybe Kyroll needed some more time to warm up to him, but at this rate, this entire trip was going to be a disaster.

"Alright, I will see you in the morning; I hope we can hunt something we can bring back to Nelya and Lysa," Martinez replied.

There it was again. Mentioning the girls back home made Kyroll visibly grimace and look away from Martinez. It was so odd. The man was a killer, or at least he had been. But his family apparently was a soft spot for him to the point hearing their names spoken by Martinez hurt.

Kyroll nodded and entered his tent, zipping it shut and leaving Martinez alone in the dark. He returned to his bivy sack, readying to sleep even with a cold knot in his gut.

What was going on? Tomorrow, he could get into the duffle and get answers. Lord knew Kyroll was not going to give him any.

OBSCURATION AND ACCEPTANCE

The suns had yet to crest the horizon; the nautical dawn had not yet concluded. The light of the twin Rentix stars bathed the horizon in orange, red, and waning purples. Refractions transformed the snow beneath their feet into equally vibrant colors.

Martinez yawned and deeply stretched, reaching for the sky, his breath puffed into steam carried away by the breeze. He had yet to completely awaken after his rude alarm clock this morning, not having had time to make coffee or eat breakfast.

Kyroll, in his infinite wisdom, decided that shooting a round into the sky was the most efficient way to wake Martinez up. Granted, this was after he had tried to wake the disgusting Vuric with a flashlight and a calm demeanor, but Martinez was unaffected by someone trying to rouse him like they were trying to wake him for fire watch.

The Human hadn't stood fire watch since he became a Doc; the Marines had granted him that waylay of responsibility since he was constantly patching them up. So when Kyroll tried that tactic, Martinez treated it like one of them was being an asshole—curling up and telling him to fuck off.

After Martinez had freaked out and dove into a fighting position in his skivvies, Kyroll chuckled at the sight of someone so close to his species preparing to fight specters. Kyroll likely would do something similar—if the Human was bold enough to try.

In retrospect, Martinez could admit that the situation as a whole was somewhat comedic; the sight of him clutching a bolt action knee-deep in the snow, wearing nothing but his boxers, certainly would have made him laugh—if he had not immediately begun to shiver from the cold clawing goosebumps on his skin.

"So how much further is it?" Martinez asked at the end of a yawn.

Kyroll stopped for a brief moment and looked up at the hillside, then back down towards his datapad. "About another kilometer, we should be able to see where the Stags are eating and getting their food for the morning."

At least that was some good news. Martinez might be able to sit down and prepare some of the freeze-dried coffee he had brought along; thank God the Marines had given him that in their care package for him and Lysa.

Lord knew he had missed the sweet black ichor, and the jar in his bag was likely the only source of coffee within several light years.

"Lead on," Martinez replied, trailing behind Kyroll, who had already stepped off.

At least he was honest about how long it would have been; the rest of their journey only took half an hour before they were setting up in a small hide.

Moving shrubbery and digging down into the snow took only a few minutes. To Martinez's surprise, Kyroll showed some uncharacteristic patience, instructing Martinez on where to set up and how to conceal their position. Martinez had never been hunting, so this was all new, and he was willing to help where he could.

The suns had not yet crested the horizon by the time they had sat down into their camp chairs at the bottom of the small fighting position they had built. While yes it was meant to be a hunting blind, Kyroll had instructed Martinez to make it like one would a fox hole, but only half the depth.

They slumped down and looked out over the valleys below, resting their rifles on their backpacks between their legs.

The vista below them was quaint, pristine, and tranquil, likely undisturbed by sentient life for thousands of Standard years. It was an example of what nature and life were long before the GU considered Renoral a location to settle.

A glacial river ran east to west inside its western flank, spreading into a small river delta. Amidst the delta, thousands of trees and shrubs offered fantastic cover, concealment, and sustenance to any creature within the area.

Like the other plants within the region, these were built for the frigid temperatures that befall this region several months of the year. They were hearty and dark green even though many less resilient foliage had already been grayed and browned.

The sight reminded Martinez of sagebrush that you would find within the mountains in California, but at 300 meters, looking through binoculars, he could not tell precisely how similar they were. If they shot a stag and went to retrieve it, he could compare the plants then.

Where they were was very similar to those mountains. No matter how far you looked in either direction, the resemblance to Earth's mountains was uncanny. Slate-like rocks crumbled and cracked under the wind, barely clutching at their perches.

A kaleidoscope of colors peaked through the snow-coated hills, hinting at the thousands of metamorphic rocks below the frost. Other than his company, Martinez knew this was the type of place he wanted to live in one day: serine and unmolested by the expansion of sentient species.

With shivering hands Martinez fished from beneath his gear an old Human-issued MRE, one of the few he kept since moving. Inspecting the package, he couldn't help but smirk: menu number 12 beef stew.

Human MRE menu options have greatly expanded since Humans were a single-planet species and now include food from all over Mother Earth. But most Marines, Sailors, and Soldiers had their favorites—and ones to avoid.

Martinez enjoyed the things that were more American. Yeah, some of the MREs that were soups, canned meats, and other delicacies from more adventurous climates and pallets were good; they just weren't the same and didn't give him the feeling of being home.

The only menu item that Martinez liked more than good old 12 was 17 chicken tacos. However, calling those tacos was a bit of a stretch. There were tortillas, cheese, hot sauce, and spiced meat. But it was just not the same.

Yet what can you expect? MREs were shelf-stable for decades; the one he was about to eat was likely prepared before he was born. At least it was better than any of the GU MREs he had sampled when the Jericho was waiting on resupply from Earth.

He pulled the friction activator on the auto heater, laid it on the ground, and waited for it to heat up. While Martinez poured coffee crystals into his heating cup, Kyroll did the same, pulling out his breakfast and readying it.

Unlike Martinez, Kyroll was eating dried nuts and what looked like a bit of jerky, likely homemade by Nelya.

Martinez didn't know why you wanted to eat something so plain when he could eat some of the canned food from camp, but he wasn't about to ask.

After a few gulps of warm coffee had woken Martinez up, and he opened the simple Mylar bag to spoon a succulent morsel into his mouth, Kyroll surprised him. He willingly started a conversation. "Why are you insisting on trying here?"

"I'm sorry, what?" Martinez replied, setting his spoon down.

"Don't act like you didn't hear me," Kyroll growled.

"No, no, I did hear you. I just don't understand what you mean," Martinez replied before sipping his coffee.

Kyroll hung his head and looked down into his own cup, steam wafting off of it. "Why are you trying to make all of this work? I've made it evident I don't like you. But you are still here—I don't get it."

Martinez rolled his eyes. How could this man not understand that he was struggling through these interactions and was out in the woods with him because his daughter and wife cared about him and their getting along?

If it were entirely up to Martinez, they would cut him all out of their lives and never look back. The man doesn't seem worth the effort. Martinez cared about Nelya and Lysa and would suffer for them.

"Because you matter to my Ruh'ah. And dealing with you this way is the right thing to do. You might hate me and everyone who's not an Aviex. But I'm not like that; most Humans aren't," Martinez admitted.

Humans were just too new to the GU to have any long-standing grudges. But what the GU thought of the Aviex was beyond a grudge.

Now that Martinez had a full perspective of what the Aviex did, he could understand why so many in the GU hate the species. However, he firmly believes that forgiveness should be given and that one shouldn't be held to the sins of the Father.

That old lesson was something the entire GU needed to learn; Lysa, Nelya, Kyroll, and the whole Aviex species were not the ones who committed those atrocities.

The Aviex war was hundreds of standard years ago. Save for a few long-lived species, no one who would have fought in it is alive, and their grandchildren are likely not alive anymore. It was time for everyone to move on.

"I suppose you Humans are better than I am, at least that way," Kyroll sighed, scanning the valley with his two remaining eyes.

"What do you mean by that? I thought I was the only Human you knew?" Martinez asked, genuinely curious. Kyroll's answer might explain why the old Aviex had a Human Marine flag in his den.

"That's complicated," Kyroll replied, trying to rebuff the digging.

"Well, I figured. You are basically a walking enigma. So, just get to the point, man. No point beating around the bush here," Martinez insisted, not caring that Kyroll was attempting to deflect.

Kyroll tossed some jerky in his mouth as he pondered the idea of letting Martinez know a little bit more about the events of the past. What Nelya had told Martinez already was essentially forbidden knowledge. Why did Nelly have to tell him? If she had not, Kyroll might have had options to eliminate the Human.

Now? Not so much; there was only one option for those who knew the reality of the Aviex and the GU—unpersoning. Death was a solution, but that was just the start. His old Unit would erase him from existence.

Destroying his records would be easy enough. But the trouble Kyroll faced was Nelya and Lysa. How in all the universe could they accept that Martinez never came back? They would know too much—more than he could cover up or ask them not to talk about.

Kyroll knows he is a monster, a boogeyman lurking in the shadows of the GU. But could he kill his own family to hush up information? Could he stomach that? Pondering it, even for that brief moment, hurt more than any gunshot.

"I worked with one for a while. It wasn't for very long, but he was a good lad, fought like hell, and knew when to keep his mouth shut. But I was still subject to his rants and raves about trying to be nicer," Kyroll said, ending his sentence with a dry, raspy chuckle. "You might have given him a run for his money with your stubbornness."

"You'd be amazed how often I hear that I'm stubborn," Martinez replied.

"Likewise," Kyroll retorted, "Nelly tells me that the only thing more stubborn than myself is gravity."

Both of them chuckled briefly; it was something they could agree on. Kyroll was almost as stubborn as gravity, with Martinez coming in a close second.

"So you worked with a Human for a while; what did you guys do?" Martinez questioned.

"Nothing fun, kid. I understand you were in the military and had some time in combat; I did, too, but none of that prepared me for what went on when I was working directly for the Aviex government," Kyroll admitted, sipping at his drink. "Stuff like that never leaves you, and you can't leave it—at least my commander told me that."

Kyroll was not sure why he added that at the end. Was he essentially begging Martinez to leave? Was he trying something to avoid having to do what he had planned? The memory of Emil was not infecting his decision-making here—Right?

"My old lieutenant told us the exact opposite. Raleigh emphasized that when we were out of the military, away from combat, we needed to let it go and be ourselves for a while," Martinez replied, stuffing the empty food container into his trash bag and then into his rucksack.

"If I hadn't followed Raleigh's advice, I wouldn't have ever asked Lysa out. I'm glad that I did listen to him." Martinez finished by zipping his bag up and looking out into the valley.

Instead of immediately responding, Kyroll grunted and looked down at the valley, hanging up instead of using binoculars to scan slowly from horizon to horizon. Using the moment to ponder the idea that Martinez might not have to die without everything falling into place so perfectly.

It was almost tragic. If Raleigh had not told him that, the Human would have stayed clear of Lysa and out of this grim mess. But the die was cast, and Kyroll had to pick it up.

After he was confident that there were no Stags in the immediate area, he lowered the binoculars and continued to speak. "So, are you going to get out of the military?" Kyroll asked, aiming at alternative solutions.

"I mean, yeah, I will. I have Lysa and am able to start a career working fully in medicine. Don't get me wrong; I love the Marines and the sailors I worked with, but lately, I've been seeing other options. But—" Martinez started but paused, unsure of what he was going to say.

Martinez loved the Marines but couldn't fully quantify why he was ready to move on to a new life.

"But you did your time," Kyroll added. "Plenty of guys that I worked with did the same thing. A few of the ones you saw at my place did one or maybe two contracts, but then it was their time."

"Yeah, I suppose that's one way to put it," Martinez muttered, reflecting on his life up to this point and how much it had changed since arriving on Renoral.

Draun, Renoral, the Trauma Center, Lysa, his friends, and now Nelya and Kyroll had changed him; they gave him new perspectives on what mattered and essentially had given him a new lease on life.

When he was first assigned to Draun, he thought nothing of it; it was just going to be another assignment, another place to wait for the next deployment for the next war, but not anymore.

Yes, Martinez still had specters lurking within his dreams, memories that would gradually fade. But he no longer felt that yearning desire to return to the field, to return to fronts where his friends—no, his family—slowly but surely bleed out, be vaporized, and die in a war that they truly didn't understand.

But they were Marines, Sailors, Soldiers, Warriors. They had answered the call to a war the GU and Humanity had justified.

Martinez supposed it was time for him to face the reality that he was ready to move on. He admitted it to Kyroll, which he hadn't even done with Lysa. Maybe the old man was more of a kindred spirit than he initially thought.

That reflection pushed him further and made him think of the positives and negatives of what would happen if he decided not to go back; he could easily remain here on Renorall in Draun and never go back to Earth.

Many of the Marines always spoke of one day going back home and settling down, but there were those few who, once their contract was done, simply got off the ship at whatever port the ship stopped at.

His friend Dee was thinking of doing just that, jumping ship in Draun and settling on Renoral, so living here until he was old and gray was a prime option for the Corpsman.

Kyroll recognized the look in the young man's eyes all too well. Martinez was deep in thought and weighing his options. Kyroll had done that many times throughout his life: before leaving the military, before joining it, before becoming a security detail or Special Operations. Every man had to go through that thought process once or twice in life.

Kyroll bit his inner lip, the thoughts of what he had to do swirling like a dark vortex, nipping at his heart and soul, cracking what little amounts of it remained.

Even he had to admit Martinez was not a bad person by any means, in fact he doubted his initial worries as a father will hold any weight. Martinez was not the type of man to hurt Lysa, but that was not the issue here; it was what Nelya had told him.

Nelya knew, and no one was allowed to know that. They were both not supposed to know; Kyroll just happened to learn it and told her when she was angry about him always leaving.

Kyroll would rather keep those secrets buried in the darkness where they belonged. But what if Martinez had already told Lysa? That's just another loose end. And his fucking family, no less.

Martinez was a different story; Kyroll did not know him, didn't care about him; if it wasn't for Nelya or Lysa caring about this Vuric, Kyroll would have already taken him out back, shot him, and buried him deep.

It would have just been another body, another life snuffed, and someone else to be forgotten about. But Nelya and Lysa would know and would not stay silent.

The weight of their thoughts buried them throughout the rest of the day. Neither truly paid attention to the valley, the wind, the cold, or the snow; none of it mattered.

Both of these men of violence and resolve had to think about what they were going to do with one another.

Neither liked their realities.

MOONSHINE IN MOONLIGHT

Kyroll and Martinez's day flew by, which was surprising considering they never saw a single stag from their first hide or a half-dozen others they moved to and set up throughout the day.

There were some fleeting glimpses of other smaller creatures, but none they were after or that Kyroll was willing to shoot. That was a shame. One of the animals they spotted was called a Eurila; it was a fat-looking bird that reminded Martinez of a chicken, other than its bright blue and green plumage and the fact that it had four wings.

Kyroll insisted they were in their mating season and should not be shot for the time being. If there were any stags around, the rifle fire would send them running. Martinez had no frame of reference regarding the mating season part but could understand the later warning.

In the right conditions, rifles like theirs could be heard firing for dozens of kilometers, so it was better not to risk it.

By the time they returned to camp, they were under the light of half a dozen moons orbiting Renoral. The hike down from the hills was deathly silent. Neither spoke, neither had fully grappled with their strife.

Martinez still could not fully trust Kyroll. Too many things raised red flags over the trip: The duffle bag, his treatment of Lysa, and the forced, almost plastic way he acted. None of it added up.

Kyroll knew what he had to do, and with them only being out here for one more day, he had to decide what he was going to do. Could he trust Martinez to keep his mouth shut? Was the risk worth it? How would he explain this to Nelya and Lysa? Could he even return to them after ensuring Martinez's knowledge dies with him?

As Martinez lit a fire, Kyroll secluded himself inside his tent, leaving the Human alone. While Kyroll dug inside the tent, likely changing his socks and underwear, Martinez poked and prodded at the fire.

He looked at the lake and wondered why those beautiful little insects had not returned. It was only then that Martinez remembered Kyroll had not retrieved that metallic orb. Was that thing some kind of insect repellent?

If it was, that was disappointing; having those cherubic orbs dancing on the glass-like lake would be a pleasant addition to the area and add a little life to the otherwise overbearing darkness just beyond the flickering firelight.

After Martinez had sat stationary long enough for the cold fingers of winter to crawl into his boots and claw away any warmth, Kyroll joined him at the fire. He groaned loudly, his knees cracking louder than the firewood as he lowered himself into his chair.

"Here," Kyroll said, extending his hand across the fire, clutching a bottle of a clear liquid. "It's some homemade liquor."

"You are offering me a drink?" Martinez raised a brow.

"Well, yeah, Vuric. It's not like I stuttered," Kyroll shook the bottle.

Martinez could not help but feel like he was being set up here. Kyroll had pulled that bottle out of the duffle bag that other Aviex had passed off to him, and Martinez had yet to get a good look at its contents. For all he knew, that bottle was filled with acid.

"Sure, but after you. It's your bottle; you should get the first drink," Martinez said, insinuating some abstract tradition.

With a slight narrowing of his two remaining stacked eyes, Kyroll glared suspiciously at Martinez. After analyzing Martinez, Kyroll shrugged, uncapped the bottle, and took a swig deep enough that it made Martinez's spine shiver, imagining the burning liquid sliding down his throat. But Kyroll simply inhaled sharply before exhaling and reextending the offer.

"See no poison," Kyroll coughed.

"I never said it was," Martinez argued, grabbing the bottle.

"You didn't have to. Your face said it all," Kyroll shrugged. I've done that before, but I could not get away with it here—it would be too obvious, and Nelya would kill me."

"Don't forget about Lysa. She would peel your dick like a banana," Martinez quipped.

"Banana?" Kyroll replied, tilting his head in confusion.

"It's a fruit," Martinez replied, gasping after sipping the burning liquid.

The liquor was nothing special, but it was nothing weak by any means. It was more potent than vodka and just as tasteless. God, how do people drink like this?

"Do you have anything to mix it with?" Martinez asked, passing the bottle back.

"Nope. What, are you too good to drink it straight?" Kyroll challenged before taking another sip, but this time, it was far less exaggerated. "Just enjoy that I'm sharing this with you at all. Normally I would have just kept it all to myself."

"I never said that but just drinking straight booze is usually not my style, plus I have had some issues in the past," Martinez admitted.

Raising an eyebrow, Kyroll keenly plucked apart what he knew about the Human and what he understood about warriors who fell to the drink. He was not confident about what Martinez meant by issues, but the insinuation was obvious.

Seeing Kyroll's mocking look, Martinez took another steadying drink. "Shut up, like you are perfect."

Martinez could have used many words to describe the next half hour: unexpected, strange, perhaps out of the blue, but in all honesty, the most poignant descriptor was surreal.

Kyroll was not acting like the man that Martinez had come to know over the last three days. The old Aviex was actually pleasant company. Kyroll regaled Martinez with tales of when he was just a young lad and first joined the military—his time in boot camp, advanced infantry training, and all the way up until he joined Aviex special forces. At that point, the conversation quickly drifted for reasons Martinez understood—most people in that line of work are tight-lipped.

Martinez had to admit the Human and Aveix training experiences were comically similar: screaming drill instructors running endless upon endless drills and tests, weeks of never-ending marches, and non-stop corrections of the slightest error. Apparently, looks weren't the only thing that the two species had in common.

As they continued to drink and relax with one another, the moons rose higher into the sky. Martinez started to believe that Kyroll had finally broken down and relented, having finally admitted to himself that unless something soiled Martinez and Lysa's relationship, the Human was here to stay.

"So tell me, what exactly do you feel about my daughter?" Kyroll questioned, steepling his fingers and leaning forward. "Considering the conviction you've shown, I'm a little curious."

That question was a shift in the left field, which Martinez never expected. Kyroll giving Martinez the dad talk right after telling him about how some of his soldiers once got lost while out in liberty and ended up drunk and naked in another city was a bit of tonal whiplash.

Martinez, of course, had heard about fathers interrogating a potential suitor while cleaning a weapon. It was a staple in hollow flicks. Some of the Marines Martinez knew had done just that with their daughters.

But given Lysa and Kyroll's distance, Martinez assumed they would have forgone this almost cliche conversation.

Casting his gaze towards the serine lake Martinez pondered the idea for a moment, not because he was unsure of his answers but because he needed to gather the words and string them together in a way that would not piss off any father.

No father wants to hear: oh, your daughter has a nice ass, I want to eat chocolate off her abs, or how watching her break alien bones while in a fight turns him unreasonably on. Martinez might be dense, but he was nowhere near that stupid.

"I think Ruh'ah is one of the gentlest, most caring people I know. Yeah, her sense of humor can be cruel at times, but she never crossed any lines with anyone," Martinez started but paused to gauge Kyroll's reaction.

For his credit, Kroll kept his cards close to his chest, not flinching or looking as though he was dissatisfied with the conversation piece. He was stalwart as Martinez expressed his feelings for Lysa.

Martinez sighed and scratched the back of his head slightly; this next portion was just a little bit awkward, even though Kyroll undoubtedly would understand. "She is amazing, if I was going to put it simply. She's helped me through some rough spots at work and some personal problems. She was right there with me through it all, pressing me on. And since we started staying over together more often, I have had way less nightmares, which is something I enjoy."

As Martinez spoke that time around, he was intently watching Kyroll to see if he could spot any indications of a reaction to him mentioning Lysa or their intimacy. Through the dancing shadows and Kyroll's hands concealing most of his face, it was difficult to spot, but there was a twinge, a slight flicker, and an unmistakable change in his eyes.

Guilt replaced his usual stoney visage and lingered there for several seconds. Martinez continued to speak and compliment Lysa in every way he possibly could.

Kyroll's shoulders slumped and sagged further and further with each compliment Martinez gave Lysa, praising how wondrous and magnanimous she was. It was like each word weighed down on him, and crushed his soul.

After Martinez had finished, they sat there in silence, Kyroll watching the fire crackle and pop, flames dancing with sparks fluttering away, joining the cacophony of starlight above. In contrast, Martinez wondered if Kyroll was not a cold-blooded killer.

There were a few Marines Martinez knew who had not changed after the strife and tribulation the forges of combat had sent upon them. Perhaps Kyroll was the same.

"Hey, are you all right?" Martinez asks, picking up on Kyroll's look of woe and clearly pondering his family. "You seem different whenever I mention Lysa or Nelya. Is something on your mind?"

Kyroll bit his tongue, his spine straightened, and his muscles flexed, readying to fight like he was caught in an ambush in some dark alley on Heavalun.

Martinez's acknowledgment meant one of two things to the old veteran: that he was dangerously sharp for someone who was just some knuckle dragger and that Kyroll was getting sloppy.

Maybe the years away from work caused him to be out of practice and unable to keep himself composed. The booze might also have something to do with it, but he doubted it was that.

This Vuric, something about Martinez dug under his skin, stabbed into him like a knife, and fileted him open, leaving his emotions and thoughts to bear. It was like the Human could read his mind.

A sudden reflection, a thought, surged forth in Kyrolls mind: the whispers of someone he had not thought of in nearly a decade resurrected from the deepest point of his mind— the only other Human he had ever known.

Emil.

He recalled Emil's rants and raves about his desire to be better, an outstanding friend, ally, husband, and warrior all at once. Back when he was subjected to those talks, Kyroll thought it was nothing more than the rantings of a madman, someone who didn't know what they were genuinely asking for and had no semblance of reality.

Emil was ignorant and didn't see the darkness that awaited him while on the team. The stupid Human's optimism would be crushed after a deployment or two.

But he never did change—quite the opposite. Emil changed the team. His thoughts infected the team Kyroll had spent years cultivating, selecting, and preparing for the rigors of what was to be expected of anyone working for the Aviex government.

One by one, the team all resigned, having learned from Emil there was more to life than never-ending combat and snuffing the lives of those who had learned too much.

Even Kyroll fell for Emil's advice to support Nelya and the soon-to-be-born Lysa. Back then, he did it without question; all it took was telling Kyroll to be with his wife, to love life and what he had.

Why are Humans like this? What was going on? Kyroll couldn't put it into words or dredge up what was crawling through his mind and digging at the chipped, cold heart in his chest.

Fucking Humans, they just did something to him. They dig into him, crawl across his skin, and change him. No, they change everyone around them.

"I'm alright," Kyroll said, hoping to end this conversation and these strange effects. But just like Emil, Martinez was relentless.

"Bullshit, it's obvious something is bouncing around in your grape. Just say it," Martinez insisted.

They held each other's stares, neither willing to be the first to break contact. Each was stubborn and bull-headed. But as Kyroll looked at Martinez through the flickering fire, he didn't see his daughter's Ruh'ah; he saw Emil smiling and jokingly telling him to calm down and relax, assuring him that no one wanted to hurt him.

"Fine," Kyroll growled, disturbed by Martinez's insistence and eerie similarities to a man he knows is long dead. It was funny, almost as if Emil was getting one final laugh out of his stubborn friend's strife, just through this other Human. "It annoys me that you and Lysa have what Nelly and I couldn't when we were young."

"Wait, hold the fuck up. You, Kyroll, great warrior, special forces commander, and spy, are jealous of your daughter?" Martinez said exaggeratedly, emphasizing the magnitude of titles Kyroll once held by gesturing high to heaven.

Kyroll grumbled and tried to think of what to respond with, but

Martinez was right; he was jealous. He was almost vindictive that Martinez was there for his little Huntress in a way he never could be or could have been. Between work, trying to protect her and how shaded his past was, it was never an option. He never could have been forward with her, unlike this Human.

"Come on, brother, you should be happy for Lysa. She's healthy and has plenty of friends. We agree to go to a fertility clinic to get some groundwork for us moving forward together. How would you be jealous of any of that? That's perfectly healthy and normal?" Martinez questioned, leaning back and genuinely not understanding why Kyroll would ever feel that way.

Perhaps it was because Martinez had only ever known being in a relationship with Lysa, but still, this didn't seem like something one should be jealous of, especially of one's daughter.

Kyroll gripped his pants hard, trying to stay composed. At this point, he was treating Martinez as if it was just Emil on the other side of that fire, calling him on his bullshit and telling him why he was lying to himself and everyone around him to keep himself in his little Happy Box.

"Because she's my baby girl, my little Huntress," Kyroll hissed through his teeth.

Martinez responded just as Emil would have in the past. "That doesn't change anything. The fact that you still think of her as your daughter and she wants you to be her father will help you be better with Lysa. All you have to do is try with her."

Stars damned it, why are Humans so damned stubborn, and why did they always seem to have an answer for everything.

"You just don't get it!" Kyroll snapped, standing and pointing at Martinez vindictively, trying to shut out the Human's prodding.

The sudden outburst surprised Martinez, causing him to flinch and raise his hands. He expected Kyroll to jump over the flames and attempt to flog him; neither moved for several seconds, both gauging the other's reaction.

"I'm going to go take a piss," Kyroll said, turning around to escape this scenario.

Before Martinez could respond, Kyroll made it near his tent and paused, looking at the closed flap and then back at Martinez. He opened his mouth about to speak but shut it, shaking his head before vanishing into the overwhelming gloom, leaving Martinez alone.

That pause and hesitation distracted Martinez from the perceived propinquity he and his would-be father-in-law were building, thrusting him back to the reality that the older Aviex despises him.

Kyroll left Martinez alone, and his duffel bag was in that tent. It was time to settle things.

"You mother fucker, get out of my head," Kyroll groaned, slamming his head against a tree hard enough that blood oozed from an open wound, getting deeper with each strike.

Emil and Martinez, why did they both have to make everything so complicated? Normally, this would be easy.

Get the target to trust you enough to get close, drug them up, then dump them somewhere or orchestrate some other method for their demise. It was no different than getting Recaf.

"But why does deciding to kill this one have to be difficult," the old Aviex muttered, leaning his head against the tree.

Kyroll thought back to all he had done, the people he had killed, the missions undertaken, and the names he had erased from history. They were all easy: a quick pull of a trigger, stepping off VTOL, or a few black lines on paper.

Kyroll couldn't see him doing that to Martinez. Even if he erased everything about the Human, Lysa and Nelly would know, and they would have to be dealt with.

No matter how he tried to justify or logic the issues away, Kyroll simply couldn't figure out how he could kill Martinez.

He could try to lie to himself that keeping the Aviex history under wraps is for the greater good of the universe. That didn't work, so what if someone else knew he knew, and Nelly knew, and neither of them were supposed to?

Martinez was trying to take away his dear little daughter. He was hardly a father to Lysa, but without Martinez, there was no chance he could ever be a father to her. Everything Martinez said was true; without Martinez's approval, Lysa disappeared.

Kyroll slumped into the snow, lying on his back, and looked up at the starry night sky, sighing. "Dammit, Emil, even from the grave, you're still right."

Kyroll lay there until he eventually surrendered to the reality that he had to be better for the sake of Nelly and Lysa. He thought back to one of the last things Emil tried to teach him: You can't fight and kill everything. Too many things need acceptance, care, and nurturing in love.

"Fine, Emil, you goddamn win," Kyroll grumbled.

He would ensure Lysa, Nelya, and Martinez were happy and safe. Slinking back to his feet, he started stepping back towards camp, wanting to start again and truly make this strange life work.

He would start out with Martinez by returning to camp and extending a true gamut of peace. Kyroll just had to make sure Martinez could never see what was in that duffle bag.

> SECTION TWENTY-SEVEN

COYOTE CHEWING ON A CIGARETTE

"That son of a bitch actually was going to try to kill me," Martinez exclaimed, looking in sheer horror at the contents of Kyroll's duffle bag.

Martinez had some thoughts of what it might have contained, but nothing came close to this. The bag was essentially a kill kit you would see in the second-rate spy drama or some bad in the hollow flick: handcuffs, syringes, gloves, a jug of lye, bleach, a tarp, and some scalpels.

That was just what Martinez could immediately identify when opening the bag; there were dozens of technical marvels he had no concept of what they were for. The horrible reality that Martinez was facing only worsened when he dug past the tarp.

A knot formed in his throat, damn near gagging him when he realized what that taped-up plastic bag of gold and yellowish powder had to have been.

Visage.

How Kyroll, or anyone for that matter, was willing to use such a horrible substance was unfathomable. One whiff of this stuff, and you would forget the next several days, all while being so impressionable you would gladly chop your arm off if someone asked.

Martinez had seen plenty of people under the effects of this drug since working at the trauma center. None were ever stable, each usually near death or permanently maimed and often across to the other side of the Galaxy from where they were drugged.

If Kyroll had a chance to use this on him, Martinez could easily have woken up on the far side of the galaxy. But if Kyroll was willing to use a drug like this to silence him, there was no doubt that he would maim Martinez. Martinez likely would end up like Ruhinley: missing a limb, cold, and alone.

Pushing those dark thoughts aside, Martinez returned to the kit and continued looking through it. Just beneath the bag of Visage, there was another thing he did not recognize. It looked like wet granola shoved into a sandwich bag and soaked in oils.

But the colors were all wrong.

Instead of grays and browns, this was a mixture of deep reds, oranges, and purples. By look alone, it reminded him of wet cat food.

Whatever it was, it really didn't matter; it was going to get tossed out with everything else in this kit. Martinez was not going to give Kyroll a chance to use any of his preparations on him by scattering his equipment to the wind and booking it as fast as possible.

He could be home within a day or two; all he would have to do is manage to navigate back. Navigating back by hugging the roads would be easy enough, even if being in the semi-tundra would suck.

As quickly as possible Martinez draped one of the handles over his shoulder and fished the items out at random and began tossing them into the night, never to be found by Kyroll again.

Putting the kibosh on that horrible man's plan gave Martinez that warm and fuzzy feeling in his stomach. One, someone would only get it when they truly beat someone at their own game.

He hated to admit it, but Lysa was right about Kyroll being no good, and now that Martinez had given the man a chance, he felt like an ass and realized that even trying was a horrible mistake.

All was going well until Martinez grabbed hold of the bag of kibble-like substance. It squelched and exploded oily juices onto his hand, soaking the bag through. He gagged from the overwhelming rot and decayed overflowing from the substance; as quickly as possible, Martinez chucked it off into the woods, pulling in every muscle possible, and oil dripped into a slick trail from where he stood off into the darkness.

Just as he grabbed the Visage, Martinez was stopped by a firm grip on his wrist. "Martinez, stop!" Kyroll shouted, looking at Martinez in confusion and then down into the empty duffle bag covered in slick goo. "Do you have any idea what you've done?"

"Yeah, I stopped you from using this shit on me!" Martinez yelled, shoving Kyroll back and throwing the bag of Visage off into the pond before turning back around and then glowering at the older man, looking flabbergasted at him.

"Not that you stupid Vur---" Kyroll started but groaned and collapsed to the ground when Martinez brought a firm kick straight into his crotch.

"Shut the fuck up, you sociopath," Martinez barked while Kyroll collapsed down and tried to stay steady with one hand, a task that was nearly impossible as he began to vomit, spewing bile, alcohol, and food slop in the snow.

As a man, Martinez felt the slightest twinge of sympathy for Kyroll. No one likes getting hit in the nuts, after all. But as a realist, he could not have cared less; a nutshot was the bare minimum that he deserved.

Kyroll gagged and attempted to look up towards Martinez. His hollow, red eyes were vapid, looking as if he deserved what he was getting and accepted it.

The older Aviex looked pathetic, and rightfully so. Anyone willing to use those drugs as a weapon was an enemy, and the Marines had taught Martinez what you do with enemies: you give them no quarter—and make them submit.

Martinez stepped forward to enjoy giving Kyroll what he deserved—a firm ass-kicking. "Get up!" he challenged.

Kyroll tried to get to his feet, pressing up and out of the snow, but the moment his legs found an unstable purchase beneath him, Martinez drove a kick into the hunched man's diaphragm, knocking him back into the frost.

"I said get up!" Martinez barked before stomping down onto Kyroll's back. Martinez's hefty size twelve boot cracking the man's rib was audible through the night.

Martinez quickly removed his foot and let Kyroll try to stand up—the keyword was try. No matter how the older man attempted to scramble away and regain his composure or however many times he broke his lips and attempted to mutter more lies, a swift boot, fist, or shove was given as an answer, keeping him on the ground, and adding uncountable contusions to his body.

"Come on, is this all you can do? Weren't you going to try to kill me?" Martinez roared, demanding a challenge from the man.

"I don't want to fight you," Kyroll managed to squeeze through his teeth after recovering just enough from a hit, but he was still on all fours in the frost. "You have to listen to me."

If anything, his pleading made the situation worse, turning Martinez's treatment from punishment to cruelty. That Kyroll did not want to fight back earned him a swift boot straight into his face, leaving an imprint across his forehead and cracking his nose like an egg, blood pouring out and into the snow, mixing with the vomiting and bile.

"I don't have to listen to shit from you," Martinez yelled while stepping off to the side a moment before driving a soccer ball kick straight into Kyroll, several of his ribs buckling and snapping underneath the force, leaving him supine and gasping like a fish out of water.

"You know I was more than happy to give you a fucking chance for the sake of your wife or your daughter," Martinez started as Kyroll lay there gasping for air. "But now I don't care anymore," Martinez continued, placing his boot firmly atop Kyroll's chest and grinding it against his ribs. "But you—you just had to not even extend a fucking olive branch back."

Despite the apparent amount of pain Kyroll was in, he hadn't even yelped once as Martinez thrashed him. Maybe it was a matter of adrenaline coursing through him, or Kyroll was legitimately just that much of a hard ass.

Either way, Martinez didn't have any of it.

Martinez pushed more weight onto his foot atop Kyroll's chest, leaning in closer.

Air escaped Kyrolls lungs as the weight on him increased, making breathing all but impossible. "Unlike you, I'm not just going to kill someone and think that solves all of my fucking problems. But don't get it twisted here. I am not above hurting you."

Kyrolls gripped Martinez's calf and pushed, alleviating the slightest amount of pressure, but he still made no attempt to fight back; he just kept himself breathing.

This was different from how Martinez pictured a confrontation between them. Yeah, Martinez was a decent fighter, But Kyroll was a former Special Forces operator and had more combat experience than Martinez could fathom. Kyroll was almost double his age but still should be able to put up a fight; it shouldn't be a one-sided beatdown. Something was off here. But in Martinez's sadistic rage, that thought did not register.

Before Martinez could ponder the idea further, Kyroll lifted his leg just enough so he could croak out his warning.

"Run Away!"

"Run? Run from what, you? Or is there something else out here that you also planned to try to kill me?" Martinez replied, gesturing around himself into the darkness and re-engaging his hold on Kyroll. "Are your friends out there ready to blow my brains out now?"

Before Kyroll could elaborate on the dangers present, a roar as loud as a jet fighter echoed through the night, shaking the timbers and rattling both to the core.

"From that," Kyroll assured, using the lapse in Martinez's focus to slip out and lever up from the ground, taking the chance to spit blood and a broken fang out his mouth. "That bag of Brigal rang the dinner bell."

"For what?" Martinez replied, rushing past the fire to retrieve his rifle, understanding that an animal is often more dangerous than a sentient—at least in a pinch.

Kyroll hoisted himself out of the snow, every muscle screaming and in agony, and began to limp to his tent to grab his rifle."Any Milurt within several days' walk," he answered plainly, not wanting any embellishment to make the danger they were in any less evident. It also helped because just breathing at this point was agony.

Kyroll wanted Martinez to feel like he wasn't much of a threat anymore and thusly took the thrashing he gave him. But in retrospect, with that bag of Brigal having been opened? He should have actually fought back, but either way, they still would be in the same situation, and if he had fought, they both would be wounded messes, not just him. So it did not matter.

"So what, were you going to feed me to that thing?" Martinez said, checking for a round in the chamber. Upon seeing the small orange straight-wall caseless round, he sent the bolt home and continued to scan for wherever that roar came from.

Kyroll shrugged, knowing there was no point in explaining the details of the plan he had given up on. If they made it through this, he could explain his thought process to Martinez, but he knew very well that was a big if. For now, survival was the only thing that mattered.

Limping as quickly as his battered body could, Kyroll moved past Martinez toward the trail leading to the truck while leaving the majority of his gear where it lay. They wouldn't need it, and gathering it would take too long."Come on, we need to go."

Martinez shot his hand out and grabbed Kyroll's shoulder, earning him a venom-filled glare."You must be high if you think I'm following you anywhere."

"I'm not high, and you will follow me if you want to live," Kyroll argued, rolling his shoulder free of Martinez's grasp, continuing down the path, and starting a slow jog.

The millisecond, Martinez's hand was wrenched from Kyroll's shoulder, a roar louder than the first vibrated his teeth; looking off into the distance, Martinez couldn't see hide nor hair of what was creating those whaling roars.

But more joined the first two and quickly became a defiant chorus. Like watchmen on an old bastion's front, one after another rose up, calling for violence; the cacophony shook the bows, each new tone announcing they had joined the hunt.

Before long, Martinez couldn't even tell one from the other. There were dozens of them, likely stretching out hundreds of kilometers, all answering the call to find the liquid soaking his skin.

Deciding that survival was more important than their fight, Martinez pivoted and followed as quickly as possible. "Can't we scare them off like last time?"

"It wouldn't work," Kyroll plainly replied. "Any of that Brigal would have alerted them to kill anything nearby."

Hearing that, Martinez paused, his heart as still as a statue while he looked down at his right arm glistening in the dim moonlight; his heart sank like a stone, understanding fully what Kyroll had just told him.

"I'm covered in it," Martinez admitted.

Without even looking back to confirm, Kyroll took Martinez's words as gospel and accelerated from a jog into a full-bore run, his wounded body moving as quickly as possible as the wan moonlight would allow. "Double time Doc, we have to move."

TACTICAL RETREAT

They barreled through the icy forest, Martinez and Kyroll pressing their bodies to the limit. The frozen air stung like knives with each breath, cutting into their throats and lungs. Each step was as calculated as possible as they rushed through the thick bows with the dim moonlight glittering overhead.

"Faster," Kyrolll shouted just after the pursuing beasts knocked over several trees, the heavy thooms, roars, and snapping wood timing the creatures' approach.

"No shit," Martinez heaved, struggling to keep pace with Kyroll.

It was unbelievable. Despite Kyroll limping and having just received the flogging of a lifetime, he was still setting the pace for their retreat and not even breaking a sweat. Martinez knew it wasn't because of any preternatural ability of the Aviex because they were almost identical to Humans.

Kyroll was just that much of a stubborn mule. Even with all of those injuries, fractured ribs, and likely inconceivable pain, he still was putting the young Human's abilities to shame.

The last kilometer of the run was undoubtedly the easiest part of the night if you could call fleeing bear-like aliens in the dark, while wounded, in the snow, and covered in a scent that easily attracts them.

Now that the duo reached the winding foothills, the terrain became more unpredictable. The snow and rocks crunched under each football, slowing their dead sprint to an agonizing crawl.

None of this would do; they were moving too slowly, and the enemy was gaining on them too quickly. One of them was more than willing to take a stance to make it back home and protect his family in the only way he knew.

Whipping around, Kyroll aimed up the hillside, hoping to delay the Milurt with some precision fire or at least harass the overly intelligent animal, warning them to keep away. "Keep moving," he yelled as Martinez passed him.

"You had better follow," Martinez replied, doing as he was told and continued to rush through the verdant pines.

With his fields of fire clear, Kyroll aimed his rifle and peered through the thermal optic. It did not take him long to find his first target: the chilly backdrop and the warm blood flowing through the Milurt made it easy to see them.

Dozens of massive creatures glowed white hot against the vanta black background projected in his scope. The Milurt weaved in and out of the trees, hiding amidst the thicket, roaring their hatred and desire to destroy anything in their path.

With a steady hand, Kyroll curled his finger on the trigger and began to release slack. Slowly but surely, as his breath released, so did the millimeters keeping the rifle's fury at bay. Once his lungs were empty, he fired.

The old Parucian eight-millimeter rifle gently pushed against his shoulder and clapped like thunder. The slug splattered against the horror, white-hot spawling cascading off the creature's armor-like hide, similar to what one would see when a tank round ricochets off another's armor.

Kyroll knew the rifle had no chance of killing a Milurt unless he managed to get lucky enough to shoot right down its mouth and hit several of its five hearts or sling a few salvos into the creature's soft underbelly.

But from where he was, all he had for targets was the thick hide. Knowing that his rounds might as well be spitballs, he followed up the first shot with three more in quick succession. After the first Milurt ate a few rounds, he switched to another target and repeated the process as quickly as the rifle bolt would allow.

Turning around and dumping the empty twenty-rounder on the deck, Kyroll felt pride swell in his chest, having seen several beasts avert their pursuit, tucking behind hardcover or moving away entirely.

Kyroll knew they would re-engage in a few minutes, but that damn well bought them several minutes they desperately needed.

Casting his gaze through the thicket, Kyroll was glad that Martinez had done as instructed. Only a fleeting glimpse of the Human could be seen through the bows. Kyroll decided to compliment the Human once this was all over.

Kyroll slammed a fresh twenty-rounder into the Magwell and dropped the bolt release.

A damn near orgasmic metallic clang rang out when the round chambered as he took off to catch up with the little hunter.

Careening through the trees, leaping over logs, and swerving through the thicket, Kyroll could not help but crack a wide, vicious grin.

Gods above this was the rush he had missed.

Working as a lumberjack for the last decade might have kept him fit and pockets filled, but that job's supposed dangers were nothing compared to the ecstasy of combat.

No drug could compare to the sheer rush of bounding, maneuvering, concealing, and scanning in the high-speed dance of death, where any heartbeat could be your last. The only thing between you and the reaper punching your time card is a few millimeters and one wrong move.

Kyroll even had Martinez around, who was likely more than willing to help him fire at the Milurt.

Basking in the thrill of finally having something threaten him, Kyroll neglected to remember the most critical part of combat: that you had to be perfect. All the rust he had built up over the years of not flexing his warrior muscles caught up to him in his moment of bliss.

As Kyroll leaped over a patch of bramble, one of the thorny vines reached up and snared his ankle, pulling him to the ground. His broken rib slammed into a protruding rock, causing a wave of agony to crash through him like a tsunami.

If not for his face burying into the rocks and snow, filling his mouth with coarse grit, Kyrolls scream of agony would have eclipsed gunfire.

As he tried to stand, Kroll attempted to call out to Martinez to shoot the Milurt while he caught up, but only another scream escaped his lips. As soon as he put weight on his ankle, it shattered like glass contorting to an unnatural angle, bone popping from the flesh.

Looking ahead, Kyroll could not see a sign of Martinez anywhere near. The Human had likely almost made it to the truck by now.

"Fuck me," Kyroll muttered, accepting he was alone.

After all of his training, Kyroll would not mope or sit idly by, especially now that his body was in tatters; there was no point in denying reality. He took a deep breath and focused, ignoring his heartbeat thumping in his ears and the fire-like pain erupting from his entire body.

With one arm and his good leg, Kyroll crawled away from the bramble, gaining distance—just enough that he should be able to get one round off when a Milurt arrived.

Aiming with his rifle propped on his knee, Kyroll waited, knowing the end was here. He had written dozens, if not hundreds, of post-mortem commendations with a similar beginning to what he was doing: A lone warrior staying behind and giving it all to fight until his last breath, allowing others to retreat.

The nearby trees cracked and snapped as the dozen animals flowed down the hillside like an avalanche, all to rip Martinez and him to shreds.

Thinking about the Human, Kyroll chuckled, wholeheartedly understanding how much Humans had changed him. Before meeting Emil or Martinez, Kyroll would have called what he is doing now stupid and a waste of effort.

But somewhere down inside his soul, he knew this was the right thing to do.

Kyroll silently prayed to whatever god would listen to an old, cantankerous monster like himself. He begged that Nelya, Lysa, and even Martinez would live well and that they would understand the only thing he could do for them to make everything alright at this point was to die.

Martinez was a good man who would care for them in his stead.

With no warning, a firm hand gripped Kyrolls' shoulder as Martinez slid in and began to speak: "Don't worry; I'm going to get you out of here."

"What are you doing? Leave me here, you idiot," Kyroll groaned, barely able to speak.

"Not happening," Martinez replied, quickly noting Kyroll's injuries. This task was frustrating in the dark. Martinez would give anything for some night vision or the flashlight he had left at camp.

"No, it is, you idiot," Kyroll barked, trying to push Martinez away and interrupting the Humans' triage.

Martinez angrily shoved Kyroll's hands away and continued his observations, being used to triaging Marines insistent on returning to the fight despite their injuries. Kyroll was similar enough that the standard Doc tough love would do.

What was visible made Martinez's stomach churn.

Kyrolls foot was touching his calf, and based on his sputtering gags, he likely had a punctured lung. That was bad enough, but Martinez knew there were innumerable more minor wounds he could not see under moonlight alone.

Martinez clicked his tongue, fully accepting that the situation was beyond fubar.

With no real options and Kyroll being moronic and still fighting him, Martinez chose to rely on the good old Doc attitude mentality, and he would do what needed to be done to save the wounded—even if that man did not want to be saved.

"This is going to hurt like hell, so grit your teeth," Martinez began stepping between Kyroll's legs and squatting.

"Hey, hey, what the fuck are you going to do," Kyroll protested. "I'm a lost cause here."

"I'm going to save you. Now be a good patient, shut the fuck up, and let me be a Corpsman," Martinez ordered, having had enough of Kyroll's bullshit about leaving him here.

You usually would never fireman carry someone who has broken ribs; that is just begging for a punctured lung or more than just a mere fracture. But Martinez was alone and did not have the time to make a stretcher or drag sled—so Kyroll would just have to tolerate being manhandled and rushed to the hospital after they were safe.

Being in pain was better than death, after all.

"Go damn it, leave me," Kyroll started but stopped and yelped when Martinez hoisted him over his shoulders like he weighed nothing.

"Stop complaining and let me work," Martinez grumbled, beginning to step off.

"What part of don't, do you not understand?" Kyroll badgered, instinctively pushing a palm into Martinez's lower back to support it.

"All of it, I'm a goddamn Corpsman. I'm going to save you even if you don't want it,"

Martinez chuckled, stepping over an overturned log.

"We are going to be—" Kyroll began to argue, but Martinez stole his words.

"Slow? Yeah, I know. So do me a favor and shoot back at any of those things that come close. Because I'll tell you this: We're making it home. Nelya and Lysa are waiting—for both of us," Martinez emphasized as he moved from a simple walk to what was almost a jog.

Kyroll did not argue, not because Martinez was right about saving him and who was waiting at the far end; no, the little Hunter just decided to adjust key role again, driving his shoulder into his fractured ribs, causing him to cut any argument short.

Just as they reached the edge of the small clearing Kyroll had fallen in, one of the Milurt burst through the treeline, snarling as it searched for the oil soaking Martinez's arm. Without missing a beat,

Kyroll gestured the rifle roughly in the creature's direction and sent out a salvo of rounds.

Several managed to strike the target and deterred it from following. But just before Kyroll updated Martinez on what was happening, another burst forth from another angle and nearly barreled into them as he fired several more rounds, its maw only centimeters away from clamping down on Martinez.

"That sounded close," Martinez gasped. "Is all good back there?"

"Don't worry about it, just run faster," Kyroll yelled.

"Easy for you to say!" Martinez shouted as he listened to the man's instructions.

The rest of the run to the truck was very much the same. Milurt came within arms' reach, and Kyroll barely managed to keep the animals at bay. While Martinez tucked them in and around the trees, avoiding thicket and ice slicks, he only stumbled and nearly ate it a few dozen times.

Martinez had not slowed in the slightest as he pushed every fiber of himself to save the man who was planning on killing him.

By the time they reached the truck, Kyroll was down to his last magazine, and the sound of the Milurt had lowered in intensity.

"Toss me in the bed," Kyroll shouted as he dumped the last of his magazine into one of the Milurt just a few feet behind them.

In a motion that was not graceful by any stretch of the imagination, Martinez slid on the ice and rolled Kyroll into the bed. The old man landed with a heavy thud and a pained groan, having fallen right on top of the ammo can filled with magazines. At least he knew where they were and could reload, as painful as that was.

Rolling himself into the truck's cab, Martinez frantically searched for the keys. After a few moments of overturning everything, he realized that Kyroll had them.

"I need the ke–" Martinez started, sticking his torso out of the truck to look back at Kyroll, but was stopped when one of the Milurt slammed into the side of the cab, snapping Martinez's arm in half between the door and frame.

Martinez's roar of agony was overwhelmed by the sounds of shattering glass and crunching metal. Thankfully, Martinez had winced; otherwise, the razor-sharp glass shards serating his face would have surely blinded him.

The impact caused the truck to list and nearly roll onto its side. But it just barely maintained its center of gravity and slammed back to the ground, rattling both Martinez and Kyrolls brains like eggs.

Though he was rattled, Kyroll levered himself back up to the bed's side, propped the rifle to its side like a gunnel, and fired at the creature before it entirely recovered. "Say that again Doc?"

"I need the keys," Martinez yelled, fishing his mangled arm from the swinging door.

Kyroll abated his gunfire momentarily, reaching into his pocket for the keys. Thank god they were still in there. As he turned to hand the keys over, a Milurt slammed into the cab, its massive head not quite fitting through the window.

From Martinez's point of view, the Milurt's split lips lapped and searched for him inside the cab, its thick drool falling onto his lap while he laid flat to avoid its maw.

Kyroll shoved his rifle through the broken rear window, muzzle thumping the Milurt in the eye. It exploded with blood and viscera before Kyroll ran the trigger like a man possessed, draining his entire magazine into its head.

To both his and Martinez's surprise, the Milurt jerked and grunted in pain as the rounds dug through its thick skull and buried in its brain. It spasmed and thrashed, trying to escape the window, but it was too late.

The massive animal breathed his last as Kyrolls bolt locked back.

Not having time to celebrate the little victory, Kyroll threw the keys inside, landing them on Martinez's chest. "Drive!"

"You don't have to tell me twice," Martinez groaned before he slammed the keys into the ignition and started the truck.

The old engine roared to life, and the wheels squealed while Martinez slammed his foot on the gas. The truck lurched forward, tossing Kyroll against the bed like a ragdoll, having not been braced for the movement.

As they pulled away, the Milurt's corpse fell free from the window, letting Matinez sit fully upright as they drove down the old icy road and away from the animals that Kyroll kept firing at until they could no longer be seen or heard.

After Martinez had driven several kilometers and had slowed down, Kyroll stuck his head into the cab, "You alright, Doc?"

"My arm is fucked," Martinez replied, tilting his head to the left, toward his fractured arm. "You?"

"Nothing you did not see already," Kyroll replied before pausing momentarily and smirking. "Thanks for not leaving me back there."

"Don't worry about it. It's my job. Besides, you had the keys."

HALF DEAD, WHOLE HEARTED

The drive out of the woods to Celna's hospital was absolute hell. Once Martinez and Kyroll had come down from their adrenaline highs, reality slammed into them like a sledgehammer.

In an instant, both went from alert and ready for a fight to absolutely exhausted and fading in and out of consciousness.

Luckily, both men had medical training and experience in high-stress environments and understood very well what they had to do in their predicament. Each had to ensure the other stayed calm and did not fall into shock.

To do this, they followed one of the basic tenets of medical treatment and first aid: keeping the patient talking.

Both understood that the conversation subjects did not matter. What mattered was that they kept communicating, keeping their minds occupied, and keeping themselves from drifting away into the darkness.

They started with prominent subjects, their military careers, aspirations, and family lives, but that could only last for so long. As the blood flowed, more arduous topics were no longer available to their cognitive abilities, so they changed to telling corny jokes and funny stories to one another.

Each lacked context to fully understand what the other was joking about or what some puns were; they had lost so much blood and were concussed so horrendously that they were more incoherently babbling to one another than properly delivering punch lines.

By the time Martinez had parked the truck and assisted Kyroll in limping through the emergency room doors, neither was speaking; just staying conscious took their entire holistic focus.

It was as if a wave of safety and serenity crashed into them and forced them to their knees. The second the nurse manning the desk realized they were there, all the fight flushed from their bodies in a euphoric wave.

Later, Martinez and Kyroll learned that the little Prinoral manning the desk screamed bloody murder and fainted when they stumbled up and looked like they died on the floor. From her point of view, two corpses had stumbled in and fallen upon her desk, muttering that they needed help.

The rest of the night and the following morning was a blur, filled with fading glimpses of nurses, doctors, X-rays, injections, and a million other treatments.

Both had to be rushed into emergency surgery for their injuries. Martinez's ulna and radial looked like they had been sent through a wood chipper, his forearm having swollen to the size of a balloon by the time he had made it into the OR.

Kyroll was in no better shape; if anything, he was far worse. That he was suffering from massive hemorrhaging was in no way a surprise; between his punctured lung and an open fracture, he was lucky to have survived as long as he had.

Given a few more minutes, the outcome of his survival very well could have changed for the worse.

Luckily, the GU's medical prowess and Celna's incredible familiarity with injured Aviex equipped them to keep Kyroll's heart beating and the lungs filling with life-sustaining fluids throughout his struggles—at least once they drained all the blood from his lungs.

Both Human and Aviex patients were expected to make a full recovery; they would just be stuck wearing casts for a few weeks and were prescribed a potent cocktail of painkillers, muscle relaxers, and nanite capsules.

Those nanite capsules were the blessing that ensured they would make full recoveries, taking the recovery and rehab time from months to days at most.

Unlike old Human medicine, neither would require pins and bolts or external framing to hold their bones together.

But like all things in the medical field, the nanobots are a give and a take. Having one's body forcibly stitched together from the inside was not pleasant by any means; it was painful to the point where most passed out repeatedly, but because of their hardy constitutions, stubborn as mule personalities, and the cocktail of medications, they were forced to take, they just needed bed rest for the next few days.

The following afternoon, they were both conscious, caught up on what had happened, and could be identified as more than just a pair of strange John Does who limped in during the darkness of night.

Once identified, their emergency contacts and the police were called.

Until told by a nurse, Martinez did not know who his emergency contacts were in the GU; as far as he knew, he didn't have any. Setting some up just never crossed his mind. If he did, he would have chosen Harnsis, the Director, and maybe even Chloe. At least then, some solid minds could handle his affairs while in the hospital.

The GU thought similarly to him. Shiksie was his primary emergency contact, but she'd never answered, no matter how much they attempted to reach her. Martinez was worried to learn that his mentor, of all people, wasn't answering her phone. It was so unlike her to not be Johnny on the spot for others.

Shiksie might not have made the best choices during their last interaction, but that didn't mean he didn't care for the woman; they were still friends, at least he hoped so. Had she abandoned him entirely? Or did something happen?

Harnsis, his secondary contact, did answer. The doctor was understanding and very professional about the situation and even made some recommendations to the doctors and clinicians here in Celna regarding Martinez's treatment and recovery plan.

It made sense that Harnsis did so; he was a Human expert in all but title. He had more experience working on injured Humans than anyone else on the planet save for Martinez himself, but while the Human was high on drugs, he was useless.

With all of that out of the way and a few more vacation days added to Martinez's leave to cover how long he would be in the hospital, Martinez was left alone in his hospital room, with nothing but the TV and the view of snow falling outside to keep him company.

For some reason, the sheriff decided that Martinez should not be allowed to use his datapad to contact Lysa or Nelya, insisting that he wished to speak to both Kyroll and the Human before they were allowed any exterior communications.

Martinez knew how well that would go over with Lysa. If she was on the warpath, it was bad enough, and if Nelya's past actions showed her cunning, open combat in the lobby was not out of the question.

No force from sentients or God could keep those two passionate women from what they wanted.

A short time later, just as Martinez started investing in trash daytime TV and the woes of the contestants on 'Dating My Mate's Mother,' there was a knock on the door and an announcement of the sheriff's presence.

Martinez had to admit the sheriff was not what he had expected it would have been coming through that door, not because they were outlandish or anything along those lines but because of how average they seemed.

Sheriff Shalala was a brown Farun'se who was just starting to show their age through gray fur around his snout, ears, and dull, tired amber eyes. That, coupled with his disheveled khaki uniform, completed a picture of a man who had been around the world twice and talked to everyone once.

"So, Mr. Martinez," Shalala said, briefly checking his datapad before looking back up towards the Human prone in the bed. "I hear you had a horrible night."

"That's one way of putting it," Martinez groaned, sitting up slightly while, watching as the sheriff closed the door and moved to a seat near the bedside.

Shalala lowered himself into the chair, grumbling as his joints cracked and popped, evidence of his wear and age. "So the nurses can't tell me much about what happened. Would you care to come in and fill me in?"

"Can I ask why you want to know? It seems odd that the police are investigating us," Martinez questioned, hoping to get some information on whether or not he needed to seek a lawyer or keep his mouth shut while in the presence of this officer.

Now, Martinez was not the most versed in legal-eez, but knew if one was being investigated as a criminal, you should shut up and let lawyers do the talking.

Shalala snorted like he was cutting off a laugh and smirked at Martinez, his radar dish-like ears fluttering while his tail swayed quickly back and forth. "Usually, you're right, but bear in mind this is a big but; we had two John Doe show up half dead. One was a class red, while the other is," Shalala explained while pointing a pen at Martinez. "Is a classification black, and what are the newest members of the Galactic Union? So this situation is a bit out of the ordinary, to put it lightly," he finished while twirling his pen in the air as if to enunciate the strangeness of the event.

"Sir, that really didn't answer my question. Why are you looking into this?" Martinez repeated quickly, picking up on the non-answer that the sheriff attempted to force down his throat.

The officer's ears drooped as he was perturbed by Martinez's asking the question at all. His eyes narrowed as he scanned every detail of Martinez, plucking apart each twitch, breath, and bead of sweat on the Human.

That was curious. Was that just a trait of the Farun' se species? Shiksie would do the same when questioned or asked something that made her truly have to think.

"Because this would not be the first time a hunting accident turned out to be a targeted attack on a red species—the Aviex especially," the sheriff said, almost sounding ashamed that anything had occurred in the past. "So I just wish to assure you that it is genuinely what this was."

Martinez clenched his entire body as his heart rate spiked; thank God it wasn't on a monitor; otherwise, the sheriff would have to read him like a book.

What should he tell the sheriff? That Kyroll was going to try to kill him after drugging and leaving him out in the woods? That girlfriend's father had illicit drugs and bait to lure in the Milurt? That Kyroll's friend was complicit in this?

An odd feeling conflicted Martinez as if two animals were attempting to reach the throat of one another inside his mind.

The Marines, Navy, and society at large would undoubtedly say to turn Kyroll in under the pretense that he was an unhinged man ready to commit murder. But Martinez was unsure; they had fought together at this point. Combat was a galvanizing experience that left one's true nature to bear—Kyroll did not seem horrible at this point.

Simultaneously, images of Nelya wailing as her family is ripped apart wracked his mind. Could he condemn Nelya to living poorly? And take away the man she loved, his flaws withstanding?

Along with the reality that he and Lysa made so much effort to connect to Kyroll, their relationship was the entire reason they were in Celna, after all.

Analyzing the sheriff, Martinez tried to gauge if the man already knew anything, trying to determine if he could tell if Martinez started to blow smoke up his ass. But that was a futile effort; this old Farun'se sitting across from him was about as easy to read as a brick wall.

With no way to tell whether the choice was sound, but deep in his heart, knowing it was correct, Martinez bent one of his core values to the point where it was mere moments from snapping by omitting the details of the truth.

Over the next hour, Martinez meticulously selected details of his relationship with Kyroll, Nelya, and Lysa and why he and the old Aviex were alone in the woods.

The sheriff made no indication of spotting falsities, simply nodding and asking for periodic clarifications, mainly cultural ones such as what Ruh'ah and Gra'hu meant, along with asking him to repeat some of the events that led up to the hunting trip.

Then came Martinez's forged lies. He was not one to lie, and when it was, they were small white ones that meant nothing. Because of this, keeping a story straight when the sheriff kept digging into him like he was in search of gold was not easy.

He must have done a satisfactory job, as the only thing Shalala asked was clarification on how they got away, clearly not believing that Martinez had carried the Kyroll while the older man provided covering fire.

"So, are you certain that's all that happened?" Shalala questioned, tapping his stylus on his data pad.

"Yes, sir," Martinez nodded, unsure about the intense glare the officer was giving him.

"You're certain you left nothing out?" Shalala half hissed, leaning in.

"Positive," Martinez nodded.

Shalala's nostrils flared, taking in the scents that the Human was giving off, which only made Martinez more nervous. Shiksie could smell anything on him, even if it was days later that roused the question.

What could this Sheriff pick up on?

Leaning back and tucking away his datapad, Shalala pulled out a second one and tossed it onto the table next to Martinez. "Alright, this is yours: don't worry, it's untouched. I didn't have a warrant to go through it. I just wanted to ensure I had both your stories before letting you have this back." The sheriff finished with the slightest smirk.

"Is that legal?" Martinez halfway croaked, pulling back the data pad.

"What, holding onto your property for the sake of what I was doing? Yes, that was legal. You're under investigation and technically detainment. I just didn't feel like putting cuffs on you," Shalala shrugged before standing and heading towards the door.

Before the older man reached the portal, he turned back around and glanced at Martinez. "If you do remember anything else, give me a call."

Martinez nodded as the officer exited and closed the door.

Before Martinez's heart had managed to calm down, he had opened his datapad, wishing to see if what the officer said was true. Not that he would be able to tell anything that was tampered with— still, there were plenty of nude pictures of Lysa he would rather not have on public record.

Instead of assured knowledge of tampering, he was met with an unholy amount of notifications.

Most were from Lysa and Nelya, asking if he was all right and requesting an explanation of why neither was on the emergency contact list; the doctors and nurses wouldn't let him see them.

Both used rather flowery verbiage to explain their gripes about not being someone he trusted. Martinez could explain Nelya—as wondrous as she was, he hardly knew her.

Lysa, however, could not explain, especially from an Aviex point of view, where sleeping with someone means you love them and want kids.

He made a mental note to ask the nurse to let them see him. Interacting with those two bubbly souls would make him feel immensely better. They were the best women in his life, after all. The other notification was more unsettling.

Why did Chloe message him?

Martinez's throat dried when he opened the message and felt his heart sink.

Chloe: Hello there, Henry. I heard you were injured. I hope you get well soon. Oh, and whenever you are back in town, let's get lunch. I'm so tired of you being such a stranger.

The thought of how Chloe would pour those venomous words made Martinez nearly gag.

If Martinez could avoid that vile woman until the day he died, he would be rapturous, but clearly, she was keeping tabs on him. How was something he couldn't even grasp, mainly because he had only been in the hospital for less than half a day? But she knew where he was.

Hoping it was just Cloe being a bit neurotic, Martinez choked it up to the fact that Chloe was the truest definition of a spook he had ever met; Martinez did not want to reply and push the issue, deciding ignorance was bliss.

After reconciling Chloe's message in his mind, Martinez hailed a nurse and requested they let Nelya and Lysa in, wanting the best women in his life to visit him. Lord knew he wanted some good news at this point.

LICKING WOUNDS

Martinez was in the hospital under constant doctor and nursing staff observation for three days. For once, being a rare species was not a boon; usually, Martinez faded into the background or was only given a side-eye out of curiosity.

It was different here in Celna; every doctor wanted to swing by to poke and prod the strange alien in the bed and obviously speak with him and Dr. Harnsis over the phone about what makes Humans tick.

Hearing the never-ending influx of comments, compliments, and praise from Dr. Harnis while he prepared these doctors was genuinely sickening. Martinez was to the point where if he had heard one more question: oh, can you survive X or is Y reality, he was going to stab someone.

Luckily, the other two visitors during his stay kept him somewhat sane and didn't make him go stir-crazy.

It warmed Martinez's heart, knowing that Nelya and Lysa were happy to keep him company; Nelya and he chatted about books, helped Martinez study, and even played some cards.

She even ate lunch with him and brought some of her cooking along. That made him genuinely feel better; Nelya's blood and meat-based dishes cooking was far better than anything the hospital was forcing down his throat.

He knew the drab food was likely just an issue because the doctors honestly didn't believe everything he could eat, so they just opted to give him grayish gruel. Either way, having meals with substance was a godsend.

Unlike Nelya, who came and went, checking on both Martinez and Kyroll, Lysa essentially had to be dragged out of his room. She clung to Martinez for hours every day, eating, sleeping, and relaxing beside him.

The nurses provided her with a cot to use; they didn't want her sleeping in his bed for obvious reasons, but she never used it.

Initially, Martinez had assumed her clinginess had something to do with his being hurt, but nothing was off by far.

Typically, Lysa had reasonably solid control of her emotions; she had moments of looseness, such as when Shiksie attempted to seduce Martinez or when a particularly violent alien pushed her buttons a little too much. He might see an outburst from her at that point.

But under usual circumstances, she kept her emotions under control until she was alone and had the opportunity to express herself without worrying about anyone judging or belittling her for them.

It must have been at least a dozen times over the last few months that a particularly nasty customer or an event transpired on the streets of Draun. She would hold it in, suck it up until she got home, and would cry on his shoulder or get angry about it.

She never got wrathful at Martinez or anything, just at the world. But that was the typical way Lysa acted. These last few days, her emotions were as stable as the ocean during a hurricane.

The worst part about Lysa's seeming madness was that she had no idea why she was acting this way, which only caused further fits of crying and wailing.

Nelya was no help when Martinez finally had an opportunity to ask her alone; she just chuckled and chalked it up to her daughter being stressed and caring so much about Martinez.

That didn't seem to be the whole truth. Nelya and Lysa were similar in that they were both brilliant and cunning; Martinez refused to believe it could just be that. Between that coy smirk while answering and that when both of them were in the room, Nelya's gaze would land on Lysa just long enough that Martinez could see gears in her head spinning.

She knew something was happening and wasn't telling him for some reason. Martinez prayed it was nothing horrible—life had been arduous enough the last week.

At least the majority of that hectic behavior diminished by the time they made it back to Nelya's and Kyroll's home—not entirely, but mostly.

It was still damn near impossible to get Lysa to let Martinez go: be it drinking his blood and wanting to snuggle more than usual or dragging him to their bedroom to have some alone time. She was insatiable and unrelenting.

Despite Lysa's shifting demeanor, they were all attempting to enjoy their last bit of time before Martinez and Lysa had to return home.

Nelya, by some miracle, had managed to free Martinez from his Ruh'ah's clutches and was upstairs with her, currently going over some recipes and preparing dinner for everyone.

Simultaneously, Kyroll had invited Martinez downstairs into his man cave of sorts, with the obvious intent behind the gesture: to clear the air and decide where they stood—over a few drinks, of course.

Kyroll walked ahead and gestured to the chair for him to take a seat, "You want something hard or something a little less potent?"

"I'll have what you're having," Martinez replied, lowering himself in the chair, enjoying the plush satin surface on his bare arms, having opted to wear his PT clothes for the time being.

Martinez had given that answer because his knowledge of alien alcohols was limited, and he figured putting the ball into Kyroll's court wouldn't hurt.

"Suit yourself, but you might regret it," the old Aviex replied, pulling down several glasses and producing a bottle from underneath the counter.

Taking his time, Kyroll gradually poured each of them a drink on the rocks, mixing several different spices and garnishing them with some sort of purplish sliced fruit.

It was far more extravagant than what Martinez pictured the rough-and-tumble man to enjoy. But who was he to judge? Martinez's favorite drink when in Human space was spiced Margaritas.

The Human thought it was fruity and extravagant until they were settled and he tasted the drink.

It was like an old-fashioned, combined with the sharpest, most pungent allspice and cayenne pepper. It wasn't unpleasant, but the flavor, mixed with the sweet maple scent of the fruit garnish, was nearly overwhelming and drew his senses in alternate directions.

"So what do you think?" Kyroll questioned.

"A bit odd, but it's good," Martinez replied, leaning deeper into the seat.

They sat there, nursing their drinks for a moment or two. While there was a silent understanding between the two, putting it into words was a whole other hurdle.

"Well, now that we're settled in for the day, where do we go from here?" Martinez asked, breaking the silence and genuinely curious about where Kyroll saw everything going at this point.

Martinez certainly had never been in a situation where the man he was currently sharing a drink with had tried to kill him before. Kyroll likely had, but that comes in the territory of having been a spook, at least if the few Martinez had candor with where to be believed.

"Honestly, I'm not too sure. So, I might as well lay it out there. Thanks for not selling me out to the cops. I do appreciate the—I don't know, gesture of peace," Kyroll said with a hint of uncertainty.

"What did you tell them anyway? I figured you would have lied and have tried to get rid of me again," Martinez replied, stomaching another sip of the booze.

Kyroll hung his head ever so slightly, clicking his tongue. "I get why you would think that, but other than the drugs and the plan to kill you, everything. I wanted to leave it up to you altogether."

"Do you have any idea how long you could have been thrown away for if I had decided to still hate you?" Martinez gawked.

"Long enough that Nelly would have moved on. You and Lysa would have treated me like a distant memory, but it was nothing I wasn't prepared to face," the old Aviex replied in a surprising show of stoicism.

Martinez could not fathom doing something like that—facing one's destiny and handing one's fate to someone who might as well be a complete stranger. Kyroll proved to be more of an enigma than Martinez could have ever imagined, especially when facing decades of hard labor or life in prison as a possible sentence.

"Speaking of Nelya, did you lie to her as well? Because I haven't told Lysa anything yet." The Human said somewhat more hushedly while leaning in, knowing very well that because he could hear the girls, they likely could also listen to them.

Kyroll had no such qualms. "I wouldn't have been able to keep this secret from her if I wanted to," he wholeheartedly laughed. "If I had lied to her, she would have seen right through me and made me sing like a bird."

"You! Singing like a bird?" Martinez raised a brow.

That statement only made Kyroll laugh harder, so the air around them vibrated violently.

Martinez rolled his eyes, knowing Kyroll was just laughing at his expense. Instead of getting mad, he took another sip out of his drink, leaned back, and waited for the older man to regain his composure. This feat must have been herculean because it took him almost half of Martinez's glass to do so.

"For Nelya, of course! She just has a way about her when it comes to figuring out what's going on. She probably saw through anything you told her." Kyroll gasped, wiping away from his eyes. "Lysa can likely do the same thing for you."

Martinez didn't respond to that one. He knew very well that Kyroll was correct there; Lysa could see right through him no matter what, and there was no point in lying to her. He could easily do the same with her. That was one of the reasons they were so compatible—they had to be honest; lying was a moot point.

After fully regaining himself, Kyroll slammed back his drink and stood, extending a hand to Martinez. "Another?"

Martinez would not argue about getting a free drink, especially when he did not have to pour it.

With him and Kyroll finally having a chance to sit down, where hopefully there were no plots in the background, Martinez had to admit the situation was funny. Nelya was correct about them—he and Kyroll were uncannily similar in their actions.

They even had the same taste in women, wanting them to be headstrong, forward, and capable.

"Any idea what you're going to do with Lysa?" Martinez questioned as Kyroll began to pour one of the drinks.

Martinez saw his back and muscles tense the moment he spoke, causing him to spill some of the drinks. It wasn't lost on Martinez that this was still a sensitive subject for the older man, but this talk had to happen—for Lysa's sake.

Kyroll replied after a few moments of cleaning up the bits he spilled, not looking up from the glasses and leaving his back to Martinez. "I don't know—wha—what we could even do. I'm not exactly a stellar father."

What could Martinez respond to him with? He wasn't a father and had no plans to be one anytime soon. He could make a few suggestions as to what Lysa liked, but acting on that might come across as Kyroll desperately trying to meet her at her level, which might be a bit condescending.

"Maybe you can sit down and figure out something you both enjoy," Martinez recommended, unable to think of a better answer yet.

"You make that sound like it's easy," Kyroll said, turning around, tossing the rag on the counter, and moving to hand Martinez his drink back.

Kyroll groaned and cracked his neck before gesturing for Martinez to continue. "So how about it, wise guy? Why do you think that's easy?"

"It likely won't be that easy, but it is simple," Martinez responded.

"What the fuck do you mean simple?" Kyroll muttered around the rim of his glass, raising a brow.

Martinez took a few moments to consider how he could explain this to Kyroll—twirling his glass and listening to Nelya and Lysa's chatter from upstairs.

From his days in the military, Martinez had learned the difference between easy and simple very clearly. Going on an 80-mile ruck march with only one night's rest in between was simple. But he had never met anyone so bold to say it was easy—it was just walking while carrying a backpack after all.

But once the fatigue, ill-fitting boots, cold weather, endless steps, and hours upon hours of silent marching hit you. Dear god, the trek was arduous.

That story was just the first example he had thought of. There's also the methodology of how you eat an elephant, but Kyroll wouldn't understand that, not because he was a dunce or anything along those lines; he just doesn't know what an elephant is. Simultaneously, the GU special forces generally had a light kit, so he might not understand the troubles of being a Doc with an 80-kilogram pack on a march.

"Let's say I had a 500-kilo ball and ordered you to roll it up a hill using only your strength; would you call that order easy?" Martinez questioned, having decided upon something that would be a far more universal explanation.

"No, it's not easy by any means. And if you think that's easy, I tell you to go rub a Coylets mane," Kyroll chuckled. "But I do think I get what you're saying—it isn't complicated, but by the stars, that is not an easy thing to do."

"I'm glad you get it, so when do you think you're going to try this," Martinez smiled and gestured the glass toward the stairs. "Lysa and Nelya aren't complicated to get along with but are worth any difficulty."

Kyroll Paused and swirled the drink, tapping the glass with his finger. "I suppose after dinner. Nelly is making Orita'ke, one of Lysa's favorites; no sense in ruining that."

Orita'ke was another traditional Aviex meal. Similar enough to the blood-based cheese sauce Lysa had conjured up that Martinez knew he would enjoy it.

This one was more like a stew with rare to medium-rare hunks of meat and almost no vegetables save for a few hardy tubers. Oh, and of course, the entire sauce was thickened blood, nothing but and nothing but.

Martinez knew the dish because Lysa had wished him to eat it several times when they were in Draun but had never convinced him. He was, at the time, still cautious about their foreign food.

At this point, Martinez was almost ready to convert to a nearly whole Aviex diet. Everything they traditionally ate was hearty, rich, and filled with meat, fat, and blood, but that did not matter. Everything was succulent and filling.

"I guess we'll see," Martinez said and lightly raised his glass in a readable salute. A gesture of which Kyroll returned as they settled in the next half hour and waited for dinner.

FATHER AND DAUGHTER

"Henry, would you like to go for a walk?" Nelya questioned as Martinez loaded the dishwasher, having just finished what could be called their first family dinner.

Overall, it went better than any of them had assumed it would have. The conversations were varied and light, and the meal itself was filling. Heck, even Kyroll had no issues throughout.

The old Aviex man was in the living room and likely about to fall into a food coma after eating four whole plates of food and downing three beers. None of them minded; while Martinez and Lysa tolerated him, only Nelya loved to spend time with him.

"Sure, that would be nice," Martinez replied over his shoulder, seeing Nelya and Lysa stuffing the last leftovers into the fridge.

"May I come along?" Lysa asked, closing the fridge before leaning onto the island, a beatific smirk on her lips.

With a gentle, motherly smile, Nelya patted Lysa's shoulder but shook her head. "Not this time, my little Huntress. Your father wants to spend some time with you."

Any semblance of Lysa's smile died when Nelya told her no, morphing into a childish pout. "Must I?" She groaned loudly.

Nelya hugged Lysa gently, supporting her daughter's need to spend time with her father despite all parties present being aware of her reservations. "You promised to try to work it out with your father, and because you two are leaving soon, now might be your only chance."

Lysa sighed and tapped her nails on the counter, looking between her mother and Martinez, trying to think of some excuse she could give to weasel her way out of a solo interaction with Kyroll.

Yeah, he apologized to her, and they agreed to make an attempt to get along, but that didn't mean she wanted to spend time alone with him. She wanted Nelya and Martinez there as mediators; that had to go better than alone daddy-daughter time.

In the past, when she wanted to have a loving father, he was never there when she wanted to have a shoulder to cry on or teach her valuable skills; Kyroll only wished to take an interest when he felt like it—which was fleeting at best.

After her agreements with others, she seems to have backed herself into a corner and couldn't think of a quick, witty response to get away from this—especially not with how foggy her head has been over the last few weeks. An issue that has been plaguing her all day, along with nausea and fits of moodiness.

"Fine, I shall make an earnest attempt," Lysa concedingly said, not wanting to rebuke her promise to Martinez, especially after his reaching out for her had injured him.

Despite how much she wanted to blame her father for the injuries, both Martinez and Kyroll swore it was just a freak occurrence with hungry animals, so she believed them—her Ruh'ah would never lie to her.

"Oh, that's perfect, deary," Nelya chirped, grabbing Lysa into a deeper hug and squeezing her daughter tight enough that she gasped and struggled to return the gesture.

"Now, Henry, go grab your jacket," Nelya said after hugging Lysa, leaving her gasping for air.

Martinez nodded and watched Nelya pirouette and rush out of the kitchen, a skip in her step and giggling like a schoolgirl.

"What's gotten into her?" Martinez asked.

"I haven't the slightest clue," Lysa replied, watching her mother vanishing down the hallway toward her room, moving so fast that her pink clothes made her a cotton candy blur. "Mother is usually bubbly; perhaps mine and Father's reconciliation has her in a particularly good mood."

Martinez shrugged. That was a believable thing, but he wondered if there was more to Motherly Aviex's current mood. Ever since Martinez and Kyroll returned from the hospital, Nelya had been so sweet he was about to get cavities. It's not that her acting like that was out of character, but she seemed giddier than when they first arrived.

"I'm going to go get my coat," Martinez said, stepping toward the back doors to head to the guest house.

"I shall await you two by the door," Lysa smiled meekly, ignoring the churning pain in her stomach.

After seeing Martinez and Nelya out the door and watching Nelya tug her Ruh'ah up the driveway, hurrying him toward the woods, Lysa shuffled into the bathroom near the kitchen. Typically, she would go the extra distance to use the one in the guest house, wanting her privacy, but that was not viable right now.

Over the last week, on top of her irregular spikes of emotionalism, she also had been regularly plagued by bouts of extreme nausea. It had not reached the point of her vomiting yet, but just having the feeling of one hard jerk or a nasty flavor would trigger such a reaction.

To her regret, the nervousness of being alone with her father drove her to the point where she knew she was about to throw up. The fear of how he would act, how she should treat him, and the neurotic worry of them getting into a physical altercation once again pushed her over the edge.

Lysa barely made it to the toilet as the floodgates opened. She gripped the bowl and retched. Every fiber of her being screamed at her to expel the non-existent poison. Retching turned into gaging, gaging into erupting a vile mixture of barely digested food, blood, and bile. The red chunky spew filled the bowl as her painful groans filled the house.

The only solace that Lysa had in this horrible experience was that the blood was the few minute's worth she drank out of Martinez just before dinner. At least it should be; as far as she knew, she was healthy and had nothing odd going on. She had just been nervous and was overwhelmed the last few weeks—right?

She continued to vomit, and the sounds of her gagging, groaning, and nearly sobbing got louder. As the pain grew, a hefty thumping came from beyond the door, approaching like a rolling tide, followed by thunderous knocking.

"Lysa! Are you alright"? Kyroll yelled through the door.

"I am alri—" Lysa started attempting to lie, hoping to keep Kyroll away from her. But as if the universe was punishing the attempt, she threw up again, covering her shirt and hair in bile.

"No!" Lysa sobbed, turning her head back into the bowl.

Without thinking or asking, Kyroll tossed open the door and rushed over to Lysa, finding his dear daughter slumped over, clutching the toilet bowl.

"It's okay, it's okay, you'll be fine," Kyroll said, pulling her hair out of the bowl and rubbing her back.

Kyroll chose to do that simply because he did not know what else to do. He was not a medic or corpsman. He could triage minor issues—other than that, his training was to keep people safe until help arrived, he brought them to it, or the danger was dealt with. So, for now, trying to keep her from choking was all he could do.

Lyza couldn't help but feel humiliated; she had never had anyone see her sick, vomiting, or in any way this distraught; not even Martinez saw the effects of her time of the month that badly.

Why did it have to be her father of all people to come to her side when she fell ill for the first time in years?

"Don't worry, just let it out," Kyroll encouraged.

Lysa did not need the encouragement. Her body was still forcibly expelling anything she had inside her. Perhaps her lungs or heart would pop into the bowl, ending her humiliation.

As Lysa continued to vomit, she made no attempts to argue about Kyrolls presence; there was no point, and he wouldn't have left even if she had. His stubbornness was something she knew all too well.

After a half hour, Lysa's body had at long last decided her gauntlet of pain was over. She looked like a mess and felt just as awful. Crusted partially dried vomit covered her shirt, face, hair, and half the floor and around the toilet.

Along with that, every muscle burned, feeling like she had just gone back to back rounds of fighting Teacher, followed by letting someone hit her with a hammer.

Glancing around and up at Kyroll's patient, caring gaze, Lysa's heart clenched. Seeing the horrible state of everything and that she was clutching her father, whom she had been awful to over the last few days, cumulatively put her back into a state of mania.

"Why? You, you should hate me," Lysa quaved. "You're not supposed to be nice."

"I'll never hate you. I was stupid, overprotective, and pushed you away, but I'll always love you, Lysa; you're my little huntress," Kyroll replied softly.

"But I'm awful," Lysa protested.

"No, no, you aren't," Kyroll replied, hugging her tightly, uncaring about the vomit or tears. Finally, holding his little girl again was a dream come true.

It took Lyza a moment, but with her father unrelenting in his caring hold, she clutched him just as forcefully and buried her face in his collar.

"Come on, let's get you cleaned up," Kyroll said softly, rubbing his hand on the small of Lysa's back, just as he did when she was little. Lysa nodded and stood with him, letting him clean the floor while she prepared the shower.

By the time Lysa showered off and managed to wrangle her emotions back under control, Kyroll had already set out some sweats and a shirt for her. They were her mother's, and unlike the clothes she usually wore, they were bright pink and covered in flowers. But for now, she didn't mind, nor did she think her mother would mind borrowing some clothes.

As she slipped on the simple t-shirt, Kyroll knocked on the door yet again. "I put your dirty clothes in the washer. uhhh--- would you want to--- come relax?"

Lysa hesitated when answering that, not because she was angry or anything along those lines. She just had to ruminate on how Kyroll was being so lovely to her, especially after all she had done.

She had yelled about him, talked behind his back, and insulted him for years. She hit him only a few days ago, for star's sake.

Martinez and her mother seemed right about him making an effort, which is earnestly unreal. She was finally accepting that perhaps this trip was not a waste.

"Have Ruh'ah and Mother returned?" Lysa asked, hanging up her wet towel. She still did not trust her father entirely and wanted them to have her back.

"Not yet; Nelly texted me and said they would be a while," Kyroll explained.

That was curious. The pair must have been gone for almost an hour by now; Lysa estimated that much time had passed based on the sun coming in through the window. She wasn't precisely sure how long her vomiting and clean-up had taken.

She wondered if they had found a pleasant location to bird watch or observe some other section of the wilderness. After all, they both enjoyed nature.

"I shall be out momentarily," Lysa conceded. "Where shall you be?"

"Okay—uh, I'll be in the living room," Kyroll replied, stepping back from the door. His footsteps became quieter as he walked away, leaving Lysa to finish any clean-up she needed to.

Shortly after, Lysa found her father precisely as he said he would be. The sight of what he was doing caused her to smile and take a pleasant jaunt down memory lane—echoes of when she was no taller than Kyroll's waist flashed in her mind.

Memories of days from when she had been bullied at school and he would snuggle up with her under blankets to watch a movie and ensure that all was all right in his little daughter's world.

Those were pleasant times, and it looks as though good old Dad still knows how to comfort his little girl.

He even had the same blanket, cookies, and tea laid out while digging through her mother's shelves, looking for either a movie or a book for them to relax.

After noticing her presence, Kyroll stopped looking for a movie and looked over at her. "Too much?" he questioned awkwardly, scratching his forearm.

"Not at all," Lysa assured as she walked over to the couch and let the plush surface pull her in.

"Any idea what you want to watch?" Kyroll questioned, showing her a collection of cutesy family cartoons that they used to watch.

Kyroll was barely looking directly at her, likely unsure how he was supposed to act. Still, he was doing almost everything perfectly to make Lysa feel comfortable and to try to bridge some of the gap between them.

Lysa certainly noticed all the effort.

"Can you play Rolala?" Lysa replied, pulling the blanket up and wrapping it underneath her.

She remembers the adventure story fondly but hasn't watched it in years. It was about a young Aviex hero traveling across a fictional version of Avalon, looking for some magical artifact to bring forth the sun and cast away the darkness.

If memory served correctly, the story was a modern retelling of the myth of why the Aviex home planet experienced darkness for days on end and now existed in a near-perpetual twilight.

Lysa was too unfamiliar with old Aviex myths to confirm it, but that sounded vaguely correct. Either way, the sword and sorcery story about fighting monsters and steadfast friends was heartwarming—she found it inspiring as a young lass.

"Okay, no problem," Kyroll said as he selected the movie. After putting it on, he moved to the far end of the sofa and groaned, lowering himself to the surface.

"Do you want some tea? Maybe a cookie?" Kyroll asked, leaning forward and groaning in pain, pushing the tray of snacks closer to Lysa.

"Maybe later," Lysa said, unable to look at the food without her stomach trying to throw up again.

Kyroll nodded, unwilling to push any subject with his daughter, especially when she seemed sick.

As they sat there and the movie rolled, Lysa continued to grumble, grip her stomach, and whined, still feeling like her gut would implode. Each time it happened, she noticed that Kyroll looked over at her and winced like he was feeling the same agony.

Between her spats of pain, Lysa looked at the details of what he had set up. There was only one tea cup and tray; he could not reach them if he wanted to. Had he done this only for her?

She whined, understanding how her father was putting such effort into this attempt at rekindling their relationship. She also understood how all she was doing was giving him a cold shoulder, pushing against and fighting him; ultimately, Lysa was not helping at all.

Thinking back to her promise to Martinez and Nelya, Lysa could not justify her actions. She had to attempt to meet her father halfway, and that was just what she would do.

Lysa stood, holding the blanket tight, and moved closer to Kyroll. Sitting down next to him, she threw the blanket over their laps and leaned against her father for the first time in years.

"There, much better," Lysa said, shimming closer and resting comfortably against him. She took in the odd mix of sap, smoke, and cologne that oozed from her father and found it comforting.

His scent was precisely the same as when she was younger and pushed deep into her soul and pulled forth feelings of comfort and safety that existed before she grew up, and they had their fights.

Kyroll froze and remained motionless, unable to comprehend that Lysa was close to him. His mind was racked with a million possibilities for why she might be attempting this. Was it some trick? Was it a cruel joke she would use to stab his heart? Or, by the rare chance, did she actually want to attempt to forgive him?

It took until she leaned against him and spoke for him to accept reality and relax with her.

"Thank you for trying," Lysa breathed.

"Thanks for letting me," Kyroll replied, draping his arm over her shoulder.

Lysa smiled and sighed contently, not needing anything else to be said.

They both understood their relationship was far from perfect, and this was just the first few steps at repairing what they once had. Even though it would be many years before all was forgiven--- this was a wonderful start.

For the following few hours until they both fell asleep on the spot, both were transported back to when she was a little girl, and he was just learning how to be a civilian and father. It was a time when their family was whole, and they all knew who was there for them.

Maybe one day, years from now, they will fully recapture that feeling. Lysa, Kyroll, Nelya, and even Martinez might just be one big happy family. Both wanted it at this point.

ARMED AND ARMORED

"**A**re you certain you have everything?" Nelya asked, watching Martinez and Kyroll load the bags into the rental SUV.

"It should be all there, but we will double-check," Kyroll assured, hefting one of Lysa's several bags up, the weight causing his healing rib to pang. He knew Martinez was likely similar to him and would not have left anything behind, so he was not worried about it, but if it made Nelya happy, he would ensure it was that way.

"Don't worry, we will get everything," Martinez smiled, turning about to look at Nelya, leaning against the side door to the house, clutching a mug of steaming tea in her hands—a boon considering the weather had been getting colder by the day.

Martinez and Kyroll had taken up the role of packing everything for Lysa. They did this for several reasons: it was the right thing to do, but Lysa also felt a bit under the weather. Her sickness had been on and off for the last four days, and Martinez was starting to worry.

When he and Nelya found her and Kyroll cuddled up and sleeping on the sofa, they thought it was adorable. That was until they found the evidence of all the clean-up: vomit on the toilet, rags in the trashcan, and Lysa's clothes in the washer.

It was then that Martinez and Nelya figured out that Lysa was unwell—but that did not mean they would wake them. If Lysa had been so ill it warranted so, Kyroll would have dragged her to the hospital.

The Human just hoped that Lysa would start feeling better soon after they returned to Draun. He had never experienced her being sick before; now that he had, Martinez was glad of that fact.

Lysa certainly could be moody when sick. It was not that she was angry, but everything seemed to bring her near to tears or upset her—or her random thoughts would blurt out like she was some sleeper agent. One moment, they were cuddling on the couch; the next, Lysa ranted about how one of her coworkers upset her months ago.

It all seemed so random.

"I know you will, Deary. I'm just being a doting mother," Nelya replied in a light, self-teasing way. "I fully trust my two lovely men."

Martinez smirked at Kyroll, cringing at hearing Nelya refer to them like that. He knew that Kyroll had accepted Martinez when it came to remaining with Lysa, but the idea of a Human being entirely a part of the family must still be a bit sensitive.

At least after Martinez and Nelya went on that walk alone the other day, he knew Nelya had entirely accepted him as a future member of their family. The entire time they were out, Nelya excitedly told him about the things they could do once Kyroll and Lysa started getting along, and he and Lysa finally gave her grandkids.

He reminded her that they still had to go to a clinic and needed to graduate school, which meant nothing to the motherly Aviex. She was talking like having kids was already a done deal. It was cute that she was so confident about what their futures would look like.

Martinez knew the GU could guarantee their offspring through genetic manipulation; even then, that took years to get signed up for and even longer for the geneticists to prepare for any procedures. At least she was optimistic.

"Come on, let's go make sure we got it all," Kyroll said, stepping toward the back of the house.

"Righto," Martinez followed.

"Oh, will you two have Lysa meet me in the living room? I want to talk to her about something before you two leave," Nelya requested before they made it around the corner.

"No problem," Martinez waved.

Once they made it through the billowing snow and to the guest house, Martinez and Kyroll found Lysa moving the last of her bags into the foyer, struggling to move the heavy luggage. "Good Morning, Father," Lysa wiped her brow, letting the bag thunk onto the wood floor.

"Good Morning, Little Huntress. Is there anything else?" Kyroll replied, pointing at the bag.

"No, that is everything," Lysa shook her head.

"Okay, just leave it there. Nelly wants you," Kyroll said, pointing out the grand window toward the house. "Martinez will handle the bags."

Martinez did not comment on Kyroll voluntelling him to do something. It was just a few bags, and he would have moved the luggage anyway.

"Very well," Lysa replied before walking over to Martinez and kissing his cheek. "Thank you, Ruh'ah."

Martinez smiled as warmth spread throughout his chest. Thank God Lysa seemed to be feeling somewhat better today. She was a little bit lethargic this morning, but after some breakfast and a shower, she was back to her usual self.

"No problem," Martinez replied, watching Lysa sashay toward the door, her tight black pants outlining her flawlessly pear-shaped ass, letting him see it sway and pop with each step.

A sudden heavy hand dropped onto Martinez's shoulder, pulling him out of the short trance he had fallen into. Turning to look at Kyroll, Martinez awkwardly smirked, seeing Kyroll's two remaining eyes glaring at him.

"Sorry about that," Martinez chuckled.

"I might be alright with you—but Human, I'm still her father. Could you not do that in front of me?" Kyroll sighed. "I still find you two kissing awkward enough."

That Kyroll was embarrassed by their little forms of PDA was funny to Martinez. It was not like they did anything beyond what Nelya and Kyroll did. For god's sake, Martinez and Lysa have been subjected to them mordaining, with Kyroll groping Nelya's ass just this morning. Maybe it was just about Kyroll being Lysa's father, but Martinez doubted it.

Kyroll had been racist against anyone non-Aviex for decades; Those sorts of behaviors and habits are not unlearned overnight. The older man likely still held some lingering resentment toward Martinez because he was a Human, but at least Kyroll was clearly trying to make things work.

"Yeah, I just was—," Martinez said before Kyroll cut him off. It wasn't malicious by any means; it was just that Kyroll found the conversation he wanted to have to be more important.

"Follow me; I got something to give you," Kyroll said, turning about and walking toward the bedroom Martinez and Lysa had been staying in.

"What about the bags?" Martinez asked.

"Get them later," Kyroll replied, not turning back to ensure Martinez was following.

Once inside the room, Kyroll wandered toward the headboard and ran his hand between the mattress and the wooden headboard itself. After a few moments of muttering in annoyance, he smirked. "There that bastard is," he praised, just before a loud thunk sounded out from underneath the bed.

Leaning over with a painful groan, Kyroll pulled out what looked like a military weapons case from underneath the bed. It was about as long as the bed itself and must have weighed a ton, based on how it took Kyroll a moment to heft it onto the bed.

"What is that?" Martinez questioned, stepping beside Kyroll.

"How about I don't ruin the surprise and just show you?" Kyroll replied, inputting a combination into a built-in control screen on the case.

After a pneumatic hiss announced that the seal on this long-forgotten weapons case had been released, Kyroll tossed it open and inspected its contents. At the same time, Martinez went slack-jawed.

Inside the case were not just weapons that would cause the most war-hungry Marine he knew to get a raging hardon, but ammunition and low-profile armor to accompany them. Additionally, amidst the contents were some devices Martinez had not seen since his time in the Marines. Frag grenades, explosive charges, flashbangs, and what he could have sworn were stacks of Vreck anti-personnel drone mines.

"Why do you have all this? And why in all the universe did you think letting me and your daughter sleep on a bed of explosives was a good thing?" Martinez gawked, reaching in and checking a C-7 rifle chamber—it was loaded

The C-7 rifle and the UB-21 blaster in the box were standard-issue weapons in the GU and Human militaries. The C-7 was more common in Human hands, while the GU regulars generally preferred the lighter, handier, but slightly less lethal UB-21. That did not mean the 21 would not put you in the dirt; it was just different.

The weapon diversity in the active forces was an issue of how new Humans were to the GU and intergalactic warfare. Go figure: Generals who first joined the Human military before the GU helped Humanity rise to the stars still had skepticism about the energy-based weapon. As such, the C-7 was preferred. It used caseless ammo and was close enough to traditional slug throwers that Humanity trusted the automatic weapon.

"It pays to be prepared," Kyroll chuckled, pulling out a small gray bracelet and a pistol. "Some old habits die hard."

"What about letting us sleep on them?" Martinez asked again, not letting Kyroll get out of answering the question.

"They can't go off without set up, you know that," Kyroll shrugged, tapping the pistol onto one of the bricks of plastique just to emphasize.

"Why leave these out here then? Would you not want them in the main house? You can't use your kit if it's out here," Martinez said, setting the C-7 back down.

"I have other caches up all around the property; this one was just set up here," Kyroll commented.

Martinez did not miss the gravity of that explanation; their property was as sprawling as a city and would take him an entire day to traverse. If Kyroll had caches as set up as this dotted around his property, Martinez could see the man being able to outfit a small army.

Kyroll turned around and flipped the handgun around to offer Martinez the grip. "You familiar with the JKL and NanoFlex armor?"

"I'm not," Martinez admitted, taking the pistol and being sure to follow the four weapon safety rules by pointing it away from Kyroll and keeping his finger straight and off the trigger.

Kyroll took a few minutes to teach Martinez how to use the JKL without shooting himself or inducing a malfunction. The pistol was a ten-millimeter caseless pistol with an integral suppressor. Its operations were similar to any other autoloading slug thrower pistol that Martinez was used to using. So, that period of instruction was simple and straightforward.

A piece this slick almost felt wrong in Martinez's hands. He had never seen the JKL in person but had heard that special forces and mercenaries across the galaxy coveted the weapon for its reliability and concealability.

This pistol model had cult status in the Human Marines, rivaling the now-ancient Kalashnikov pattern rifle. Despite not being produced on Earth for hundreds of years, that rifle still managed to worm its way across the stars and end up in the hands of both Humanities and the GU's enemies and allies alike.

Following that, Kyroll showed Martinez how to use a piece of technology that he thought he would never be able to use— NanoFlex armor.

Considering this armor was usually reserved for Humanities, L.O.S.T troopers, special advisors, and deep recon, it was surprisingly simple to use. There were only two buttons on the wristband, one to activate it and one to deactivate it.

Martinez pressed the activation button, and the small wristband essentially disintegrated and crawled up his arm in a wave of dry, gray particles. Once up his arm, the wave spread out and covered his entire chest underneath his shirt and jacket, forming a thin layer of light nanocomposite. It stopped just below his jaw and at his waistline while covering his arms like a T-shirt, offering him coverage far beyond the rigid polycarbonate plates most Human troops wore.

"That's so fucking cool," Martinez exclaimed, peaking down his collar at the small black hexagons coating his skin. "What is it able to protect against?"

"Most threats, bullets, blasters, knives, claws, you name it. But it has limited power, so try not to get hit too much," Kyroll said, silently chambering a round in the pistol. "You know, use hardcover and whatnot."

"What do you mean limited?" Martinez said, looking up just in time to see the JKL recoil and launch a slug into his stomach.

Freaking out, Martinez jumped back and clutched at his gut, expecting that he would have to hold in his blood by shoving his finger in the hole and running away from Kyroll. But there was no blood or hole; instead, he found the armor had essentially engulfed the bullet and nestled it inside the material, keeping him safe from all harm.

Before Martinez even had a chance to react to the news that he was fine, Kyroll buckled over, laughing at him. "You should see the look on your face!"

"That's not fucking funny, man," Martinez barked, "you could have killed me!"

His argument only made Kyroll laugh harder, causing the older man to lean against the bed for support. "It would not have."

"How the fuck do you know that?" Martinez stood upright, almost ready to shove Kyroll because of his nonchalant attitude to shooting him.

Waving his hand at Martinez, Kyroll indicated he needed a moment before he could keep speaking.

While Kyroll composed himself, Martinez was livid. This motherfucker just shot him. Plenty of races have odd and downright dangerous training methods around the galaxy, with some including just this. But Humans were not one of them.

Humanity had long abandoned practices like that save for some zealots who settled outside the GU.

Kyroll took an entire minute to steady himself. Once he did, the old man explained that he shot Martinez to demonstrate the effectiveness of the incredibly light armor.

When Martinez asked about them having set it up on something and then shooting it as an alternative, Kyroll looked embarrassed but then shrugged and dismissed the idea. Insisting seeing that your armor worked was always better than just blind trust.

Kyroll then explained how his drill instructors did just this for demonstration for him and his fellow recruits. But unlike what he had just done for Martinez, they shot one another with progressively larger weapons—to the point it was knocking the victim flat on their ass.

Martinez was glad his training did not include anything like that. It was stupid, dangerous, and unnecessary, but it did explain a bit more about Kyroll's attitude toward violence.

"You're still a fucking asshole," Martinez grumbled, turning off the armor by pressing the button on the small remaining wristband, so Kyroll would not shoot him again.

Much like when it was activated, the armor slinked back down Martinez's body and wrapped tightly around his wrist, leaving him with an odd cold feeling around his chest without it. After the armor dissolved, Martinez felt an odd rubbing around his belt; He moved his shirt to look, and the smashed slug fell to the ground.

"That's kinda neat," Martinez said, picking up the bullet.

"Yeah, it will hold the round and any spall in place until you shut it off," Kyroll explained, "as for knives, it will harden and repair any cuts."

"Why the fuck don't they give everyone these?" Martinez looked down at the bracelet.

"It costs too much for the average troop," Kyroll shrugged, closing the pistol into a small case. "Anyway, I'm giving you these," he said, handing Martinez the sealed box.

"Why are you doing that?" Martinez raised a brow.

Kyroll's face took on a sudden, serious look, leaving no room for misinterpretation of his feelings about the topic. "Simple, you are keeping Lysa safe from now on–not me," he grumbled while looking away from Martinez. "Now you will have the tools for anything that might happen."

Martinez was about to speak and question why Kyroll thinks he needs weapons to ensure Lysa stays safe until he recalled what Nelya, Kyroll, and himself knew about the broader galaxy that Lysa was ignorant of—namely, the dark history of the Aviex and why so many other aliens would wish her harm. The events of their date were also cast in a new light with that knowledge.

With that in mind, even Martinez had to admit that keeping a weapon on hand, or at least in his backpack, could be helpful.

"I will keep her safe, but am I able to have this—legally, I mean?" Martinez questioned.

Kyroll wrapped an arm around Martinez's shoulder and jostled him. "I'm glad you will, and don't worry with your experience in the military, you can own it. Just ask the police at Draun or check on the data net; both will tell you the same."

"If you say so," Martinez replied, holding the case close. "Thanks."

"Now I can blame you when something goes wrong," Kyroll chuckled, letting Martinez go and heading toward the door. "Come on, let's get the last of the bags."

HOME BITTERSWEET HOME

Martinez groaned, turning from handing the keys to the rental SUV to the clerk. A line nearly half a kilometer long of impatient aliens had formed; claws flared, tentacles undulated, and teeth bared.

"Sorry about the delay," Martinez muttered, slinking out of the way.

It was not like it was his fault the alien manning the counter, had lost the record of him having rented the vehicle, causing him to have to prove he had through credit statements, his copy of the contract, and showing that he had the damn SUV.

Martinez slipped past the crowd on the thoroughfare and skirted the road's edge, allowing families and taxis to drop off and receive sentients from the Celna air/spaceport. Both were almost as densely populated as any street in Draun.

Martinez was already missing the solitude and calm of Nelya's house—but the navy had assigned him to Draun, so he had to return on time. He would not want to be shipped off to the Iron Spire on Mars to serve brig time for going A.W.O.L (absent without leave).

If rumors about that Navy supermax were to be believed, being on bread and water aboard a starship was a far more pleasant fate.

Pausing before crossing the road and entering the main terminal, Martinez was amazed by the number of aliens in the small port. It was abuzz with sentients going to and from their destinations, paying one another no mind as they did.

Through the large glass windows, Martinez could see even more. If anything, the density inside increased, something that became all the more apparent once he had joined the hellish, flowing waves of aliens inside.

Martinez slowed his pace as he neared the shoreline of the ruckus crowd, scanning over it for his found family. The task was made simple because of the menagerie's treatment of them. The crowd gave the three Aviex in their midst a wide berth, letting Nelya's bright yellow jacket and poofy pom pom hat stand out like the north star.

Martinez quickly adjusted his heading and moved through the turbulent crowd, never losing sight of Nelya. He navigated the crowd with practiced ease, a talent Draun and, more specifically, the Hospital there had taught him.

Breaching through the crowd and into the calm void to join them, Lysa was just wrapping up her goodbyes. She was hugging Kyroll tightly while he did the same; only the mangled half of his face was visible through his daughter's raven hair. If that side of his face was still emotive, without a doubt, it would be overflowing contentment—but alas, all Martinez could see was the slight upturn of his lip.

Before Martinez had recovered from stumbling through the crowd, Nelya had already grabbed hold of him, latching to him tighter than a person trying to break his rib through sheer machismo.

"Little Hunter, please don't leave!" Nelya whined, pulling Martinez down to her level, hugging around his head, burying his head against her sweater and the plush build beneath. "You two just got here."

Martinez could not deny that the time they had spent here had flown by, and despite his wish to stay, that was not possible. "Sorry, Kurenla," Martinez replied, righting himself and returning the gesture, referring to Nelya with the Aviex word for Mother. "We have to go home."

Calling her that apparently was both the correct and incorrect thing to do for the man. With more force than Martinez thought possible with her seam-splitting build, Nelya reengaged the hug around his chest, causing him to gasp.

"Gra'hu could get you a job here; Lysa could stay home with me, writing our days away. A big happy Kureal," Nelya argued. If you could call her explaining, they would be the Aviex equivalent of an extended family unit an argument.

It was not like they all had not accepted that as reality, save for Kyroll, who likely needed more time to warm up to the thought.

"Kurenla, as heavenly as the sounds, Ruh'ah has to finish school," Lysa interjected, patting Nelya's shoulder.

"You are supposed to be on my side here," Nelya complained, looking over her shoulder and sticking her tongue out at her daughter, earning a chuckle from both Lysa and Kyroll.

It was pleasant for such a mature woman that Nelya was so open with her feelings. Few sentients would be as expressive. Nelya was so willing to wear her heart on her sleeve that everyone knew what she intended.

"I am. However, I also informed you that I would not strong-arm Ruh'ah into moving here," Lysa said before gesturing at Martinez. "That is up to him once he graduates."

"Don't worry, we will visit again. Just after I graduate," Martinez added, not giving Nelya the chance to make a protest.

Without missing a beat, Nelya's cunning and ability to move things to where she wanted shined brighter than the sun. "Are we not able to attend?" She said with a bit of sing-song begging while widening her pink eyes, mimicking the cutest kitten eyes he had ever seen.

"Of course you can," Martinez chuckled, not needing the kitten begging; he would have invited them anyway.

"Thank you, Little Hunter. I can't wait to see you two again," Nelya replied, letting Martinez go but having not completed her onslaught of hugs.

She turned around and grabbed her daughter, who saw it coming this time and met her living ferocity without issue.

As they gave their final heartfelt goodbyes, Martinez turned to Kyroll and gave him a firm handshake.

"Take care of her," Kyroll smirked, "I know you can."

"I won't let you down," Martinez nodded.

"Come on, Nelly. They will miss their flight if we keep them," Kyroll said, going over to Nelya and Lysa.

Nelya looked at Kyroll and likely was about to argue the point, wanting to insist her dear daughter stay but giving the man a point; he knew Nelya. Kyroll snaked an arm between Nelya and Lysa, twisting her around and planting a kiss on his wife's lips, leaning down over her.

Martinez had never seen how Lysa melts in his arms, but now he thinks he knows what it looks like. In the span of one second, Nelya went from as stiff as a board to clutching Kyroll's shirt, lightly moaning against him, letting him support her as they leaned down.

"I guess we should," Nelya breathed once the little kiss broke, and Kyroll stood her up and wrapped his arm around her waist.

Lysa and Martinez glanced at each other, neither willing to admit aloud how uncanny the similarities between their relationship and the older couple's were—but they knew.

After another short round of pleasantries, Nelya and Kyroll left, letting Martinez and Lysa get checked in and board the shuttle.

To Martinez's surprise, the airline did not care that he had a gun now. The weapon just had to be unloaded and in his checked bag. It seems Kyrolls's shakey idea of legality was genuine when he told Martinez about the legality of owning the JKL. The airline representative just wanted to see his Military, GU, or LE ID to confirm he could own it.

Once the dynamic duo were settled in their seats, Lysa lay against Martinez and immediately fell asleep, leaving Martinez to stew in his emotions about what was to come once he returned home.

It was odd; the two times he had returned to Earth after enlisting, returning home was joyous—but Draun was melancholic.

Martinez had hardly thought about work, Shiksie, patients, or the incident since arriving in Celna. But now that he was en route to Draun, it was at the forefront of his mind; the same was true of an expected enemy brief, which made him think of what injuries he would be dealing with.

Martinez was not worried about getting in trouble for throttling Shiksie; she was molesting him and causing a S.H.A.R.P(sexual harassment and rape prevention) officer's worst nightmare.

The only way Martinez could see any backlash befalling him would be if Shiksie had gotten an aneurysm from slamming into the fridge.

"Fuck," Martinez muttered, realizing this was the first time after texting Ivron he had thought of possible injuries she could have sustained.

In all the chaos and emotions of that night, he did not even consider that she could have died from the impact he gave her. Telling Ivorn was not enough. Shiksie could have sustained a fractured skull, TBI, internal hemorrhaging, or countless other life-changing injuries.

Had he abandoned her after hurting her? Martinez had no idea how he would cope if that were the case. Yeah, he was not a doctor and did not have the Hippocratic oath—he had something else: the Corpsman's oath.

"I shall do all within my power to show in myself an example of all that is honorable and good throughout my Naval career!" The words of his instructors roared in his mind.

Martinez had said those words like gospel for months in training and afterward at every promotion and follow-on school. Had he fallen so far as to abandon Shikise when she was not only in need but also harmed?

He had beat the fuck out of Marines but still stitched them up, had a beer with and told them it was ok. But he ran away and left Shiksie alone.

The sight of her crying and belting herself as he ran flashed in his mind. If Martinez could take it back, he would—but what else should he have done? He was panicking.

What if that was the last he would have seen of her? She could have died, and he had not for one moment thought of her.

If something happened after leaving her there, Martinez might as well give up on medicine, and he would not deserve to see another patient again.

Martinez's imagination ran rampant, and he imagined his kind, quirky, and gentle mentor changed because of his actions: stuck with crutches, unable to speak, paralyzed, or even dead—all because of him.

Those thoughts haunted him, clawing at his mind like a razor blade until he reached Lysa's house in the afternoon.

"Shall I see you tomorrow?" Lysa asked, turning around in the afternoon sun, the light flaring against her raven hair, making her look positively angelic. The only thing since the flight started to pull Martinez back down to earth—or Renoral in this case.

"Maybe," Martinez replied with a shaky answer.

"Are you positive?" Lysa purred, playfully plucking at his shirt button and fluttering her four blood-red eyes.

"I want to see how studying and work go," Martinez loathfully choked out.

Lysa lost her flirty attitude and stared at Martinez, studying his expression. It was enigmatic. Her love looked nervous and sad yet had a painful grimace, like someone was driving nails under his skin.

"Are you still upset about Shiksie?" Lysa sighed, knowing Martinez likely said work and studying so as not to name-drop the Farun'se woman.

Martinez froze momentarily when Lysa mentioned Shiksie but quickly recovered and attempted to deflect. "It's not about that."

"Oh! Then what might it be?" Lysa pressed, challenging the obvious attempt at avoiding being candid.

"Well, you know, it's just getting back, getting into the swing of things, and—" Martinez started to trail off, listing things about their daily routines they would be resuming.

If the subject matter were less meaningful to him, Lysa would find the idea of drowning herself in word soup comedic, but in this case, it was annoying.

With each addition, Martinez's answers became less logical and grew in mundanity. By the time Lysa stopped him, he was going on about folding his laundry.

"Ruh'ah—please cease. I know you must be nervous about meeting up with Shiksie again; considering how you are behaving, it must be niggling you," Lysa said, draping her arms on Martinez's shoulders and pulling herself against him.

Nearly instinctually, Martinez wrapped his firm hands around her hips, holding Lysa in place. "Am I that obvious?"

"Just to me. I know you too well, just as you do me," Lysa whispered into Martinez's ear, her warm breath rolling past his neck, the beatific care of it seeping into him.

They stood silent for several seconds while Martinez quantified what he needed to say. Each enjoyed the truth in the statement of knowing the other so well. However, Lysa has been a bit more challenging for Humans to read in the last few weeks. It was not impossible, but Martinez had to adapt to her mood swings.

"I figured you would be furious if I mentioned needing to talk to her," Martinez admitted, moving a hand up Lysa's back, bringing her into a half hug. "You did say you would skin her alive."

A smirk crawled up on Lysa's lips, thankfully not visible to Martinez—she would have looked psychotic. "I did, but she is essential to your life, career, and schooling. I cannot demand you abandon her altogether—that seems a bit—selfish on my part."

Lysa stepped back and let the cold winter air fill the gap between them. "Could you please seek counsel on how to confront her? Perhaps seek out Ivorn or possibly the doctor?"

Martinez was already planning on getting one of them to broker a meeting between them to help clear the air. Lord knew he had no plans to ever be alone again with Shiksie. It was not because Martinez felt like she was a danger to him; no, Martinez could slaughter Shiksie if push came to shove.

He just felt violated. A line had been crossed, and there was no return to what the world once was. All they could do now was adapt to the new battle space.

"I will ask them," Martinez assured.

"Marvelous; tell me how it goes, Ruh'ah," Lysa purred, kissing Martinez's cheek and leaving a trace of her black lipstick just over his stubble.

The walk from Lysa's house to Martinez's apartment was not far, only clocking in at a second over fifteen kilometers. Martinez ran further than that most mornings. But with everything going on in Martinez's mind, it felt like he was back on Mars and conducting the Joli Rouge again.

The Joli Rouge, a French term for pretty red, was the cumulative event for Corpsmen in the Human Navy. It consisted of three tribulating days of constant marching, triage, physical training, and ruck marches, all against the backdrop of the Rouge desert.

With confronting Shiksie on the horizon, Martinez could not deny the conflict brewing inside him.

Had he not been clear enough? Was staying at Shiksies despite knowing she had set a trap a stupid idea? Each question rolled in his mind and conjured up a thousand ways to solve the issue. But that was all in hindsight and only made the Human feel more guilty as if he had failed one of his only friends.

"God fucking dammit," Martinez muttered, kicking a rock into a bush, a small animal scurrying out and chirping angrily at him.

"Well fuck you too," Martinez said, flipping the squirrel thing off, wanting to tell something to pound sand, even if it's just a random animal.

Once the beast had returned to the bush and Martinez felt no more vindicated, he continued to stew alone in his thoughts—specifically on the incident.

How the hell was he supposed to know the usually level-headed woman would have come onto him like a bitch in heat? He doubted anyone would have ever pictured prim and proper Shiksie doing that. It was so out of the left field it might as well have been an ambush.

Who would blame him for panicking and throttling her? Other than himself, that is.

As if Martinez did not hate himself enough for all the missteps that led to the schism between himself and his mentor, his understanding of the fallout was about to shift from guilt to being unable to deny his culpability.

Once Martinez reached the floor of his apartment, his onus was laid to bear, not in the form of a body or anything he had ever encountered. This time, it was just simple brown boxes. Stacked neatly in front of his door were dozens of boxes, each with his name written in oh-so-familiar, print-like handwriting.

Martinez drew his knife and sliced open one of the boxes, wondering what Shiksie could have dropped off. They were all filled to the brim with the notebooks Shiksie had him use to study from. The same ones she read regularly and had used to pass her college classes several years ago.

At first, Martinez wondered why she had left her notes with him until he started to move the boxes out of the way of the door and found the note taped to his door.

Reaching up with a trembling hand and pulling it down, Martinez swallowed his spit, fearing the absolute worst. While being in the military made him jumpy about suicide, it was for a damn good reason; this would not be the first final goodbye he had to read—and every fiber of him prayed the gut reaction the Navy built into him was wrong.

But seeing the uncharacteristically shaky text on the paper, it was as if the worst parts of his fears had been manifested into reality.

The scrawl was short and to the point and read like it was written by someone about to suck start a shotgun.

Henry, I enjoyed our time together. I hope you did as well. I pray you do well in life. I wish it did not have to end this way. Please forget about me for your sake.

Your friend

-Shiksie

Martinez sucked in a breath and dropped the note; pulling out his datapad, he texted Shiksie, telling her he was coming over right now, before running back out into the cold Draun evening.

BYGONE MENTOR

Snow drifted lazily around Martinez, the first snowfall this year in Draun. Celna had been under snowpack for weeks, but in this massive city, this was untimely late. Each fresh flake glowed like embers in the evening light, burning just like the Human's ragged breath.

"Get the fuck out of my way," Martinez barked at a group of aliens, ordering them to make a hole or get barreled through.

This group took the warning of the two-meter-tall man to heart and skittered away like rats, allowing him to pass.

Those were the smart ones; not all had that many survival instincts. Martinez had crashed through a group of Ruqaura, their flabby builds jiggling as they fell to the duracrete and cursed his existence.

Fuck them; they did not matter, nor did the abject panic Martinez was stirring up in his wake. The Human certainly was causing a scene in the otherwise serene city. Whether the aliens thought he was being chased, was a crazy nutter on the loose, or that he was a deranged rapist, he did not care.

They could think he was a serial killer or a terrorist for all he cared. All Martinez cared about was reaching Shiksie and ensuring she had not done the unthinkable.

By the time Martinez had reached Shiksie's posh neighborhood, sweat was flooding off his brow; on her front lawn, he nearly collapsed from vomiting, having just run the fastest he had done in years. Fuck even Raliegh could not hold a candle to the show of speed and athletics Martinez had demonstrated, and that man ran ultra marathons.

Through blurry vision, Martinez looked up at Shiksie's house. It was as spartan as the last time he was here. The house showed off the owner's simple, straightforward personality, a bold defiance of the bright pastels and gaudily decorated homes of her neighbors.

At least the house had not changed.

Pounding on the door with hammer-like fists, Martinez roared into the gloom. "Shiksie, are you there?"

The milliseconds dragged out into hours; each breath dragged into eternity. With each passing eon, Martinez repeated the process with more desperation, beating the door as if it owed him money.

Each repetition drew on more of the same. A silence so deafening it crushed Martinez's soul like an ant.

"Please, if you are in there, answer the door," Martinez barked, punching the door hard enough that his knuckles bled. "I need to know you are alive."

With no answer coming from inside, Martinez changed tactics. Between savage attacks on the door, he sent texts to everyone both he and Shiksie knew, trying to get any update on her.

No one had any answers for him. They did not know if Shiksie was alright, nor had they seen her in well over a week. That only compounded his worry. Did they not care about her?

`Therein—Nothing, he did not even want to talk to anyone.

Sursee—Nothing other than word that she did not know.

Harnsis, of all people, also had no answers, and that man kept tight tabs on his workers.

What in God's name was going on?

The only one who gave Martinez more than sorrowful nothingness was Ivorn.

Ivorn: Come over to my place; we need to talk.

Considering that beating Shiksies' door was getting him nowhere, and Martinez was not about to break in, he hurried out of Shiksies' neighborhood, destined for Ivorn and Sursees' place in the old town.

Martinez glanced over his shoulder, hoping to see Shiksie at her door, but no. All he saw were the neighbors peering from behind curtains at him. He ignored them.

"Henry, it's great to see you," Sursee purred after opening the door to her and Ivorns' place.

Sursee was a Prinoral, a small feline-like species that was sociable beyond belief. Like many of her species, Sursee stood only as tall as Martinez's chest and had traits that made her as cute as a button.

Sursee wore a long, draping dress held loosely around her dainty form. Its bright white color made her golden fur and amber hair stand out boldly. Her radar dish-like cat ears and long flicking tail made her the picturesque housecat-like woman.

"Please, come on in," Sursee said, stepping abreast of the door and bidding his entry.

"Thanks, Sursee," Martinez replied, entering and taking stock of their home, having never been here before.

Their apartment was quaint and comforting. Most surfaces and furnishings were colors like autumn, oranges, yellows, and browns, giving the space an overwhelmingly comfortable vibe. That matched with what smelled like freshly baked pumpkin pie, making the entire location breathtaking.

A menagerie of plushies was staged on shelves across the astel, adding splashes of vibrant summer to the otherwise warm home.

Martinez had no doubt the plushies were Sursee's. She was a little ball of sunshine, and they fit her personality and aesthetic to a T.

"So, Henry, can I get a hug?" Sursee asked, her tail swaying happily behind her while she smiled as bright as sunlight.

"Not now. Where is Ivorn," Martinez replied instantly.

Sursee pouted, her ears folding flat and tail tucking away. Any semblance of joy that overflowed from her died instantly.

Martinez appreciated that Sursee was listening to Ivorn's advice and not latching onto him like a heat leech, asking first. But he had not registered the sorrow in her—this was the only time she had been told no to a hug from him. She expected it at this point, even if she was being polite.

"Ive is in his office," Sursee said, pointing down the hallway.

Before Sursee registered that Martinez had moved, she turned around and picked up a plate of steaming cookies off the coffee table, hoping to help Maetinez feel better. While she did not know the man intimately, she was adept at gauging emotions, and Martinez oozed sorrow.

"Would you want some—" Sursee trailed off, realizing the Human had already left her alone in the living room.

If pouting harder could be done, she did so. His leaving her like that felt like ice to the soul. She baked the cookies for him once Ivorn had told her Martinez was coming over. But the Human did not care about that or Sursee's feelings.

Opening the indicated door, Martinez found Ivorn lounging behind a desk, reading a book with a massive smile across his face.

"What do we need to talk about?" Martinez asked.

Ivorn jumped at the intrusion and squirreled the book away. Not having expected Martinez for several hours. "Do you not know how to knock?"

"Where is she?" Martinez asked, ignoring everything but Shiksie.

Ivorn sighed, leaning back in his chair. "Not even a hello, huh? I get it." Ivorn said. "Sit," he finished by gesturing at a seat across from him.

Martinez was about to argue and tell Ivorn to get to the point, but the alien man could read him like a book and beat him to the punch.

"I get you are likely upset, but can I please explain," Ivorn insisted.

"Fine," Martinez grumbled and sat down, knowing this was the only way he would get any answers.

Over the next few minutes, Ivorn calmly explained what had happened with Shiksie after he left. According to Ivorn, once Martinez had left Shiksie in her house, she drank; drank to the point it was nearly lethal.

By the time Ivorn had arrived, she was three beers deep and was about to have liver failure. If not for Martinez telling Ivorn to come she would have died. Following that, Shiksie spent several days in the ICU, needing treatments to not die.

After Shiksie was out of the ICU, she vanished, never showing up to work again. The Director also told Ivorn not to mention anything that happened between Martinez and Shiksie to anyone, along with instructions to funnel the Human to the Director once he returned.

"So you don't know where she is?" Martinez said.

"No, I don't," Ivorn admitted.

"Then why the fuck am I here? I need to find her," Martinez replied, standing up and heading toward the door.

"No, you are not," Ivorn barked, stopping Martinez. "The Director made it clear. The only reason you were not fired, and she was not in jail, was because Shiksie left."

Martinez turned around and glared at Ivorn, knowing damn well what the Director had pulled his friend into—a cover-up. Things like that were all too common in the Military and large corporations. It was easier to hush things up than face the reality of what happened.

"So for your own sake. Forget about her," Ivorn sighed.

"Forget her! What the fuck are you on about. She is my friend; I have to help her," Martinez argued, stepping forward and leaning on the desk with both hands. "She needs help."

"Oh, does she? I don't think she does. You just want to feel better after having made her nearly kill herself." Ivorne challenged with a growl—the last two weeks of having to hold his emotions overflowing.

Ivorn might like Martinez as a friend, but Shiksie deserved more than this. She was kind, a bit aloof, but for Kilera's sake, why did she have to fall in love with a detestable asshole who thought he could solve everything alone.

Martinez paused and was taken aback by the challenge. Of course, he wanted to help her. Shiksie was his friend, mentor, and a woman he lov—er liked dearly. This was not about him but her.

"Are you high? I want to make sure she is OK," Martinez replied, pointing at Ivorn.

"Oh, shut the fuck up and stop grandstanding," Ivorn replied, standing to his full height. Usually, Ivorn, due to his gorilla-like build and posture, only stood as tall as Martinez. But at his full grandeur— he nearly touched the ceiling. "If you gave a fuck about her, you would have asked for help with her. You would not have gone into her house, knowing damn well she loved you."

Ivorn stepped around the desk and jammed a finger into Martinez's chest. "Now you have the fucking gall to think she needs you? How about you face reality and understand you fucked up and can't fix it."

"Woah Ivor—" Martinez started backing up, but his friend persisted.

"How about you get that you are not some infallible bastion? What you have done has caused so many issues. My friend and mentor is gone; now we all have to suffer because you just had to not say no!" Ivorn growled, nearly pressing Martinez to the wall.

"We all like you. Sursee, Shiksie, Therein, Harnsis, fuck even me. But dude, you fucked up and have just to let bad enough die," Ivorn said, backing up and giving Martinez some room. "Just go talk to the Director in the morning. He will tell you the same."

Martinez was going to argue to assure Ivorn he could fix this. But Sursee stepping into the room deflated any tension between the two.

"Can you two not yell at each other?" Sursee asked.

Ivorn turned to Sursee, returning to his usual leisurely posture. "Don't worry about it, Sursee. Henry was just leaving. Right?" Ivorn said, looking at Martinez, his last shred of patience visible.

"Yeah. I am," Martinez said, slipping past Sursee, who, for her lovable part, tried to reach out and grab him, but Ivorn stopped her and shook his head.

Martinez stormed out of the house and went toward his own, refusing to believe that he could do nothing to fix this. There was always something he could do. He just did not know the answer yet.

Without a doubt, even if he had to sell his soul to the devil, Martinez knew he would find Shiksie and make this all ok.

Martinez had seen enough friends die, give up, and vanish. If his actions had caused her to give up for any reason he would find her. Even if he had to raise this entire planet to the ground he would find Shiksie—dead, or alive.

ABOUT THE AUTHOR

PirateOPotato, more commonly referred to as just "Pirate," I am an aviation Marine from the glorious land of cheese curds and beer, better known as Wisconsin. I have a strong dedication to reading, writing, cheese, and making bread. If I am not doing something that involves those, I recluse in the woods to go hiking for days on end.

If you want any Updates on future projects please follow the links below for my in-progress stories or regular one-shot tales.

Links
https://www.reddit.com/user/Professional_Prune11/
https://www.royalroad.com/profile/353341
https://ko-fi.com/pirateopotato

Additionally, if you are looking to join a community of individuals who love romance, action, and good stories, I direct you to Romance For Men (RFM). There, you can interact with me and many of the other authors of romance books for a male audience.
https://linktr.ee/romanceformen

BOOKS BY THE AUTHOR

Human Trauma Universe
Human Trauma
Human Trauma 2
Human Trauma 3(coming soon)
Iced Hearts
Escape From Heavalun (coming soon)

Veil Rider Universe
The Last Tower (Coming Soon)

www.ingramcontent.com/pod-product-compliance
Lightning Source LLC
Chambersburg PA
CBHW070841260626
47170CB00007B/2456